HOUSE OF CRIMSON CURSES

A STEAMY VAMPIRE FANTASY ROMANCE

KINGDOM OF IMMORTAL LOVERS
BOOK THREE

RUBY ROE

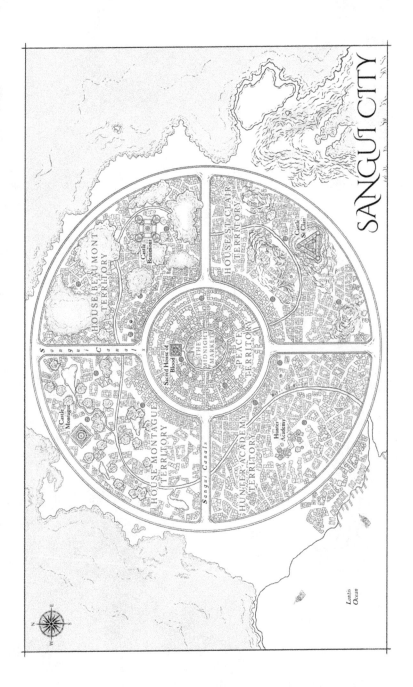

SANGUI CITY

NOTE FOR READERS

This book is intended for adult (18+) audiences. It contains explicit lesbian sex scenes, considerable profanity and some violence. For full content warnings, please see author's website: rubyroe.co.uk.

This book is written in British English.

PLAYLIST

Vampire - Olivia Rodrigo
Que Sera, Sera (Whatever Will Be, Will Be) - Hidden Citizens
I Wanna Destroy - EMA
A Little More - Rosemary Joaquin
Control - Halsey
Neon Ocean - New Dialogue
Bottom of the Deep Blue Sea - MISSIO
Oh No - Biig Piig
Don't Speak (feat. Tim Halperin) - Hidden Citizens
Kiss Me With Your Eyes - Morgan Clae
What Could Have Been - Sting, Ray Chen
You Broke Me First - Tate McRae
I Am Not Okay - Jelly Roll
Haunted - Britton
That's How You Make a Villain - Emlyn
How Villains Are Made - Madalen Duke
Mommy Issues - Cloudy June
Back with a Vengeance - Portals
You Don't Do It For Me Anymore - Demi Lovato
Stone Cold - Demi Lovato

Cruel World - FJØRA
Paint It, Black - Ciara
Long Way Down - Steelfeather
The Other Side - Ruelle
Leaving Home - Camylio
Trouble - Camylio
Monsters - Camylio
Familiar Taste of Poison - Halestorm
Love Runs Out - OneRepublic
Let Me Fade Away - Nine One One
Binary Code - Taylor Bickett
Hold On - Chord Overstreet
Strange - Celeste

To all the smutty little sapphics whose happily ever after involves a masc lesbian walking into a bar, picking them up, shoving them against a wall, and fucking them into oblivion...

This one is for you, baby girl.

CHAPTER 1

OCTAVIA

For a thousand years, I have lived under the assumption that love would very much be, *enough*.

Honestly? I feel naive. How could I place my trust in someone who, time after time, has betrayed me, hurt me, and blamed me?

I shuffle my feet, lean back against the tree Red handcuffed me to and let the sounds of rustling leaves and trickling river water in the distance calm me.

Except it doesn't. Nothing will calm me down tonight because of what she has done.

This entire time, I've fought for Red. Made choices I thought would be best for her. Well, no more. The moment Red stepped into that trial ring, she broke us. Destroyed us. I cannot subject myself to her lack of faith in me anymore.

No part of me wants to watch her fight my sister. Dahlia will beat her to a pulp. I know Red is a trained hunter and that she should be able to hold her own. But Dahlia is something else. She's vicious, mean, there's no remorse or hesitation with her. She's kill or be killed. And even though this fighting trial isn't meant to be to the death, I'm certain Dahlia would relish the opportunity to slaughter Red because she's well aware of how much she means to me...

Meant to me.

Past tense.

I squint into the distance, trying to make out the fighting ring. But the silver cuffs are too distracting. Where they're locked around my wrists, it chafes and burns, my skin blistering.

How fucking could she?

The fight begins. I should look away. Force myself to close my eyes and turn away from what Red's doing.

Intentionally losing.

Throwing away everything that we've worked for. But I can't. I'm like an addict trying to get my fix even though this fight is a carriage crash in slow motion.

They tussle. For a while, Red holds her ground. Even landing a thumping whack on Dahlia. But that only pisses her off more.

Red clings to the ring and then the blows really begin.

Dahlia doesn't hold back.

Even this far out, tucked in a copse of trees and barely able to see, I can hear the reverberation of smacks and the crunching cracks of bones shattering.

I grit my teeth. The night air chills me to my core. My teeth chatter, my fangs clattering against my lower canines. And I'm not sure if it's terror or rage. Probably a little of both.

Red knew what she was doing. And she did it intentionally. To ruin me. To fuck our chances of winning and me taking ownership of the city.

The only thing I've ever wanted was to feel like I

belonged, and this was my chance. I cannot believe that someone who professed to love me would commit such an atrocious act.

She doesn't... Love me...

It's the only answer I can come up with. Vampire bond or not, she doesn't love me.

I would never do this to her.

Dahlia's hits come thicker, quicker, harder. I bite down on my lip so hard I draw blood.

Under my skin, the shadow beat of her heart thuds. It echoes through my soul and clouds my mind.

It speeds up as she fights and then slows as she's beaten.

Now it slows too much.

Slows too quick.

She's going to die.

I am so furious with her. I can't do anything to stop it. But worse, I don't know if I want to.

She's the one who cuffed me in silver handcuffs. Unless I cut my own hands off, I'm not sure there's anything I could do anyway.

So I slide my bound hands down the trunk and drop to the ground, watching the woman I loved for the last three years throw away the only dream I've ever had.

I don't cry. I'm too numb.

My insides are cold, silent, resigned.

There's a whip of wind, the trees rustle and then a disembodied voice slices through my thoughts.

"Octavia, Mother of Blood. I've been looking for you everywhere. I tried to stop Red," Xavier, my favourite sibling, says.

His floppy black hair is slick, there's a sheen of sweat across his brow.

"My, my, Xavier, I don't believe I've ever seen you break a glisten, let alone a sweat. You must truly have been fearful for me."

He fires me an irritated stare. "What the hell are you doing?"

"Oh, you know, just having a sit down and rest while I watch the big fight," I say, stone-faced. "The fuck does it look like, Xavier? She trapped me here. So that she could sabotage the trial."

"What? No. Why would sh—"

"Sadie. I don't know what she fucking said. But clearly, I underestimated her desire to win. She manipulated Red, gave back her memories in exchange for losing this round."

"Gods," Xavier says.

"Quite. Now, if you don't mind, I'd like to leave."

"You can't leave," Xavier says, his gaze dropping to my wrists. He tugs on his jacket sleeve until it sloughs off and then wraps it around the silver cuffs. His fingers curl around the fabric-covered metal and he wrenches. His neck cords with strain. But finally, the cuffs snap, freeing me.

"Thank you, brother. I'll see you later."

"You can't leave, you're bonded. What if she dies and it fucks with you?"

"Then so be it." I step away, but he grabs my arm.

"You don't mean that. She's the dhampir, for god's sake. If she dies, that cure dies with her, you don't get the city and you lose everything."

"I already have, Xavier. She's intentionally losing this round. We won't get enough points to win."

He frowns, his eyes skittering as he thinks the situation through.

"You could still draw."

"I need. To. Win. The city hates me, remember? This

4

isn't *just* about points. I need to win them over. I'm starting from negative, unlike you and Dahlia," I snarl.

He pauses, his chiselled jaw flexing. His gaze flits across my face, searching for something, and then he squeezes my arm before letting me go.

"I didn't think you were a quitter."

I growl at him and grab his jacket lapels, ready to head-butt him.

He slides his hands over mine. "Octavia, we need to stop this. Dahlia will kill her. No matter how angry you are, you don't want that."

"You have no idea what I want, Xavier."

He tilts his head at me, pursing his lips. "You're mad. I get that, but don't take it out on me."

I relax my grip a little. "You cannot fathom the depths to which I need to win this."

"So explain it," he says, his thumb stroking the back of my hand.

I release his jacket and snatch my hand away. His gentle touch stings like a poisoned thorn.

"Do you have any idea what it's like not to be loved? Not to be wanted? You have everything. Beauty gives you everything in this world."

His forehead wrinkles.

"I dare you to argue with me."

He holds my gaze, his lips trembling as if words want to spill out, but they fall away, his lips stilling.

I continue. "You're popular, have connections and friendships. You're invited to all the noble parties. You're respected, adored. People willingly do you favours and support you."

His eyes drop to the floor.

But I am relentless, and I need him to understand. "I am

derided. Vilified. People look away from me and flinch when I pass them. I am only invited to parties because of Mother, or because of you. Not because people respect me or love me or want me there. You cannot comprehend the depths of loneliness I have reached, Xavier. So don't you dare claim to know how angry I am with Red."

I make to leave, but he grips my wrist. I glance at where he grazes my skin, sliding his hands until he only holds my fingers.

"I hear you. I see you. I acknowledge everything you have said."

I roll my eyes. "Why is that a complete sentence and yet there's a but coming."

He smiles; it's soft, warm and filled with pity. My insides burn.

"While I do accept what you're saying, I have also stood by your side for five hundred years, Octavia. Which is why I know that come tomorrow, if she is not in this world, no matter how furious you are, your heart will break again. And then the depths of loneliness you have felt will be trivial compared to the pain you will experience if she is gone forever."

My lip curls.

"Then I will relish every second of that pain."

I rip my hand out of his. But he shakes his head at me.

"If you're so fucking bothered, Xavier, you save her."

And then I speed out of the forest, and I don't look back.

CHAPTER 2

RED

I really thought dying would be a little less *fuck-me-this-hurts* and a little more, old haggard lesbian in her bed, wrinkled and cranky with the love of her life.

But this... this is something else.

Every nerve in my body is on fire. Every cell has exploded with a blaze of fire and light and agonising pain. The fighting ring blurs around me, the only thing I can focus on is the old monk in front of me. He wobbles. His eyes flutter shut, and I know I have to do this before it's too late.

I open my mouth, my fangs—because that's what they are now, I can't keep denying it—drop down.

He teeters, leaning down for me, his wrist still spraying blood everywhere. The scent of iron is thick in the air, and it makes my mouth water. My stomach curls, my chest tightening as I try to work out whether it's desire or disgust I'm feeling.

His weight bears down on me, but I'm too broken to help. As his neck brushes my lips, smearing the scent of blood over me, my instinct takes over.

There is no hesitation left.

My fangs sink into his neck, a haze of claret swims over my vision. Iron and tangy, sweet metal fill my nose and mouth, my senses overflowing with flavours. It's not just blood I'm drinking; I'm consuming him. Like drinking every memory, every emotion, every experience. It's so filling, so overwhelming.

I pull and tug and draw his blood into my mouth. I squeeze my eyes shut, wishing I could block it out, pretend it's not happening, that I'm not stealing the life of an innocent. And not just any innocent but a fucking monk—a religious man. I'm going to hell.

A wave of nausea rolls around my gut, and I have to stop, swallow, breathe, before resuming drinking. I cannot throw up his sacrifice or it will have been for nothing, and we'll both die.

I have to continue. Drain his essence, his life, his blood. I won't let his sacrifice be in vain.

What choice do I have? He cut his wrist and would have bled out anyway. This way, at least his life has gone for a cause. Though as I drink him down, I'm not sure if I really am a decent cause. And definitely not when I think about what I've done to Octavia.

As his blood flows down my throat. My body tenses up. Bones mat themselves back together. My insides rip and shred as much as they knit and heal. Internally, I'm screaming as everything forms and reforms and breaks all over again.

But I keep drinking.

It's funny, I thought I was ready to die, to give up after Dahlia landed her last blow. But faced with the end of my life, I realise I am not ready. Not even close.

I need to make things right with Octavia. I fucked up... Like royally-screwed-literally-everything-I-possibly-could up.

I took the one thing Octavia wanted, and I pissed it up the wall all because Sadie fucking manipulated me.

I really thought our only competition was Dahlia. She's the favourite, after all. But no. The real competition is always the quiet ones. What I don't understand is why Sadie sided with Eleanor and Cordelia. Has she been promised the city if she convinced me to transition? Did Cordelia hand Sadie the city as penance for what she did to her? Maybe the myths of Sadie being locked up and screaming her voice away into the walls of Castle St Clair are true.

Well, mission accomplished, Sadie. I'm the dhampir now.

Or I will be if I can drink down enough of this monk. My stomach is so full and bloated with his blood, I gag over his carotid artery.

As his body is drained and weakens, mine grows stronger and healthier. It ripples out from my stomach. A glistening energy that throbs and pulses with waves of what I can only describe as the most peaceful golden light I've ever experienced. It's like I'm everywhere all at once. I am in my body, above my body. I am in the earth and the sky. I am the forest around us, the night clouds and stars. My veins thread under the soil and flow into the wind. I am connected and yet alone.

My toes tingle, my calves and legs pinch and throb. My

core undulates as waves and pulses of energy fly around my body.

My vision whites out. All I taste is the iron tang of blood. All I hear is the roar of blood pumping through my body and the slowing beat of my heart.

Thud.

Thud.

Thud.

It no longer beats with the same fast rhythm. It slows. Slows. Slows and then...

It stops.

I'm no longer drinking. The monk is empty. My tongue tugs and pulls but instead of liquid, the squelch of arterial tissue brushes my teeth. I reel back, gagging against the fleshy pulp. I've drained him dry.

I push and his body flops off mine.

But I can't move. Not yet. My back arches off the fighting ring ground as my spine cracks. The most agonising muscle clench grips my heart. One final beat. One final scream. A sound that booms and reverberates like the city itself is crying.

As my voice surges through the forest, it breaks the tree branches, cracks teeth and shatters watches and goblets.

Spasms wrack and contort my body as I'm surrounded by a light so fierce that it blinds me. I am only sensation.

I am blood. I am energy. I am power.

I jerk across the fighting ring, my body rolling around, flipping upside down and front to back. I curl into a ball and then fling my limbs out as if controlled by a puppet master. My body fractures, reforms and floods with power.

Finally, finally after what feels like an eon, I come to rest. It's over. I am no longer human.

My hand lays on my chest and where it once rose and fell with the thumping beat of my heart, it does nothing.

And yet, my skin is still warm. I still breathe. I am no longer human. But I am not a vampire either. I am something more, something less.

I am something different.

The dhampir.

And now? The entire city knows.

There is nothing but silence in the forest clearing. I can sense the heartbeats, no, maybe I can hear them? Hundreds of fluttering raps. Each one thudding an erratic melody against the others. The people's eyes bore into my skin. But not one of the nobles, hunter elders or the monks draws a breath.

They all stand around the ring and stare at me.

It's not until Cordelia steps under the ropes and peers over me that I realise everything is going to go south.

I just transformed. I drained a monk in front of the entire city.

A city of people who have been trying to get me on their side. Who have been hunting for the dhampir so they can control them...

Me.

Shit.

I'm helpless, splayed right in front of them, ripe for the taking.

Cordelia stands upright, her arms held open to the crowd. "THE DHAMPIR HAS ARISEN. MAGIC WILL RETURN."

I try and get myself up, but while I'm strong of body, I'm weak of energy right now. The blood I drank all used up in healing and the transformation.

"GET HER," someone in the crowd screams.

"LET HER BLESS US," another shouts.

Oh, shit.

I try and roll myself over, but I scarcely manage more than an inch off the floor before my body gives out under my own weight.

Still silent, a hunter breaks rank first, lurching out of the crowd and gripping the fighting ring rope. Cordelia outright hisses like a cat and swipes her nails so fast across his wrist that his hand—still gripping the rope—separates from his arm.

It's only then that the world explodes.

His arm pisses blood everywhere, spraying Cordelia, even I get hit, the arterial spray is so severe.

He shrieks, and several vampires, not expecting the strong scent of blood, snap into a blood lust rage. Nobles stream out of the ranks. Hunters throw fists and arms and feet out to stop them. But the crowd surges forward ever closer to me.

The Chief—Eleanor, fuck, when am I going to get used to that—leaps into the ring, her fists already balled.

"You did amazing, Red. I'm so proud of you," she says.

I want to knock her out. "Fuck you," I spit.

How fucking dare she. She manipulated me for her own gains. She is dead to me. I'll take the Academy from her. She doesn't deserve it. The same way I suspect Octavia feels about me.

I need to make it out of the ring so that I can find her and explain.

Someone lands millimetres from my head, my body bouncing from the nearby impact. I crash back to the floor as the body is dragged away screaming.

This is chaos.

There are people everywhere.

The ring ropes are yanked and pulled. Someone swarms in and cuts several of the ropes, giving the crowd easier access. My name is screamed a thousand times in a thousand different voices with a thousand different requests.

"Red. Red. Come here. Let me help you."

Others scream, "Dhampir! Dhampir!"

All the while I am unable to escape. The monks that were at the front of the ring, are all kneeling in prayer while limbs and blood and bodies are flung above them.

This is absurd. I need to get out of here. But as I push myself up, my body gives way again, and I collapse back to the floor. Mother of Blood, I'm not getting out of here alone.

Amelia rushes into view. A man—human—swings for her. She growls at him to get away, but he brandishes a stake.

I scream her name but it's too late. He lunges, and just like in the market, she's lightning quick, darting out of the way. The man spins and springs for her again. But again, he misses.

This time when I bellow her name again, it's not to protect her, but in the vain hope I can stop her.

Her head rears back as her fangs descend and her eyes darken.

"No, no, no. AMELIA. NO!" I am screaming, trying desperately to haul myself off the ring floor and reach for her, but it's useless. I'm so tired.

I know I'm a hypocrite too. I literally just drained a man to death. And yet, I can't stand the thought of watching Amelia take a life. Not when she's so young. So innocent. My baby sister.

In one swift snap of her teeth, all the growth I thought I'd seen, all the change in her for the positive, evaporates away.

This isn't what I thought she was growing into. This is savage. This is ruthless and ugly. She bites not to stun or wound. But to kill.

She wants to drain him, I can see it in the glimmer in her eye. She likes this. Loves it. She kicks out a leg, tripping up another human as her lips pull on the man's skin. Her expression glimmers as she holds him in place. His body goes slack, the light fading from his eyes.

"No, Amelia," I whine.

But she can't hear me through the cacophony of noise and bodies and limbs.

Cordelia and Eleanor fight back to back. Something I'd never have dreamt of seeing but after the revelation of them working together to manipulate me, nothing is surprising anymore.

They keep me guarded. Preventing hunter or human from getting too close. But still, I need to get out of the ring. I need to leave, and certainly not with them.

I yawn.

Such a strange action to take in amongst the roaring shouts of my name and heavy thumps against hollow chests and crack of bones and slurps of blood from human necks.

I am utterly exhausted.

My eyes flit back to Amelia. Her cheeks and lips are covered in blood, she smears her arm across her mouth, wiping some of it away, but mostly making a mess of it. She smiles. "I'm coming," she says and runs towards me.

But I don't want her to get me. I no longer know who that is. It's not my Amelia, the little girl I used to know. The one full of sweetness and light who loved cookies and her teddy and would run to greet me when I returned from the Academy. I've never seen her drain a human, aside from me during her transition, I've only seen her drink from blood bags and goblets.

This is different. This changes things. The feral wildness in her eyes, the gluttonous consumption. The absolute disregard for that human life. Who is she? My sister would never behave like that. I wonder if she lost her humanity in the change to vampire. I don't know what stands before me, but it isn't my sister.

It's a monster. A broken soul and I only know one thing that will fix it.

The cure.

I have to get up. But even as I think it, my body feels heavy.

A vampire slams into Amelia trying to get away from a human wielding a stake. Amelia's knocked off course, and it gives me another chance to drag myself a few feet away. I can make all my limbs move, but I can't seem to coordinate anything. Despite the fact my muscles are even more toned, I feel heavier, thicker set with even more muscle than before. I am useless. I just want to shut my eyes.

I think I have to.

I can't make it out alone. If they take me, I wonder if they'll kill me or worship me. And if Octavia hates me, I'm not sure any of it matters anyway.

As my eyes drift shut, strong hands grip me. There's movement.

And then everything goes black.

CHAPTER 3

CORDELIA

One Thousand Years Ago

I am a prisoner where once I was free.

We should have kept running.

It's been six weeks since I was torn from Eleanor's arms, and now, as free as we were for all those months, we are now prisoners.

Or at least, I am. I would love to know what has become of her. But for all I know, she could be as dead as she is lost.

All I know is that she is lost to me, and it makes the marrow in my bones ache. She is the only thing on my mind, the only thing I dream of and the only thing my heart pines for.

I get out of bed, for all the good it will do me, and I traipse around my room. I bathe in the bath the maid left me. The water is tepid now, but I don't care for anything, so I climb in anyway.

When I'm dressed, I walk the eight paces it takes me to reach my window.

There are bars on it now. I can see the field where Teddy resided. The same field I used to escape through and in the distance on the horizon, the same woods that gave me my freedom.

All of it seems so far away now. There are three smudges on the glass from my fingers. Two dots for eyes and a smiling mouth. I am anything but happy. But I figure if I lie to myself long enough then perhaps I'll believe it.

I grip the bars; the iron is cold and bites into my skin. Winter is descending and it makes everything seem more bleak, more lost.

I breathe onto the glass. The mist makes the face smudge pop to life.

I sigh, and sit back down on the bed, taking a sheaf of paper and my quill and attempting to write another letter to Eleanor.

I've no idea whether I'll be able to get it to her, but I don't want to quit. I have to keep trying. If I give up, I'll lose all hope, and I can't live without hope. I still have a small amount of coin I scrabbled together, I figure I may be able to bribe one of the lower-ranked housemaids who may need the money more than the senior staff, who are all entirely in Mother's pocket.

I finish the letter as a key rattles in the lock of my bedroom door.

Just another reminder that I'm a prisoner now. I am only allowed out when Mother deems it necessary; either because a gentleman caller has arrived, or she fears for my sanity. Being trapped in a small room for long periods of time, utterly isolated, is enough to make me wobble.

Lest she forget, my heart is also broken.

Not that she cares.

The key—worn by my mother and occasionally by her senior housemaid—clicks in the lock and the door opens.

I glance up from my sheaves of paper, where I've hidden the letter in the middle. The last thing I want to do is risk Mother seeing or asking questions, then my chance of getting a letter to reach Eleanor vanishes.

"Good morning, Cordelia."

"Mother," I say through gritted teeth. I cannot even summon the civility I once could. There is no love lost between us. I am here to perform a duty, and she expects me to fulfil it.

Give her an heir so that my child can inherit the family fortunes and businesses, because clearly I am too much of a shameful disappointment to do that.

"You're to walk the gardens for the next hour, and then a gentleman caller will be arriving," Mother says.

"No."

This is the game I like to play. Say no to every request, just to irritate her. To get a rise and make her realise that she can't break me the way she wants to. She thought that dragging me back home would make me compliant, that suddenly I'd realise she was right, and that I should be marrying a noble of proper blood.

I couldn't give a hoot what she wants or believes, the only thing I know is that I'll fight her till my dying breath.

Mother sniffs, it's a mixture of a laugh and a huff, and it's riddled with the kind of discerning disapproval that makes my skin crawl.

"You shall, or I will make your time considerably worse."

"You've already taken everything I care about, what more could you do to me."

"My dear, sweet Cordelia, don't be so naive. Things can always get worse. Now, get your backside up, and in a coat and outside. NOW."

I grit my teeth and get up, my rebellion drained for the day. I grab my coat and shawl with my back turned and slip the note inside my inner pocket. She doesn't see, thankfully. I shove past her as I exit the room, making sure to knock into her.

"Childish," she sneers. I ignore her. It is childish, but it also helps me cope. It's a small enough rebellion she's only irritated. I make doubly certain not to let her cross to outright annoyance. She could pick some awful noble for me to marry, someone four decades my senior with some hideous body odour and a weird fetish that would make me have nightmares.

No, while my fate lies in her hands, I continue to rebel only enough to irk her.

I make my way outside and immediately shiver, even with my outer layers on. But I stroll around the garden as instructed. My eyes skirt to the horse field, but just as I watch the ponies, Mother's staff watches me.

I glance around the garden, hoping to see one particular member of staff but see nothing. So after my walk, I decide to make my way towards the kitchens and hope to find her there.

There's a chance, it's small and she would be risking her job to help me, but I think with enough coin, I can probably convince her.

I slip inside the kitchens, and the heat is instant. It flushes my cheeks and warms me from foot to scalp. The head chef tuts at me and jostles me out of the way. But the scents of roasting chicken and herbs and warm buttery vegetables make my mouth water.

How I love a roast dinner on a weekend. It must be Sunday because the chef never cooks roast chicken on any other day.

Mother has forbidden me from reading newspapers, so I lose track of time stuck in my room the way I am.

The chef bustles me all the way to the other side of the kitchen and out into the hallway. I pout at her, because the hallway is cold, the sconces are never enough to keep the warmth from leaching away through the stone walls.

She huffs but reaches back into the kitchen and hands me a warm baguette that's been freshly buttered, and then she shoos me away like you would a mouse.

I give her a small curtsey and say thank you, and she wafts a hand at me before shutting the door. I meander through the corridors and spot the maid I'm looking for. I make eye contact and jerk my head towards one of the quieter corridors, then I dive down it.

I press my back into the shadows of the corner of the hall and wait. Hoping that she will find me.

She takes her time, long enough that I worry she didn't understand my gesturing. But as I'm about to make my way back to the main corridor, she appears, and I breathe a sigh of relief.

"You can't be asking me for help like this, miss, your mother strictly forbid it," the maid says.

"I know. But I'm begging you, Mabel. I'll get on my hands and knees and plead with you."

"I could lose my job," Mabel says.

"I understand. Truly, I do. But I love her. You understand that, don't you? I just need to know she's okay. It will just be this once. I swear it. I'll never ask again. But I was torn from her, and I need to know she lives and that she's okay."

Mabel's lips press into a thin line. She stares at me for what seems like eternity. Finally, she nods, and I almost break into tears. I rub my face and pull myself upright. There's no time to dilly-dally, we could be caught at any moment.

I pull a little bag of silver coins from my coat and the note I scrawled to Eleanor.

"I beg you see that it gets to her." She nods just as Mother rounds the corner.

Her eyes darken. "What is going on?"

Mabel moves so fast I scarcely see the sleight of hand. She slips the bag of coins and note I gave her into her skirts while simultaneously grabbing me and barking, "COME ON, CORDELIA."

Her fingers slip to my wrist as she drags me out of the hall, sparing no delicacy. But as Mother's eyes linger on us, I realise what she's doing and play along.

"NO. I SAID NO. I DON'T WANT TO."

"And I said you'll be late. NOW. COME. ON." She tugs me hard enough I leap off the wall and have to stagger in order to prevent myself from falling.

She glances over her shoulder and mouths an apology, and then her face crumples into a frown as she turns back to my mother.

"Honestly, Lady St Clair. Your daughter is a handful. I should rather like to be put on a different duty."

"Hmm," Mother says. "I understand. Please accept my deepest gratitude."

Mabel bows her head in servitude and continues dragging me towards the bathing chambers.

"She needs to be ready by teatime," Mother calls after us. Mabel aggressively shoos me just like the chef did, and we head towards the household bathing chambers.

I make a show of huffing and puffing and folding my arms to make sure Mother believes she really was trying to corral me out of the corridor, praying to the witch-gods that it works.

We reach the bathing chamber door, only to find a suite of other maids waiting for me. "Ugh," I groan, knowing precisely how childish it sounds and being unable to hide it anyway.

Mabel winks at me and scurries away. I watch her totter all the way down the corridor, quietly praying she manages to smuggle out the note. The first chamber lady drags me into the room and begins undressing me.

"I'm capable of taking my dress off, thank you," I say, my tone a little ruder than she expects.

"Very well," she snaps. "See to it that you're quick about it. We have much to do before the gentleman caller arrives."

My top lip curls at her words. "Well, I hope he's completely unsuitable," I snap back and drop my dress.

She hands me the soap bar and nudges me towards the steaming tin bathtub. "I did bathe this morning, you know."

Mabel tuts and says, "Mother's orders."

I pout but climb in and wince against the heat of the water. It scorches my skin, no doubt an intentional punishment from Mother.

She nudges my back and then three more ladies crowd around me, one with soap, one a loofah and the other with a razing device.

"For the love of the gods, I am capable of washing."

"We know," the maid who shoved me into the bath says. "But your mother thinks you'll intentionally sabotage the tea. So we're having to tend to you like you're a child."

The one holding the loofah pipes up next. "We're as

unhappy about this as you are. So why don't you make it easy on all of us and comply?"

I grit my teeth but accept that she's right. This is not their fault, and they are just doing their job. I do make it easy for them, raising my hands and arms when requested. Presenting my legs for razing and only snatching the loofah away when she reaches for my private regions.

"I am doing that myself," I bark and grab the sponge.

"Fine," she says and presses her lips together.

When I'm out of the bath and dried off, they tend to my hair, brushing and airing it out, twirling it and attaching flowers and decorative hair pieces and curling it with hot tongs.

Finally, after they smear a line of kohl across my lids and blush on my cheeks, I'm presentable.

All three of the maids have lightened up considerably now I'm dressed and ready. The first maid, the one who shoved me into the bath, grips my hands.

"He's got a kind heart, this one. While your mother's cross with you, she isn't entirely heartless. Plus a few of us maids suggested a handful of lords we thought suitable. We did our best."

I could cry, my eyes sting with gratitude. I squeeze her hands back. "Thank you," I say and stand, ready to meet my fate.

CHAPTER 4

I made a mistake.

Once upon a time, a thousand years ago, I made a mistake that cost me dearly.

I've worked for a long time to fix it.

And things are almost in place.

Everyone believes Cordelia has power, but she doesn't. She's as much a pawn as Red is.

I'm the one really controlling this game.

And it's almost time for me to win.

Before the end of this, you'll know who I am. And I hope... that maybe you'll understand why I did it all.

CHAPTER 5

OCTAVIA

I creep through the shadows of Xavier's mansion. My skin still pulsates with the hot, slick rage of Red's actions.

I was almost back to my castle when I smelt Xavier. Then came the sensation of *her* crawling under my skin— instead of silk and obsession, it was crickets and fire ants. She was alive.

I don't know what made me turn around and follow their trail. Perhaps morbid curiosity. Perhaps the need to know if she'd transformed.

The reason doesn't matter, I suppose. I'm here. Xavier drops her in a suite as a hoard of healers swoop into the room and guards position themselves by her door.

Xavier flurries around ordering guards out to the perimeter of his grounds. He speeds this way and that through the mansion, grabbing guards and ordering instructions. I peer down into the foyer as the group of his staff are huddled together.

A furious line carves his brow as he speaks. "There will be protestors and worshippers crawling all over the city in the next twelve hours, we have to widen the mansion's boundary. I don't care who you have to bribe, pull all the security from the other house. We cannot afford to be penetrated here."

I peel back into the shelter of an empty room. He doesn't know I'm here, probably best I just leave. I slip out of the room and retreat further down the corridor, hoping this perpetually bright, white marble obscenity of a property doesn't give me away as I head towards the rear staircase.

The air frissons, a breeze rushes over my arms, goosebumps rising. I halt, glance over my shoulder. Nothing.

When I turn back, I yelp and throw an instinctive fist out.

Xavier catches it.

"Hello, favourite." He smiles.

"I was just leaving." I snatch my hand back and fold my arms.

"I thought you didn't care..." He lets that hang in the air.

I bristle.

"I don't."

"Then why are you h—"

"You're in my territory, Xavier."

"Nothing to do with her then...?" His eyes glance in the direction of the room he put her in. Bastard.

I refuse to bite.

"It's okay to love her even though she's hurt you," he says, his expression soft.

I clamp my mouth shut so hard I taste blood. My nostrils flare. The fact there are small pieces of me that still love her is a complexity that I will never understand. But I suppose, just as one doesn't grow to love a person overnight, nor do they stop loving them in an instant. It's a gradual process of hurt, mistakes, unspoken words and secrets kept locked away. Until they all coagulate into resentment. And I do resent her. Very much right now. I hate every inch of her because she hurt me, and even if I love her, I can still choose to walk away.

"I'm leaving," I snarl and step around him, but he moves with me.

"Xavier," I growl.

"Don't do this," he says. "Don't let this break you."

I shove a finger in the middle of his chest. "What do you know? I've spent my life in the shadows, hiding parts of myself in order to placate others. Pretending to be less than I am in order to not scare children or offend the sensitivities of civilians. I've spent years trying to be a fair and reasonable leader, looking out for those in my territory. And they can barely afford me more than a trembling nod. Well, I am so fucking tired of it."

"Then don't be the monster they think you are. You're better than that."

"Am I? I'm tired of bending the knee and mollifying the sensibilities of people who are less than me when they give not one ounce of respect. So. If they want me to be a monster, I will be."

He stares at me and changes tact.

"When are you going to confront Cordelia? She killed your mother..."

"Cordelia *is* my mother."

"Your birth mother, Octavia. You had the vision from the Mother of Blood gifted to you for a reason. Do you not think you should at least ask her about it?"

I purse my lips; this is no better of a conversation topic than Red. "No." My jaw flexes in warning.

"So you're not curious?"

"She drained her because she was transitioning. What's there to ask?"

"Then why are you so hurt over it?"

I grunt in frustration and shove past him, speeding out of the mansion before he can catch me up. And I don't stop until I make it into the heart of Sangui City.

I drift through the streets and canals. My hair is up, wrapped in a bun I only wear when I want to hide. Tonight, I am hunting. For the weak, the evil and those in the wrong place. If this city can't be mine, then I'll fucking ruin it for everyone. If I can't win this competition, then I won't even bother trying to fit in.

I am sick of trying to fit their mould.

Tonight, I make a new one.

I stalk the streets of Sangui City. My footsteps float their way over the cobbles. Silent. Invisible. Just like me.

Though, I swear the gargoyles know a predator is loose. Their eyes follow me, judging. As if they know who I really am, what I'm about to do.

I wander down another alleyway, another street. Hunting. Sniffing out prey. Victims. That's what monsters do, right?

The city is on edge, it vibrates around me. Whispers drift like ghosts through the streets. *She has arisen. The dhampir is here. Magic is coming.*

It sets my teeth on edge, makes my skin prickle. Word travels fast, then again, there were thousands of onlookers watching her transformation, and the city has waited a millennium for this day.

I perch on a balcony a floor above street level, determined not to think about her. I peer inside the windows; the apartment must have been abandoned years prior by the looks of the layers of dust coating the furniture. The room is small and uniform-like, clean, simple furniture. It looks like the sort of room a student would live in. Or a hunter.

My thoughts turn back to her. I ball my fist against the window, determined not to pursue them. I shake the thoughts away and turn to discover my first prey of the night. He follows two young women, a knife flashing in his hand. Disgusting. I leap from the balcony, land on his back, plunge my nails into his trapezium and wrench his head to the side as I consume him in one long inhalation. The women run screaming and don't give me a backwards glance. Good for them. This could have been the other way around. When I'm done, I drop his carcass to the street and step over it.

I don't bother to wipe my mouth, and I don't bother to clean him up. Fuck him. Fuck the city. Let them see.

Another victim appears a few streets down, and I drain her. Then two more—drunks this time, trying to sell doses to minors. Pigs.

I leave their bodies in the street, pleased to let the pigeons and crows pluck their innards out and feast.

Already I'm full. I don't need any more blood, but gluttony is the theme of the night, so there will never be enough blood. Besides, I just want to make people hurt.

I halt when I see one of Mother's staff hanging a poster on a wall near the market. It's Red's face, the poster is advertising a reward for finding her.

Mother of Blood, she doesn't fuck around. It's only a few hours since Xavier took her, and already Cordelia is searching for her.

The more streets I go down, the more posters I find. One after the other, her face peers out at me. Can I never escape her? Dozens of Mother's staff are out patrolling and questioning the people of the city.

Then the posters shift, and instead of rewards, they say 'found dead or alive.' The further I go, the more the messages on the posters change. Some wishing her dead, others blessing her.

I turn a corner and come face to face with what I can only describe as a party. I glance around, realising I've hit the back of the Church of Blood.

Music blares, monks with drums and shakers and metal instruments dance and sing around the church square. I grab one of the humans standing on the edge of this chaos and tilt my head so he can't see my eyes.

"What's going on?" I say.

"Haven't you heard? The dhampir has arisen, we're giving thanks to the Mother of Blood and praying for the dhampir's safe return to the church."

"The church?" I ask, frowning. I nearly glance up at him until I remember I'm not wearing contact lenses.

"Of course, she'll be our direct connection to the Mother of Blood. She's a living deity, she must join the church and lead us."

Fucking hell, the city has lost its shit, this is bizarre. I edge back from the crowd wondering what the church would think if I fucked their precious deity in the middle of the pulpit. The encounter produces a sour taste in my mouth and an unease that won't leave my gut. Red is screwed, she's not going to be able to go anywhere.

I approach the main market square only to stumble back into the shadows.

A pair of vampire nobles I don't recognise stroll past me, their voices low enough only a vampire could hear.

"I heard Lady St Clair said if a vampire finds her, she won't just offer monetary rewards but blood rewards and favours. We really ought to ask the cousins and aunts to help us. This could put us in good standing."

"I agree, this could elevate our status. I'll put in a note with my messenger woman at dawn. Tomorrow, we hunt."

They disappear down another street. I focus on them, straining to hear their conversation and work out whether I recognise their voices, but I don't, and they've walked too far too fast for me to follow.

There are monks from the church sat praying and chanting about the dhampir in every square I walk through. Residents and citizens are clustered around them making offerings, many more of them joining the monks to pray for the dhampir to be found.

The city really is losing it. I've never known anything like this. There are as many people praying for her reappearance as there are putting up posters hunting her, calling for her death by beheading, bleeding the magic from her and all manner of other ugly forms of torture.

None of this is my problem anymore. Red isn't my problem. Why my gut rolls with unease at the thought, I don't know. I stalk back into the shadows determined to find some peace and preferably a new prey to drain.

That's when I notice a young woman. She's an addict. Her eyes hold that glazed look that's reserved only for blood lust. Too bad for her, she's done nothing wrong save being in the wrong place.

I've gone past caring about right and wrong. I just want the pain in my chest to stop. I want to cut Red out from my heart and leave the drying carcass of our love out in the sun to desiccate. And if I can't, then I'll bury my pain in the hunt.

Yes, this woman will do nicely.

I stalk her, following the line of shadows the building roofs provide. I will punish her because I can't punish Red. I want to. Fuck, every ounce of my body wants to hurt Red in a way that is unhealthy. But I won't. I can't. Because I'm afraid of who I would be if I do.

So instead, I choose an unsuspecting victim. One that doesn't deserve it any more than I deserve what Red did to me. Unfortunately, collateral damage is a peril of being human in Sangui City.

The woman stumbles towards the same park bench that I fucked Red on. Gods. Can the Mother of Blood not give me a fucking break? I feel like Red is written into the cement of this city. Written in the cells of my pupils, my heart. Everywhere I look are reminders of her. Of us. How the hell am I going to exorcise her out of my life?

The woman drinks something distinctly claret coloured from a glass bottle. Blood. Definitely an addict then.

I rush past her. She halts, her eyes wide, the fear writ clear in her expression. Good. I like my victims afraid. I smile, hidden in the cover of a bush. She stumbles as the blood kicks in and staggers to the bench.

I'm done waiting. I pounce like a cat. Gripping her by the neck and dragging her into the bushes. All while she screams into the palm of my hand.

I dig my nails into her shoulders and wrap a leg around her body, pinning her back to my chest. She stinks like week-old sweat, hints of piss and stale fish.

I regret my choice.

This won't do. I drag her to the pond further in the park and dunk her head under, scrubbing my hands over her neck. She screams but the water drowns out the noise. I rub her neck until I hear the gurgles slow. I'd rather eat fresh fish and algae than have to taste this woman's festering flesh.

I pull her out just as I think she's going to drown. Her chest heaves. The scent of piss is stronger now. I glance down to see a dark stain marring her crotch and trouser legs.

Vile. But the terror washing over her eases something inside me, a loosening, uncoiling of all the tension. I was always a monster, I just played the good girl for my mother. I'd forgotten how good it is to really be myself, to unleash the predator inside me.

I pull her back to the darkened bushes, her heels leaving drag marks in the gravel.

"Please," she whines. "Please don't."

I flinch at her words. I'm a monster, but I recognise that this is beneath me. She is beneath me. Yet, I can't stop. I'm a carriage attached to spooked horses. Galloping, galloping, galloping towards their doom.

Her neck, though, looks decidedly cleaner than it did. Part of me wants to apologise to her. For stealing what little shred of a life she called her own. But staring at her, at the acceptance washing over her expression, I'm not sure she cares. There's no resistance left in her.

Pathetic. The least she could do is fight for the meagre years the Mother of Blood gave her. I will show no mercy, I will feel no pity.

I sink my teeth in hard. Savagely drinking her down and gulping at her life force. I guzzle and guzzle the warm liquid, hoping to replace the coldness in my bones, in my soul. But as fast as I can drink, the warmth is sucked away and I am left icy all over again.

I shake her, frustrated and drink quicker, desperate. More frantic. Biting again, again, again. I change positions. Drink more. Take everything she can offer.

"Octavia." A smooth, deep voice drifts from the other side of the bush. "It's time to stop."

I know this voice. I know exactly who it is, and my eyes instantly respond, stinging and tingling.

Fuck him. Fuck Red. Fuck this whole city.

I keep drinking.

He appears, haloed by the park lights, his wavy locks coiffed to perfection. I shake my head as I sink my fangs in deeper.

"You need to let her go," he says, his voice like silken blankets.

I pause only long enough to growl at him. "No. Don't do this to me, let me take her life. Let me hurt her. Just let me play the fucking villain I'm meant to." I resume drinking, and the woman tenses underneath me, realising how close to the end she is, how futile resistance is, how easily I can snuff her life out.

"Tave," Xavier says.

I crack. Pull off her, a giant, heaving cry wailing from my throat.

"You don't want to do this." He holds his hand out, pleading.

"Fuck you," I whimper and then I bite harder. Drink faster.

"Let her go, Tave. It won't stop the pain. It won't stop the ache."

I can't even speak. My whole body is on edge. I don't cry. Won't show emotion. Refuse to break. My face tingles, my eyes prickle and sting like they've been sprayed with acid.

34

"She still loves you," he breathes.

"Stop it. Just fucking stop it," I bark.

His words have penetrated my ribs. Driven a blade straight to my heart. My fingers release their grip on the woman, and she makes to run.

Funny how humans don't value their lives until they're under threat of it being taken. Xavier grabs her and compels her to forget what happened, he tells her to get some iron supplements and gives her coin, forcing her not to spend it on blood but the iron she needs, and then he sends her on her way. And I stand there shivering, smothered in blood, my mouth and hair and fingers sticky with the life force of the countless humans I've drunk.

I feel nothing and everything. He comes to me.

"Don't," I say, unable to look him in the eye.

Xavier doesn't listen. He wraps his thick arms around me and there, hidden in the shroud of the park's hedges, I break in two.

I sob, the heaving breaths rocking my chest, and all the while he holds me as though he were the elder sibling and not the other way around.

We sink to the ground, leaning against the bench, and he holds me, strokes my hair and tells me it's going to be okay.

I wail into his chest until there's nothing left but hiccuping sobs and sore eyes.

He kisses my forehead, takes my cheeks in his hands and makes me look at him. "You are enough."

That makes my bottom lip wobble. An aching lance spears through my ribs for so many reasons.

For the truth that I have never felt good enough, worthy enough. For the fact that right now, I believe him. And for the realisation that this may be the first time I have ever felt like I am enough.

Last, for the knowledge that all I ever wanted was to be enough for *her*.

"I promise you, Tave, when she wakes up, she will have seen the err of her ways. It's not for me to apologise on her behalf. But I know you and know how deep your love for her goes."

"It's too late, she broke a piece of me."

"Yes, and what did you do to her? You took her control away. She had the choice to die in that ring or change into the thing she hates. And why do you think she drained an innocent?"

I shrug in his arms.

"Don't be petulant. She didn't transition for herself. She might be unconscious, but we're intelligent enough to recognise the truth. You know her. She wouldn't have turned willingly. You have to recognise that you both fucked up. I know she needs to do more than just say the words. But you, too, need to be open enough to hear them and accept her apology when she wakes up."

"If..."

"She will. My healers are with her."

"And if she doesn't?" I whimper, more tears rolling down my eyes, only I don't know why I'm crying at the prospect of her dying. Relief probably.

I rub my face with the sleeve of my shirt.

"I just wanted this city to love me the way I love it. I want to feel like the place I call home wants to be my home. I really thought that this competition would be my chance to influence it for the positive."

"It will be. It's not over yet," he says, brushing a loose lock of hair back towards my bun.

"It is over. I'm done, Xavier. There's no way I can win. And look at what's happening in the city centre? It's chaos, Red isn't safe. She may never well be again. She can't stay here."

He pulls me in tight. "Don't think about it. Just focus on me and breathing and remembering that at some point we weren't broken or lost. And that version of Octavia is still somewhere inside you. But more than anything, remember that I love you, and you will always be enough for me."

I hate that he's made me feel better. What is it about the love of a sibling that can repair hurt faster than anyone else?

"Thank you," I say, and wipe my face.

He shrugs.

"No, I mean it, Xavier. Thank you for this." I gesture at our sitting position. "Thank you for stopping me from killing that woman. I would have regretted it and felt awful."

He nods. "What are brothers for?"

And this time, I kiss his forehead and together we stroll back through the streets to his mansion. Despite the city collapsing around me, with every step I take, another brick rebuilds itself inside me.

CHAPTER 6

RED

I slip through the ether. I'm not sure whether I'm still alive. I don't remember what happened, all I know is that I dream of *her*.

The love of my life. The one I've lost. The woman I broke because I let myself be manipulated.

And then I dream of Eleanor. The way she caressed Cordelia a thousand years ago. The stone arbour. The intensity of their love.

Amelia flashes through my mind. Her savage maw and fanged teeth plunging into a human. Her eyes wild and alive, twinkling with a feral kind of joy as she drains him dry. Sucks the life from him until his eyes go dull and his fingers slacken their grip.

All of it swills and merges with what happened in the ring, my body aches even in my dreams. My muscles flex and spasm and twitch even in my sleep.

I have no idea how long I stay under for. Long enough that the tension in my body finally eases and I have to wonder whether I'm being kept asleep. But eventually, the light seeps into my eyes, a warm, milky light. Not the rays of sun, but of warm fires, burning embers and lanterns.

"Ugh," I say. Not exactly the most profound thing to say on waking up after what feels like an eon of sleep. But it's the only thing I could manage.

"Hey," a deep husk of a voice says.

That makes my eyes shoot open.

"Xavier?" I say and then frown hard. "What the fuck?"

I shoot up, realising I'm in a silky bed, one almost as smooth as the vampire in front of me. His wavy black locks skim his chiselled cheek bones. He rubs his sharp jaw, his salt-white teeth smiling at me. If I even had an inkling of interest in men, I'd find him a delightful specimen. Unfortunately, mankind just isn't for me.

"What...?" I start and then stop because I'm not sure that's the question I really want to ask. "Where is she?" I try again.

His shoulders slump, he pulls his eyes away from me.

"Great," I say, leaning back against the soft headboard. The room I'm in is cream, the bed too, in fact, by the looks of the hallway outside the room, most of the house appears to be white.

"Amelia?" I ask.

"She's been here, but I sent her away when it was clear you'd sleep for a while. The fewer people in this building, the better. She's in the city and staying at the Whisper Club, I believe."

"Okay," I say and take in more of the room. "You're a strange vampire to like white so much."

He pulls his gaze back to mine. "Light is beautiful and unfortunately too much sun isn't great for my complexion, so I make false light with colour. Hence the cream walls, marble, lanterns and lights."

"This is your house?" I ask.

He nods, his chest puffing up.

"One of them. I have two, one in the Beaumont territory and one in the St Clair. We're in the Beaumont house right now. I didn't think staying in the St Clair territory would be sensible given your... er..."

"Transformation?"

"Exactly." He nods.

"How long was I out?"

He swallows. "Three nights."

"Fuck." I wipe a hand over my face, running it through my knotted hair. I need a shower. The pleasantries are great, but he knows as well as I do that it's not what I want to talk about. My fingers skim the silk bedding—it's as creamy as the walls.

"Has she been to visit?" I ask.

He presses his lips together.

"Mother of Blood," I curse.

"What did you do? I want to know in your words because she won't speak of it," he says and then gets up, moving to a table at the back of the room. There's a clatter of glass, a pouring of liquid and then he returns to the bed holding two goblets and my heart sinks.

"You should drink something," he says and hands me the cup.

I can tell even without taking a sip that it's human blood. "I don't want it."

"Red..." he says, his tone dropping, accusing.

"I. Don't. Want. It."

He sags. "Not only were you an addict, but you literally drained a monk in order to stay alive, and now you're making out like you won't continue to drink blood in order to survive?"

"Do I *need* to drink it in order to stay alive now?"

He shrugs at me "I don't know but I suspect so. It would be better all around if you did, given you just slept the better part of three days. And given the state of the city..."

The words hang in the air.

"What does that mean?"

Xavier looks away and out the window. "It's bad out there. Everyone is hunting for you, whether it's to pray at your feet, beg for a blessing or sever your head from your body. The city is quietly losing the plot, and we're not sure how to stop it."

"We?"

His eyes slide back to mine, but he doesn't answer. The silence is answer enough: Octavia.

Finally, he speaks. "Answer the question, what did you do to her?"

I tut at him and lower my eyes to where I hold the goblet in one hand and fiddle with the silk sheets in the other. "You witnessed what I did. I fucked the strengths trial and screwed our chance of winning."

"Yes, but why?"

I can't look at him. "Because I was mistaken. I was led to believe that Octavia had viciously stolen my memories. That she'd done it with the intent to control and manipulate. And I was too fucking cross to see through the ruse."

"So you wouldn't have done it had you known the full truth?"

"God no, Xavier, I love her. She is my entire world. I just want her back."

"Thought as much."

"It's over, I'll never get her back." My eyes water at the

thought, and I have to bite down on my cheek to stop the flow.

"I can't make any promises, but I think I can orchestrate a conversation. In the meantime, there's someone else here to see you."

He holds out a hand and I pass the goblet back. Then he slides his palm against mine, and we struggle to manhandle me out of bed. It's a full two minutes before I'm up. I'm not in pain so much as I am super stiff from lying in bed for three days straight, and all the muscular changes in my body from the transition mean I can't quite control my limbs right. I imagine I look a bit like a teenage boy who just went through an overnight growth spurt, all clumsy and gangly. Only I'm all muscle and stocky bones. More than any of that though, I'm fucking famished. My eyes keep drifting to the goblet. I hold out despite Xavier rolling his eyes at my stubbornness.

I stand just assessing myself. The density of my muscles is different. My shoulders feel bulkier, my thighs thicker. Everything faster. Stronger. This must be the vampire elements in me. I wonder what the dhampir pieces do. It reminds me of the man in Octavia's club and the strange energy that pulsed from my fingers into his stomach.

Xavier lets me lean on him as he guides me to the window and points down. It's dark, but I don't have to squint the way I would have before.

"That has been there for three days," he says, a note of disgust in his voice.

"You're kidding me?" I say, peering down at Xavier's garden. "He slept outside?"

Xavier nods. "Unfortunately, he got in before I got the guards in place. But I can't trust him. He's on the other team, and I had no idea what he would do. He's lucky I didn't throw him in the dungeon, frankly. I was peeved enough that he worked out where you were. So I refused entry, and he refused to leave because he said he knew you were here."

"You left him in your garden for three days?"

He shrugs, nonchalant at me. "I'm not callous. I sent food."

I raise an eyebrow.

"I may have given him a blanket too."

"Really generous there, Xavier."

He pouts at me.

I sigh. "I'd better go and see what he wants."

I hesitate, glancing at the goblet on the bedside table, not having drunk any of the contents. It smells divine and my mouth waters.

"Just drink it," he says, his tone bored.

I shake my head. "I can't."

I may have had to drain a human in order to stay alive, but I'm not sure I'm quite ready to accept my fate as a hybrid. I don't think drinking human blood is something I'll ever get used to or accept.

I push it to the back of the bedside table and pull my eyes away, all the time, ignoring the fact my mouth is salivating at the smell.

Xavier looks at me the entire time, his usually plump lips pressed flat and thin. He says nothing though, just quietly observes.

It feels like judgement. But he'll just have to wait. I'm not going to be pushed into breaking everything that was important to me just because I did it once to survive. That was different.

Wasn't it?

Wasn't it?

Fuck.

I wipe my face not wanting to process what's happened and struggle after him. I'm a little unsteady on my feet but I make it to the bedroom door and into the hall.

As I expected, the mansion is more extravagant than is polite. Everywhere I look there's white and cream marble threaded with golden rivulets and glass.

Even though it's dark outside, the mansion—though it's more like a palace than a house—is bright. There's a crystal chandelier dangling from the ceiling in the centre of an enormous foyer. A giant marble staircase swirls around the huge, open-plan foyer, splitting into two and sweeping towards different wings of the mansion.

We follow the hallway around until we reach the stairs. It's slow going, but my body eases into its new form, the muscles finally warming up. My skin crawls like someone is watching me. I glance around, all confident and vibing with my new body until I take a step onto the stairs. Suddenly what was down is now up.

There's a swoosh of air. I land in a set of thick arms.

"Mother of fucking Blood, Xavier. I never thought I'd see the day when I was in a man's arms."

He chuckles as he steadies us against the banister.

"Right, you can put me down now," I say and attempt to wriggle. But his arms become solid iron bars, and I huff at him.

"Listen. Octavia might be pissed at you, but I have known that woman for five centuries. I reserve hope that one day she will forgive you, and if that day comes and I was the one that let her human plaything crack its head open on my marble stairs and stain them pink... well, I shan't like to think of the consequences."

I glare up at him, but he just laughs at my indigence and carries me the entire way down the stairs.

"I am gay, you know." I continue huffing at him.

"Oh darling, I'm as pansexual as they come, but you are most definitely not my type. This is all manners and graces."

Finally, we reach the bottom of the staircase, and he puts me down on solid ground. His eyes flit up to the second floor. I follow his movement, but there's no one there.

"As long as you're inside my compound, you'll be safe. I've imposed quite the barrier around the outskirts of my property and the land is guarded. But I warn you, do not step outside the property alone."

"Super," I say, unable to hide the sarcasm.

"Red..."

"Yes, Xavier?" I drawl.

"Do. Not. Leave the grounds." He folds his arms at me.

"Oh, come on, it can't be that bad."

"A lot has happened. The city is... well, let us discuss once you have dispatched of your guest. Besides, we need to work out what to do with you and the trials."

"And Octavia?"

"That's a whole other situation we'll need to discuss. Now go on. Get that thing off my property. He's dirtying up my white roses."

I laugh as I wander out of the enormous, white, studded oak doors and find Lincoln on a bench a little way into the garden. Movement in the corner catches my eye. It's a vampire very much standing guard and watching Lincoln's every move. The more I scan the grounds, the more vampires I see. The whole property is crawling with guards.

"RED, GODS. YOU'RE ALIVE," Lincoln says and leaps off the bench, sprinting over to me, his arms open wide.

The vampire guard appears in front of me in a flash. Lincoln crashes into his enormous chest and bounces off, landing a few feet away. He brushes himself down, and I grab the guard's arm. "It's okay, honestly, I'll be fine."

He glares at me, stoic, his features unmoving and then nods. "So be it."

The guard steps out of the way, but I notice he doesn't return to his original spot. He stays a little distance away, enough that he would have to strain to hear our conversation but not far enough that if Lincoln were to attempt to attack me, he could still sever every one of his limbs before either of us blinked.

"Hey," I say, suddenly uncomfortable. It's been a while since Lincoln and I were together in a non-hostile environment.

He shoves his hands in his pockets and kicks the ground with the toe of his boot. "I thought it would be easier when I saw you for the first time..."

He lets that hang in the air. I don't know that I have anything to say, though. It's not easy when we parted the way we did.

"I've been here ever since Xavier took you. I tried his St Clair property first, but you weren't there. I knew he had another one here in Octavia's territory because of hunter surveillance. You're safe, though. I was the only one who saw him take you after..."

"After I transitioned publicly in front of the entire city?" I ask, and again, I'm unable to keep the dread from my voice.

"Yeah. After that. Look..." he nudges the ground with his toe again. "I am really sorry."

I fold my arms, push my weight onto one of my hips.

"What are you sorry for, Linc? A lot of shit has gone down in the past couple of weeks and honestly, I'm not sure where we are or what we're doing anymore."

He hangs his head low. "I'm sorry, okay. I got caught up in the thought of winning. That maybe I might make something of myself for the family. Neither of us come from an elder family... We both need this."

"I get that, but that doesn't mean you abandon your friends," I say and then regret it.

He pouts. "You weren't a great friend the last two weeks either. You hid a pretty big secret from me."

I guess he's right, I'm not sure I was any better than him —hell, look what I did to Octavia. But I was also protecting my life.

"You're right. I was a pretty shitty friend. But I couldn't trust you, Lincoln, you were literally pitted against me and weren't showing any signs of loyalty, and let's be real, the secret I was holding was protecting my life. From what I hear, it's not exactly safe for me in the city right now?"

He flicks his head towards the perimeter of Xavier's property.

"No. I haven't been out since I broke in to get to you. But I've heard the guards and staff whispering. It sounds like a war zone out there."

He just brushes off the fact he broke into Xavier's house. "Yeah, and breaking in was the most wise and safe choice you've ever made," I say, sarcasm dripping off me in waves.

"I had to." His lip twitches like he wants to grin, and it makes my mouth quiver too. The ice between us is finally broken.

"Why come to me now?"

He sags. "Because even though I wanted to win, I never

wanted to see you hurt. Not like that. I would never support Dahlia to do that to you. I thought she would fight Octavia, and we'd be the ones sparring, and then Cordelia changed the rules and decided to only have one fighter, and then you... I don't even want to know how you managed to get Octavia to not show up. But I had to stand there and watch Dahlia pummel the shit out of you. I thought you were going to die. I thought that was it and I'd never see you again. I was sick to my stomach and... and..." Lincoln waffles and stumbles his way through his stream of consciousness.

"And?"

"And I'm sorry, okay? I never, ever want to see you injured like that again. I was a fucking coward. I should have jumped into the ring to stop it, and I didn't. I'll never forgive myself for that."

I reach out and pull his hand into mine. "I forgive you. And I'm sorry I kept my secret from you. I can't promise I wouldn't make the same choice again, but I am sorry that my choice hurt you."

He nods and pulls me into an embrace. The vampire rushes forward several feet until he realises it's a hug and then settles down, although he doesn't return to his position, he stays close to us.

Lincoln holds on for a long time, rubbing my back and squeezing me hard enough it feels like he's still convincing himself I'm here and breathing. When he finally lets me go, he tilts my chin up.

"Where's your heartbeat?" he asks.

"Gone."

His eyes flash. "What are you?"

"That is anyone's guess. A hybrid. Not quite human, not quite witch, not quite vampire. I am something new."

"The dhampir," he whispers.

I shrug and nod. "I guess so." What else is there to say? It's a big ugly truth between me and the rest of the city. Between me and him. Me and Octavia.

He softens and gives me a fist bump to the shoulder. "So, we're okay?" he asks.

"That depends."

"On?"

"On whether you still want to win."

He presses his lips shut and stares at me for a long time before nodding. "I do. But not at the expense of your life."

"Good answer."

He shrugs. "A truthful answer. I debated whether admitting it would make you hate me, but I figured I needed to be straight with you. Besides, I know for a fact you still want to win, so there's no harm in me wanting the same thing."

I nod. I do, only I'm not sure why I want to win anymore. It used to be for Amelia. To get her the cure. But seeing the delight in her eyes in that forest. It shifted something. It made me as sick as it did push my understanding of who she is, what she is and what she wants. And how much that diverges from what I want.

"Where did you go?" Lincoln says.

"I'm here. Sorry."

He carries on. "I want to win, yes. But I think it's more about whether or not I'm willing to step on our friendship to get it. And I'm not... And I think that's what's important."

"It is. Thanks for waiting for me to wake up. I'm sorry he made you sleep in the cold."

"It wasn't too bad. Besides, it was worth it to see that you're alright."

"What's that?" I say, noticing him scratching a crusty wound on his palm.

"Oh, nothing. I got it during the aftermath of your transition. There were a ton of fights that broke out. I was trying to protect the humans, but there were so many protestors and vampires it all got very confusing at one point, and I nearly got staked. And this—" he waves his hand around, "—was a stray blade someone threw. I batted it away with my hand and unfortunately, it was sharp side up."

My hands tingle, like they're urging me to reach for his wound. It's instinct. Like compulsion, only I'm leaning forward willingly. I reach for his hand more out of morbid curiosity than anything else.

"Wh—" Lincoln starts as my fingers curl around his palm and a strange heat nestles between our skin.

It tingles like electricity and scratches like dry sand between your toes. It makes the most incredible golden energy flare out from where we touch. The air fills with the soft scent of mint and lavender.

"Woah," Lincoln says, and when he pulls his hand away from mine, the pair of us gawp at his palm. The wound is gone.

"How the hell did you do that?"

My mouth hangs slack. "I have no idea. It happened once before, but afterwards I was completely drained, and I couldn't fully heal it. I guess it's part of being a dhampir, they were healers..."

He flips his hand this way and that, noting the fresh skin and smooth texture where once it was mangled and scabbing.

"This is off the chart," he says, still examining his hand.

"How about you don't tell anyone until I've worked out

exactly how to control it and what the consequences are for using it."

"That would be my honour and the least I can do."

There's a pause; it's sticky and thick. Though the air doesn't feel as awkward as it did when I first arrived. But it's clear now that both of us have apologised, neither of us know what to say. Our friendship is healed, and yet a scar still remains.

"I'll see you around," I say.

"At the next trial."

"When is it?"

"Few days' time. Listen, the whispers I've heard here... Cordelia is hunting you, Red. The Chief too. You need to be careful. They want you out of hiding and in the limelight."

"Like a plaything they control."

Lincoln nods, his expression souring. "And if it's not them, it's the church. The monks are... well, they want you found just as much as Cordelia."

"Great," I say and sag on the spot.

"There's a ball, the same one that always opens the start of the Festival of Blood at the Whisper Club. We suspect that's where the final trial will be held. But it's not safe for you out there. Not yet, anyway."

He squeezes my hand and takes off at a jog towards the exit of Xavier's property. I stare after him for a long while, until my back burns like I'm being watched. I glance up at the palatial windows. One of them has the curtains pulled, but there's no one there. It's dark. But the fabric moves like it was just tugged.

Someone is watching me.

CHAPTER 7

OCTAVIA

Xavier marches into the room I've commandeered in his mansion, slams the door shut and huffs his way to the end of my bed where he plonks himself down and folds his arms, glaring at me.

"You can't just watch her forever," he moans.

"I can, and I shall do whatever pleases me." This time, I fold my arms, and I'm quite aware we both look like teenagers having a tantrum at each other, but he doesn't get to push me into this.

"If you hate her so much, why bother coming back to my mansion with me?" He raises a smug eyebrow at me, and I want to rip it off.

I open my mouth to answer and stop. Why am I watching her? Because I'm furious. Because I did want to know if she survived, not because I cared if she was alive, but because I care if we get magic back. If we get the cure. I *care* about who takes control of this city.

When I don't answer, he continues droning on at me.

"She nearly fell down the bloody stairs because she felt your eyes on her."

"So?"

"Octavia!" Xavier says and kneads his temples. "You are very close to slipping from your status as favourite."

"Don't bullshit me. There is no way in hell any of our other siblings would be your favourite. What do you want from me, Xavier? She betrayed me."

"Yes. Because she thought you'd done the same to her. And let us not forget, you *did actually* take her memories... Repeatedly... and against her fucking will."

"To protect her."

He flings his arms up.

I pout at him. "I'm not talking to her."

"You have to." He pulls a piece of card out of his pocket and chucks it at me.

"Fucking gargoyle whisper network. Cordelia might not know where Red is, but the goyles do. So this has found its way here."

I snatch it out of the air and stare at the gold embossed text on it. It's from Mother.

Lady Cordelia St Clair cordially invites you to the final trial and opening ceremony for the Festival of Blood. It will be a masquerade ball. You are required to attend as part of the trial. Further instructions will be given in due course.

"There's a second invite for Red."

He pulls another card out of his pocket and throws that

at me too. I snatch it out of the air for the second time and read the words on her card.

It's the same except it says:

> *In order to protect your identity, we will not allow anyone into the building without wearing a mask. Your attendance is mandatory or both you and Octavia will be eliminated from the prizes at the end of the trials.*

"Fuck," I hiss.

"You need to talk to her before the trial."

I drop both invites onto the fire burning in the hearth of the room I'm in. Xavier follows my hands, his eyes lazily landing on the fire.

"Was that necessary?" he asks.

"No point in keeping trash. And all Mother is doing is using the pretence of a 'masked' ball to draw Red out. If we thought the hunt for Red is bad in the city now, that entire ball is going to be a trap. Mother of Blood knows how we're going to get her in and out safely without someone finding and capturing her."

Xavier's eyes narrow at me. "I thought you didn't care...?"

I stiffen, standing a little straighter. "I don't."

"Mmmhmm," he says, the sarcasm practically dripping off his smirk.

"Fuck you, Xavier. She's quite literally ruined my chances of winning this thing. What's the point of evening going to the ball?"

"And yet, the very fact you read those invitations mean

you haven't given up on trying to win. And frankly, it seems like you haven't given up on her either."

"I have."

Xavier takes a seat in the armchair in the corner of the room, crossing his legs and leaning against the back. His head tilts to rest against the chair back, and he heaves an exaggerated sigh.

"Ever the dramatics," I say.

"Takes one to know one," he says and drags his head off the chair to look up at me. "It's a long life, Tave. Do you really want to spend it alone?"

My jaw clenches. "I will not forgive her. Not after everything I've done for her."

And truly, I have. I have made so many sacrifices for that woman, I don't think I could even count them if I tried.

"Fine." He wafts a hand in my direction. "Go say goodbye, then. Seems like you're over her. You might as well tell her you're going to search for a way to sever the bond and be done with it."

I fold my arms, fire a pointed stare his way. He glares right back. An impasse.

Neither of us bends.

It's me that cracks first.

"FINE. I will."

I march to the door. But his words stop me.

"You go do that… I mean… It's not like you've stayed in *my* mansion for the last three days or anything. It's not like you've lurked in every corner, every darkened hallway and door, waiting for a glimpse of her. It's not like you've stubbornly refused to ask for updates and then hovered around my staff, hoping for them to drop breadcrumbs about her progress."

My teeth clamp down so hard I actually pop a bubble of

air in my jawbone. He's wrong. I mean... Okay, he is theoretically correct. I have done all of those things, but not because I give a shit about her. But because she's bonded to me, and I was looking out for myself. Putting me as number one.

I have no idea what would happen to me if she died. Stupid fucking bond. I should have done far more research before agreeing, but apparently my brain was in my pussy that night and not a cell lived anywhere else. I don't bother glancing at him as I march out of the room. But his shit-eating smirk crawls over my skin anyway.

"Wanker," I breathe.

He hears, of course he does, he's a vampire. The same as I hear his breathy laughter all the way down the hall. I make my way downstairs and just as I hit the bottom of the sweeping staircase, Red enters through the double oak doors.

She freezes. What little colour she has, drains out of her face.

Loving someone is a bizarre experience. People speak of humanity. Of the complexity of holding vast and conflicting emotions simultaneously. But humans understand nothing of the depths of a vampire's heart. The levels to which we will suffer, the sacrifices we will make. The intensity with which we love.

We live for millennia. We must hold vast entanglements inside us so that we may continue. If we were to break as frequently as human hearts do, we would not survive the long years—and yet, I stand here before her, breaking.

I stare at her, my entire body aching. I never thought I would look at her and feel such poisonous rage. I want to hack her pretty fucking head from her neck. I want to slap her arse until it bleeds. I want to punish her, to make her orgasm over and over until she's begging me to stop. I want to make her comprehend how much she has broken me.

My fingers itch with the need to slide around her neck, choke her, watch the life fade from her gaze.

And all the while, my traitorous fucking heart is pleading with me to do the opposite. I want the explanation. I want her to make me understand why she did what she did. How could she? My heart clenches and spasms in my chest so much I want to fall to my knees and be sick. I wish I could tear the useless muscle from my ribs and discard it. Because loving her is too hard when I am so furious with her. And yet, so too am I desperate to lift her up and wrap my arms around her. I refuse to hold both of these things, so I push the desire down and cling to the fury.

"I can—" she starts, but I hold my hand up to stop her speaking. Her pert little lips fall closed.

Better.

I prefer her silent right now. She's not the only fragile one in the mansion. I will not break, though. No matter how much Xavier might meddle, I will not forgive her. Not this time.

I spin on my heel and march off towards the rear of Xavier's mansion. I halt when I realise she hasn't followed me. I sigh, turn around and she's stood exactly where she was.

"Are you coming?"

"Wh—I—Well."

I don't stop to listen to her mutters, I take off at a rate of knots. If Xavier is so intent on us speaking, then she can jolly well speak to me on my terms.

Her feet patter against the marble tiles. So I make my

way through a side door, down a set of stairs and into the belly of the house.

Xavier gave the majority of his staff the week off. He wasn't sure when Red would wake, and he didn't want anyone who wasn't a long-term member he trusted here when she did. Not with the flow through of people. The risk of information leaking out was too great.

I meander down the corridor until I reach the kitchen. I need blood, preferably mixed with whiskey. Or better yet, Sangui Cupa.

By the time she enters the kitchen, I've already procured two goblets and a bag of human blood mixed with essence of jealousy. I pour two goblets and put the carton away in the warmer.

She eyes the goblets, her nose wrinkling.

"You smell it?" I say.

She nods. "My senses are... different."

"Heightened, I suspect. You are half vampire now."

Her nostrils flare like she's unimpressed by this information.

"Have you drunk since you woke?"

She shakes her head, her little lips pressing flat like she's resisting.

"You need to drink," I say. My tone is cold, sharp and unforgiving.

Her eyes drop to the kitchen island counter, she fingers the base of the goblet, swirling her fingers in semi circles around the stem.

"You don't want to?"

"I've only just woken up, Octavia. After killing an innocent man."

"And fucking our chances of winning," I say.

Red winces, and I take a sick sort of pleasure seeing her flinch away from my words. Good.

She sits on a barstool. Her eyes drag over the contents of the goblet, and she swallows hard. Her brows furrow, her lips part. And a flash of heat washes through me—as if I *want* to watch her drink. It's infuriating. I can see she's struggling with the conflict of what her body wants her to do and the old human mindset she's still clinging to of 'blood is bad.'

"Do you know what happens to a vampire that doesn't drink?"

She swallows again, harder this time. "They desiccate?"

"It's considered to be the most hideous form of torture. A feat of psychological and physical pain like no other. Your body is clever though. It will try to survive, try to eat itself from the inside out, it will drive you to commit atrocities all in the name of getting blood. Or, you could drink a little of..." I reach under the counter and down to the warmer and pull out the same carton, "this barrel-aged B-type with essence of jealousy and all of that can go away. Lest you forget, all of the blood I drink is donated willingly. You can drink that way too."

She screws up her eyes as if that will make the reality of what she needs to do go away. It won't. She needs to get over this or her life is going to be rather uncomfortable.

Breathing out one long puff through her nostrils, she grabs the goblet and throws back half the glass.

"Impressive," I say as she slams it down, a single drop bouncing out of the goblet and onto the island counter. I reach over and wipe it up, pressing the droplet into my mouth. It's a travesty wasting any essence of jealousy.

My eyes scan the carving block on the edge of the counter, it holds a set of knives the chefs must use when they're cooking meals for the staff or for whatever human guests Xavier has.

She follows my gaze.

"Are you going to kill me?" she says. Her skin has flushed, the blood clearly having an effect. Perhaps this transformation has left her with a little more vampire than I thought.

"Not today. But I am curious as to your healing capabilities."

She shrugs. "Seems I can heal others. I know nothing about me. But I don't think that is what we really need to talk about, is it?"

"No." I pick up one of the knives and twirl the point around the pad of my index finger. She watches me like a hawk, constantly flicking from where my hands play with sharp objects to my expression. Gauging, calculating. Am I going to kill her? Hurt her? Play with her?

I want nothing to do with her. Not anymore.

She places her hands on the counter, her head dropped. "I need to apologise."

"No," I snap, and in a flash, I bring the knife down to the back of her hand, positioned between two metacarpal bones. The point of the blade pushing just enough to make her hiss, but not enough to cut the skin.

Her shoulders rise and fall with her rapid breathing. She looks up at me, slowly. "Do it. Just fucking do it if it will make you feel better. Is that what you want? To hurt me? The way I hurt you?"

I snarl. Push the blade, just enough to cut the skin. She tenses but her gaze never leaves mine.

It's a game of chicken. Who will last out. Who will win?

"I am sorry, Octavia. Sadie lied to me. Or not lied, so much as misled."

"No," I snarl and push the knife in a millimetre more. This time her teeth clench against the pain. A bead of blood wells up and over the back of her hand. The scent is divine, sweet summer rain, blossoms, iron and winter fires. I feel drunk on the smell.

She breathes hard, her whole body tense.

"Try again," I say.

"I'm fucking sorry, okay? I fucked it. I fucked up. Sadie only gave me half my memories. She made a deal that she would give them back if I threw the fight with Dahlia. She gave me half my memories and chose which half very strategically. So she made it look like you were the villain."

"Ha," I bark out on a sharp laugh. "I've always been the villain in your world, Red. Don't you get it? Everything I've ever done has been for you. To make your life better. To support you, protect you. And at the first fucking sniff of foul play, you decide to fuck everything."

I slam the blade all the way down and into the kitchen counter.

She lets out a high-pitched squeal which she cuts off instantly, refusing to let me see her agony. But her eyes squeeze shut, water pooling at the edges.

Her silence, at least, goes in her favour. She doesn't get to play weak right now. She was a fucking coward in the forest when she sabotaged our chance of winning.

Red takes two giant gulps of air and then reaches for the goblet with her free hand, gulping down the other half of the blood.

Interesting.

When she looks at me, her eyes are watery and bright. The green of fresh leaves and spring buds. She slams the cup down.

"When Sadie finally gave me all of my memories, I realised the mistake I'd made."

"A mistake?" I laugh, and I hate the way it comes out, all shrill and hysterical. "I think that is the understatement of the millennia, Red. Gods. You're just like everyone else. You see me as a monster and because of that, I will never be enough for you"

"That's not tr—"

"It's exactly how you looked at me in the Blood Woods. Don't even try to deny it. Do you know what that's like? To see the woman you have fallen for look at you like you're less than? Like you're the monster from her fucking nightmares?"

"I didn't—"

I step closer and she flinches. The same sick twist of pleasure coils in my gut as I step closer, closer, closer.

"So you fucked our chances of taking this city for our own on a whim?"

"It wasn't a whim," she says through gritted teeth.

"Oh, I'm sorry, because of the half-addled memories of a dhampir."

That makes her tone switch. She prods me in the chest, pushing me back. "Don't you fucking use what's happened against me. Sadie manipulated me."

"And you fell for it. You trusted Sadie over me. You ruined us because you *thought* I'd taken your memories forcefully."

She bares her teeth at me now. "YOU DID, OCTAVIA."

I step back, shocked at the fight, the rage, the resentment still in her. Both our shoulders heave as we take each other in.

"Fine. I did. What, once? Twice? And only in the name of helping, supporting or saving you."

This time, she sneers. "You don't get to justify your wrong doings if I can't do the same. You're not innocent in this."

"And you're clearly not sorry."

I lean down, grip her chin between my thumb and fore-finger. I want to stop breathing because every time I inhale, it's her I smell. Leather, damp skin and hot muscles. She smells of the outdoors, of life and the sea and living things.

My eyes fall to her lips. Fuck. Every ounce of me wants to kiss her. But I can't. I shouldn't. Even if I do, it doesn't change anything, I am still furious. I still can't forgive her.

She's breathing hard now; I don't think she can hold back the pain of the knife between her hand bones much longer.

I inch forward, my cheek skimming hers, as if I'm going to kiss her. I don't, and I'm punished with a bristle of electricity passing between us.

I yank the knife out, and she hisses, immediately grip-ping her palm in her good hand. But before she can examine the damage, I've brought the blade between us, licked her blood from the shaft.

"Delicious," I say, tasting the sweet notes and deep, heady allure of magic thrumming in her blood cells.

I lift the blade to her throat.

"Either kill me or stop threatening me," she says, leaning against the glinting knife's edge.

"You'd like that wouldn't you? For me to just end it all. Put you out of your misery. Well, I'm not that merciful, Verity. You don't get off that lightly. I'm only here because we're bonded, and Xavier forced my hand. You fucked up. I don't forgive you."

"I did fuck up. But I'm trying to apologise."

"You think a pitiful 'I'm sorry' is going to make up for what you've done? You. Ruined. Everything."

I slide the knife higher under her neck, forcing her to tilt her head up, forcing her eyes to meet mine.

"What do you want from me? How am I meant to fix this?"

"I want to be enough. I want to feel like I'm enough. To feel loved. To feel, for once in my godforsaken life, like someone chose me."

She swallows against the blade, and it nicks her throat. A tiny droplet runs down her neck and pools in the dip between her clavicles.

Before I know what I'm doing, I've bent down and licked it and the entire river all the way up to the source.

As I pull my tongue away, I notice the cut has already healed. She's panting. Practically begging me to fuck her.

Mother of Blood. I made a mistake tasting her. My pussy clenches between my thighs. This time, it's me who swallows... Swallows down the giant fucking mistake I made savouring a drop of her blood. The sweetest, most enticing liquid I've ever consumed. It surpasses even essence of jealousy. It's like summer and the heavens and every type of blood in the city. It tastes of a thousand witches that came before her. Of magic whispers and ripe fruit. Like sunsets and dawn and waves cresting on a winter beach.

But I'm not going to let her know how exquisite she is.

I steel my features. "You taste different," I say as coldly as I can, trying to hide the fact I feel like I just took drugs.

"Well, I'm not the same person anymore. I'm on my knees for you, begging."

I pull back... scan her face and then purr out my next words. "I don't see you on your knees, Verity."

She hesitates but then she falls to the ground.

Gods, the sight is ruining my will power. "Mmm, see? Same old good girl you always were. Not so different after all, are you?"

She slides her thighs open a little, placing her hands palm up on her knees.

I wave her off, disinterested. "If you're going to grovel, you could at least do it naked."

She hesitates, her brows pinching.

"Or not." I shrug and speed towards the door.

"No. WAIT," she shrieks.

Trembling, she lifts her top off and discards it on the kitchen cobbles. She scoots up, tugging her trousers down, pulling her shoes off and her socks, then she sits back in the Nadu position in her sports bra and boxers.

I hop up onto the kitchen counter and open a jar of nuts coated in blood yogurt. I chuck a handful in my mouth and cock my head at her.

I ogle her body. Observing, objectifying. She's right, she is a different person. Her shoulders bulge, the curved cut through her biceps more pronounced. As are her traps, her thighs. Her stomach is flat in some places, ridged and muscled in others. Fuck, she is a specimen sent from the Mother of Blood herself. That thought halts me in my tracks when I remember the Mother of Blood is *actually* my mother. I must remember not to thank her at all in future.

I swallow down the blood nuts, my mouth suddenly dry as I gawp at her extremely defined abs.

"That's not naked," I say.

She huffs, but obediently pulls off her sports bra and boxers. And then she really is naked. She rests her palms back on her thighs and spreads her legs an inch more, knowing I can see. Then she lowers her head. Leaving me with a delightful view of her pretty pink pussy.

I swallow hard, a war fizzing inside me. Fury burning my throat as I try to make myself leave. Try to force my eyes away from her flesh.

But her blood is in my system, and I want to ruin her.

I glance at her palm. "You are healed."

Her head continues to hang low. "So it seems," she says and tilts her head up to me. "I am sorry, Octavia, I am begging you to forgive me."

I want to. There's a piece of me that does, but I cannot. I have spent too long broken by this city's rejection. Shadows linger in my soul; she was supposed to be the light that cast them away. The one person I thought would love me the way I loved her, and she failed.

Despite all of that, her blood is in my system and our souls are bonded. There's a significant part of me that hates myself for wanting her right now. I lick my lips. But I know this isn't the right thing to do.

"Get dressed. You don't want this," I say.

"I do. I need you."

"You don't know what you're asking for. If I fuck you, if we do this, you won't like it. I won't hide how I'm feeling."

"I would crawl to the ends of the city if it meant I got to keep you."

I cock my head at her, a single eyebrow raising.

"So be it. Crawl to me. Show me how sorry you are…"

Her eyes glimmer and deepen, lust making them groggy, and then she leans forward, placing her freshly healed palm on the kitchen tiles.

CHAPTER 8

RED

I lean forward, put myself on all fours. She could ask me to lick the kitchen clean and I think I'd do it. I'm that desperate to get her back.

I crawl, inch by agonising inch.

"I'm sorry, Octavia. I'm sorry," I whine all the way across the cobbles. I can't hide the desperation in my voice.

The cobbles make my legs ache. The bite of the cold, uneven stone gnaws into my kneecaps. Before I transitioned, I'd have been bruised for days, now all I'll have is the memory. It doesn't matter what I have to do, how many scars I have to create as long as she will take me back.

Octavia's sitting on the countertop on the other side of the kitchen. She leans against the wall. "Safe word?" she says, not even bothering to look at me.

Instead, she examines her nails like they're the most interesting thing in the room and I am nothing but an irritation.

"Villain," I pant, desperate for her attention, knowing

that the more she ignores me, the tighter my body winds and the more aroused I am. My core heats, my breathing grows laboured, and as if she can sense what her indifference is doing to me, a smile draws across her expression. But still, she doesn't bother to spare me a glance.

I want to scream. I want to touch myself. I want to yank her off that fucking countertop and demand she believe my apology.

Her eyes, despite focusing on her nails, flicker with delight as I edge closer. She takes her top off, exposing her breasts and pierced nipples but leaves her leather trousers and boots on. She plays with her nipples and piercings, refusing to watch me, as I edge closer.

As her nipples harden, I have to close my mouth and look down to stop myself salivating.

When I make it to her feet, she hooks her boot under my chin, tilting my head up to her and finally looks at me.

"This is your last warning. I cannot hide how I feel."

"I want you. I will always want you," I say, my hands sliding over her leather-clad calves. I reach up to touch her, but she slides her boot to the top of my head and pushes me forcefully down and into my submissive position. I gasp, panting at the shock of her action. My fingers slip between my legs and when I pull them away, they shine with my excitement.

I glance up, desperate for any scrap of attention she'll give me. "I truly am so fucking sor—"

She places the sole of her boot against my mouth, cutting my apology off. She sneers down at me; the heat from her gaze could penetrate marble. I've never been so vulnerable. Utterly bared, naked, stripped of any façade, any armour. It's humiliating, and yet my body is hot, tingles swarm in my clit, my breathing is laboured. I like it? I want the degradation. Gods, if this is what she needs, I'll give it to her over and over.

"Enough, your words, are meaningless when it's your actions that ruined us," Octavia says and removes her boot before leaning down and brushing her lips over mine. "Now, you have to earn an orgasm."

The same frisson of electricity that's always between us fizzes in the air. That is something. The knot of anxiety that was aggressively growing in my stomach unfurls a little. She leans back, popping the sole of her boot against my mouth again.

"Well?" she says, staring down at me. Her nipples are tight little peaks. As if the more she humiliates me, the more she gets off on it. She's not the only one, I'm practically vibrating.

I'm breathing hard through my nose, my cheeks on fire. She's degraded me before, but not like this. My clit throbs, just as much heat pooling between my thighs as in my cheeks.

"Are you going to earn your orgasm?"

I nod against her boot.

"Seeing as you're a filthy little blood slut, then you can kiss my filthy little boot, can't you?"

I whimper. I'm one word from exploding. My clit pulses in a rhythm, hardening from the rush of electricity flowing to my pussy.

I swallow and kiss her boot. Then I move onto the leather.

"Mmm," she purrs. "That's my good little blood whore."

She reaches down and grabs me by the throat, hauling me to my feet. Her grip is just tight enough I know I'm not allowed to move. She slides her other hand down my body and between my legs. A little whimper of pleasure escapes my lips.

"You like it when I remind you how much of a little slut you are?" she says, slipping two fingers between my folds and coating them. She pulls them up and examines the sheen. Then her eyes snap to my face.

"Open," she says.

I do as I'm told and open up. She thrusts her fingers over my tongue. "Clean up the mess you made."

When I don't move, she grips my throat harder and my entire body tenses up, my pussy tingles, slick excitement pools between my legs and I tremble trying to hold back the rising orgasm. How can I be this excited when she's barely touched me? My nipples are so hard they ache. My clit so sensitive I swear if my thighs rub together, it will be enough to push me over the edge.

I close my lips around her fingers and suck. It's strange tasting myself when I'm so used to her flavour. When Octavia's fingers are clean, she releases my neck and pulls her fingers out of my mouth.

She scans her hand as if to check whether I missed anything.

Maybe it's the brat in me, maybe it's the fact I'm desperate for forgiveness, maybe it's that if she gives even an inch I'll slide in and steal the power, but I don't wait for her to decide what's next. I curl my hand around her neck and crush my lips to hers. She hesitates, and then slowly closes her eyes and pushes back against me, actually kissing me.

At first, I think everything is going to be okay. She's kissing me, there was that spark between us. I can make this better. If she just kisses enough of me, drinks enough of me, fucks me long enough, she'll realise that we're meant to be. That I'm sorry and that everything will be okay now.

But hope like that never lasts long in the face of reality.

Her fingers grip me, her hands make their way around my body and at first, I'm comforted. Her touch, her warmth, the familiar scent of Oud and cool wind and warm fire wraps around me. But then her fingers dig into my back, my waist, my shoulders. Her nails grow sharp and instead of a caress or embrace of ownership, it's more like punishment. Like she hates me and wants to hurt me.

I pull away, and look at her, my body heaving as I breathe deep. But I refuse to give up, I love her. I will always love her.

So I try again. I unbuckle her trousers and help her slide them off. I tug her ass to the edge of the counter and then I step between her legs.

She tilts for me, giving me access, but her normally glistening core, is not. My stomach sinks, disappointment slides over me like a noose. I always turn her on.

"Are you sure you want this?" I ask. No matter how much I need to apologise, I won't fuck her if this isn't what she wants.

"Yes, but I told you I can't fake how I'm feeling."

Okay, that's fine. I can handle this, I just have to work for it. I lean in and slide my tongue over her clit, kissing and lapping and caressing until I elicit a first moan. Her head falls back, her long raven hair drifting off her shoulders.

"Oh god," she breathes. But none of her usual tone is in her voice. I refuse to give up that easily.

I pick her feet up and slide them onto the counter, giving me better access to her. Then I push a finger inside her. She responds, her body relaxing into me, and at last she's wet enough I can slide another finger in. Then she rocks and tilts and grinds against me.

But it's not like normal. It's perfunctory. It's fucking for the sake of an orgasm. And I can't help the way the tears spring to my eyes. I force them back. If I show any weakness she'll leap on it.

I slide in and out of her, tilting my hand so I can reach the point inside her pussy that I know will make her spill over into orgasm.

I locate it and rub, adding a little extra pressure, and her pants grow stronger. She doesn't look at me, instead her eyes roll shut, and she disappears into the waves of pleasure. Or maybe it's the same waves of pain I'm feeling.

She moans and whimpers, but she doesn't say my name. And as her pussy tightens around my fingers and she spills over into an orgasm, I know she isn't coming for me, she's coming for herself.

I pull out when she's spent. I'm not sure I gave her this orgasm. She took it from me, and suddenly my nakedness isn't just humiliating, it's shameful.

I cover myself, awkward and unsure, and retreat to gather my clothes, knowing I did not earn myself an orgasm. My cheeks are blazing now but with the heat of a thousand unshed tears.

Octavia adjusts herself and pulls on her trousers in silence. The air is stiff and cold and nothing like the way it was between us. It crawls under my skin, infesting my mind. My brain switches into overdrive. This can't go on. We can't have a relationship like this. But I also can't live without her. I don't know where this leaves us. It's clear we both know what just happened was wrong. What am I supposed to do now?

When we're dressed, she leans down and kisses me.

This time, the kiss tells me everything I need to know. It's hard, too hard. Bruising in a way meant to punish. And then something shifts.

Her demeanour, her kiss changes. It's so sudden, so sharp, my heart breaks in two. Her lips lighten, her tongue roams my mouth, caressing mine. But it's automatic, meaningless. All the feeling sucked from between us.

Tears spill down my cheeks as I remember the way we used to kiss, the heat and passion. The way her fingers would pull and tug at my body, desperate to make it hers. Now her arms hang limp at her sides.

This is a punishment worse than death. Worse than becoming the dhampir. And as awful as it is, I don't want it to stop, because if she lets go, I don't think she'll ever kiss me again.

I need her.

I want her in my life and as pathetic as it sounds, if this is all I can have, I'll take it even if every kiss she gives me breaks another piece of my heart.

She pulls off suddenly and I am bereft. Her touch lingers on my mouth like a ghost. My fingers come to my lips, but I'm not sure if it's because I want to keep the sensation or wipe it away.

"You're crying," she says.

There's nothing I can respond to, it wasn't a question, and I don't much feel like explaining that I understand exactly how she feels: hurt, angry, hateful. All of it directed at me.

I can't even bring myself to look at her.

"I warned you, did I not?"

I nod, two more tears spilling out. This time they plop on the kitchen tiles between us.

"I thought if I apologised. If I could explain..."

73

Octavia sniffs, and wipes her mouth, erasing my kiss from her lips. It stings. But not as much as my heart does right now.

"Sometimes an apology isn't enough, Red. I heard you. But that doesn't mean I forgive you. I let you get close to me. I gave you a piece of my soul and you threw me away. You hurt me more than anyone else has in a thousand years. You think grovelling, crawling along a kitchen tile and a quick orgasm is going to fix that? You failed to believe in me. You thought I wasn't good enough just like everyone else."

My mouth parts but the only thing that escapes is empty air.

She huffs. "Exactly, so why should I treat you any different than I treat the rest of the city?"

She turns and strides away. I reach out, desperate to grab her hand and make her believe I'm sorry, but she moves too fast for me to grab her, and my fingers skim her sleeve.

"Octavia."

She keeps walking.

"OCTAVIA," I scream.

Still she walks, but she hesitates in the kitchen doorway.

"Please. I'll do anything. Don't leave. Let me make this up to you."

Her head sags, but she doesn't turn to face me. "Perhaps in another life, we could have worked. Maybe we should have in this one. But some fates aren't meant to be ours..."

I gasp, sharp and ugly, as my heart seizes over her words.

"We almost made it... The hunter and the vampire. It

would have been legendary. A love story they would have written about for another millennium."

I fall to my knees, sucking in giant gulps of air, unable to stop the juddering sobs now.

"Please don't do this," I beg, but she doesn't turn to face me, and this time, instead of humiliating, it's fucking devastating.

She sighs, a crack finally appearing in her voice. "The worst bit is, I do love you. But more than that, I'm grateful to you..." She turns her head an inch towards me, but her hair still covers her face. "Grateful for the lesson you taught me: that I need to stop trying to be good enough for everyone else. And instead, realise that I'm already good enough for me."

I shatter. "Octavia, please..." It's more of a howl than real words.

She takes a single step, putting her on the other side of the doorframe.

"What about the trials?" I shriek, one last desperate attempt at getting her to stay.

"Fuck the trials. And fuck the city too. I'm out, Verity. It's done. We lost... I will always love you, but I am choosing me...

She hesitates, and maybe I should have done something. Said something. Screamed an apology so raw that my lungs fell apart. Begged her to continue the competition because if we don't finish together, then we don't finish at all. Which means we don't open the door, and Octavia won't get the city.

But I do nothing because I know in this moment, she is lost to me, and if I want her back, it will take a feat far greater than two spoken words.

"Goodbye, little hunter. And goodbye to who I was with you..."

I blink, and when my eyes open, she's gone. The door stands as hollow and vacant as my chest.

I wail for her, I beg and plead with her to come back to let me explain, but she never returns. I slide down the kitchen counter I just fucked her against, tears pouring down my cheeks. My chest tight, my eyes burning.

I cry, because I've lost her. Sob because I had her. And scream because I have no idea how to get her back.

I wrap my arms around my legs, my eyes dropping to the silvery line in the middle of both my palm and the back of my hand.

I might heal quickly, but unlike vampires, I still scar like a human. Scars are the past. They're everything that came before. All you're left with in the present is the fading memory of how it happened.

I refuse to let Octavia become a scar in my life.

I will not back down. Will not give up.

The sadness morphs, my stomach hardens, and in its place, steel coalesces. I roar, and this time when I do, I fling my elbow back and smash it into the cupboard door. An almighty crack echoes around the kitchen. Fierce, hot pain radiates down my arm. I yank my elbow out of the splintered wood and stand up. This time I kick the cupboard door. My foot goes all the way through. I lash out, rip it off the hinges and launch it across the kitchen. I don't realise my strength. It flies the all the way to the other side and clatters into the cupboards.

I ball my fists and slam them onto the kitchen counter hard enough to break it. Fuck, it hurts.

I bellow to no one, to everyone. It's not the pain of my hands or the devastation of Octavia.

Not anymore.

It's rage.

It's white-hot, filled with fire and fury and the burning heat of a million angry women before me. It's fuelled by mistakes and betrayal and the knowledge that retribution is what makes an angry woman sleep at night.

There's only one person I need to see.

"Sadie fucking St Clair..."

I'm coming for you.

CHAPTER 9

CORDELIA

One Thousand Years Ago

The rate at which I'm being introduced to new lords and barons is truly the most dreadful and exhausting thing I've ever experienced. Mother has set about finding me a husband with a fervour that I don't believe I've ever seen her hold. If I weren't so furious with the fact I'm her project, I might be delighted to see her so full of life.

Day after day, I meet with new potential suitors. Once there was even a fae prince from another city. I have to say Mother's one saving grace is that she's not *just* passing me off to the first man she finds. That, at least, is something.

Though she's scarcely spoken to me in all the weeks I've been back. A few words here and there. I truly thought that if I obeyed and did as she requested things might perhaps go back to normal. But it appears her fury is as deep rooted as her hatred of the Randalls.

Their family have set alight some of Mother's uncle's

farmland on the outskirts of the city, so there's been a slew of aggressive family meetings and late-night plotting between the elders. There's sure to be a retaliation in the next few days.

Honestly, when will they learn that an eye for an eye only leads to misery and blind men? I wish there were some way we could find peace. If not for Eleanor, then the loss and devastation these battles are causing to the city.

Unfortunately, Mother is still insistent on my being smothered by the ladies who work for her. She makes them bathe and dress me, raze my legs and pamper my face with creams and blushes. It's quite ridiculous.

But it's made worse by the fact all I want is word from Eleanor. I haven't seen Mabel in days and the last time I did see her, she told me to back off and that she was working on it.

But I cannot rest until I know that she is safe and living. I know that no matter how furious my mother was with me she would never kill me. Marry me off for a tortured existence the rest of my living days maybe, but not death.

I know nothing of Eleanor's family though—the only things I hear are the whispers of attacks from the elders that visit the house.

I am, once again, in my room. The door locked, but the fire is dying, and the embers are no longer warming the room sufficiently. There's no one outside my door though, so I'm stuck here in the cold until someone deigns to visit me.

I pull on a shawl and hope it keeps the bite of winter at bay when I notice the fire flickering.

"What on earth?"

I scoot off the bed and shuffle across the room. I kneel beside the fire and watch as the embers spark and dance.

Usually, the coals just glow orange for a few hours before shedding their ashy skins—which they did about half an hour ago. They should be cool, but the coal remains are positively sparking and crackling. It's almost as if...

"Oh my gods," I say as an envelope materialises in the fire. I reach out instinctively and pluck it from the embers before the smouldering coals relight and whatever this magic is, is lost.

I almost drop the letter; the paper is hot and crispy on my fingers. I fling it at the window, but it immediately sticks, condensation forming between the cool outside glass and the heat of the paper.

"Oh no!" I squeal and dart for the window, realising that if there are words between the pages, I shan't be able to read them if the condensation makes the ink run.

I dart across the room and pull it from the sticky glass.

Thankfully, only the exterior has been tainted. I glance at the smudged word.

Cordelia

My heart beats in my mouth. I know this writing. I remember seeing it scrawled in dozens of grimoires lined up on shelves.

I remember when those same grimoires had lighting fluid poured over them. I remember the flames that ate the pages and crinkled the corners. The same flames that ate their magic.

Eleanor.

I'm trembling. I dare not speak her name, not even a whisper in case someone listens. I lay on the ground and strain, peering under the doorway. Most of the time, I can see feet in the shadows. But I want to be doubly sure there's no one lurking before opening the letter.

There's nothing, no shadows, no boots and even when I tip my ear to listen beneath the door, I hear nothing. Not even the skitter of mice feet on floorboards.

My heart rate slows and I ease myself into my desk chair. As quietly as I can, I slice my letter knife through the corner of the envelope, all the while listening for anything out in the corridor.

Nothing.

With my heart beating in my mouth once again, I pull the sheaf of paper out. Blood pounds in my ears as I try and fail to open the sheets. My fingers are shaking too much, and I nearly drop the paper.

I take two steadying breaths and then I start again.

I get them open this time, and my eyes instantly well. I knew I recognised the writing, but a piece of me didn't want to hope for her words.

But there across the page are her scrawled letters.

I press the page to my cheek; I inhale the scent of ink, and I swear I can smell wildflowers and herbs.

Eleanor. My sweet Eleanor.

I pour over the pages, reading the words slowly and consuming the letter over and over until every word has imprinted on my mind.

Dearest Cordelia,

How I have missed your sweet smile, your heart, your body. My soul is incomplete without you. I have been fraught trying to find a way to get you a note or letter. Anything so that you may know I am thinking of you as much as you are, me.

It took your maid a few attempts but she finally got your note to me a couple of days ago.

I sit bolt upright. What a genius Mabel is! I shall have to find a way to thank her. Perhaps see if I can scrounge a couple more coins for her. I'd given up all hope of her being successful.

I turn back to the letter.

I have so few details coming in. But from what you've told me and what I've heard from the scullery maid whispers, you are in a much more dire situation than I.

I have my freedoms to roam the grounds and mansion. I have been permitted to work. But only under the watchful eye of a cousin, or uncle. It is a small joy.

But there is something I must confess. My mother has given me these freedoms under the condition that I marry.

I am certain this won't come as a shock to you, though I suspect it will be as disagreeable as it is to me to know that you too are being wed.

I, though, am being allowed to choose a wife. I wanted to be truthful with you as I've been made aware that you are not being permitted the same liberty.

My heart breaks for you, Cordelia. If we cannot be together, then that is not the life I would wish for you.

There is one more matter that I wanted to address. Before we were torn apart, I had raised the question of stopping. Of giving up running.

I fear that it was cowardly of me. And I wanted you to know that I regret ever speaking those words. I do not mean them. I would never give up the fight for you.

Do you agree? If so, then write me back. Use the reverse side, prick your finger with a single drop of blood and set light to the note.

This is the only safe way we can communicate. Do not trust the maid again. I fear she read the contents of your letter. No one can be trusted.

Yours always, E.

I place my hand against my chest, my heart beats like horse hooves. Thunderous and cantering. I scramble for the ink and quill and immediately begin penning a response.

But as soon as I start, I stop.

I wonder what it is that I should be saying. Can I trust even this magical mode of communication?

I re-read the note again. My eyes fall to the only question she asked.

Do you agree?

I frown. Re-read the sentence prior. *I would never give up the fight for you. Do you agree?*

Do I agree?

What a strange question. I turn the two sentences over and over in my mind. They don't fit together. It's like jamming a puzzle piece into the wrong slot, it's slightly too big or slightly too small.

Do I agree?

It's the only question, so she must mean for me to answer. My eyes widen as I pour over the words again, moving them and putting them together until they do fit.

Do I agree to not give up the fight?

My fingers tingle, I swear on the witch-gods my heart stops beating. I scan the rest of the letter. She regrets telling me she was giving up. She's asking me if I still want to fight. Oh my, oh my.

I dance around the room, my whole body practically pulsing with excitement. I want to scream and sing and cheer and holler across the fields that of course I don't give up. Of course I'll never stop fighting for her, that I'd risk my life, my soul, every coin I had in order to have one more moment with her.

So instead of penning an entire letter—which, trust me, I want to explain my situation. I want to tell her every waking second of agony I've been in thinking of her, missing her. Instead, I write two words in large script.

I agree.

Rummaging around, I find a dress pin from an old sewing kit I had in my drawer, and I return to the hearth. I prick the end of my finger and squeeze, making a bead of blood well, and then I drop it over the words. I place the letter in the hearth just as footsteps echo in the hallway.

Oh fuck.

I scrabble to hide the sewing kit, the ink and all the items I had out. I shove the envelope onto the fire too, hoping that it just burns up.

The footsteps grow closer, and I plead and pray with the witch-gods to take my blood, accept the offering and let their magic work.

A key slides into the lock, and I swear my brow glistens with sweat as the door turns, my heart now beating like hooves again. The door opens, I glance at the fire and swallow hard, silently thanking the gods.

The letter is gone, and only embers and my hope remain in the fireplace.

CHAPTER 10

RED

It's over. Those two words ring through my mind again and again as I head for the exit of Xavier's mansion.

I can't believe after everything, everything we've been through, I've lost Octavia. I mean, I know I fucked up, like severely. But somewhere, some stupid part of me didn't think she'd ever leave. More fool me for taking it *and her* for granted. She deserves better. Maybe we both do.

Well, I'm going to fix it. Starting with Sadie.

I march my way into the foyer and towards Xavier's front door. He, being the smarmy smug vampire that he is, speeds past me to lean against the doorframe—tall, dark, arms folded and obscenely handsome—blocking the way.

"Move," I bark.

"I don't think so. It's a blood bath out there. You haven't been out. You don't know what you're heading into. I can't let you leave."

"I didn't think you were the type to keep prisoners."

He frowns, holds a finger up to me. "Now, hold on a second."

"Just move, Xavier, I've got places to go."

He kicks off the doorframe and rounds on me. "I mean it, Red, you can't just go out there alone. Everyone is hunting you, whether it's to worship you or end you, the result is the same. The entire city is looking for you. You need an entourage if you want to leave, and that's going to require organisation. Otherwise, how exactly do you propose to roam the city without being mobbed by people?"

I huff, an exasperated sound that pops out of my mouth.

"Exactly. Now, before you leave, I have something for you..."

He hands me a box. I scowl at it, wishing I could just leave, but dutifully manhandle the box open. There's a masquerade mask in it. What the hell?

I pick it up by the ribbon and glare at it as it twirls and glints in the candlelight.

"One wears it," Xavier drawls.

"I'm aware of that," I mumble and slide it onto my face.

As soon as I do, a vision plays in front of my eyes. It reminds me a little of the holographic-type projections I saw in New Imperium with Remy and Bella when we were using their RuneNet.

Eleanor appears alongside Cordelia. Together they stand in the middle of one of Cordelia's ballrooms. The rooms are enormous, with long, arching windows and rich velvet drapes in a ruby red so dark, it's almost black. The floor is decorated with chequered black-and-white tiles. Chandeliers hang from the ceiling every few feet, their shimmering crystals leaving mosaics of glittering light on the floor tiles. And along the edges of the room are marble pillars, jet black and shiny and threaded with white veins.

Cordelia opens her arms. "Hunters, vampires, competitors. It is time for the final trial. We have the amulet we need to break the boundary. We've been given a gift of foresight from the Mother of Blood thanks to Sadie's win. We now know there are demons and creatures that lie within the boundary. And now we've seen your strength play out. It's time to see who is the greatest leader among you."

Around the ballroom, the shadowy figures of the rest of the contestants appear. I think I spot Octavia, but the moment I lock eyes on her, her form flickers in and out of focus. I scan the rest of the group, but they, too, are hard to discern, all twisting shadows and morphing mist.

The Chief speaks next. "No matter who wins the race to the door, it is the people's favour you need to earn, and so, we thought our final trial should be a test of just that."

Cordelia steps forward and a table appears with our five glass jars filled with blood stones. The Chief waves her hand and the glass jars empty. Then she turns to us.

"At the beginning of the ball, each vampire noble, hunter elder and human in attendance will be given a blood stone."

She waves a hand again and the jars we had grow, morphing and extending until they're each five times the size they were. When they're large enough she's satisfied, the Chief continues explaining.

"By the end of the evening, each attendee will vote on which of the teams they deem the most suitable to run the city."

At this, the Chief steps down and Cordelia grins, her eyes molten like warm coal.

"How you get the people of the ball to vote for you is

entirely up to you. Be that idealism, negotiation, persuasion, coercion or otherwise. There are no rules. But by the end of the night, the votes will determine the winners," Cordelia says, her smile bordering on vicious.

She glances at the Chief. They share a look that makes me uncomfortable. I don't care whether they used to be lovers or not, for as long as I've been part of the Academy, the Chief has hated Cordelia, and Cordelia has quietly plotted war against us. It concerns me seeing them sharing any kind of conspiratorial look.

Cordelia's expression darkens, practically septic. "The winning team will be granted the amulet. You shall be the ones to break the barrier and enter the boundary, gaining yourselves some lead time on the others."

"What's more," the Chief interrupts, "every vote behind the leader you are, will incur a time penalty before you start. The more votes behind, the longer the delay will be before you can enter."

I swallow hard hearing this news. After I overheard the Chief and Cordelia talking about what Sadie learned, I'm not sure I want to enter the boundary first anyway. Especially now everyone knows I'm the dhampir.

I guess it doesn't matter who gets to the door, I'm the only one who can open it. And if I'm the only one who can open it, then everyone is going to want to find me during the race to the door. And with a time delay, that is going to make reaching the door together, and securely, extremely difficult. The thought occurs to me that if Octavia were still competing, this would have been the most important round to win. Because even if we lost the trials overall, we still have to get the door open.

So if the people supported her... actually chose her this

round... maybe she'd realise how amazing she was. Maybe she'd finally feel accepted.

This just became paramount. It changes everything. We don't just need to win, we *have* to. And she needs to be the one to pull this trial over the line. This is how she wins the city.

I sag where I stand. She's quit. Said she was out, done. With me and the trials.

And even though I want to help, want to fix the fuck-up I've done, I don't think I can. Because if I fix this, I know she's going to think that I don't believe in her. If I fix it for her, she'll think that I believe she's not good enough.

Mother of Blood. My hands are literally tied. How the hell do I help without making things worse?

There has to be a way.

"One more thing," Cordelia says, making me jump as I focus back on the vision. "Clearly, we have a celebrity dhampir in our midst. She's listening to this very invitation. Quite the surprise, since we didn't expect her to transition so quickly."

Fucking liar, they pushed me, they're the ones that colluded to put me in that ring with Dahlia. They gave me no fucking choice but to transform, and now I'm stuck like this forever.

"The dhampir is critical to the success of the boundary break. But with the tension in the city, and the desire from all sides to... partner with the dhampir, it's imperative that we keep her location secret at all times. Therefore, as indicated by the mask in your box, we will be hosting not just a ball but a masquerade ball. Please make sure that you attend wearing a mask. Entry will not be permitted without one. Of course, we understand that this makes convincing those in attendance that they should vote for you a little bit harder... But such are the perils of being a leader."

The Chief takes over. "That's it for now, we will see you on the first night of the Festival of Blood. We're almost there, team. We will be crowning a new leader of this city in just a few nights from now."

The vision dissolves and I glance at Xavier.

"None of this matters because Octavia is out-out."

"Define out-out..." he says.

"She as much as bellowed it at me when she broke up with me," I say, my eyes stinging all over again.

"But you still want her back?"

"Obviously." I eye roll him.

"You can't help her win the votes."

"Yeah, unfortunately, I already worked that much out."

Xavier scratches his jaw. "I'll keep thinking."

"Well, if you don't mind, I have somewhere to be." I shove past him and head for the door, but he speeds past and blocks the way.

"Xavier," I growl.

"Are you senile? Or just in denial... did you forget about the blood bath out there? Aside from the fact everyone is looking for you, I've heard whispers of demon attacks. So, delusional little hunter, where exactly do you think you're going?"

"To get Octavia back in the game. Even if I've lost her, she still needs to compete. She deserves the city. She needs to win."

He puckers his mouth up. "I get that, but you can't just walk into the middle of the city. Everyone knows your face..."

Knows my face... Something clicks. He's right, maybe I can't show my own face. But even before I was the dhampir,

I had forgery magic—albeit low level. We blended it with Remy's magic to capture Roman and Marcel. I wonder if now I've transitioned that magic is stronger.

I close my eyes, let my senses drop into my body, feel for the magic coiling inside me. I'm sure I should probably have training or something, but who the hell is going to teach me when there hasn't been a dhampir in a millennium? Fuck it.

What have I got to lose by trying?

I keep hunting deep inside me until I find what I'm looking for. A little thread like the ones I've seen attached to mansion walls in New Imperium. It makes me wonder where my magic stems from. I tug on the thread, and it comes spooling loose.

I imagine wrapping it around my fist, and then I pull my hand over my face, picturing Sadie's features instead. My skin tingles, the faint scent of mint and lavender and a dash of burnt cinnamon wafts under my nose. There's a rushing sensation of pins and needles that drops from my forehead all the way down my neck. Quite suddenly, the magic releases and slithers back to my core.

"The fuck," Xavier gasps, stumbling and hitting his back against the door.

"My face isn't a problem anymore. I got that part covered," I say.

Xavier, white as a sheet, his face scrunched up, stretches his fingers out to poke my face.

"Do you mind," I say, swatting at his digits.

"I don't mind at all." He continues to poke at me. "This is so weird. How the hell did you do that? It's bizarre seeing my sister's face on the wrong body but more to the point, talking."

Ah yes, if I wear this face, I can't talk or people will know it's not Sadie.

"You're also half her height," he says, smirking.

"Alright, you heightist prick. For that, you can lend me a carriage."

"That I can help with. But I still don't think you should go alone. What if the magic wears off? What if someone realises who you are?"

I take him by the shoulders. "Listen, I appreciate the support, really, I do. But I have to do this alone."

He shakes his head. "She'll kill you. Sadie is stronger than you think. I'm assuming that's where you're going, given that." He points at my face, barely able to look at it.

"I might not be able to beat her as me, but wearing her face. . . At least she won't see me coming. And as much as I want to kill her, that's not what I'm going for. Do you trust me?"

I pull my hand back over my face, releasing the magic and letting my face return to normal.

He pouts. "I trust you to do the right thing for Octavia."

"Then let me go..."

"Fine," he sighs and points to the right of the mansion. "Use the carriage at the front of the queue. He's compelled into silence so even if he could tell someone where you were, his insides would liquify. You'll be safe."

"Thank you for everything," I say and give him a squeeze, hiding my stinging face in his shoulder.

"Why does that sound like goodbye?"

I tear my gaze away, trying to turn the sad smile I'm wearing into a don't-worry-I-will-see-you-later smile. But I won't see him later, and that's the worst bit of this.

Once I've gotten Octavia back in this competition, I'm

leaving. I'm no good for anyone, not when all I do is hurt the people I love.

"Goodbye for now," I say, but the words taste like the lie they're concealing.

I head outside towards the carriage area, not looking back at him. The breeze hits my cheeks, brushing away the remaining magic and cleansing me. I tell the driver where I want to go, and then I climb into the carriage. I don't even realise I've fallen asleep until the driver shakes me awake.

"Miss, we're here. I think you should take my hat though, your face is everywhere."

He offers me his cap and I smile kindly at him. "Don't be alarmed," I say before I repeat the movements I made in front of Xavier, reaching inside to pull on my magic and transform my features. That same sweet scent wafts through the air and then vanishes once I know my face has settled into the shape I want it.

The carriage driver gasps and staggers back, almost falling off the carriage steps. But I grip hold of his arms.

"It's okay, it's still me. You can't breathe a word of this, can you?"

He shakes his head. "Compelled." But now he can scarcely bring his eyes to meet mine.

Excellent. That means my forged face is good enough to terrify the population. They'll leave me alone. I hop out, but as soon as my feet hit the stone cobbles I freeze. The fuck? In a few short days, this city has been plastered with images of my face, my real one, not Sadie's forged one.

It's just like Xavier said, only now that I'm confronted with it, my arms freckle with goosebumps, and my spine tingles like I'm being watched and about to be caught. Until I remember that my face is hidden beneath the magical Sadie mask, and no one will think otherwise.

Wearing her scornful grimace, my snow-white hair flowing over my shoulders, I head for the Church of Blood, a million sets of paper eyes tracking my every step.

CHAPTER 11

The little hunter's face is plastered across the city. You can't hide, Red. Unfortunately for you, I don't care whether you live or die now you've transformed. What I want, is for you to open the door...

The door has to be opened, no matter what. Or everything I've worked for was a waste.

Where oh where are you hiding, little hunter?

I'll catch you soon, even if I have to stalk my way around this whole city to find you.

I've got everyone where I want them, at last.

The boundary is thinning, I can feel it.

It won't be long, and then I'll finally be free of the mistake I made.

I'll be able to come for you and explain... Perhaps I'll write you a letter.

CHAPTER 12

RED

I drift through the streets, staying where possible to narrow alleys and dark streets. I don't want to give anyone an excuse to question me. I reach an open square, where some of the smaller sellers sometimes frequent. Open space is not good. I pull my hood over and keep my head low. I'm about to break into the square when I hear a voice I recognise. I slam back against the alley wall, my heart in my mouth.

"Oh, stop it, Ash," Amelia says, giggling. "We need to tear down these posters. Help me."

I peer around the wall and see Amelia and another vampire yanking posters of my face off the square's walls.

The vampire, and I can't make out whether they're male or female from this distance, rips down three more posters and then hands Amelia a blood bag.

She grins, practically falling over herself to take it.

My stomach twists remembering the Blood Woods, how she'd torn into those humans.

"Thanks," Amelia says, drinking some of the blood and handing it back to the vampire who steps into her personal space. They push a lock of her hair behind her ear and then lean in. As their lips meet, I know in my gut there's no way she's taking the cure. Not if she's dating a vampire.

As they break apart, the smile on her face stretches all the way to her eyes. Gods, not just dating, she's falling in love?

How the hell did I miss that? Have I been as shitty of a sister to Amelia as I have been a girlfriend to Octavia?

I pull back, hiding behind the wall and slide down it. This whole time I was charging towards a cure she doesn't even want. She's happy, and I was going to take that away because of my own moral judgements?

What is wrong with me? I've fucked everything for everyone. And I'm meant to be this city's saviour? Meant to be the one that brings back magic? I can't even be a decent sister.

It solidifies my decision. Amelia will be fine without me. I kick my head back against the alley wall. A swell of pain blooms out of my skull. I'm going to fix this once and for all. I stand, give my sister one final glance, and retreat, leaving her to her romance and head in the other direction for the church.

I turn down another alley and halt. My neck tickles. I glance over my shoulder, but the alley is empty, so I scan up. But there's no one on the rooftops either. My hunter instincts kick in and my feet carry me into the shadows, my back against the wall. This way I can see anything coming. But nothing does.

I'm just paranoid. The only company I have is a creepy poster of my face glaring at me. The eyes follow me as I keep my spine pressed to the wall and edge down the street.

I peer in the direction I came and then towards the church. There's no one there, I don't know what I'm panicking about. Bloody Xavier putting the wind up my arse.

I pull off the alley wall and make my way to the church, cussing myself out for being a pussy.

Only, as I march down the alley, my skin crawls again. I halt. A rush of wind washes past my cheek. My hand automatically goes to a blade in my trousers.

Not so paranoid.

But I don't want whoever the fuck it is to know I'm on to them, so I keep walking, only slower.

My skin heats as they get closer. I'm not taking any chances, stab first, ask questions later. I can always heal them.

A breeze washes over me, bringing the stench of decay and rotten skin. The fuck? Someone needs to clean their teeth. Gods.

When I feel the heat of their body disrupt the air, I take a breath and swing around, unsheathing my blade and stabbing up and towards their neck.

I land my blow dead centre over their carotid.

Only, I am not staring at a human. My fingers run cold, my eyes widening as I take in the sight of a demon.

Its vertical eyes are the orange of molten embers, its skin is mottled, in some places it's almost human-like, and in others it appears more like rotten bark. When it opens its mouth, I nearly pass out from the stench, its teeth are spiked and smeared in what looks like the remains of blood and flesh.

"The fuck are you...?" I whisper.

Its hands come out to grab my neck. "You're coming with me," he snarls. Or I think he does, the words are addled and gritty and hard to make out. He tightens his grip on my neck until my vision smatters.

I can't breathe. The tingle of panic loops around my gut. My defence training kicking in, I twist the knife in its neck. Fuck going anywhere with this thing. It shrieks a godsawful sound that makes me want to slap my hands over my ears.

"You must open the door," he says, his voice like nails on glass and the screech of metal grinding over metal.

"How the hell do you know who I am?"

"Dhampir," he says. "You're running out of time..."

He grabs at me and walks backwards. Fuck this shit. I push the knife, plunging it deeper into his neck before dragging it across the rotten skin. A grey liquid spills from his throat. I gag as I'm covered in it. The demon sways and then drops to the alley floor, jerking and twitching.

I stagger back and freeze.

"What. The. Fuck?"

It's body writhes on the floor and then it lays perfectly still. As the light drains from its orange eyes, the creature shifts. The eyes turn blue, round pupils replacing the vertical ones. Its skin ripples and flakes, the bark-like decay flaking off until it reveals the supple skin of a man beneath it.

A human man.

Grey liquid runs between the cobbles and when it comes to rest, it too, shifts. Colour seeps back into it until the scent of iron hits my nose and my clothes are smeared red.

Horror rushes over me, settling in the pit of my stomach

like an iron weight. I drop to my knees and throw up. Then I crawl my way to the body.

Because that's what it is now: a human body.

It wasn't. I swear. I rub my eyes trying to make the demonic creature I saw reappear, but it doesn't.

But it was, wasn't it? Whatever magic gripped it has vanished.

"No, no, no," I breathe and place my hands over the man's decimated neck. I reach for my magic, desperate to repair the damage I've done. Stop my body count climbing.

"I didn't mean to hurt you... I thought you were..." I shake my hands, pleading with the magic to work faster, better.

But it's pointless.

No matter how golden my hands glow, the skin doesn't heal, and he doesn't breathe.

I slump and the glistening glow dims until it's just me holding a dead body in an alley. A group of people singing and chanting 'The dhampir has risen,' cross the end of the alley. I wrench around to cover my face until I remember I'm wearing Sadie's features. Fucksake. Xavier was right, this is a nightmare and there's no way I can stay here. I get up and drag his body to the side of the alley and close his eyes.

"May the Mother of Blood bless you," I say and leave. The faster I get out of the city the better.

I am even more cautious now, waiting for streets to empty before moving down them. Finally, I creep towards the back door of the church. The gargoyles stare at me, their eyes squinty and narrowed as I draw near. It makes my skin itch, and I wonder whether they, too, can sense I'm not who I appear to be.

The goyle on the ancient oak door scowls but opens his

mouth, his spike extending, ready to accept my offering. If I give him my blood, he'll know who I am. So I decide to give him enough to knock him out. I push the pad down hard, and several beads of blood roll down the spike. His eyes widen as the truth of who I am flows into his veins and then his eyes tip into the back of his head as he passes out.

I push the door open. It's dim; a flickering lantern hangs on the wall, and the stale smell of damp stone and old books hits me. I creep through the corridor until I remember that if I were Sadie, I'd be confident because this is my territory. This is why I never went undercover as a hunter. I'd have been useless.

I pull myself together and stand a little straighter, a little higher as I try to embody her floating grace.

A monk appears at the end of the corridor and pauses to incline his head at me. My blood curdles as I wonder whether this is the moment I get caught. I have to physically bite my tongue to prevent myself from speaking.

Instead, breathing heavy through my nostrils, I lower my head, helping my hair to fall across my features and obscure the absolute terror coursing through me.

He wanders off, and finally the knot in my stomach releases.

I hurry through the corridors, realising I probably should have looked at a church map before breaking in. But it's too late now. I find what looks like a staff corridor and decide to wander down it.

The Mother of Blood must be looking over me because finally, I spot a door with a plaque in the middle that says:

SADIE ST CLAIR

I press my ear to the door, but I can't hear anything, not even the scratch of a quill. I slide inside.

Her office is as dim as the corridor. Four lanterns hang in the corners, their flames open. I'm amazed she allows that given how many leather-bound books reside in here. Her desk is tidy, a quill, ink and a few scrolls and letters lay tied together. There are only two windows in here. But both are imposing, their long, arched bodies tattooed in blood-red stained glass telling stories of old.

The room is lined with bookcases tall enough to scratch the ceiling and filled with enough tomes you'd need three lifetimes to get through them all. Last, a full-length mirror, arched like the windows, sits just to the side of the door.

A painted scroll hanging on the wall catches my eye. It's contains three family trees. The St Clairs the Randalls and the Montague's. There's a small symbol in the bottom of it, all concentric circles and strikethrough lines with an M.

A scuffling noise drifts in from the corridor. I race to stand behind the door and pull out two blades, grateful I didn't have to wait for Sadie long.

It swings open and she glides in, silent save for the shuffling of her feet and rippling of her gown. The door swings shut, and I move faster than I ever have. My arm swings out and around her neck, the other coming to hover over her breast.

I realise now, I have a problem. She can't talk, and therefore if I want to communicate with her, I need to see her hands and there's no way I'm letting go, she'll rip me in two.

"Mirror. Now. Move," I snap and shove her forward. It makes the blade bite into her neck, and she inhales a quick breath.

We shuffle to the mirror, and I force her to face it, then I step to the side of her so she can see my face—*her* face.

She startles, her eyes wide as she takes in two of herself.

"Go on... speak," I say, nudging her hand with my knee. I'm not removing these blades until I know we have a deal.

The shock morphs, her expression deepening, lines furrowing into her brow and eyes. There she is.

"Who are you to wear my face?" she signs.

I close my eyes and let the magic fall free, my features twist and contort but eventually, I'm left in my own skin and her face darkens even further.

"You." She points at me.

"Yeah, me."

"What do you want?" she signs, her hands move fast enough it's hard to focus on both the blades at her neck and her movements, which are also reflected backwards in the mirror. But I manage to keep up.

I suppress the urge to growl at her. "I want to give Octavia what she deserves. You didn't just fuck me, you fucked her too."

A sneer curls over her lips. An expression I can't read washes over her. Rage? Regret? I settle on disinterest when she shrugs and then raises her hands, "I just want to win. You all dismissed me, now who's in the lead?"

"Aren't you clever," I snarl.

She shrugs again. "I want that door open as much as Octavia. I wouldn't be competing if I didn't want to win."

I hoped she'd say something like that.

"Yeah... and how do you think the city is going to respect you as leader if you win by default? If you want to win the people, you need to *win* by beating the others... who wants a cheat for a queen?"

She stiffens in my embrace. I hit a nerve. She knows I'm

right, just like I know Octavia needs to win this round fair and square. She needs to convert the people to her, and this is her best chance.

She sags, relenting. "I'm listening," she signs.

"Octavia quit. She's done. Out. Caput."

"No." Sadie shakes her head.

"Yeah. We did that. You and me fucked it. But I'm making it your problem. So if you want to win and actually be queen of this city, then you're going to have to fix what you broke. Get Octavia back in the competition."

Her eyes narrow at me in the mirror. "Even if I do, that doesn't mean she'll win. She still has to get across the boundary, make it to the door and then keep you safe long enough to open it, seeing as your blood is the only thing that can do that."

This time, it's me that falters. In the mirror, my face crumples into a frown. "My blood?" I breathe.

She laughs, or I think she does, no actual sound comes out, but her expression crinkles and lines form around her eyes. "Come on, when is it not about blood?"

I purse my lips. "So I'll give her my blood, and she can open the door..."

Sadie moves suddenly, smashing my hand away from her neck and using her full body weight to shove me. I go tumbling into her desk. She rounds on me her hands up, but not to fight, to communicate.

"Why are you really here, Red? Retribution? Go on then, hunter, end me. I can't even scream for help." She flings her arms wide as if inviting me to kill her.

"You're fucked up, you know that..."

She tosses her head back, laughing, and this time a whisper of a sound that could break glass and corrupt minds flows from her chest.

105

RUBY ROE

"Get her back in the competition yourself," Sadie signs.

"I would, but I can't. You made sure of that. Drove a giant wedge between us, and now she won't even speak to me."

Her eyes glimmer. "Well, if you weren't so self-obsessed and maybe gave something up for her for once, perhaps she wouldn't have frozen you out."

Self-obsessed? How fucking da— But I don't finish the thought because she carries on, and I have to pay attention to her hand movements.

"I'm not going to do what you want," she signs.

I glower at her, "You are." My tone is an outright threat.

"Make me..."

"I don't have to. If you don't get Octavia back in this competition, then . . ." I slide the knife under my own neck. A clear warning, but not to her this time... To what she *wants*. And I'm just pissed off enough to do it.

I glare at her. "I've lost everything and everyone I love. Getting Octavia what she wants is the last thing I can do, even if it means ending my own life."

Sadie startles, her expression wide. I have her attention, so I continue.

"Get her back in the competition. Or I'll vanish and take every last drop of my blood with me. Then no one gets the door open."

Her lips pull back, as if she's growling, only no sound escapes.

"Fine," she signs. "But I won't forget this. Watch your back, little hunter."

"It's dhampir now," I say and march out of her office. I keep marching until I'm out of the corridors and back on the main street.

I forget I'm wearing my own face. And a kid who can't be more than eleven or twelve gasps as she passes.

"You're... Oh my gods, it's you!" The girl opens her mouth to shout, and I clamp my hand over it.

"Don't scream," I hiss.

She trembles beneath me, but I hold her tight.

"I don't want to hurt you, okay? I just need to escape without being seen. Understand?"

She nods against my hand.

"If I remove my hand, are you going to scream?"

The girl shakes her head against me, her body relaxing. Tentatively, I remove a finger, and then another, until her lips are free and she could scream if she wanted.

She doesn't.

Instead, she falls to her knees and takes my hand. I freeze, and glance around us. The closest people are the other side of the square. I'm safe for now, but I need to get out of here.

"What are you doing?" I say and tug my hand, but she holds on.

"Bless me," she says and looks up at me, her big eyes watery. "Please, dhampir? Bless me and my family..."

The actual ever-loving fuck? Is she on crack?

"I'm not what you think I am."

Her eyes drop to the floor, and she stands. "You might not believe it yet, but I do... you've come to save us all. May the Mother of Blood bless you in your quest."

She bows her head and then breaks into a run, heading straight for the group of people on the other side of the square.

"MUM," she shrieks, and that's when I make my exit.

I break into a run and replace my face with Sadie's as I

bolt for the carriage. I don't think I take a breath until I'm locked securely inside.

"Where to now, miss?" the driver says.

"The Academy," I say.

Much as Sadie's words hurt calling me self-obsessed, they burrowed in, and now I can't let them go. I think she's right. This whole time I was doing everything for me. Chasing the cure because *I* wanted it for Amelia. I sabotaged the last trial because of *my* emotions. I haven't once done something for Octavia, or Amelia.

That changes tonight.

CHAPTER 13

OCTAVIA

It's not often I get blind drunk. But I am, exactly that.

I swill my Sangui Cupa and stare out my glass office window. The Whisper Club is heaving tonight. I push the scraps of paper away from me. Piles of reports from Cordelia and residents of the city. Whispers of demon attacks, pleas for protection. Our city is falling apart.

I sigh and move to the glass window. There's something distinctly reassuring about being invisible in a crowd. I can pretend for a brief moment that I'm one of them, part of a collective. That I belong to this city.

And then I blink, and realise the glass is between us, and I'm still alone. I swallow hard, my throat thick with all the things I wish I'd said to Red. Maybe I shouldn't have left the way I did. But I was... *am* still so angry with her. No matter how much it hurts me, I have to choose myself this time. That's what I've learned from her, to choose myself for once.

I collapse in my office chair, unbuckle my trousers and

tug them low enough I can access myself. I slip my hand inside my underwear and slide that down too, then I rub my clit over and over.

I need an escape. Anything to take my mind off Red.

I dip two fingers inside my pussy and circle them back over my clit. But it's not enough. Fucksake. I wrench open a drawer in my desk and grab a bottle of lube and drizzle some over my fingers.

I resume rubbing, but images of Red flash through my mind.

"Fuck," I groan and kick my leg out, making the bin crash over. I rub harder, letting my other hand join in and slip two fingers inside myself.

I pump hard, wishing it would hurt the way my chest does.

Red.

Red.

Red.

Her naked body in the kitchen, her palms up, head down. She is divine.

"No!" I bark and slap my cunt in frustration. It stings, but I like it and moan into the tingle. I want to scream in frustration as images of Red's lips sucking on my clit wash through my head. Her plump mouth, swollen and bruised from licking me till I come on her face. Her fingers slide inside me as her tongue drags over my pussy. Will I never be able to rid myself of her.

"FUCK," I scream as my body tightens.

The tunnel. Her slapping my arse, fucking me from behind. Me tying her to the hook, smearing an O between her breasts.

"Oh gods." My pussy clenches against my fingers as I

fuck myself harder. Faster. I don't want this. I shouldn't be doing it. Not when it's Red poisoning my thoughts.

Red. Red. Red.

Her rock-hard abs, her pink little nipples. Images of her straddling me. Her breasts rising and falling with the bounce of her riding my strap.

My clit throbs between my fingers. I squeeze it. Punishing. But that only dredges up the memories of Red using a paddle, her palm, her body to make mine melt. Her legs either side of my cheeks as she lowers her cunt to my mouth.

Her sweet, sweet taste.

"Shit." I spill over, my thighs shaking as I jerk in my chair, pumping once, twice more before pulling my fingers out.

I'm drenched.

"Fucksake." I head to the bathroom at the back of my office and clean myself up. On the way back to my desk, I pick up whatever whiskey dregs there are and a definitely-not-clean tumbler and pour myself a glass of it.

I swallow down half in one go as my office door clicks. I frown then get up reluctantly to shut it. But a breezy rush whips around me and by the time I turn to face it, a woman is sat in my office chair.

"Sadie," I say, my blood instantly boiling.

She ruined everything. I ought to cut her throat where she sits. Her demeanour, though, is so relaxed it takes me by surprise. She rests in the chair the other side of my desk, her head leant against the velvet back, which makes her hair look grey in this light. It ages her, almost makes her appear exhausted. Her legs are crossed, a long gown draped over her equally long limbs.

"What do you want?" I say, shutting the office door and making my way back to her.

"Peace," she signs.

"Should have thought about that before you manipulated my partner."

She shrugs. "I want to win. You would do the same."

"Would I?"

Her eyes narrow at me, and she gestures for me to sit. I do and cross my legs, peering at her.

"Is this just a social call, or do you intend to tell me why you are here?" I ask again.

Her lips press into a thin line.

"I hear you quit..." Her hands remain in the air, motionless, shaping the last sign.

"I can't win the trials, so what is the point?"

"I didn't take you for a sore loser."

"Did you come here just to berate me? I always thought we were above the petty tactics of Dahlia."

She deflates, her shoulders drooping before she very slowly and intentionally signs, "Please re-enter the competition."

"Why do you care? You were the one who orchestrated me out."

She stands, turning her back on me and leans her forehead against the office glass, watching the dancers and club goers beneath. The silence is thick and tacky. I don't have a lot to say to her. The thin relationship we had, the mutual understanding, was broken the minute she screwed with Red.

"I'm not changing my mind. I'm done," I say, hoping that will get her to leave.

She faces me, leaning her back against the glass.

"You will re-enter the trials," she signs like she's scolding me.

I huff a laugh out. "Who are you to dictate to me what I should do? Don't act like our mother. You're not Cordelia, Sadie."

Her eyes darken.

"No. I'm not. But I do know who *your* mother is."

I freeze, vampire still as I try and process the information. I don't blink, I don't breathe, not a cell moves in my body.

That's impossible. No one knows who she is.

"Your birth mum was the Mother of Blood, right?" she signs.

It takes me three beats before I'm able to force myself to unfreeze and answer. "How—"

"The trial of spirit."

Her answer comes quick and easy. I narrow my gaze at her, searching for falsehoods, or trickery. "What are you up to, Sadie? You fought so hard to get me out of this competition, and now you want me back in? Do you want to win or not?"

"I want the door open."

"Don't we all." I sniff.

"Re-enter the competition and when it's over I'll tell you who your mother is."

I shake my head. Do I really want to know? Does it matter after all these years? "She left me, I'm not sure I care anymore."

There's a flicker in Sadie's expression but it's gone before I can identify what it was. She holds my gaze, her eyes boring into mine. "Everyone wants the answers that plague their hearts. And the identity of your mother has always plagued you. The pain is rent through your expression. Don't lie to me, Octavia."

I grit my teeth. "Fine. Maybe I want to know." I feel like a teenager stropping and throwing her weight around.

"Once the door is open, I will tell you all that you need to know." She floats across the office to stand before me. Her forehead crinkles. "I'm sorry that I ruined things between you and Red. That wasn't my intention. I merely wanted to win and..." Her hands pause, she opens her mouth as if she were going to say something else. Her lips flicker and move as if spilling whispered secrets. But the words never reach me, her hands never move, and whatever she was going to say is lost.

I'm suddenly uncomfortable, so I fill the silence. "I appreciate the apology, but it's not on you to make up for Red's mistakes. She could have chosen to listen to reason. She could have asked me. Instead, she reacted and hurt me."

Her lips thin. "But you'll rejoin?" she signs.

I fold my arms, taking her expression in, trying to scan for any lies. "No tricks, no deceptions? You'll tell me who she was?"

Sadie nods, a curt little thing. "Yes, I'll tell you who your mother is."

She leans down and kisses me on the forehead, lingering a little longer than normal. Then she squeezes my shoulders and floats her way out of the office. The shadow of her lips still cool on my brow.

CHAPTER 14

CORDELIA

One Thousand Years Ago

The house has never looked so regal. Even if it is for an occasion I'd rather die than attend, the house is exquisite. In order to get the nobles back on our side, Mother is throwing a marriage ball to end all balls. No expense has been spared.

I snuck out while the staff were drawing my bath. There is a marquee of sorts, extending what was Mother's ballroom into a long dancing room. I'd guess that it's now three times the size. Chandeliers hang from the ceiling, smothered in crystals and enchanted candles that never burn out. The glimmering light reflects the crystals, showering rainbows over the walls. There are dozens of tables, all dressed with candelabras as tall as I am. Flowers hang from the walls and form arches in the doorway. In the corner, musicians set up their instruments and musical stands.

There are servers fluttering here, there and everywhere,

and already, the rooms swarm with Mother's lady friends and noble family members. I'm about to wander the gardens when Mabel grabs me. "Come on, we must get you ready."

I nod obediently and give the room one last glance, recognising it for what it is. My execution room.

Not literally, you understand, but figuratively.

Much as I'd hoped Eleanor would come to my aide, given the fact she has more freedoms than I, I've not heard from her in weeks.

I thought the note meant that we would try again. Find a way. But perhaps she meant it as a way of apologising and healing her heart and guilt. I've tried to puzzle the truth from the letter, re-reading it so many times the paper is worn thin in patches and so crinkled some of the words are frayed and faded.

My stomach sinks as I follow Mabel through the mansion towards the bathing chamber. Tonight, a husband shall be chosen, and in the morning, I shall be wed, and my mother will finally be free of me.

I shall become no more than a cow, bred to produce heirs and shoved away to be quiet the rest of my waking years.

What a life I will lead.

"Here, miss," Mabel says and holds open the door for me.

I dutifully undress and step into the warm water. Like the caged animal I am, I don't even try and rebel anymore. I lie still while they pull me about, yank a brush through my locks and raze the hair from my body. I don't even resist when she nudges my legs apart to wash clean my private areas. What's the point of keeping my modesty when I'm going to be sold for my womb? I have no dignity left.

"All done," she says and holds a towel out to me.

I take it and wrap it around me.

"Oh," she says and brings a small cloth to my face and wipes beneath my eyes. "I'm so sorry."

"Don't be," I say and dry myself, dropping the towel and exchanging it for a robe. I walk through the bathing rooms towards the empty passage that leads to my bedroom, where another two staff wait for me, holding my dress.

"Great," I say, unable to keep the resentment out of my tone as I approach them.

"Let's make this quick, shall we?" the first staff—I think her name is Harriet— says and adjusts her skirts before unzipping the dress and holding it out for me.

I sigh, de-robe myself, walk naked across my room and step into the dress. It's made of a heavy satin adorned in glittering crystals that match the chandeliers. I wonder if that was on purpose. Whether Mother sees me as no more than a piece of furniture to show off.

When I'm secured in the dress, Mabel comes and nudges me towards a dresser where she makes me sit.

"This won't take long, you have a natural beauty," she says.

"Thanks," I mumble, not really caring. Only praying for a swift death. A piece of poisoned meat perhaps, a short fall from the balcony. I do not want to live a life with a man. I would rather cease now, this night, than continue to have him force himself upon me just to bear his children so my mother has an heir.

She's right, she can force me to marry. But she can't force me to stay alive. I will not let her take that from me.

I decide tonight is the night I die.

Harriet wipes powders and lacquers over my face until I

stare at myself in the mirror and wonder who the beauty is looking back at me. At least I will die beautiful. A morbid thought, but a comfort when nothing else is.

Both Harriet and Mabel look at me, their eyes drooping, as if they know I'm walking to my death, and I want to scream at them to keep their pity.

"Good evening, miss," they say in turn, and then I am alone.

I consider ripping the curtains from my four-poster bed and attaching them to the ceiling, but I have nothing to cut them with. I glance at the window, but it, too, is locked so I cannot even throw myself from it.

Beneath me, the musicians kick off, a dolorous melody sweeping through the halls and matching the tune of my heart.

The door unlocks and to my surprise, Mother stands before me. Her eyebrows rise. "Wow," she says. "You are beautiful."

I want to say thank you, but I can't. This façade of beauty is a bridge leading to my demise. I will not thank her for my death.

Instead, I press my lips shut and incline my head at her. She offers me her hand, and I extend my gloved one back. She pulls me into the corridor and leads me towards the main ballroom.

"I don't want any funny business this evening, do you understand?" she says. And all the niceties have evaporated. Any warmth in her tone eradicated as the thorny hackles I recognise in my mother's voice appear.

"I do."

"I mean it, Cordelia. This is your last chance. I have gone out of my way to persuade as many nobles as I could to give you a second chance. There's a sizeable dowry attached to you now. You will come out of this evening wed. As much as we've had our disagreements, I will do you the honour of letting you choose from the shortlist."

"How gracious of you," I say and immediately regret it. My tone is far too sarcastic, too impudent.

She opens her mouth to scold me, and I immediately jump in. "Forgive me, Mother. It is hard for me, you understand, when this is not what I desire. I will do my best to honour your wishes this evening."

That cracks a little of her ice. "And that is why, despite all of your misdemeanours, I want to work with you. I don't want to give you to a man that will make you miserable. I do not wish that upon you. You are my child, and I love you."

I glare at her, willing my eyes to soften. She's delusional. None of this is about me, if it were, she wouldn't be forcing me to marry a man at all. But I see now she's so wrapped up in her own status and reputation that she's forgotten how to listen, how to be a mother.

"I am giving you your freedom this evening, do not abuse it. You'll be watched. I have several guards here whose sole job is to watch over you. So please, don't make this any harder than it needs to be."

She kisses me on the forehead. Her lips are warm, not like cosy fires and duvets in winter, but like the fever from acids, burns, and lightning strikes.

She makes to leave, but I grab her wrist. If this is to be the last time I lay my eyes upon my mother, I should like to take her in one final time. And I do. I notice the way crinkles line the corners of her eyes, and I wonder whether it was the stress I have given her these last weeks that created them or whether she has aged without me noticing.

I recognise the shape of her mouth and curve of her lips as my own. Her eyes too. Dark like ravens.

"Thank you," I say quite suddenly.

She frowns at me as if it's an odd thing to thank one's mother, but then I guess she doesn't realise what I'm thanking her for.

Life.

The one I shall take before the night is done.

Mother vanishes then, into the throng of nobles. I stand for a moment, taking in the crowd of people. Many are sat eating and collecting drinks or food from the extensive buffet.

Some already dance in the middle of the exterior portion of the ballroom. The musicians seem to have multiplied and there's practically an orchestra in one corner of the room. I scan the crowd trying to work out who is guarding me. Whose eyes never leave my body. I think I find one and take note of their appearance so I know who to slip past later.

A gentleman approaches me, and I stiffen.

"Good evening, Lady St Clair," he says.

"I'm not interested." I don't mean to be rude, but what is the point of engaging in these marriage conversations if I intend to end things for good this evening?

"I do understand, only, I've heard of your proclivities, and I'm rather interested in discussing them."

I round on him. His features are so refined they're practically sculpted. Not rugged and worn like most noble men. Is that a dash of blush powder I note on his skin?

I frown. "Are you like me?"

"In a way," he says. "I think we could perhaps make an arrangement. One that is more suited to both our needs. I fear the other men who have tried to propose have not realised your preferences."

So he likes men? I narrow my eyes at him.

"Explain, sir."

He nods at me and ushers me away from the bulk of the noise and into a corner of the dance floor.

"I rather think we would be in a loveless marriage, but one where we make an heir and then are free to live as we wish, discreetly."

I sag inside. "Making the heir is the bit I do not wish to do."

He nods. "I understand, it will cause me a level of great difficulty too. But perhaps if there were others involved, we may find it easier to... do what is required?"

I stare into his eyes, they're a rich brown, like autumn forests and burnt leaves. I have to admit, his proposal is the most appealing of all I've received. But still, I do not wish for a man to touch me in any capacity. Whether it be for heir making or otherwise.

Another man, slightly taller and sporting a neatly trimmed beard, approaches. "May I have this dance?" he says.

And I can tell he's here reluctantly, he's fighting the disdain and from wrinkling his nose.

"Sure. Do excuse me, sir, I will be back to discuss this with you further," I say, and I do mean it. Of all the men that have approached me, he does have the most promise.

I dance with nobleman after nobleman until my feet hurt and I am desperate to sit. When I'm glistening from effort, I excuse myself from the dance floor and make my way to the exit. But when I reach it, a man dressed in a black suit puts his arm in front of the door, blocking the way.

"Excuse me," I say.

"I can't let you out. Lady St Clair's orders," he replies, not even bothering to look at me.

Bastard. I want to shove him, slap him, bite him and force him out of my way. How in the gods will I fling myself from the roof if I can't even escape the ballroom?

I tut and spin on my heels, stomping back into the dance area. But I don't get far.

I halt, my skin tingling, my arms rippling with gooseflesh.

A sign.

A warning.

An omen.

Something is wrong.

It's the last thought I have before the world lights up. Explodes.

Noise. Glass shattering. Sharp fragments and splinters spray down like a thunderstorm as more explosions rip through the air. Balls of fire lick up the side of the ballroom. Table legs and chair backs fly in all directions, and I stand there immobile. I am motionless as the world around me tears in two.

Fires lick across the carpet and up the walls, and I wonder whether I manifested this. Did the gods hear me? Were my prayers answered?

I sit down. Waiting for death to consume me.

Fire is an abysmal way to go, but if that's what the gods deem for me then I accept their gift, and I will lay down willingly.

Bodies run past me, knocking into me. Screams rend the air. Men holler as they drag their loved ones to safety.

The musicians have stopped playing. But still there is a

melody of piercing cries and shrieked names that sounds like a song of death. The wood cracking rings out a beat and the shattering of glass is the crescendo. And all the while I watch the chaos around me, smiling for the first time in weeks.

As I sit down waiting for my life to end, I realise that there are as many bodies running from the ballroom as entering it.

Why would people run into the fire...? Unless... my blood runs cold. I scan the room again, trying to catch sight of the men and women darting through the ballroom. None of them are dressed like us. They all wear dark combat clothing and masks. This isn't an accident. This was intentional. It wasn't the gods at all.

I *would never give up the fight for you. Do you agree?*
Eleanor.

Oh gods. Eleanor.

I'm up in a flash, the prickle of panic erupts over my skin as I realise my dress has caught fire. Dropping back to the floor, I roll myself over and over to suffocate the flames. I manage to get them snuffed out, but my heart now hammers in my chest. I scan the crowd, but even though it's thinned, the smoke and smog from broken things and explosions swallow the light in the room and make it hard to see.

I'm an idiot. I should never have sat down. I should have run like everyone else.

"Eleanor," I shriek. But the word gets jumbled and caught in my throat as I cough and splatter my guts onto the ballroom floor.

Run.

Get out.

I stagger forward, spluttering and choking against the

growing smoke. How could I be so foolish as to think she'd abandoned me? Of course she didn't.

I make it to the marquee but it's so long and already fire consumes a huge part of the exterior. The flames would take me long before I reach the other side. I glance back and see the internal ballroom is already aflame. I can't go back either. The dark-clad combatants are hunting and attacking the remaining nobles left inside. Slaughtering them all. But none of the nobles fight back. No one resists. In fact, most of them seem to be on their knees before the men in combats force blades through their backs. What the hell is going on?

I stumble forward, I can't give up, not if she came here. I refuse to quit on Eleanor. Not this time.

But as I stagger through the heat of the blaze, my lungs burn. I scan the room, realising it's not really fire, or it is, but fire that seems to be somewhat under control. The smoke is gas.

"Oh gods," I say as my vision swims. And then my eyes roll shut and I'm falling, falling, falling.

But I never hit the ground.

CHAPTER 15

RED

T he Hunter Academy looms before me. It's high-walled stone perimeter and grey turrets an ageing symbol of what is now lost to me. It takes me a moment before I can move.

For as long as I can remember, this building symbolised everything good and right and worthy. I was barely a day over thirteen when I came here the first time. It's shaped me into the adult I am today.

But as I stand in front of it now, the grandeur, the privilege, the honour has waned. What was once a regal oil painting is now an antique watercolour. My chest tightens, air struggling to reach the bottom of my lungs.

I love this place.

It's my home.

More so even than Oriana's, or my childhood home. That thought makes my eyes sting. How can one place hold so many emotions simultaneously?

"It's you..." an older lady says. *Shit.* Even before I turn around, my stomach sinks. I should have been more careful.

I glance at the woman; her skin has wrinkled so much she looks like crinkled paper. Despite the fact she seems well fed and healthy, her clothes are worn and tatty.

"The Mother of Blood has blessed me," she says and bends to kiss my knuckles.

Fuck my life. This is awkward and uncomfortable. The carriage driver raises an eyebrow at me, and I internally scold myself for not forging a new face before I got out. I will never get used to this kind of behaviour. Doesn't she realise I'm just as fallible as her?

"Please," she says, and then raises her wrist to me.

I frown. "Please?" I ask.

"Take it. My blood. It would be an honour."

My eyes bug wide. "What? No. I don't... I mean, I wouldn't." I take a step back and her demeanour falters, her eyes glassy. Fucksake. I didn't mean to upset the old woman, but I am not what they think. Or maybe I am, but I can't do this or be what they want.

She reaches into her pocket and pulls out a sculpture. It's small and carved from a blueish stone. It's a head, and when I look at it, I recognise the reflection.

I gasp.

"Take it, please... it would be an honour."

I nod and clasp my hands around hers. "You are too generous. May the Mother of Blood bless you."

Her face beams, "Oh, thank you, thank you," she says and trundles off. I grab her hand and turn her back to face me.

"Can you keep this secret?" I ask.

Her brows furrow, her eyes droop.

"I know you probably wanted to tell your family and friends, but please?"

"For you... anything." She dips her head and walks away. I don't trust her. I'm not sure I trust anyone right now, but what can I do?

Get in and out of the Academy fast, is what I can do. I slip the sculpture of my head into my pocket. That was too close, I have no doubt she's going to tell everyone and anyone that she saw me. My time is limited. I steel myself against what's to come and close my eyes, reaching deep into my magic to pull threads out and wrap them around my fist. I draw my palm over my face, pooling my magic in my hand. My features contort and pinch and twist until it's no longer my face I'm wearing, but the Chief's.

I can't believe I'm here to do the unthinkable. Three months ago, if someone told me I'd betray the very foundations of everything I believe in, I'd have knocked them out. Today, I'd have to bend the knee and accept their truth.

I wipe a hand over my face only to discover it's wet. I glance at my tear-streaked palm. It doesn't matter how much this hurts, how much it's cutting me up. I have to do it.

I stand a little straighter and march into the grounds.

Several younger students are training in the courtyard. There's a chorus of, "Hi, Chief. Chief, over here."

I smile and nod and try very hard not to open my mouth. There's only so far my magic will go, or at least while I'm untrained. I navigate my way through the castle, wandering halls so full of memories. Laughter echoes off the bricks, memories dance like ghosts next to me the deeper I wander. Each one a lance. Each one breaking another piece of my heart.

Around one corner, Lincoln and I are laughing. Around

another, Winston, my favourite third year, is smiling in his far-too-big first-year uniform. That memory in particular makes me grit my teeth. He was so scrawny, hell he still is, but my gods is that kid strong. Maybe he'll make head of security one day.

Several trainers pass me, all of them do a double take. I am shorter than the Chief by several inches. Damn.

"Chief." One of them nods at me, and as I pass, I feel their eyes crawl over me. I cock my head back, but he's already shaking off the confusion.

As is the way for most people. Happy to ignore the splinter, the awareness that something is wrong. Gods forbid we upend the status quo.

Which is how I end up in the Chief's office waiting room in front of her assistant.

I clear my throat and attempt to deepen the tone a little and mimic the Chief's accent. "Take a break," I say.

"But you have a—"

"Are you listening?" I bark. It's better this time, more like her on a bad day.

"O-Okay," she says and quickly gathers her notebook and files and runs out of the room.

I take a deep breath knowing that once I cross the threshold into her office, that is it. I can't come back from this. I'll be a traitor. Betrayed my own kind for our enemy.

How things change. A couple of months ago, it would have been inconceivable to me that I'd be standing here willing to betray everything I fought for for almost two decades.

But here I am. Hand on the door handle, stomach in the floor, ribs trying to suffocate me.

I close my eyes. I can do this.

I push the handle and cross into her office.

It's just the same as it always is. The rounded room, grand, arched windows, the stakes behind her giant desk and tall bookcases.

But none of that is what I've come for. That remains behind a hidden wall. Only three of us know it exists. Me, the Chief and the head of recruitment.

I stroll over to the bookcase and pull a book down. It's not real, rather attached to a hinge that's actually another door handle. There's a creak and half the bookcase shudders as it breaks apart and swings open.

It's a tiny room, barely wide enough for me and the cabinet inside. But I pull the drawers and search for what I need.

I think that's the worst bit about this—because of my rank and status I can just walk in and take what I need. Or I could have if it weren't for the fact the whole city is looking for me. Gods. If it weren't me stealing our secrets, I'd be fuming at the theft and implementing a multilayered security system. Hell, maybe I'd ask Remy to come and install some fancy RuneNet thing for us.

The pile of files is huge. But I've got what I need. I close the cabinet drawer and shut the bookcase behind me.

Prickles spread down my spine like I'm being watched.

I freeze. Someone is here.

"I told you to take a break," I bark in my best impression of the Chief.

"Oh gods," a young man says. "I hoped it wasn't you."

"Winston..." I say and turn to face my favourite student.

He staggers back, confused at my face and the disconnected voice. "I could tell by your walk."

But even as he retreats, my magic weakens and all the woven layers of the Chief's features fall from me.

"It really is you," he says. And then his eyes slowly fall

to the pile of quite clearly secret files in my hands. He frowns, locks his eyes on me.

"What are y—"

"Do you trust me?" I say.

"Red, don't do this." He shakes his head at me, his eyes glassy. His whole body trembles. "I don't want to hurt you."

I cough out a single laugh.

"Three years, and this is what it comes down to?"

"Fuck, you were my favourite. I respected you so much. Hell, I wanted to be you."

His words cut something deep inside me. My throat thickens. "You don't understand what's happening."

"Then tell me. . . Make me understand..."

I shake my head, there isn't time. How do I explain that everything he ever believed was a lie? He's too institutionalised. Fuck, it took me long enough to believe it. It wasn't until I saw Cordelia and the Chief together that I really accepted that the Chief could be betraying our entire species.

I remember how loyal and militant I was at his age. No, it doesn't matter what I say, he won't believe me until he sees it for himself. Finally, I look at him and his expression cracks, he shakes his head, realising I'm not going to explain.

"Why, Red? Just tell me why..." he asks and his voice breaks, a tear rolls down his cheek.

I never wanted to hurt him, or anyone. But I do have to do this no matter what. Octavia is the only one who should be ruling this city. She's the only one who will do it with truth in her heart and a desire to help. Everyone else wants the city for power and privilege and control. This is the way it needs to be. And as soon as I deliver these files, I'll be

131

gone. Winston and all the trainees will be better off without me.

"I can't," I say and take a step towards the door.

"And I can't let you go with those files. Not without an explanation."

I sigh and slip into teacher mode. Don the tone I used to take with the kids when I was done with their bullshit.

"This is bigger than both of us. I do not want to hurt you. Don't forget, I am no longer just Red anymore. You've seen the posters, you must have heard the rumours. What am I, Winston?"

He shakes his head.

"Winston... What. Am. I?"

There's a beat. Another. Three more. Then finally he answers.

"The dhampir."

"That's right. You've seen I have magic. I can and I will get past you in whatever way I have to. Do you understand?"

He nods.

"And I don't want to injure you. So how about we agree to this. You're going to stand right there. You're going to count to one hundred, and when you get there, you're going to hit the security alarm. Okay?"

He nods, tears falling down his cheeks. Oh, my sweet boy. With every tear that falls, another cut rips me from the inside out. I swallow down the lump in my throat.

"I know where your rooms are, Winston. I am the most powerful person in this city, and unfortunately for you, I drink blood."

I bare my teeth at him and he flinches. This is the moment I truly hate myself. How could I do this to him?

Break his spirit? Even if it is for the greater good and his benefit in the long term.

I shake it off, I don't have time to mollify or pander to his emotions. I have to get out before the receptionist comes back.

I grab his shoulder forcing him to look at me. "What are you going to do?"

He blinks up at me and finds his voice. "C-count to one hundred."

"Good, and then what are you going to do?"

"Hit the um. Umm. Hit the button."

"Well done, Winston, still top of the class." I reach for my magic and pull my hand back over my face replacing mine with the Chief's.

Winston gasps and tries to step away but his back hits the wall. I hold his gaze for a moment longer. Internally apologising. Quietly sobbing to myself as I watch the image he had of me crumble.

"Ready?" I say.

He trembles as he nods.

"Goodbye, Winston." I say and it takes everything I have not to let my voice crack as I walk out of the office. I have to grit my teeth the entire way down the corridors and all the way out into the courtyard and back to the carriage. I never look back. I never stop. I march my way out of the Academy, my home, my life, for the last time. And every step I take, my breath gets shorter, my heart pinches a little tighter.

And right on queue, as I shut the carriage door, the security alarm shrieks to life.

"GO," I shout. The horses whinny as the driver cracks the whip and I jerk back into the seat.

And then I slide to the carriage floor and shatter.

CHAPTER 16

RED

We arrive back at Xavier's and I press my thumb over the gargoyle's spike. It's odd seeing a white goyle, all the others I've met are grey stone or black. If I had time, I'd stop and ask his name and chat. But I need to get in and get out.

I push open the door and glance over my shoulder. Dawn is kissing the horizon, the darkness ebbs away in streaks of purple and blossoming oranges. This was either the best timing or the worst.

I step inside and close the door. "Xav—" I shout, but before I can finish his name, he appears.

"Where the hell have you been? It's been nearly a day. I was going to run out to try and find you but it's almost sunup.

"I had shit to do. Listen. I need a favour."

"Why does that sound like a bad thing?"

I shake my head. "It's the easiest favour you'll ever do. I just need you to give Octavia this..."

I hand him the files and a paper bag that clinks and clangs as I pass it over.

His eyes narrow at me. "And what, pray tell, is that?"

He prods the bag as if it will explode on him, so I lurch suddenly forward.

"Oh," he yelps, and I laugh my head off.

"You're an arse," he says and jabs me in the shoulder.

So I nudge right back. "And you're going to do me this favour."

He shakes his head. "Nope. I'm out. I'm tired of being your middleman. You two are grown-ass women more than capable of talking to each other. And in fact, that's exactly what you need to do."

I pull my eyes away, examining the ornate tiling in his foyer. "She's made it very clear what she thinks of me, and that she's out of the competition. I really don't want to hurt her anymore. So will you please, just do this one last favour for me?"

I pray he agrees. I have nothing to persuade him with, no favour I can do him, no tactics for coercion and honesty. Xavier has done so much for me already; it feels like an imposition asking him to do this too.

I don't think Octavia would even entertain me trying to give this to her; it's better this way, at least she'll listen to Xavier. Besides, if I can't fix us, I can at least help her win. She doesn't need me to get in the way and fuck anything else up. So there's really no reason for me to be in the competition anymore. Not if I don't need the cure.

Which makes Amelia my last stop, and then... I'm gone.

Xavier huffs and snatches the files from my hands. "Gods, Red. Must you look so pitiful. It really is quite the fucking guilt trip, you know."

135

I smile, but it doesn't reach my eyes. One of those half-hearted attempts to make both of us feel better.

"I need to go," I say, still unable to look at him.

His expression stiffens. "I can't change your mind?"

So he's figured out what I mean. I shake my head no. "I need to do this. She needs to win this thing on her own and make the city hers. I'm just going to get in the way. You've seen it out there. Everyone wants a piece of me. If I stay, her win will become about me, and I'm not going to do that to her. Besides, I want to get out, everyone is hunting me... including, apparently, demons."

"De— wait, what?" he says, his face scrunching. "Mother mentioned that there's been a spate of weird attacks in the city, but I thought it was just the usual hunter-demon brawls."

I shake my head. "I was attacked, or sort of, I don't know. It was trying to drag me to the boundary. You should tell Octavia."

"Or maybe you should grow up and have a conversation about it."

I glare at him.

"Fine, but did you at least kill it?"

"Yes, but that was the weirdest part. Once I killed it, it shifted into a human. I... I don't think they're real demons. I think maybe they got caught in the formation of the boundary and it did something to them."

Xavier whistles. "Okay, thank you, I'll tell the others. But... You're wrong... about Octavia and leaving."

"All I've done is cause her pain."

"Maybe. But you also gave her love... *made* her love. And that is a price worth paying a million times over. I don't think you should leave... And, I do think you should give her these files yourself."

I press my lips shut and shake my head. "I can't. She won't even see me. When we last spoke it was very clear how over it was."

Xavier sighs, deep, breathy and exhausted and I swear in that moment, the bags under his eyes darken.

"Then at least tell me where you're going..."

"I'm leaving because it's the right thing to do, not because I want to be found..."

"You're making a mistake."

"The mistake was sabotaging the last trial. This... this is the first time I'm doing the right thing. Just make sure she gets those files, okay?"

He nods and then pulls me into his arms and squeezes me. "It's been real."

I squeeze back, then break away. "Move left, the sun has risen, and I don't want you to get blasted."

He steps out of the way of the door's light path, and I slip outside, the sun warming my skin.

I climb inside the carriage and ask the driver to take me to the Whisper Club, where I assume Amelia will be.

As we pull up to the club, part of me hopes that Octavia is there. That I'll accidentally stumble upon her as I make my way inside. Maybe I can persuade her to give me one last chance. But that's not what I deserve and unfortunately, luck isn't on my side.

I keep my hood up high and my head bent low as I reach Broodmire. I tickle him under the chin, and he gobbles up two drops of blood. His skin ripples and he shivers with excitement.

"Wow," he says.

"It's a little different now, hey?" I say.

"Sure is. She's not here, I'm afraid. Octavia... if you're looking for her, she left after Sadie St Clair visited."

My stomach drops. The little seed of hope fizzles out. Probably for the best. I don't deserve to see her again, let alone a chance at convincing her I'm sorry.

"That's okay, I was hoping for my sister."

He nods, and the door swings open. "Octavia's office, last whisper I heard."

"Thank you, Broodmire."

I slip inside and the first person I see is Erin. "Morning," I say, hoping she doesn't freak out that the dhampir is standing in the middle of the club.

She hesitates for a split second and then says, "Octavia isn't—"

"It's fine, I'm looking for Amelia."

"Office upstairs," she nods and indicates where I should go. I'm quietly grateful she treats me the same way she treated me before. I'm already over the looks I keep getting, it makes me think of Octavia and how she's always been treated. But that makes my heart clench and my throat constrict.

I push the thought away. Just like the Academy, these corridors are trodden into my mind likes the veins in my body. I'll never forget this place. It might even be the one place I miss.

I traipse upstairs and push open Octavia's office door. I find Amelia sat at a small desk in the corner with a pile of paperwork, her hand smushing her forehead in concentration.

She doesn't move, her eyes focused on the pages in front of her, so I clear my throat.

She yelps and jumps up from the desk. "Gods, Red, you scared the life out of me."

I smile, trying to suppress a laugh but it bubbles up anyway. "And here I was thinking vampires had super hearing. So much for the benefits of turning."

She rolls her eyes at me and gets up from behind the desk and comes over to give me a hug.

"Xavier wouldn't let me stay. He said the fewer people there the better, and I just figured I needed to prioritise your safety not my selfish need to see you."

"He told me." I rub her back and disentangle.

"How are you?"

I shrug.

"Don't give me that bullshit. How are you really? Sister to sister..."

"I've been better. Things are wild out there, the whole city is feral. I've never seen so many images of my face in all my life. . . They all think I'm some kind of fucking deity. I'm just glad I've only run into the ones who want me to bless them and not the vampires hunting me."

Amelia gets stiffer the more I say, "It's terrifying that half the city would bleed for you and the other half wants you to bleed for them."

She's trembling, so I take her to a sofa and plonk us down.

"I'm fine. I'm here, aren't I?" I say.

"I guess," she says, and a bit of the tension seeps out. "So... things with Octavia?"

I look away, unable to even bring myself to speak of it.

"That good, huh?" she says and takes my hand to

squeeze it. "You'll get through this and find your way back to each other."

"We won't. Not this time."

Amelia sighs and changes the subject. "It's funny, I spent the whole of last night ripping your face down from the city walls like, how the hell did my big sister get so damn famous?"

She tilts her head at me, the laughter crinkle in the corner of her eyes gone. "I'm sorry... about Octavia."

"It's not your fault. It's my stupid fault for reacting too quickly and not thinking anything through."

"She'll forgive you..."

But I shake my head. "She won't. She made that abundantly clear."

"You risked being attacked to come here, so tell me what's going on."

"I came to apologise."

A frown further dampens her usually sunny face. "We already made up for you not talking to me after I turned. What on earth could you be sorry for now?"

I squeeze my eyes shut, wishing I'd been a better sister, a better listener. Wishing that for once, I hadn't been so selfish. But I can't undo the past, I can only make it better going forward.

"I didn't listen to you."

"What do you mean?" she says, her blue eyes scrunching in concentration.

"The cure, Amelia. The fucking cure, okay? I only entered this competition to get the cure because I wanted you to take it."

"Oh," she says and fiddles with a loose thread on the sofa cushion. The ensuing silence hangs so much heavier than our conversation.

I reach out and stop her fiddling with the thread. "I know you don't want it. You never did. I recognise that now. You're happy as a vampire and I need to respect that."

She blinks at me a few times, taking a few more deep breaths, and then says, "I never wanted this... to be a vampire... But when I was in Octavia's arms and dying, I couldn't think of anything worse than leaving you. I wasn't ready to die. And of course I can't forget what they did. Vampires took everything from us. But maybe I see this as a chance to rectify that. To do some good."

I lean back, because while her words sound beautiful, I'm not sure I believe them. Not after I watched her tear a man's throat out in the forest.

"You're becoming one of them. I saw you in the Blood Woods. You killed a guy without blinking."

"He was going to stake me. What would you have me do?"

I turn to the club and stare out the glass window. "It's not what you did. It's how you did it. The pleasure in your eyes. You revelled in taking an innocent man's life."

She's silent a moment, then gets up off the sofa to return to her desk, sliding back into her chair with a thud. "Was he? Innocent, I mean?"

I open my mouth to respond and find myself unable to.

She fills the void for me. "It was kill or be killed. And yes, I might take a little pleasure in my newfound skills. It's invigorating, hell, it's fucking empowering being able to defend myself. I was never the strong one. You were. I always had to rely on you, Red. You were older, stronger, and better than me. I was the burden, the little one incapable of anything and for once, I was able to care for you. Or indirectly, at least. Xavier's the one who deserves the real credit for that night, anyway. He got you out."

I fall silent, let her words sink in, turning them over and over. It's the right thing, to leave. She's going to be fine. I need to let her spread her wings, empower herself.

"I came to say goodbye..." I say, filling the quiet.

"What?" she says, frowning. "What the fuck do you mean 'goodbye'? You can't leave, this whole city is looking for you."

"Who? Me?" I say and reach deep inside, searching for those familiar threads and pull my hand over my face. The tingle of my features morphing washes over me. "I have a feeling they'll never find me," I say.

She gasps, her hand flying to cover her mouth. "Holy shit. How the fuck did you..." And just like Xavier, she strides over, her fingers outstretched, ready to prod and poke my face. Well, her face, really.

"That's fucking spooky. Damn, does my nose really tilt to the left like that?"

We both burst out laughing, because of all the shit she could say, that was not what I expected.

"Don't be vain," I say and put my whole palm over her face and shove her playfully back.

She smirks and then her expression falls. "Please don't go," she says and all of a sudden, we aren't adults anymore. She's a kid and I'm a tween just back from the Academy for the first time. She's holding her well-loved teddy and crying for me not to leave, and my heart shatters in two because I know that leaving her with Oriana is the right thing to do, just like I know leaving her with Octavia is the right thing now.

"You don't need me anymore, Amelia. You're all grown up. And I was going to make you take a cure because of my own selfish desires. I can't do that to you. I'd never want to force you into a way of life that you didn't choose. I think I just need to be on my own for a while. To figure out who I really am and who I'm meant to be."

"Fuck." A tear rolls down her cheek. I wipe it away. "Oh gods, you're really leaving," she says, but it's strained and her voice cracks.

"Come here, you idiot, you're going to be fine." I pull her into my arms, and she lets out a whimper.

"I love you," she says.

"I love you too. I won't be gone forever."

"You promise?" she whines into my chest.

"I promise."

She grumbles into my shoulder and when she pulls off, there's two little wet patches from her eyes. "I forgive you... in case you needed to hear that. You didn't make me take it..."

"But I could have. And honestly, if I stay, I'm still not sure if I'd try and convince you. It scared me what I saw in the woods. And I've never felt like that about you. And then I saw you taking down the posters with..."

Her back goes ramrod straight. "You saw me with Ash?" Her cheeks pink.

"Are they your—"

"No. No. I mean. Not that they're not. It's. We... They..."

I chuckle. I can't help it. It bubbles up and spills out like cloud puffs and candy. "Oh my gods, you fancy them."

"I do. They're the nicest person I ever met, and they just get me."

"I thought you were straight..."

She glares at me. "Is anyone actually straight?"

"I mean... some incomprehensible people are, sure. But I guess I just never questioned it with you... never had a reason to."

"I just fell for them. The way their eyes light up when I

walk in a room. Or when they have a romance book in their hands. Or when they're building some ridiculous luxury carriage. That's what they do in their spare time and..."

"Gods, Amelia... are you falling for Ash?"

"I think I am."

I smile and pull her into a hug. "And that's how I know you're going to be fine without me. I'll send word when I can and when I've settled in a location."

"You're not going to tell me where you're going?"

I shrug. "I haven't decided yet."

"Be safe. And I swear to gods, if you wear my face better than I do, I will hunt you down."

I laugh and ruffle her hair and take her face off. I'll let her wear it alone, besides the carriage is right outside the club.

I stroll out and down the stairs and corridor all the way to the exit, my heart a little lighter for the first time in weeks.

I find the carriage driver waiting for me. My blood runs cold. There's a huge group in front of the club. They're brandishing banners and posters held up on wood. They're chanting and holding wooden sticks lit aflame. It's a sea of contorted faces. All of them spitting with fury and lined with hate.

"Death to the dhampir!" someone shouts, and the crowd jeers and screams with delight. The carriage driver touches my hand and I startle.

"I think we need to leave. Where to?"

"Edge of the city. I've got an old friend to find."

"Yes, ma'am."

I drag my eyes away from the crowd, a cold unease settling into my gut, when someone screams, "IT'S HER. SHE'S HERE. KILL THE DHAMPIR."

"Fuck." I scramble into the carriage as the crowd roars. Gods, if I didn't need to leave before, I really fucking do now. For a thousand reasons and about a hundred more right outside the carriage window.

"Make it quick," I shout through the window. He cracks the reins and the horses race off, the crowd bellowing and chasing after us.

CHAPTER 17

OCTAVIA

I take the underground tunnels to Xavier's property. By the time I make it there, it's broad daylight, the afternoon sun crisp and fiery. I have to take extra precautions before opening the carriage and stepping inside his mansion to make sure there are no stray sunrays about to desiccate me.

I stroll across his underground carriage station and up into the belly of his house. I break into the foyer to find him pacing like a wild animal. He visibly relaxes when I enter.

"Rather dramatic for an afternoon, don't you think?" I say.

"Where the fuck have you been?" he says, strolling over to me carrying a pile of files and a bag.

I quirk an eyebrow. "What is this?"

"It's for you." He shoves the pile of files and bag at me. I grapple to take them without dropping it all.

"You planning on explaining?" I say, my eyebrow descending into a frown.

I open the bag and find two vials of blood and a short note.

> *For all the blood you gave me, it's about time I returned the favour. This will open the door. You deserve the city. I wanted to be the one to give it to you, but now, I realise you need to take it for yourself. This is my way of apologising. My way of saying I believe you can win this.*
>
> *I will always love you, Octavia.*
>
> *You will always be in my heart and my veins.*

I freeze. My blood coagulating as I stand there.

"Why isn't my bond hurting?" I breathe.

"Because you told her you were done. Because you're both consenting to be apart from each other."

"I... I don't consent."

"Mother of Blood." Xavier flings his hands up. "You choose now to decide you're not over her?"

"I am," I snap. And then immediately change my mind. "I mean. No. Well, sort of. I don't..."

"Stop blabbing and open the files. What has she given you?"

I peel open the covers and find page after page of secrets. Drawings and renderings and accounting files and slips.

Xavier whistles. "Gods, that's a lot of blackmail."

My stomach sinks, the fleeting tickle of hope dissolving as I stare at pages and pages of blackmail.

147

"How could she?" I breathe.

"What's wrong?" Xavier says a crease forming in the middle of his eyebrows.

"For fuck's sake. She gives me the blood in one hand and breaks my heart all over again in the other."

"I don't get it. She's given you a file of blackmail so you can convince everyone to vote for you. She's handing you the keys to the city, Tave. This is everything you wanted."

My stomach is in knots. And I'm not sure if it's devastation or fury. Either way, I want to throw the files in her face.

"You don't get it. I don't want to win this city because I blackmailed everyone into fearing me. I want to win this city because I'm accepted."

I throw the files on the floor. "How am I ever going to do that if everyone who's anyone fears me and only complies because they're worried about the consequences? That is not how a city is made."

"I guess she thought she was doing you a kindness by handing you what you needed to win."

He kneels to pick up the files I threw, tutting and pressing the creases out of his trousers where he bends.

"Well, some fucking kindness. Where the hell is she, anyway?"

"Gone."

The word smashes into me like an anvil.

"What do you mean gone?" I spit.

"She thought it would be best for everyone if she left. The way she was talking... it... I thought she was doing this to support you. Not make things worse."

He trails off, all the while, my heart breaks in two. If this is what she thought an apology was... Then maybe I never really knew her at all. How could she think me blackmailing everyone would help me be accepted?

"She must have thought I couldn't convince them. Couldn't get anyone to accept me. What if she's right? What if I can't? How the hell am I supposed to convince a city that hates me, to love me?"

Xavier's silent as he pulls sheaf after sheaf together and then he stops. His fingers hover over one handwritten piece of paper.

"Oh," he says.

"What's she done now?" I snap, unable to keep the irritation out of my voice.

Xavier stands and hands me the piece of paper. "I only read the first line, but I think you need to see this."

As my eyes scan the words, my mouth goes dry. There's a roaring in my ears and bile claws up my throat.

Dearest Octavia,

Don't get mad. If I know anything about you, you'll jump to the conclusion that I've handed you these files as a way to blackmail the hunter elders and vampire nobles. But it's so far from that.

See, I really do believe that our city needs you. That you are the one true queen meant to rule over our people. The queen who will finally unite our city. And if I ever gave you cause to doubt that, then I want you to know that I am deeply sorry. With every cell in my being, I am sorry.

So, too, am I sorry for entering this competition under the guise of getting the cure for Amelia. I've gone to give her my apologies and tell her that I'll never force her to do anything. I think it's best if I leave the city and give you all the space to become the people and leaders you were meant to be.

I do believe in you, Octavia. You will win this competition and that's where these files come in. I've given them to you not to use them for blackmail. But to use them for good.

These are the only files and only evidence we have on these people. It's everything the Hunter Academy had. And I stole the lot. All you'd have to do is destroy the evidence and everyone in those files is free from whatever hold Eleanor had over them.

Or you could agree to negotiate with them, solve their problems. Either way, these files are an olive branch. I've taken what the Academy had and I'm gifting it to you because I believe you will do the right thing with it. That's how I know you'll make an incredible leader and why I know you'll be able to convince everyone to vote for you.

I am so, so deeply sorry for everything I did to wrong you. I'm sorry I fucked our chances, but you have everything you need to win now. My blood, the method to convince everyone to vote. The boundary will be a formality. All you need to do is believe in yourself the way I believe in you. Do that and you'll be unstoppable.

Just like you said to me the other day, "Some fates aren't meant to be..." I think you're right. We really would have been legendary. I hope that in another realm, they write our love story and in that author's world it lasts a millennium. And in each one of those thousand years, I will yearn for you until I find you again.

I wish things had been different.

But no matter, I will always love you.

My queen. My Sovereign. My soul mate.

Verity

My hands are shaking so hard and my eyes so blurry by the time I get to the end of the letter that I can't read her name. I can't breathe. I can't think straight. I can't do much of anything. My entire body trembles.

Someone calls my name but I'm too lost to hear it.

The only sound is the screaming inside my head. The cries for her, for the clusterfuck we've become and the loss of the love we should have had.

"OCTAVIA," Xavier bellows, shaking me by the shoulders and bringing me back to attention. I hand him the letter and his eyes scan the rest of the page at vampire speed.

"Oh, Tave," he breathes.

But I can't respond, because every syllable I try and make comes out as a jumbled blob of tears and whimpering. When I've calmed down enough to speak, I whisper. "Where is she?"

"I told you, she left," he says, his eyes droop, matching the soft, pitiful tone of his voice.

"Yes, but where did she go?" I say, my mind suddenly clearing and a burning desire swarming my insides. My chest heats, my stomach tightens as if my own ribs are now a vice. Oh gods, I have to find her.

I run for the door, but Xavier leaps in front of me. And shoves it shut.

"Still daylight. You can't go out there."

"What?" I glance up at the foyer curtains, still pulled closed. "No. I have to leave. Right now."

"It's too late, Octavia. She gave me these this morning. You can't leave and run across the city for another three hours, and even if you pushed the carriage horses as fast as they could go, you wouldn't reach her."

"I have to. I fucking have to, Xavier. I know I told her we were done, but... but..."

He folds his arms. "You both fucked up and now you want to rectify it?"

"I can't run this city without her. I can't finish this competition without her. This..." I point at the letter and gesture at the remaining files on the foyer floor. "Is genius. I would never have thought of it. She deserves to take credit for it too."

"She does, but she won't unless you forgive her."

"I think we need to forgive each other."

He sighs. "Take the carriage through the private tunnels, they should be clear at the moment. But I think you're going to be too late. I don't even know where she's gone."

I pause, my chest thumping as if I had a heartbeat.

"There's only one place she'd run to... I just have to get there before she crosses out of our city boundary..."

Xavier pulls the letter out of my hand and shoves me towards the back of the foyer. "Then go already. What are you waiting for?"

And with that, I speed out of his mansion and down into the carriage station, praying to the Mother of Blood that I can make it before she's out of my reach.

CHAPTER 18

RED

The carriage jerks forward but rioters are already on top of us. They rock the cabin, tipping it this way and that as I try and press my hands to the roof and steady myself.

This is not good.

Not fucking good at all.

"GET US OUT OF HERE," I shriek. The horses whinny, and then we're moving and galloping out of the square and hopefully to safety. I hope too soon though, the rioters aren't finished with us. Worse, when I pull the curtain back and peer outside, there are vampires in their midst. And they are as fast as the carriage.

"Shit." I throw myself back from the window, my fingers prickling with the tinge of panic. I grab hold of the handrail and cling on as the carriage veers one way and then another. It rears up as we wheel over a rock that should have been taken much slower.

There's a thump on the exterior wall and a moaned cry.

"Oh gods, the driver."

The carriage slows and then stops with a lurch. I'm flung forwards, careening into the wall with a crack.

The door is wrenched open, and I'm unceremoniously dragged out of the carriage. I kick out, smashing the vampire holding me in the face as I land on the ground. I whirl around and jump up. I cannot stay on the ground if I want to stay alive.

I'm grabbed by the shoulders and thrown through the air like a projectile. Fuck me, the vampires are strong. They must have all fed recently. I crash to the ground and skid across the cobbles, landing on the bridge. Three of them round on me as I scramble up and edge further on to the bridge. Behind them, I spot the rest of the rioters, their placards bobbing as they run through the streets to catch up to us. This is not fucking good.

The horses whinny and neigh and shy away in fright as a fourth vampire rushes past. One of the horses spooks enough to break free of the carriage wreckage. I hate that the animal was scared, but I'm grateful that as it shreds the reins, it tramples one of the vampires, who gets crushed under the feet of both horses as they dash for freedom.

The carriage driver lies a few feet away, his body unnaturally still on the path, a puddle of red oozing out under underneath him.

Internally, I'm screaming at myself: run Red, just fucking run. But as I check over my shoulder, I realise one of the vampires already made it to the other end of the bridge. I'm trapped. Blocked in on both sides. So fight it is.

Three vampires won't be easy, but I've faced harder odds and at least these guys aren't original vampires.

I slide my hand to my knife sheath and unclip it. The first vampire charges at me, he leaps the last little way, but that was his first mistake. I rear back and spin around, landing a savage turning kick to his ribs as he drops down. He goes skittering back.

But the next vampire is already in front of me, and the one behind me is creeping dangerously close. The one in front swings out. I block the blow, but the force of it shunts me back.

My ankle slips on one of the cobbles, jarring me and enabling him to land a godsawful blow to my jaw.

The strike is so hard, my brain and teeth rattle in my head. It takes me a long second to shove the stun away. He, however, wastes no time letting me recover and lands three quick jabs to my ribs. One rib cracks so violently there's no question it's broken. I stagger back, sliding the blade out of the sheath and knowing that I need to get a grip of this fight. Fast.

But I made a mistake and didn't keep an eye on the vampire behind me. He grabs my hair and yanks me backwards at the same time the vampire in front of me lunges for me. I use the weight of the vampire behind to counterbalance me and I kick out, smashing my boot into the oncomer's face. His nose splits open and he cries out, momentarily blinded by pain and blood.

He staggers back and slips and falls over the edge of the bridge.

One down, two to go.

I twist my body around and thrust the knife out and push up. It stabs into his gut and tears flesh and organs; I can feel things pop and release. He shrieks and lands a nasty blow to my eye socket. But I'm already reaching for his innards and yanking them out. Sure, he might be able to recover, but it won't be quickly, and it will be minus half his insides.

Cunt.

He stumbles back, which leaves me with the last remaining vampire. . . and the rest of the humans and rioting hunters, who, unfortunately for me, have caught up with us. This isn't good. I have two choices. Stay and try and fight with a hundred-to-one odds or run and pray I'm faster than most of the humans.

I don't hesitate; I leap up onto the bridge wall and run with my arms out, trying to keep my balance so I don't fall over the side. My eye is fuzzy where I was hit, which makes keeping my footing sure extra difficult, especially when I glance over my shoulder and see the rioters on the bridge. The remaining vampire stopped to help re-insert his friend's innards.

Finally, I reach the end of the bridge. I could drop into the alley or I could climb. I decide climbing is the fastest way to get away from the bloodthirsty group bearing down on me. The problem is, they're screaming and shouting so loud that more city dwellers are opening their windows and clocking on to what's happening. A line of sweat forms on my brow as I reach for the drainpipe, my ribs protesting. The sharp, searing pain makes me falter, and my hand slips off the pipe. I try again, bracing myself for the pain and this time, manage to clamber my way up and onto the roof of the line of stone terraced houses.

I hoick myself up and over the roof lip and lay on my back, panting and letting the searing heat in my ribs fade. I might not die easily, but unless I drink blood, I'm also not going to heal too quick either. I need to get myself to safety and fast.

The jeers below are growing louder, so I push myself up and start running. As I dart over the tiles and chimneys, I assess my body. My ankle twinges, my ribs are excruciating.

My eye is still blurry, and it throbs around the socket, I wonder if the bone is cracked.

I pick up the pace and spot a stray piece of pipe along the way. I grab it, it could be a useful weapon, and sprint over the roofs, leaping from one to the next. It's only when I hit the end of the street and realise there's no easy way across to the next roof that my insides run cold.

"Fuck."

I glance below and the alley is filled with pissed-off humans coming for me. I have no choice, I can't wait it out up here. I hoist myself over the edge and jump down. My ankle screams at me when I land badly and agitate the already irritated ligaments.

"There she is!" someone cries, and I make a run for it. I pound my way through street after street until I skid to a halt, realising I made a catastrophic fuck-up.

"Dead end, little dhampir," one of the humans says. He runs a hand through his greasy hair and pulls out a wooden baton. I swallow hard and scan the area. Terraced houses rise on both sides. Behind me is a brick wall. But if I remember the route I took, on the other side of the wall is the river. It's not a smart idea to try and swim to safety when there's a hoard of people after me, but I'm betting that the wall is too high for most of them to scramble up. As it is, I think I'm going to have to springboard off the terraced wall.

The human advances on me as the rest of the group flood the street. I'm not waiting. I run at the terraced house closest and leap, using it to kick off and twist. I land hard against the wall. My fingers scrape down the bricks, but I hold on, barely. I want to cry out, and I'm pretty sure I ripped all the skin on my palm, but I haven't got time to wait. I haul myself up and onto the top of the wall.

YES! I was right. The river is underneath me, but it's a lot further down than I expected. I glance over my shoulder, the rest of the crowd are closing in.

"Get down here, you little bitch," the man says, brandishing the baton at me.

"Fuck you," I shout back and crouch, ready to leap. I'm not hanging around for them to attack.

I spring up, but as I do something fucking hard smashes into my head. My vision smatters, and then I'm falling, falling, falling and everything goes black.

I wake, my entire body bruised, broken and aching. I'm in a boat, a young woman wearing a brown, bohemian-style skirt and loose-fitting shirt leaning over me.

"Hey," she says.

"Hey, yourself," I reply.

She stares at me, blinking, expectant.

"Sorry, do I know you?" I ask.

"No. I know who you are, though."

"Apparently so does the entire city."

She gives me a hand and pulls me sitting. I groan as white-hot lances spike through my body.

Once I'm upright, I take in my surroundings. I'm inside of a barge boat, and we're drifting along the canal. Most of the curtains are closed, thankfully. So she clearly recognises me. The decor is simple, fresh flowers adorn several surfaces, the seat fabrics are awash with browns and oranges and the curtains contain a bold floral print.

"Here," she says and hands me a glass of blood. I take it, my stomach growling. It's still warm.

"What is this?" I ask.

She shrugs. "My mum is religious. She hasn't stopped banging on about you since the news broke. I figured with the amount of injuries you had when I pulled you out, you'd probably need blood if you're half vamp."

Her mum? The woman in front of me is at least a decade older than me, she must be heading towards fifty, so her mother must be significantly older. I wonder if she looks after her. She holds her wrist up to me and there's a nasty gash on it.

"My ma wouldn't forgive me if I told her I had a chance to save you."

My fingers itch with the need to mend, heal, fix. I put the glass down and reach for her arm. A golden light blooms where I touch her. She gasps and goes to pull away, but I hold her tighter.

"Don't panic," I say. It tickles and itches in equal measure, like sand between the toes only fluffier.

When the light dims, I pull away and reach for the glass, drinking it down. She gawps at her wrist, turning it this way and that.

"How?" she breathes.

"That's the gift I was given when I transitioned."

"So it's true, you really are the dhampir, and magic really is coming back."

I slouch against the seat. "The truth is, I don't know. I wasn't born to change the world, I'm just another girl trying to survive."

She holds her hand out to me. "Madeleine."

"Red." We shake hands.

"Thank you," I say and raise the glass to her.

"It's nothing."

I shake my head. "No. It's much more than nothing. You must have single-handedly hauled me out of the river."

She shrugs like it really was nothing and then flexes her bicep. "I work out a lot."

That makes me laugh.

"Where are you going?" she asks.

"Away."

"Need a lift?"

"You'd aid and abet the most wanted person in the city?"

Madeline shrugs again, and then rolls herself a cigarette. She sprinkles some herbs inside it and when she lights it, I recognise the smell.

"Listen. If I can help a girl out, I will. The city is wild right now, and it seems like you need a break." She takes a drag on the cigarette, her eyes glazing a little. She brushes some ash off her skirt and focuses on me, taking another drag and then handing it to me.

I really should not dabble right now. I take it anyway and when I inhale the hit, it burns down my throat, but I immediately feel more relaxed.

"Wouldn't your mother be disappointed you had the chance to ferry me back to the church?"

"Probably." She shrugs and takes the cigarette back.

My limbs are far more relaxed, the blood she gave me flowing through my system and knitting my wounds back together.

"But I'm not my mama. And honestly, you look like you need someone to cut you a break."

I smile. "Edge of the city, if you don't mind."

"Edge of the city it is." She gets up and makes her way to the stern where she steps up and outside, takes the wheel and guides us out of the city.

CHAPTER 19

OCTAVIA

S at in the carriage, I leaf through the files Xavier raced into the tunnels to give me. He figured if I was stuck in a carriage for the next few hours, the least I could do was go over the files and construct a plan. But I'm restless. I stand, sit. Stand again. Switch sides in the carriage.

None of it helps.

I churn over what I'm going to say. I compose sentences, only to rip them up and start over. None of it flows the way I want because all I want is to stop the sheer panic rushing through my system that I'm too late.

I have to stop her from leaving. I'm so furious with myself, gods, with her too. With the pair of us.

Am I still angry with her for sabotaging the trial? Yes, of course. But does every cell in my body still love her?

Always.

By the time the carriage reaches the tunnels, I'm vibrating with irritation. The horses slow, having run the entire length of the city. They're exhausted.

"Stop," I bark, as we creep into the tunnels far enough that the sunrays don't reach me.

I scramble out of the carriage and approach the driver.

"Give the horses a rest at the first watering station. And then I want you to continue. Take the carriage as far as you can, and I will meet you there, okay?"

His features wrinkle. "Yes, Lady Beaumont. City's edge it is, where the tunnels split?"

I nod, and then I turn and run—vampire fast—into the darkness. I sprint as hard as my legs will carry me. Tunnel after tunnel rushes past me. Locks of my hair flap like whips behind me. My eyes leak tears from the rush of wind. But Red left hours ago. She'll be so much further ahead of me, I doubt I can even reach her in time.

And then what if I'm wrong? What if she didn't go to Bella?

No.

There's no way and I can't think like that. It's not going to help me run any quicker through these bastard tunnels. Besides, where else would she have gone? The tunnels split, some veering left and others right to other cities. But there's only one border I need to make it to.

I pump my legs harder, swing my arms. Dig into every ounce of vampire strength and power I have. A line of sweat trickles down my neck as I round a corner and finally, finally a speck of dim light appears in the distance. The sun is finally setting. I dig deeper, run harder. Shadows whip up, but I ignore them, pushing until my lungs hurt and I swear I'm going to puke up the blood bag I drank earlier.

I skid to a halt a few feet from the entrance and scan New Imperium, the city standing before me, the one I cannot step into.

Red's not here. The street is empty. I missed her. My stomach drops through my feet. I fall to my knees.

"Fuck," I shriek and punch the ground. "Fuck. Fuck. Fuck."

I smack the floor until my knuckles split and re-heal numerous times, leaving crusty flakes of blood over the back of my hand.

A breeze whips into the tunnel. Leaves skitter into the darkness, dragging pieces of the city with it.

I lean against the wall, watching a city I'm forbidden from entering. More and more lamp lights yawn awake. This is the end of the line; I failed. I was too late.

Unless I ignore that directive and initiate a war between my city and the magicians... I'd do anything to reach Red right now. Would I go to war for her?

I edge towards the tunnel opening... Maybe I could sneak in unnoticed. Just for one night... I can't give up. This *can't* be it for us. Like Red's letter said, I'll spend the next thousand years yearning for her.

I stand, step closer to the entrance, my toes on the boundary edge, a millimetre from the light. It's the right thing, and I'll be quick enough, stay at vampire speed so that no one will notice me...

I lean forward, my fingertips edging into New Imperium, when a voice freezes me.

"I wouldn't do that if I were you..."

I gasp and pull back, my arm sliding into the shadow of the tunnels. I turn, slowly, and finally come face to face with her.

"Red..."

"Octavia."

"I thought I'd missed you, that you'd already made it into the city... I was going to..."

165

I jerk my finger in the direction of New Imperium.

"I can see that. You flew past me about half a mile ago. You were going so fast, you didn't see me in the shadows."

I laugh. The relief is palpable. It tickles its way through my body, into my fingers and toes, and all the way to my throat until I am laughing hysterically.

I run my hand through my hair. But Red stands there, arms folded, staring at me, and suddenly none of this is funny anymore. That's when I truly take her in. Scan her face, her clothing. She's bloodied and dirty, her jacket ripped. There's a shadow of bruising around her eye socket and she's holding herself awkwardly.

"What happened?" I say, my tone serious.

"Does it matter?" she says, resigned.

"Of course it fucking matters."

She rolls her eyes. "I was attacked, I had to escape, it got messy, I fell into the river and a riverboat woman pulled me out and gave me a glass of her blood."

My jaw clenches. A bubbling pit erupts in my chest. I'm not sure what I'm more pissed about: the fact she was attacked and I wasn't there to protect her or the fact "some woman" pulled her out of the river and gave her some of her blood.

"Are you okay?" I ask.

"No. Not really. But I will be when I can have a shower and drink a few glasses of blood because apparently that's the only way I heal."

Her expression steels, as if she's daring me to comment on the fact she's willing to drink blood. I decide to pick my battles and that's not the one I'm here for.

"I got the files," I say.

She shifts on the spot, the stiffness leaking out of her expression as she kicks a tunnel cobble with her boot. "I figured you'd be able to negotiate some positive deals, make problems go away." She wafts her hand like that's the easiest thing in the world.

"You make it sound like the monster everyone has hated for a millennia can just convince them just like that."

She looks up at me. "You're not a monster, Octavia, you never were. And I do believe you can do just that. If you believe it, you'll make it happen."

I pause, letting the silence blanket us, while Red gazes steadily at the floor, waiting. When she looks at me next, I utter a single word.

"We..."

She hesitates, her eyes examining my expression. "I have to leave. I just cause everyone problems. You have the vials of my blood, you can open the door yourself. You don't need me."

"You're wrong."

Kneading her forehead, she takes a step back. But I match her, pacing forward. "You're a coward for leaving."

She flings her arm down, the same fierce fire in her eyes that I'm used to. That I want to see.

There she is.

"Fuck you, Octavia."

But I'm relentless. "You're a coward for not handing me those files yourself. For leaving me a note and for not facing me."

"Facing you? As if you would have listened. You're the most stubborn, pigheaded—"

"That's not an apology, *Red*." I fling a hand on my hip in frustration.

"Well, you're shouting at me."

"And you should have tried to speak to me."

I take a deep gulp of air and breathe out the irritation. I'm not here to argue, I'm here to get her back.

She slides a foot into New Imperium. My body twists, I lurch forward, grabbing her hand and pulling her back into the shadows. "Wait."

She tugs her hand out of my grasp. "I need to go. I'm no good for anyone."

"You can't leave," I say and step forward, laying a foot into the forbidden city. Red flinches like she's going to recoil but instead shoves me back into the tunnel's protection.

"Do you have a death wish?" she growls.

The first frisson of energy sparks between us. It's hot and electric and throbs in the air like lightning. I can win her back.

She lowers her eyes, her feet edging towards the boundary like all of this is inevitable. Like I'm not standing here trying to fight for her.

"There's no life for me here. I'll never be able to go back to the Academy. Those files make me a traitor. This kid caught me, so it's over for me. I've lost everything. My home, my sister, the competition. You..."

"What if you didn't... lose everything, I mean."

I inch closer, the warmth from her body radiating into me. Gods, I want to wrap my arms around her, inhale the heat, drink in her smell, her taste. I want to devour her, but first I need to convince her to stay.

"Amelia would never hate you," I say.

"Maybe not, but I wasn't a good sister. She never wanted that cure, Octavia. And I was going to force it on her."

I reach out, skim my little finger over hers. Such a small touch, so delicate it's barely the touch of a butterfly. But it makes her look up.

I give her a half-hearted smile. "And I bet she's already forgiven you."

She squirms on the spot, so I take the opportunity and lunge for her hand, lacing it through mine, tugging her three steps back into the darkness and away from yet another city that hates me.

She inhales a short, sharp breath. Her chest rises and falls as if my hand is a current. She drags her eyes from mine to where our palms touch.

"We haven't lost the competition. Or... not exactly. The ball aside... We still have to open the door, and you're the only one who can do that."

She chews her lip before answering. "I gave you my blood, you don't need me."

I pause, realising she's determined to leave despite my desperation to make her stay. I release her hand. If this was a few months ago, I'd have stood here and compelled her into doing what I wanted. But I won't do that, not again, and yet, I also can't make her stay. My insides shrivel, my mouth dries. I don't think I've ever been so helpless.

So I try the only thing I can think of.

The truth.

"Maybe I can open that door on my own. But... what if I don't want to? What if I can't think of anything worse than winning this city without you by my side?"

Her eyes go watery, her lips press together. "Why? I took everything from you. I ruined your dream. I shouldn't have done that no matter how mad I was with you. It was unforgivable."

"And so was taking your memories without consent, Red. We both fucked up. Both of us."

A tear rolls down her cheek, but she stays silent. If my

heart beat, it would be thunderous. Her silence sucks all the stars and hope and joy from the tunnel. I've lost her. She's still going to leave. My throat is so thick I'm certain I'll mess up the next words. But I have to try, so I push the trembles away and take a deep breath.

"I don't think I can do this without you. And even if I can... I don't want to."

She drops to her knees, pulling me down with her. "I'm so sorry, Octavia, I swear I will never do anything like that again."

"I'm sorry too," I say, and wipe the tear away with my thumb.

"I love you more than anything. I swear I'll never doubt you again." She leans up, cupping the back of my neck and brushing her lips over mine. I almost die. I swear her touch is like the sun and moon and every happy moment I've ever had. And she hasn't even kissed me.

Her sweet scent drifts between us, leather and hot skin, the outdoors, and—what is that? An odd undertone of stagnant water. Yeh, she's right, she does need a shower. But right now, in this second, I don't have a single fuck left to give. I want to consume her, devour her essence. Hell, I'd rebond with her all over again if I could.

She tilts her forehead to mine, until we touch.

"Let's make our love story legendary," I say. With a nudge, I press my lips to hers.

Our kiss is fire and air and salt and sea. As if our bond can feel us finally reunited, an explosion erupts in my chest. A firework of sensations as she moves her lips over mine. Her hands wander over my body in gentle caresses, soft at first, then more insistent, pulling and stroking.

Then harder. Tugging and needy. Her mouth moves faster, her tongue sliding over mine, desperate for more.

I kiss her back just as insistent, running a hand through her hair, up the back of her neck. I want all of her. To touch every inch of her smooth skin. I need to breathe her like she's oxygen. Two hands can't consume her fast enough. My every breath fills with the glorious scent of her. My molecules fizz and burst to life as her hands caress my skin. She kisses me like she's starved. And she is, but so am I. Ravenous lips and teeth and tongues, hands and flesh, heat and lust.

I grip her short, shaggy hair and yank her off me.

"I need more," I pant.

"Yes. More," she says, her eyes doe-like and lips swollen pink from all the kissing.

"I'm putting you on my back and running you to the carriage."

"Okay." She doesn't even hesitate. I haul her onto my back and speed back through the tunnels.

It takes an unreasonably long time to reach the carriage, but when I do, I wrench open the doors and drop her inside.

"Home," I say to the driver. "And make it quick. Take the private tunnels when we get to the city."

"Yes, ma'am." He slaps the reins and the horses rear up, taking off at a gallop through the tunnels.

I round on Red. "You're mine, do you understand?"

She nods at me, biting her lip, and looking up from under her lashes. Such a fucking tease.

I step close to her and slide my hands to her jacket, unzipping and helping her out of it. Next are her top and sports bra, which I pull up and over her head, leaving her standing topless before me.

"Fuck. I can't believe I nearly lost you," I whisper and as if her breasts hear me, her pink nipples harden.

My mouth waters at the sight of her. I reach out and tug

171

her towards me, running my thumb over her hardened bud. She gasps as I run it back the other way.

"Mine," I say and pinch. She squeaks but her eyes shut as I drag my fingers down her sides, making her skin fleck with goosebumps. She flinches and I stop.

Her eyes fly open. "It's just a rib. Don't stop. Blood will sort it out later."

I do as she says and reach for her trousers at the same time she grabs the buttons on my shirt. Together we peel the layers of clothes off, until we're both standing there naked. The carriage rocks as the horses canter through the tunnels, and Red wobbles on her feet. I nudge her back until she's perched on the edge of the carriage seat bench.

"Open," I command, and she slides her legs apart.

I nestle between them and take her mouth with mine. I kiss her hard and soft, and prise her lips open with my tongue. She sucks my lip, making a bolt of electricity shoot straight to my pussy, right up until she bites down hard enough to draw a drop of blood. A happy sound squeaks out of her, and she licks up the droplet. I pull away, hissing, but she grins like she knows what she's doing.

I tilt my head. "Are you going to be a brat?"

"Maybe," she purrs.

I pick her thighs up and flip her so her knees are on the bench and her ass is sticking out—which, I promptly proceed to slap.

She shrieks until it dissolves into a moan then cocks her head over her shoulder to look at me.

I pick up my shirt and use it to tie her wrists together and then toss it over a jacket hook attached to the carriage roof.

"My, my, don't you look marvellous strung up like the

172

little fuck toy you are," I say, admiring my work. Not bad improvisation, if I say so myself.

"Should I punish you, Red? Give you what you deserve for hurting me?"

"Oh gods," she pants, her legs trembling.

"You'd like that wouldn't you? For me to punish you. Make you pay for all the anguish you caused me?"

She nods, struggling against the makeshift handcuffs.

"What's your safe word?" I ask.

"Elysium. Yours?"

"Villain."

I reach out and slap her arse hard enough to leave a print. She rears up, her tied hands thudding against the carriage wall.

I stand behind her. "Spread," I demand. And she hitches her knees wider. I slide down until my face gets the view I've been waiting for.

"Look at that pretty pink pussy." Her neat little slit glistens at me, her skin cleanly shaved and pink.

"Mmm," I mumble. How delicious she looks.

I lean forward and run my tongue all the way down to her clit. She jerks against my shirt restraint as I touch her for the first time.

"No moving," I snap and bring my hand down on her arse cheek. She yelps, but it quickly descends into a moan as I slide my tongue between her folds.

"Oh fuck," she breathes.

I draw my tongue up and down her pussy, licking and caressing every inch of skin. I worship her, showering her cunt with long swipes of my tongue and nibbles with my teeth. I suck her folds into my mouth, then her clit, applying pressure on and off, on and off.

She arches her back, tugging and pulling on the

restraints. I lick the other way, all the way up, up, up, until I reach her other hole.

"Fuck!" Red squeals as I make contact with an unexpected region.

"Do you need to use your words?" I ask.

"No, gods, no. It's just... different, is all."

I smile and lower my tongue to her hole, swiping this way and that, drowning it in saliva. When it's nice and wet, I position myself on the ground between her legs, my back resting against the bench lip. I locate her clit with my tongue and then reach around and up to place my fingers over her arsehole.

"Oh gods," she pants. "Are you going to..."

But I don't let her finish, I slide to the ring of muscle I soaked and run the tip of my finger in circles, teasing it and encouraging it to relax. I move my tongue quicker and harder over her clit and when I feel her body loosening against me, I slide my finger inside her tight entrance, the ring of muscle finally relaxing for me.

"FUCK," Red moans. "Oh my gods, Octavia..." She's panting and gasping as I thrust another finger inside her. She rocks against them, driving herself onto me as I continue to lick and lap at her clit. Her legs shake as her clit swells against my tongue.

I devour her, licking up every drop of excitement that leaks from her pussy. She grinds against my hand, thrusting her arse against the pressure of my finger. I push another one inside her. She rears up, her body tightening, so I pull her back down. I'm not quitting until she tips over the edge into orgasm. My teeth graze against her clit, and she cries so loud I swear the driver will stop the carriage to check if I'm hurting her.

I thrust my fingers harder into her arse, licking quicker and lighter, and as she spasms and jerks, tipping into bliss, I release her clit and sink my teeth into her thigh.

She moans as I guzzle down her blood.

"Fuck, Octavia," she shrieks as the intense pleasure of my bite shoots into her system. I pull out and stand up behind her. I'm not done with her yet, I'll never be done, but right now, I want to wring another orgasm out of her. Blood drips between her thighs as the wound slowly congeals. I lean over her back, find her pussy and tease her entrance. She's soaked and ready for me, so I slide two fingers inside her and thrust hard, ramming her into the carriage wall.

"Fuck, I don't know if I can come again," she whines.

"You can and you will." I use my other hand to grip a fist full of her hair and pull her head to the side so I can gain access to her neck, and then I sink my fangs in, greedily.

She moans, panting and swearing and screaming my name. Just the way I like. I thrust, using my hips to shunt her forward and fuck her deeper, curling my fingers until I find that delicious spot deep inside. Her pussy finally clamps around my fingers, and she arches into me as she comes. My fangs sink into the other side of her neck, enabling me to take my fill of her. Own every piece of her— body, blood, heart.

"Mine," I growl as I pull out of her and release her neck.

"No," she says, and yanks her hands down from the ceiling so hard the wooden beam cracks.

I quirk an eyebrow up. Interesting. "The transition has made you strong."

She shoves me, pushing me until the backs of my knees hit the opposite bench and I'm forced to sit down.

"Yeah. It did."

Gods, she is magnificent. Standing before me, covered in my bite marks, blood dripping down her breasts and between her legs. It's enough to send pulses of pleasure to my clit. The scent of the carriage is exquisite. Sweet claret, orgasmic sex and hot bodies.

She comes to me, leaning down and brushing her fingers over my jaw.

"This time when you come, you will come for me, do *you* understand?" she says. Command laces through her voice. The power, the tone, all of it has me shorting out and instantly submitting.

She grips my jaw, tilts my head and bears my neck. "I said, do you understand?"

"Yes, fuck. Yes, I understand."

"Who owns your pleasure?"

"You, Verity. It's all yours."

I run my hand over her abs, trailing it through the blood.

"It will always be mine, because I will never let you starve of pleasure. But I swear, it had better be my name on those pretty fucking lips of yours, or..."

"Or what?" I purr.

She smiles, her eyes glimmering.

I whimper, I can't help it. This woman before me... the only one that could get me to my knees in a thousand years. And I hope to gods I stay here for the next thousand.

By the time the carriage reaches Castle Beaumont, it's fucked, in a word. The driver slows to a stop in the main foyer, and when he opens the door, he flushes pink from his collarbones to his scalp.

"Ah," Red says, and extracts two fingers from my pussy.

I lower my leg and we both stand. I glance from her to me. We, also, appear fucked, both literally and figuratively.

We're butt naked, both of us covered in rapidly healing bite marks, streaked with drying blood. There are hand-prints on thighs and arse cheeks, our hair is strewn and both of us are a hot, sweating mess. And as for the carriage, none of the ceiling beams have survived. The walls on both sides are cracked, the seating bench is broken in two and one of the curtains hangs loose.

Well, might as well embrace it. Bold as brass, I stride down the carriage steps and incline my head to the open-mouthed driver who promptly averts his eyes from my flesh, until he realises looking down is actually no better, given my pussy is also on show. So instead, he plucks up the courage to look me in the eye.

I smile, not just because I'm amused, but because he's looking right at me. "I will, of course, pay for a full refur-bishment of your carriage, and there will be a gratitude bonus for you for the inconvenience."

"Thank you, Lady Beaumont."

"Red," I call. She glances down at the pile of trashed clothes, probably wondering what other imaginative ways I'm going to find to shred yet more of her wardrobe. *Plenty, darling. It's a running joke now, can't let the side down.*

She sighs and follows me out of the carriage and into the house. We stroll right through the main hallway, leaving bloody footprints as we go up to my private quarters.

"We're not even close to being done. Get in the shower," I say, and her eyes glaze with lust.

"Yes, Mistress Beaumont."

My body warms. Oh, how I am going to ruin her...

CHAPTER 20

Y ou forget, I've been watching you all. Following your every move. I saw what Red gave Octavia.

The power she handed her. And she just left it in Xavier's mansion.

Fool.

So trusting.

While you were all distracted with riots and files and saving your relationship... I snuck in and took what I needed.

I have the blood.

All the pieces are in place.

Now it's just a waiting game.

Tick-tock, the boundary is going to fall. And when it does, I'll be the one to open the door, not you, Cordelia, or any of your children.

It's my door. And I'm going to take what's inside.

CHAPTER 21

CORDELIA

One Thousand Years Ago

I wake with a rag over my face. It's soft cotton but smells sweet and sharp and a little acrid, like unripe fruit and blossoming flowers.

I sit bolt upright, coughing and spluttering.

"Where...?" I say, unable to get the rest of the sentence out without sharp pains in my lungs and throat. I realise I'm in a set of thick, warm arms. Familiar ones. I glance up and see Eleanor's blue lagoon eyes.

"Oh my..." I cough and splutter but manage a croaky, "gods, Eleanor." I shriek her name and fling my arms around her neck, squeezing tight. When I open them again, I notice my home over her shoulder. Flames consume huge portions of the marquee, black scorch marks singe glass as windows smash. Bodies litter the ground, and people run like ants streaming from the property. I pull back and gasp, my hand coming to my mouth.

"Wh—" I start to ask what happened, but my lungs burn so raw, I end up throwing up over the side of the cart.

"Just breathe," Eleanor says. "Here, inhale more of this in."

She raises the cloth back to my mouth and nose and covers it. I gulp a few more ragged mouthfuls of oxygen laced with whatever this sweet-acrid scent is and find the tightness in my lungs easing.

"What?" I say, wafting the rag. But cough all over again. This is getting tiresome.

Eleanor touches my hand as if to say don't speak.

"It's healing magic, to draw the soot out and clear your airways. Look at the cloth," she says, pointing to it.

And sure enough, where I've coughed into it, there are black marks and flecks of soot spittle on the fabric.

I take several deep breaths while staring at my home. The flames are aggressive licking up the side of the bricks. Stretching all the way into the sky. A thick, dark plume of smoke swirls around the growing evening sky, covering the star's attempts to wink to life. What little moon we had is swallowed by the cloying black clouds.

Even from here, several hundred feet away, the horse and cart taking us further and further with every passing second, the heat of the blaze sizzles against my skin.

"They'll never forgive your family for this," I mumble into the cloth. Keeping it over my mouth seems to help and enables me to get more words out.

"I know, but we won't let it destroy the whole building. We're letting it burn until we're into the forest, and then my family will use magic to snuff it out. Speaking of which, Arnold..." Eleanor says.

The driver cracks the whip, urging the horses on, which

makes the cart jolt forward, and me fly backwards into Eleanor's arms.

"Why do it in the first place?" I say and haul myself upright.

"It was the only way to get you out. I sent my cousins to try and negotiate with your uncle and father. But they were under strict orders from your mother not to accept any deal. We tried finding ways into your property, even using some of the staff. But none of it came to anything. We had no choice but to use force."

"They'll have the whole city looking for us. It will be just like last time. We can't hide," I say, shivering. A chill settles over me as I realise how much trouble we're in.

I flinch as another window shatters in the mansion and the flames crawl out like tentacles.

"Arnold, get us into the damn forest," Eleanor shouts. He glances behind and then cracks the whip again, urging the horses on.

"I didn't want anyone hurt, but it was this or let you go... I was never going to do that."

I wrap my arms around her again. "I was so lost. So desperate. Gods, Eleanor... I was going to..." but I can't finish the sentence. I try again. "I'd been considering drastic measures to stop me from having to live a life my mother chose..."

"Oh, Cordelia," Eleanor says and untangles herself from me, pulling the cloth from my face and looking into my eyes.

"I will never stop fighting for you. No matter what. I will fight until my dying breath."

And then she leans in, her soft lips brushing mine, a loose curl flopping onto my cheek as she deepens the kiss. I pull and tug at her arms and back and waist. Trying desperately to get her closer. To make up for all the time we lost. Even when our bodies are pressed against each other and we're laid flat on the cart bottom, it isn't enough.

I wish I could stitch her soul to mine, consume every cell, bind her essence to mine so that we were never parted. She is my everything, and I cannot live a life without her.

We stay entwined until we breach the forest perimeter. The last image I have of my home is flames swallowing the mansion roof, the smoke wiping out the last remnants of the sky in giant billowing plumes.

My clothes stink of smoke and burnt wood. My dress is shredded and stained, my arms are covered in cuts and bruises and the odd burn mark. But none of it matters because I am with Eleanor.

"What do we do now?" I ask, rolling to face her.

She smiles and brushes a lock of my hair behind my ear. "Whatever we like."

I smile at first, and then it falls. "I mean it, we ran for two years and look where it got us..."

She nods, very serious this time. "We did, but we never really left *here*. . . When I say we're leaving, I mean for good. We're moving to another city. Maybe the fae? Or perhaps the magicians. It doesn't matter, I have three options, one that would take us right to the edge of the known world, to an ancient Academy where we could retrain. I've also negotiated a safety deal in the fae city. Plus, I know the magician queen because we shared some magics a few years ago. I think I could negotiate us moving there too, though that city feels too close to be truly safe."

"I like the idea of studying something new. I think we should go to the Academy. What's it called?"

"Finis Academy."

"Finis Academy, I like it. Then that's where we shall make our home."

Eleanor sits up and pulls me upright, then drags two rucksacks between us. "I gathered supplies."

She opens the rucksacks and pulls out a few items, showing me everything she packed.

"It should cover us for a week. I've organised horses, they're deep in the forest waiting for us. We'll ride till midnight, sleep, and continue in the morning. I've set up some dogs with my clothing to run through the woods to send our families off track. They'll be chasing dead ends for days."

"You did all of this just to rescue me?"

Eleanor smiles, dragging her fingers along my jaw, her cheeks flush pink as if she's embarrassed by what she's done.

"You're incredible, Eleanor. I am so grateful to have you."

She leans forward and kisses me, and then turns behind her and pulls up a tarpaulin. It's on hinges and pivots to create a roof over us, separating us from the driver.

Placing her finger over her lips, she pushes me down by the shoulders. Her mouth comes to my ear and she whispers, "Don't make a sound."

I giggle against her as her breath trickles over my skin and down my neck. Eleanor's fingers slide deftly over my dress, unfastening and unlacing every ounce of fabric and ribbon and each button. When I'm finally free of my clothes, she kneels above me, taking in my body. Her tongue flickers over her lips, and she drags her hands from my throat all the way down my body, over my nipples and to the hem of my lace underwear.

"Magnificent," she says and then pulls them down too.

She takes a blanket from the corner of the cart and flings it over her shoulder like a cape and then she leans down and cups the back of my neck, kissing and nibbling my throat, and collarbones. I bite down a laugh and hiss when she makes it tickle, Which only appears to encourage her.

She places her hand over my mouth and kisses and licks faster. But when she removes her hand and slides it between my legs, I promptly stop giggling and take a sharp inhale instead. She stares at me, our eyes locked together in a hard gaze.

One filled with weeks of longing.

Filled with the fear we'd never see each other again and the futile hope that we would.

"Gods, I love you more than life, Eleanor, I never want to be separated from you again."

She sweeps down, brushing her lips over mine before she ravishes every inch of my skin. Like a pirate, she plunders pleasure from my body. Dropping heavy, hungry kisses everywhere, my shoulders, my jaw, my breasts. She sucks my nipples into her mouth, one, then the other. Every place she caresses is raw and alive where I've been deprived of touch. Waves of excitement wash through me. Pleasure tingles where her tongue licks. My nipples harden to aching buds and when she releases them, a cool breeze rushes in, making the peaks tighten.

Her hands massage my breasts, tender caresses brushing over the sides and cupping their heft. I bite my tongue, using all my strength not to cry out at the blissful things she's doing to me. Heat pools between my legs as her fingers move swift and rhythmic over the hot space between my thighs. She massages that tender spot at my apex, rubbing and flicking until I'm bucking underneath

185

her. She lowers herself until her face drops over my hips, then drags her lips over my skin, drawing her wet tongue over my flesh.

She slides between my legs, her tongue tracing a trail of exquisite sensation, and I have to squeeze my eyes shut to hold back the cries of pleasure.

I shove my hand in my mouth and bite down in order to stop from screaming her name. Her tongue circles where her fingers once were. She devours me with devilish speed and precision. Everything is hot and wet and incessantly electric. It consumes me, sets my body alight, every nerve on fire, every cell pulsing.

My vision smatters, my body tightens, goosebumps rush over my skin just before my back arches off the wooden cart and everything shatters as I tip over the edge and fall into a blissful paradise.

I'm breathing heavy when she crawls up my body and kisses me. She tastes sweet and delicious as she plunges her tongue into my mouth.

"My turn," I whisper against her lips. I tug at her belt, and she allows me to undress her, but when she goes to lie down, I shake my head.

"No, come here," I say and point to my face.

She raises an eyebrow at me, and I smile.

Her eyes never leave mine as she hitches up my body and places her knees either side of my face. I reach up to help lower her down onto my tongue.

Her scent is exquisite. I want to stay here all night, feasting on the best bits of her. But I know once we reach the heart of the forest, we'll have to be dressed and ready to run for as long as we can.

I swipe my tongue between her folds and her head falls back. It makes a delighted grin spread across my expression, my eyes glimmering with delicious pride. I lift my head up to reach her apex and suck her into my mouth. I want to whisper filthy things to her, all my sordid desires, but I'm too busy ravishing her core. I draw my tongue up and down, over and over until her hips begin to move in rhythm with my tongue.

The faster she rocks on my face the more I enjoy myself, licking and lapping harder and faster. Heat builds and blossoms again between my own legs.

She leans back a little, as if she knows what's going on, and slips her fingers between my thighs. The sudden rush of pleasure from her hand causes me to almost bite her apex. I gather myself and continue sucking and kissing her.

Eleanor bounces on my face, her short little breaths doing unholy things to my body, while her fingers flick over my core as fast as my tongue does over hers. Together we rise, we fly, and then we bloom. Her mouth parts, her eyes roll shut and the sight of her falling into an orgasm drags me with her. My body stiffens, a white-hot bliss as she gives me every drop of her own pleasure. Waves radiate out from my core. I have to force myself to focus my energy on my tongue to wring every last ounce from her. She jerks on my face, her hips driving into my mouth as we both see stars, filled with the promise of our future—safe, together, in an Academy far from here.

And it's the first time I really believe we can escape.

Because tonight, we are finally free. Tonight, we flee our families for the last time.

CHAPTER 22

OCTAVIA

Twelve hours ago, Xavier strolled into my rooms and demanded we stop fucking and create a plan. There was a growing swarm of protestors outside Castle Beaumont, and he was getting twitchy. It seemed that while Red and I were gorging ourselves on orgasms, the city had caught wind of her comings and goings and was now hunting her in the most obvious places. My castle being the obvious option.

Not even bothering to avert his eyes or blush, Xavier handed me a folded note from Mother:

Dearest Octavia,

I know you know where she is. If you want to win this competition, you better ensure she attends the ball, otherwise you're disqualified. And I'll prevent you from running the boundary.

Find her. Make her attend and you're still in the running.
Love always,
Mummy

"Bitch," I snarled and shoved the paper at Red.

She read it and paled. There was a disagreement, and I lost. Red and Xavier agreed that we couldn't do this alone. So, she used her odd little orb calling device thing and summoned her friends from New Imperium to the city. Xavier sent his compelled staff off to collect them.

Which is why, now, twelve hours later, there are no less than four magicians in my castle. *Four*. It must have been more than a thousand years since we had this many magicians in our city in one go. But they're here for a reason.

Quinn, Scarlett, Remy and Bella stand in my main living room, all of them wearing some kind of scowl. Scarlett's hand is permanently attached to a blade pouch on her hip, her eyes sporting an expression that could murder on sight. Quinn runs her hand through her curls, her eyes darting to —and practically salivating over—all the books on my bookcases. Remy has her face buried in yet another weird orb device. Bella is the only one who even seems remotely relaxed—though Red tells me she has been to Sangui City multiple times.

"Thank you for coming," Red says.

"The least we could do," Remy answers, finally sticking her head up from the device with strange symbols crawling all over a holographic screen thing. When all of this is over, I'd really rather like to ask her about the technology. Perhaps in a different life, we could even create some kind of trade agreement between New Imperium and Sangui

City. I wonder if we could open up the tunnels and live a life of peace again. I add it to my mental file of plans and goals for the city.

"So, Red... what is the plan?" Bella asks, strolling around my living room. The others, by comparison, seem to be very much stuck in their spots: Scarlett a pace in front of Quinn, arm bent on her hip so her elbow nudges her partner, ever vigilant and defensive, and Remy absorbed in her device, but not oblivious.

Gods, I'm already developing a headache. "We can't function like this. Look, no one is going to be hurt while you're here. I swear it. You're here because we need your help... I need your help. And Red does too."

Red strolls over to Scarlett and pries her fingers off the blade at her hip. "No one gets harmed while you're here. If anything, the only person this city wants to injure right now is me."

Scarlett sags a little but gives her a nod and eases into a more relaxed pose. Eventually she takes a seat, dragging Quinn with her.

"In a few hours, we're going into a ball where there will be hundreds of vampires, humans and hunters. We need your help, which means you're going to need to get comfortable being real close to vampires..."

I stare pointedly at the four magicians sat in my living room and grimace. The only one who seems remotely excited by the prospect is Bella, who has thrown her legs over the arms of one of my chairs and is chewing some sort of gum thing, blowing and popping bubbles with her mouth.

"We got you," Quinn says, "but, ahh, you may have to reassure us some. We weren't exactly brought up to think being in the vicinity of a vampire was safe, and currently there are three of them in this room..."

"Three and a half." Red shrugs. "But Xavier has something that can help."

"I do," he says, standing and approaching our group. Scarlett visibly stiffens and I sigh, wondering how the hell we're going to get them ready for the ball when they can't even sit comfortably in our presence.

Xavier pulls a bottle from his jacket pocket. "Vampire pheromones, the most beautiful and exquisite scent in the universe."

Remy's eyebrows shoot up. "So you want us to smell like you?"

"Only for a short while," Amelia says, finally joining the discussion. "It will wash off in the shower. But if you're in a room full of vampires and you don't smell like one of us, a human or a hunter, then it's going to cause problems. We need you to blend in, not stand out."

"Right, and how exactly are we blending in?" Quinn asks.

"Oh my gods," Bella says, flicking her legs down. "IS IT MAGIC, did you finally get some magic?"

"I did. Watch..." Red says and then she steps up to Bella and squints at her face, examining her features. She closes her eyes and takes a deep breath. When she opens them, she runs her hand over her own features. Her skin ripples, her skin morphing and shifting and when she pulls her hand away, the whole room takes a collective breath.

"Holy fuck," Bella says, her jaw hanging loose. She reaches forward and prods Red's face.

Red tuts and smacks her hand away. "Always with the fucking finger."

"It's wild. I'm literally staring at my own face, but like *not on* my own face."

Red rolls her eyes. "Yes. It's magic. Keep up."

"It's insane!" Bella squeals in delight

Red turns to the rest of the magicians. "What I need you guys to do is wear my face. I'll use this magic on you, and then there will be five of us wandering around the ball all looking like me. In case I'm discovered or need to escape, I want there to be enough of us we can confuse everyone and get out."

"What if someone attacks us?" Scarlett says.

Quinn nudges her. "I brought poison powder."

"Poison?" Amelia gasps.

"Well, not exactly poison, but it will stun anyone that gets too close. There's enough for us all."

Red points at her sister. "Amelia, I need you to wear my face too, is that okay? That will make six, and you're probably the closest to my actual height so it makes sense."

"Sure." Amelia shrugs.

"And what are you going to be doing while we're wandering around this party?" Remy asks, closing her device and pocketing it.

"I'm going to be trying to convince the hunters, vampires and humans to vote for me," I say.

"And we're going to help," Xavier adds. "We'll work with you, following after you. You'll have to be quick, speak to as many as possible, and then move on. We can mop up the details of how we will rid them of their blackmail evidence. Negotiations, etc."

"Yes, but Xavier, I need you to promise me not to use compulsion. We all know you are the best charmer of us all. But you have to swear you'll do it above board. I don't want to use coercion to win them over," I say.

Red nods. "I think you should focus on the hunters, Octavia. Most of the vampires already know what you're about, Xavier can easily vouch for you with them. But you have no existing relationship with the hunters. So that's where you should focus your time."

"Good idea." Xavier nods.

"And you're going to be doing what?" Quinn asks Red.

"I'm going to be trying to stay inconspicuous. I can't help Octavia because they'd know I'm in there. The gargoyles will no doubt inform Cordelia once I've entered the mansion because they'll know my blood. Better them tell her than she sees me with my mask off."

"Then it sounds like we have a plan," Amelia says.

"Wait though, I think we should distribute out the files. Make sure we've all studied them, just in case," Red says.

"We don't know anyone, though," Quinn says.

"How are we going to convince anyone of anything?" Bella asks.

"This is when we need my sister, Stirling. She's an expert negotiator," Scarlett says.

"We don't have time to get her across to Sangui City. Hopefully, it won't come to that. But if it does, you'll have to embody your inner Stirling," I say, not really knowing who this Stirling woman is.

"What of the other teams?" Xavier asks. "Do we know what our siblings are going to do?"

Red shakes her head. "I haven't seen Dahlia since the forest. Sadie seems hell-bent on winning, but I've heard no word on how she's going to do it."

"And Gabriel?" Amelia asks.

The magicians swivel their heads between us trying to keep up with the slew of new names and information.

"I imagine Gabriel won't even bother. He'll probably sit

himself in the corner of the ball and read while Keir sucks him off," I say, trying not to roll my eyes.

Xavier smirks, and Red presses her lips shut, trying not to giggle. He takes a seat at the dining table, giving the rest of us space, and quietly leafs through the files Red stole.

"Then we all need to get ready. Amelia, go and get all the outfits we have from the closets below. Hopefully there's something that will fit everyone. I need to work on their faces," Red says.

"Me first." Quinn hops up, shoving Bella out of the way.

"Oi, she's my bestie, I want to go first," Bella snaps, giving Quinn a friendly nudge out the way.

"Neither of you are going first," Scarlett says. "I'm going first so that I can make sure this is safe before it goes anywhere near Quinn."

"Ever the romantic," Remy drawls from her seat.

Scarlett fires her a glare "Like you'd let Bella go first."

But Remy shrugs. "Red's her best friend, she's not going to do anything to hurt her."

Scarlett presses her lips together, clearly unimpressed at the answer but proceeds to push the other magicians out of the way until she's standing before Red.

Red examines her face and then makes her sit in the armchair Bella was in, and kneels in front of Scarlett. There's a twitch inside me, a little spark of fury at the sight of her knelt in front of another woman. I have to tell myself to stop being ridiculous; Scarlett is taken and her girlfriend is in the same room as us, for goodness' sake. But it doesn't stop the possessiveness that floods my system.

"I don't exactly know how to do this as I've only ever done it on myself."

"You inspire such confidence in me," Scarlett says, her tone dripping with sarcasm.

Red glares at her and examines Scarlett's features. "Okay, I think I just need to... yep, and then... okay, right. I've got it."

Red closes her eyes and takes a deep breath. Scarlett glances at Quinn and mouths the words "I love you" at her.

Quinn mouths them back, and Scarlett closes her eyes and steadies herself.

Red's eyes flash, her skin brightens as if it glows golden, and then she runs her hand over Scarlett's face But slower than she did her own. Her brow scrunches in concentration, a line of sweat forming at the peak as she burrows deeper into her magic. When her hand reaches Scarlett's chin and finally pulls away, she opens her eyes and the whole room gasps all over again.

"Fuck me, this is so cool," Bella says. "Look at you, Red, you're so tall now." And she bursts out laughing.

"Oh fuck off, Bella," Red says, laughing. "I am kind of impressed with myself, though."

"It's reversible, right?" Scarlett says.

Red shrugs. "Hopefully."

"Hopefully?" Scarlett sits bolt upright. Red laughs and pulls her hand over her own face, making Bella's features melt away and returning her face to its original beauty, followed by removing her face from Scarlett's.

Scarlett sags in the chair and mumbles, "Thank fuck for that. No offence, but I'm fine with my face, I've had it long enough."

Red laughs again and yanks Scarlett out of the chair. "Right. You're off to Amelia. Who's next?"

Amelia walks in with a trolley of clothing, racks and racks of options. Scarlett strides over to her, still hesitant to be so close to yet another vampire.

"Wait, we should all wear the same thing... just in case our masks slip," Scarlett says.

Amelia claps her hands together. "Good point. Red, how do you feel about forging clothes once you're done with faces?"

She sighs, her skin growing pale, and I realise she's probably flagging. She's not expended this much magic before, and I suspect needs blood to top her energy up. But I doubt she's going to want to drink that in front of everyone.

I make a mental note to ensure she's fed before the ball begins. "Blood," I mouth at Amelia, who nods and disappears out of the living room to fetch it.

An almighty crack booms outside. All eyes shoot to the window.

"I'm on it," Xavier barks and speeds from the room. He returns a few moments later, his skin a rosy colour, a stark contrast to the darkness in his eyes.

"We have a problem," he says.

"Say more, Xavier," I say, my skin already prickling.

"There's an enormous protest outside the grounds. And it's growing."

"Just dissenters?" Scarlett asks.

Xavier shakes his head. "No. There's religious ones there too, fanatics that want to take her to the church."

"Is the perimeter intact?" I ask.

"I think you had the stone reinforced, but the castle is also three hundred years old. There's nothing to say they won't be able to smash through it. And if they don't, they may still attack each other out there anyway."

Remy heads to the window and flings an orb out of it, then she puts her device on the table and waves her hands around until a translucent projection appears of the outside of my house.

"Woah," Xavier says.

Scarlett, Quinn, Bella and Red don't bat an eyelid. But the more I'm exposed to the magician's technology, the more I want to win this damn competition so that we can modernise our city. Developments and technology will always help foster progression.

Scarlett examines the projection and gives Remy the side-eye.

"We're not safe here, are we?" I say.

Scarlett shakes her head. "From the size of the crowd, I'd say no. It's only a matter of time before they—"

Boom. The roar of the explosion is so loud it rattles the foundations of the house. One of the windows shatters and rains glass down on us. I leap to cover Red, dropping my body on top of hers. Scarlett lunges for Quinn and both Remy, Bella and Xavier dive behind the sofa. Fragments of sharp glass twirl in the air as they flutter to the carpet. Delicate like snow, deadly like knives.

There's a ringing in my ears, followed by the thunder of my ragged breathing. I tug Red over until she's on her back and staring at me. My eyes rapidly scan her body for any injuries.

"I'm okay," she says, caressing her hand over my cheek.

We all dust ourselves off and stare at the place the window used to be.

"Is everyone alright?" I ask.

There's a thick pause, where we all share surreptitious glances and a string of nods. We can't stay here. Everyone is thinking it.

It's Bella that finally cuts through the shock. "So... you have a way out, right?" She adjusts her ponytail and shakes out her clothes, a few stray shards of glass tinkling as they drop to the carpet.

I glance at Xavier. "Prep the carriages. Oh, grab the files." I frown, glancing at the pile of paperwork Red stole. "Where's the blood?"

He hesitates and glances at the pile, the paper bag Red's blood was in is missing. He dives under the table searching for it.

"No time, just get the carriage ready," I shout and frantically scan the room, but I know I put it with the files. It's gone. The fucking blood is gone.

Xavier rushes from the room grabbing the huge pile of files Red stole, and I turn to the rest of the group, vowing to find the blood later.

"We'll take the underground tunnels and use carriages to get out of here. We can continue the meeting on the move," I say.

No one moves.

A brick comes soaring through the open window and clatters into the table, scratching the antique piece.

Mother of Blood. "Go," I bark.

Scarlett moves first and takes Quinn's hand, dragging her from the room. Remy picks up her device from the coffee table and follows Bella, who slides her fingers over everything as she saunters out.

I catch her pocketing a trinket and roll my eyes. She glances at me, and I cock my eyebrow at her.

"What? It looks cool," she says.

I tut at her, walk over and slip my hand into her pocket. "I am more than willing to let you have souvenirs, but please ask first. Honestly, where did you find her?" I ask Red.

She smirks and says, "Bella is chaos incarnate."

Remy tugs her partner into the hall, and I nudge Red out after them.

Xavier appears at the other end of the hallway, gesturing for us to follow him.

We make our way through my mansion, all the while, the clamouring from outside seems to intensify. Each of our expressions grows more concerned. Red smiles, but I see right through it. Beneath her forced grin is a tremble, her eyes flit this way and that, always scanning back to the windows.

We make it as far as the main foyer before the front door explodes off its hinges. There's a crescendo of screaming from the gates. The crowd surges against the iron rails, rattling and shaking them until their hinges loosen. Shit. Dust fills the air from the explosion.

Scarlett is lighting fast, drawing two curved swords from the holsters on her back.

"Octavia," she shouts.

But I'm already on it, shoving Red in Xavier's direction. "Go," I shout at her. "Xavier, she's yours."

Remy and Bella react instantly and grab each of her arms, forcing her in Xavier's direction.

"GET OFF ME, I can protect myself." She scowls in my direction.

"There isn't time," Scarlett shouts, and I glance at her. So odd to be agreeing with a magician.

"OCTAVIA," Red shrieks, but Remy and Bella lift her off the ground, kicking and screaming as they haul her towards the carriage station.

Scarlett seems to think the same as a flicker of surprise slices through her brow.

I give her a half smile. "You and me?" I ask.

She nods. Quinn appears by her side, bottles of glittering powder in each of her hands.

"No, you go with Red, get her to the carriages. We'll deal with this and come after you," Scarlett says.

Quinn pouts but jogs after the others. Then it's only Scarlett and me.

"Never in a million years," she says, shaking her head and barking out a crisp laugh.

"I'm as surprised as you. Thank you... by the way. For protecting Red."

She inclines her head just as the gates shriek their last breath and snap off the stone walls.

Scarlett leans a fist wielding a sword in my direction. I glance at it, and she tuts at me.

"It's a fist bump, Octavia. Gods, do vampires not do them?"

"I..." I shake myself and give her a bump. There isn't time to explain the million things rushing through my head. The fact that, yes, sure, we fist bump, but no one fist bumps me. They're all too afraid. That people don't voluntarily touch me, or team up with me. If the adrenaline pumping through me wasn't keeping me completely zeroed in on the surging crowd, I might feel choked. But as it is, the first human crosses the threshold and it's game on.

Scarlett grins at me, and I smile back. My fangs lower, which startles her, but the crowd is gaining on us. Scarlett lurches forward, her swords drawn as she slashes her way through the crowd. I knew she had magician powers, but fuck, she's almost as fast as I am. It's an unnatural speed. She darts this way and that, landing blows on kneecaps and jaws. Her leg flies in a roundhouse, her fists jabbing in quick succession.

I'm practically a neanderthal in comparison. She moves with such dexterity and deftness it's like visual poetry. I grab, rip, punch and drink, more savage than anything else.

I lunge for the first vampire attacking. I catch his fist and wrench it around, snapping his wrist. He shrieks and kicks out, the short blade lodged in his toe cap sinking between my ribs. I cry out and lunge for his throat, ripping his windpipe from his neck. Then I sever the rest of his head from his shoulders.

I shove a human into the hallway wall, knocking him clean out. Two more vampires attack me simultaneously. But just because they're untrained doesn't make them less deadly. One of them clumsily throws himself at me, all fists and fury. I kick him out of the way, but it allows the other one to jab a brutal blow to my ribs in exactly the same place the blade just penetrated. My skin parts as the broken bone protrudes. It makes me want to puke. I can't heal if there's an open wound.

I rear back, elbowing his face and smashing his nose in. He howls1§ and stumbles to the floor where I land a foot on his temple and knock him out. The floor is covered in protest debris, banners and posters, wooden polls and disgusting signs asking for Red's head.

Someone lands a blow to Scarlett's chest, and she flies past me, clattering to the foyer floor, landing at a godsawful angle on her foot. She curls her legs up, kicking them out, and suddenly she's standing again. But as she dashes forward, I can tell she's hurt her ankle and it's the adrenaline keeping her going.

We stand side by side and march on the group. With a dozen bodies already dead, bleeding or unconscious smothering the hallway, the group is reconsidering and retreating. I drip blood on the carpet as we approach the last two humans standing.

I glance at Scarlett.

The humans look at each other and decide better of it.

Spinning on their heels, they dart out of the mansion to rejoin the rest of the crowd still protesting outside the grounds.

"Come on," I say, wincing as I turn to go. I'm not sure if I can make it down to the carriage station without healing. And I can't heal with a bone poking out of my side.

Scarlett flushes.

"What's wrong?" I ask.

"You're not the only one with a broken rib, and possibly ankle too," she says. It's only then I realise she's panting, but not in an exercise way, in an 'I can't get enough oxygen into my lungs' way.

"We're going to need to help each other," she says.

I raise an eyebrow. "You sure you're okay with that?"

"Not much choice," she says through gritted teeth.

I open my arms and we each slide an arm around the others neck and slowly hobble our way to the others.

CHAPTER 23

OCTAVIA

Scarlett and I make it to the carriage, thankfully without incident. Xavier prepped the largest one, but with six of us inside, it's still a little tight. Remy and Xavier lean down the stairs to help Scarlett and me inside.

"That is vile." Bella grimaces, pointing at my rib.

"Fuck," Red says, her hands already glowing gold. She's up and at my feet, examining my ribs this way and that. Scarlett winces taking a seat behind her.

"I need you to stand," she says.

I do, groaning as a hot lance of pain shoots through my side and blood oozes down my clothes. Her nose flares, her tongue skittering over her lips.

"No, I mean stand up straight," she says.

"Can't. Hurts too bad."

She tuts and climbs onto the seat behind me. Her hands slide under my armpits and then keep sliding until she locks them behind my skull.

"Do you have any idea what you're doing?" I groan.

"Instinct. It's magic," she says and then she wrenches back, lifting me into the air until my feet rise off the floor.

Pain, white-hot and all-consuming radiates from my rib. The bone shoots back into my abdomen, and I gasp at the relief. Red drops me back down and I point at Scarlett.

"I'll heal now," I say as Xavier passes me a blood bag from a warmer under the bench seats.

Red's hands glow brighter as she kneels in front of Scarlett, who is still panting, her skin a little pale compared to when she arrived. Quinn eyes her. "What are you doing?"

"I don't know. But it's not failed yet."

"What kind of healing magic is it?" she asks.

"Blood magic. Other than that, I don't know because most of the dhampir records were lost a thousand years ago."

Scarlett leans back and points at her own broken ribs.

"I found it," Red says as Scarlett's eyes go wide.

The air fills with the smells of mint and lavender and a hint of overcooked cinnamon. Scarlett's panting reduces until she takes several long, deep breaths, her skin rushing back to normal.

"Can you do that to any wound?" Scarlett says, lifting her ankle and dropping it on Red's knee.

"I can, but it seems to work instinctively on the really acute injuries," Red says.

"Gods, when all this nonsense is over, you and I need to go on a study retreat," Quinn says, clapping the air.

"You think?" Red smiles.

"Yeah, are you kidding? If we could combine our healing magics, I think we'd be unstoppable."

"At least it would stop you pilfering all my business." Scarlett smirks.

Quinn elbows her in the rib and Scarlett yelps.

"Easy, babe, don't want to break it all over again."

The horses whinny outside, and the door opens. Amelia stands before us. Scarlett's instantly on her feet, her hand at her hip again.

"Mother of Blood, sit down, Scarlett, it's just Red's sister." I grab Amelia's hand and tug. "Get in, stop standing there gawping." When she doesn't move, I tug her inside and slam the door shut. I knock on the driver's window and the carriage lurches forward, shuttling us into the gloom.

"Sit down you two, you're making everyone nervous," I say to Amelia and Scarlett.

Red kneads her temples. "I am getting really tired of being attacked or worshipped or asked to drink from someone or given random gifts. I tell you what, Quinn, we can do the retreat if it's in a different city."

Quinn grins. "Deal."

We circle the tunnels for a few hours, until we received word from one of the staff who tracked us down on horseback to inform us that the property was safe to return to. We didn't spend long at home. Just gathered our clothes and belongings and headed straight to the Whisper Club so we could arrive before anyone else.

As the carriage draws up to the club, Red's face pales the nearer and nearer we get. The streets are so much worse. It's like the entire city stepped over the edge into frenzied madness. There are prayer parties—giant groups of church goers praying en masse—in the middle of the squares. Protestors occupy all the other open areas. If the city's walls were plastered with her features before, it's nothing compared to now. Every board, every storefront, every lamppost, even the doors are smothered in pictures displaying her face. Some praising and worshipping her for the transformation. Others offer goods, money and bribes in exchange for her location. The worst ones are calling for her death.

It doesn't matter which direction you look, she's everywhere, either being vilified or venerated.

She swallows hard. I reach over and take her hand, giving it a squeeze and rubbing my thumb over the back of her palm.

"It's going to be okay," I say.

"Is it?" She glances at the sea of her faces across from us. There are five other versions of Red sitting in this carriage, and it's disconcerting to say the least. I, of course, can tell the difference, not least because our bond calls to me under my skin, throbbing and humming the way it did when we first created it. As for the rest of the world, I just hope Red's forgeries are good enough that no one will be able to tell which one is which.

"Everyone have their masks?" Xavier asks as he slides a navy blue one over his marble-sculpted face. The rest of us follow his lead, pulling them on. We reasoned full-bodied masks would be preferable to cover as much skin as possible.

Quinn goes first. Red uses a painting forgery trick to make Quinn's hair bleach to the same dirty blonde colour as hers. Scarlett is wearing a wig already because she didn't want Red fucking with her long hair.

Remy is close enough that she only needs a hint of colour put in hers, which Red sorts with a lazy waft of her hand in Remy's direction. Like Scarlett, Bella is wearing a wig to make her hair short enough. Each version of Red is wearing a dried blood-coloured suit, again trickery from Red's clever forgery magic. It's bizarre staring out across the carriage at the same face over and over in identical outfits.

If you hadn't met Red and didn't know that she was quite clearly the shortest one of the bunch, then you would have no idea who she was.

I just hope and pray to the Mother of Blood that it's enough to keep those hunting her at bay.

"Are you sure you should go in?" I say.

"Cordelia made it clear that if I didn't enter the competition you'd be disqualified. We're a team, we need to finish this. Together."

I nod, my lips thinned to a narrow line. We get out of the carriage and Erin frowns as she gazes at five identically masked people. Her eyes flit from me to the group and back again, and she decides better of asking.

She guides us to the rear entrance and safe passage. But when we get there, one of Mother's staff members greets us.

"Sorry, love," he says to me. "Lady St Clair's orders were for us to cover every entrance and exit. And everyone is to hand over their masks and instead wear one that we provide."

"I beg your pardon?" I say, trying to swallow the growl rising in my throat. He falters, realising who I am and immediately drops his gaze from mine.

"As I said, miss, I'm under strict orders not to let anyone in unless they're wearing one of our prescribed masks."

He shifts from foot to foot, his eyes flicking up to mine and darting away again. I can tell he's trying to look at me but is hesitant. He adjusts his shirt collar and tucks the bottom of the fabric into his trousers.

"Fucksake," Bella says from behind me then she snatches the mask and turns her back on him to swap it out so he can't see her face, or I should say Red's.

"It's still good coverage," Scarlett says and takes another mask off him following Bella's method of spinning to hide her face while she places it on.

I grit my teeth, but take the masks he offers from him and hand them out to the rest of the group. The one good thing is that they're large. Larger even than ours and all identical and black as ink. Small eye holes and a cut out for our noses. But the mask material stretches down our cheeks, hiding most of our faces. Feathers stick up at the tops, and ornate black crystals embellish the surfaces. They are pretty.

"Thank you, miss," he says and then taps my arm. "Good luck tonight, may the best leader win."

He inclines his head to me and smiles in response. Perhaps I can win people around after all.

There's a scream somewhere distant in the city, it's barely audible, though Xavier catches it and narrows his eyes. It's not the sound of a human, but one that sears through the night like metal cutting glass. It's the sound of nightmares and darkness.

"I'll investigate," he says and zips off into the night.

The real Red touches my arm, her eyebrows raised as if in question.

"We heard something... it will be fine, I'm sure."

I place my finger on Broodmire's tongue and dispense a few drops of blood to enable all of us to enter, the last thing I want to do is let him taste magician blood. Red follows suit, Broodmire cocks his head at her and grumbles that he'll let Cordelia know she arrived.

I lead the way through the nightclub and the dim lighting. I, unlike the rest of the team, am wearing a claret-coloured dress. It's strapless and corseted around my chest and torso. My cleavage is on point, if I do say so myself, and clearly Red agrees because she keeps dropping her eyes and licking her lips.

I lean in to her ear and whisper, "You know if you wanted to fuck me, all you had to do was say so."

CHAPTER 24

RED

"Now is hardly the time, Octavia," I hiss.

"Of course it is, look at you," she purrs at me.

"Me? Have you seen that dress?"

"Exactly. Ladies, please, the bar is yours, it's open and the tab is on me. We have something we need to deal with, we'll be back momentarily." Octavia nods at the barman who acknowledges her, and Scarlett, Quinn, Remy and Bella gladly retreat to the bar.

"Follow me," Octavia says and takes me by the hand, leading me into the corridor and up the stairs to her office floor. Only she doesn't take me to her office, she leads me down a corridor I don't recognise.

"Expansion," she says, answering my question before I'd even vocalised it. "I like to think that you've become somewhat of my muse."

"Muse?" I frown as she drags me into this new area of the club. It's a long corridor with black doors, each one with different symbols. When we come to the last door, there's just a piece of rectangular mirror on it.

My frown deepens. But she just grins at me. "I had this made for you." She pushes the handle and swings the door open and my mouth drops.

I step into a room of mirrors, my jaw on the floor. Everywhere I look are versions of me.

Octavia steps in behind me, her lips tracing my ear, kissing down my neck. "Right now, it's not safe for you to be watched, but you can watch yourself. And one day, when the city isn't imploding, I will put you on display for everyone to see. I'll show them exactly how pretty my little dhampir's cunt is."

"People can see in?" I whisper.

"Mmmhmm," she breathes into my neck. It tickles and I laugh, shrinking away from her. I step up to the mirrors and the closer I get, the more I can see through them into the dim corridor. There's a corridor and even some viewing sofas.

"Mother of Blood," I breathe.

"You like it?" she asks, suddenly quiet.

I stride over to her and tug her chin down until she's looking at me, "I fucking love it."

"Happy early birthday, Verity."

And for the first time in what is probably a thousand years, Octavia Beaumont blushes.

"You're adorable when you're embarrassed." I grin and stand on tiptoes to kiss her. I press my lips to hers and she makes a delighted little trilling noise. I grin as I push my mouth over hers. Soft at first, like petals and silk, and then hungrier. Needy.

"Gods, I never want to fight with you again," I breathe.

"Me either," she says, her fingers working at my jacket buttons and then my shirt.

"We don't have time. What if we're caught?" I whisper.

"This area isn't open to the public yet. It's just me and you, and I'm pretty sure I know exactly which buttons to press to make you come as quickly as I want."

It's my turn to flush pink. "Confident much?"

The embarrassment vanishes, her demeanour switching as fast as lightning. She straightens, her eyes darken, her tone drops to a low purr. "Safe word?"

"Elysium. Yours?" I say.

"Villain. Though, I think perhaps that will need to change. Now, mask stays on. But I want you to strip for me like the little blood slut you are."

Fuck.

I untuck my clothes, and slide out of my jacket and shirt, letting them drop to the floor. I'm not wearing a sports bra tonight, so I'm topless. My shoes next. I kick each one off without even undoing the laces. Then my belt, I unbuckle it and pull my trousers and boxers down, leaving me in only my mask.

Octavia circles me, staring at my body with the eyes of a starved lion.

"Look at yourself, Red. Watch as I do exactly as I please with you. I don't want your eyes on me tonight. I want your eyes on you."

She takes my hand and leads me to the middle of the room where there's a large, mirrored cube, big enough for both of us to lay on, much like a bed.

"Sit," she commands.

I do as I'm told, the mirrored glass cool against my skin. It makes goose pimples rush over my legs and my nipples tighten. I glance around the room, seeing myself reflected over and over, a kaleidoscope of infinite versions of me.

"Spread your legs…"

I hesitate, glancing up at her. If I spread my legs, a million versions of my pussy will surround us.

"Don't act demure, Red. Be a good girl and spread your fucking legs for me. I want to see what's mine."

I do, slowly.

"Wider," she barks.

My cheeks heat. I'm completely on display, my cunt reflected back at us over and over, from every angle possible. It's obscene. But it's so hot. Fuck, she's absolutely right. When this room is public, I will have a field day knowing the corridor is full of onlookers. The thought makes my pussy clench.

"Now, lean back for your audience. Show them what belongs to me."

There's no one out there, but it doesn't matter. We're creating a scene, and the fantasy is enough to make me wet as sin. I lean back, baring more of my pussy; the slick stick of excitement already coating my folds.

"Mmm, that's it. Show them exactly how filthy you are…" Octavia comes around behind me, resting her knee on the cube and leans an arm over my body. She slides her palm between my breasts and all the way down to my cunt.

I'm panting against her touch by the time she reaches my clit. I glance up. But she growls and uses her other hand to grip my jaw and wrench my face back in the direction of the mirrors.

"What did I say? Eyes on you."

She runs her fingers through my wet folds and then spreads me apart. I can't work out if it's humiliating being laid out on display like this or empowering.

I think a little of both. She stares at my cunt in the mirror, her head tilting this way and that as her fingers drag down my folds and spread them wider. Her corseted breasts press against my skull. Fuck, I want to shred the dress off her and take each pierced nipple into my mouth. I want to fuck her against the wall. Make her sit on my face until she squirts all over me.

I pull a hand over my face trying to slow the thoughts. I'm winding myself up so tight, she's going to touch my clit and I'm going to explode all over her.

"Messy little slut. Look how wet you are for your audience," she says and then drags her fingers through my soaking flesh, bringing them up to my face and shoving them into my mouth.

"Clean up the mess you made."

Fuck. I breathe hard through my nose. My nipples are rock hard, blood flows in hot waves into my clit, making it swell. I have no choice but to suck my juices off her fingers. My whole body is on fire. This is degrading, humiliating and it just makes me wetter.

She pulls her fingers out of my mouth and runs them over my body, playing with my nipples, pinching and caressing them, all the while her wild eyes never leave my pussy. It's like she's possessed and the only thing that will exorcise the demon is my orgasm.

Octavia steps away from the cube and walks to a specific mirror by the exit. Crouching down, she presses one side to open a cabinet and pulls out a strapless strap-on. She slips it under her dress and pushes it inside her. I have to suppress a laugh at the sight of my voluptuous woman with a raging hard-on poking out of her dress.

Sauntering over, she kneels in front of me. "What do I want you to do?"

"Watch myself."

"Good," she says and then grips both my thighs and pushes my legs wider. She leans in and I watch in a thousand mirrors as she draws her long tongue from my arsehole all the way up to my clit.

"Oh gods," I cry out. It takes everything I have not to shut my eyes against the swelling rush of pleasure. This is sordid and filthy. Being defiled like this in front of so many people. My pussy clenches, waves of heat pooling between my spread legs, which Octavia hungrily laps up.

She's ravenous tonight, lapping and licking. And because I'm watching the whole thing, I'm so fucking wet that her face is smothered in my glistening excitement.

I rock my hips against her mouth, desperately trying to take some control back. But I have to fight against her hold on my thighs. It's fraught, the pair of us vying for control. Fuck. I love the way my pussy rubs all over her face and she just takes it, knelt beneath me, lapping at my cunt, milking the pleasure out of me. I rock harder. My hand finds her scalp and I grip, pulling her in, riding her mouth, driving my pussy up and down, up and down as if her face is my own grind pad. I smother her, but she's relentless and doesn't stop licking every inch of my pussy. I watch in the mirror at the filth on display. The way her tongue flicks over my clit, each stroke sending bolts of tingles shooting around my body.

She releases one of my thighs and brings two fingers to my entrance. I'm so wet and so fucking turned on she doesn't even need to warm me up. She pushes a finger in, and I moan. I'm not going to last long.

"Do you like what you see?" she breathes against my pussy. "Me filling you up?"

"Yes," I cry as I rock on her hand and watch her sliding

in and out of my pussy in the mirrors. Gods, I'm already twitching and jerking, my body climbing so hard and fast to the precipice, I don't know if I can hang on.

"Mmm, I think this pretty little cunt can take more of me. I think it needs filling."

She shoves a second finger inside me, and I'm gone. Her mouth descends over my clit, her fingers curl as she drives in and out and as my head rolls back, I'm given a delightful view of watching her fuck me from above.

My pussy clenches, my clit pulsating as she throws me over the cliff, and I swear I black out momentarily as I spill into the most intense orgasm I've ever had.

But she's not finished with me. While I'm still riding the aftershocks, she's hitched her dress up and lifted me off the cube, sliding herself onto the seat and dropping me on her lap. My back pressed against her breasts. I'm half delirious with post-orgasm haze when she notches the thick blue cock at my entrance.

"Octavia, what the f—"

But she drops me onto the dildo and seats herself to the hilt. Shit.

"Fuck," I whimper as the intrusion makes another wave of pleasure wash over me. It's fucking huge. I've never taken a dildo this big before. It takes me a few seconds of inhaling deep to adjust to the enormous size.

"Octavia," I pant, my eyes still wide as I try and relax enough to be able to handle the fucking huge cock inside me.

She shrugs at me. "What? I knew my filthy little whore could handle it."

She forces my feet either side of her thighs, forcing me apart. I don't think I can cope. My eyes slide back to the mirror, I am spread obscenely wide by the blue cock.

Octavia's eyes practically salivate over the view. Her fangs descend, and I can tell she's fighting the urge to bite me. She can't, though, not in here, and not tonight. The last thing we need is my blood in the air.

The cock flares to life, vibrating inside both of us. But it's me on display. She runs her fingers through my folds, mopping up any remaining wetness and then she brings it to my clit, circling and rubbing. I jolt and jerk against her, still so sensitive from the first orgasm.

"One more, for our audience," she says, groaning as she begins bouncing me on her lap, and I get a front row seat to her fucking me. She drives the dildo in and out harder, faster. Thrusting and pumping in time with her fingers on my clit.

The view is extraordinary.

"That's it, Red. Show your audience exactly how much you like me fucking your dirty little pussy."

My body is still wound so tight from the first orgasm that it doesn't take much to reach the cliff once more.

Octavia is panting, whether from the pleasure of owning my orgasm or that the end of the dildo vibrates inside her too, but I can tell by the way her eyes glaze that she's close.

Halting mid-thrust, she pulls out, lifting me off her lap and spinning me around. She pushes my face onto the glass cube we were sat on and takes me from behind instead. I get a view in the side mirrors of her as she fucks me from behind, still fully dressed, the fabric of her outfit hitched up lazily as if she couldn't be bothered. Fuck, the thought tips me a little closer. She pulls me up by the hair and instead, knocks my knee shoving one of my feet onto the cube, displaying my cunt all over again but from a side angle.

And that does it. The view of my breasts rocking, my

pussy spread wide by her cock and her fingers all over my clit as she shunts into me from behind.

"Fuck," she says as she drives harder and faster before her eyes close and she spills into her own pleasure. Her fingers pinch my clit, shoving me over into another orgasm. It radiates from my head to my toes as I grip the cube to prevent us from collapsing, both of us moaning and swearing as we come together.

When we've caught our breath, I pull her around and bring her mouth to mine. I plunge a bruising kiss on her.

"Thank you, best present ever," I say and kiss her all over again.

CHAPTER 25

OCTAVIA

Dressed and suitably de-sexed, we enter the main club area. It's full to the brim of people. Humans, hunters and vampires fill the space.

I notice Amelia in the corner with someone, their hair shorn short, wearing a sleeveless top, their strong hands cupping Amelia's jaw. They kiss her, pinning her against the wall.

"Oh, my," I say.

Red glances over and then cringes. "Gross."

"I didn't know Amelia was seeing anyone."

"She's... they. Gods, I don't want to see that." She spins me around so her back is to them. "Yeah, I think she's dating them, their name is Ash. I don't want to know the gory details though. I'm just happy for her."

The magicians spot us, wave and make their way back over to us from the bar. Their eyes are as wide and frantic beneath their masks as Red's. In the heart of the room sits a table containing the five glass jars, one for each team. But in the central two jars, there are already two dozen stones apiece.

"I didn't think you were supposed to start until Cordelia gave the word..." Amelia says catching up to us. Ash, I notice, has made themselves scarce. I smile to myself; fresh love is kind of cute. Not that I'm an old romantic at heart... but, perhaps.

"I wasn't aware we were allowed to campaign before the start of the ball either," I say.

"Motherfucker," Red growls. "She also said there were no rules. I bet Dahlia and Sadie have been convincing people since the announcement."

"Fuck, they'll be days ahead, if that is the case," I say, and my heart sinks. Why did I choose this trial to start playing fairly? For fuck's sake, I've probably signed our losing ticket. My teeth clench.

Amelia grabs me by the elbow and ushers me away from the main group. I nearly slap her hand off me for disobedience, but then I see how stressed she is. "There's no time to mess about, you need to start greeting people."

"Fine, fine," I say and do as I'm told, for once.

"Everyone spread out," Red says.

And we do. The magicians meander off into the crowd, and I make my way around to the hunter nobles as Red suggested.

I approach the first one, an older man Red said she thought had an affinity for vampires because his favourite niece was turned and he never ousted her from the family.

"Good evening, elder Rothman," I say.

He inclines his head in a polite nod but doesn't seem interested in talking to me much further.

My stomach drops. I can't do this. I'm never going to get enough people to vote for me this evening, no matter what I do. But especially the hunters, they hate our kind. This is utterly pointless. I want to give up. Throw it all away. The hunters are going to be bad enough, but the human leaders not from my territory will never bow to me, no matter how many of their problems and issues I offer to solve.

I spiral hard. My chest tightens, I can't seem to get any oxygen into my body. My fingers tremble, pins and needles attacking the tips. Thoughts turn vicious. I stand before this man silently telling myself I'm useless, pathetic, I'll never win and don't deserve this city when the elder Rothman, to my surprise, touches my hand.

"Are you okay? Did you have something to say to me... I know who you are, Lady Beaumont, and I'm not afraid of you."

His words startle me out of my thoughts long enough I'm able to find my voice again.

"I... Listen, I am here to solicit your vote, as my siblings will be too. But rather than dish out a laundry list of promises and politics, I wanted to offer to solve a problem for you."

His eyes narrow. They scan my face, searching for the lie or catch I'm going to hold over him. But he won't find it because I'm here legitimately, and I really will sort out his problems. If he agrees to support me.

"Go on."

I take a deep breath. "I request that you hear me out fully before making a judgement..."

"Fine." He nods, a little less friendly faced.

"I'm aware of your niece and that her situation has endeared you to our kind. But I also know that you've been taking bribes from her to let her crew feed in your territories."

Rothman's face turns beetroot purple. His expression

trembles as much as my fingers do, flickering from wide-eyed horror to scrunched fury. He looks left and right, scanning the room for anyone close by.

"Do you mean to blackmail me?" he says, his voice low and full of threat.

I shake my head. "Quite the opposite. I mean to go to your niece and control this situation so that you need not have to take the bribes anymore."

His face crumbles, he puts his head in his hands. We stand like that for a few moments, and I wonder whether I've made a mistake, whether this is all futile and I shouldn't have bothered even trying to win this trial. But I can't extinguish the seed of hope in my gut. That I do have the ability to create a better city.

Finally, he looks up at me. "Why would you do this?"

I breathe out, my shoulders relaxing as I realise that perhaps not everyone is as resistant as I'd thought. And as the seed grows a stalk, I just pray that by the end of the night, a tree blooms inside me. I see now that this was all as much a me issue as it is them. If I just give people a chance, they, too, may give me one in return. I take a deep breath and confess my truth.

"Because I believe in unification. That we're better as a city aligned across our species than separate. But we can't do that if we carry lies and deceit. We can't do that if the burden of our secrets weighs too heavy on our hearts."

"You're not who I thought you were. You're not the monster they make you out to be."

I smile. It's true and genuine and reaches from my scalp to my toes. "I'm not. And you, sir, are not as hateful as the vampires tell me the hunters are. I hope that you'll consider this offer when voting this evening."

I turn to leave but he places his hand on my forearm, stopping me.

"And there's no expectation from me? You won't hold this over me or expect a favour later down the line?" he asks, his eyes darting to the people around us.

"Your favour is voting for a 'monster.' Remember... I expect nothing in return except your honesty and values brought to the table with an open heart when I bring this city back to its true potential."

His mouth breaks into a grin, and it takes me aback. I think it might very well be the first time anyone who isn't a vampire has looked at me like that.

I bid him good night and move on to the next person. Hunter after hunter I speak to.

They aren't all as kind as elder Rothman. One grabs me by the throat.

"You piece of shit. You don't deserve this city. You ought to do us all a favour and euthanise yourself." He shoves me back and spits at my feet.

It is testament to the fact that I want to win this fairly that I don't rip his limbs from his body right there in the middle of my club.

"I was hoping you'd say something like that," I snarl, and speed into his personal space. His eyes widen as he's forced to lean back. I whisper into his ear.

"See. I was willing to give everyone a second chance, no matter their secrets and crimes. But there are certain things I find abhorrent."

He shakes where he stands, his voice a tremor when he breathes his threats. "You don't know what you're talking about, you disgusting monster."

"Is that so? Bleeding underage humans for vampires

with certain proclivities... I promise you, when I take this city, the only place you're going, is to hell."

He steps back and darts straight to the jars, his eyes narrowed to slits as he drops his stone into Gabriel's jar. Wasted. But I don't care. I will see him imprisoned.

I move on. Trying humans and hunters alike. Some are hesitant, but do listen. More than I anticipate actually give me eye contact, and a surprising number offer me their hand and promise of a vote at the end of our discussion.

Each positive interaction gives me a little more confidence. I promise to erase gambling debts and give pardons to those running illegal blood farms. I swear to sort out the humans who have been bribing vampires to compel other humans into doing their bidding.

On and on the list grows. Each time I barter for another vote and another deal, my heart grows with pride as I realise that perhaps I really can do this. Politics is nothing more than people management. And while the people have hated me, I think that I, too, may have judged them too harshly. I've been standing in my own way. The humans are admittedly quite a lot harder to convince, but it's not impossible. But when Xavier returns to me an hour later, his face is grave.

"What's wrong?" I ask.

"I found the source of the screaming."

His face pales, his Adam's apple bobbing when he swallows hard.

"Demons. It seems the boundary has thinned enough to allow them to pass through, and they're running around the city..."

He doesn't finish the rest of that sentence.

"Running around the city doing what... exactly?" I ask, lowering my voice.

"What do you think?"

"How bad is it?"

"Seventeen dead already. And I don't think they're all like the one Red saw either. I caught glimpses. She said hers was human-like. The one I saw very much wasn't."

"Have you informed Mother?"

He nods. "Came from her to you. She's sending a ton of her staff out. But there's more. Red said that she felt like the demon was targeting her."

My eyes narrow. "You better hurry up and finish that sentence, Xavier, I'm losing patience."

"She thinks the demon that attacked her was genuinely hunting her, it wasn't a coincidence. And if that one was hunting her, with the triangulation of the sightings this evening..."

"Spit it out already."

He pulls his hand through his wavy locks. "I think they're heading for the club."

My mouth runs dry. "Shit."

"Quite."

The pair of us glance at the glass jars in the middle of the dance floor. Sadie is quite clearly in the lead, Dahlia isn't far behind her and of the three of us, I am most definitely in last place. But I'm not without any stones.

There is a surprising number piling up in there, and as we watch the table, another hunter elder places their blood stone in my jar.

"I'm so proud of you," Xavier says and squeezes me.

"Thank you, favourite."

"But if there is trouble heading our way, we need to move faster."

"The pressure isn't helping," I say, trying to keep the irritation out of my voice.

Xavier runs a hand through his locks. "I know, but if a demon is coming our way and it disrupts the entire event, then what? What if Mother calls it at halftime and we haven't had a chance to get enough points?"

Red appears, her suit tailored so perfectly to her new shape. Defined muscles and tiny waist contoured by the fabric. She's as handsome in this ensemble as she was beautiful when she was naked earlier.

It's a distraction to say the least; I'd rather like to pull her out of those clothes and ravish her in the middle of the dance floor. But Xavier's right, Mother could pull any kind of shit and create any excuse, especially if she is working with Sadie or Dahlia. And that's without the prospect of a potential demon attack on the club.

As if on cue, a monk strolls into the heart of the dance floor. I glance at Xavier, he frowns.

"I didn't think they came out of the church..." he tugs his hand through his hair.

"They don't. Or at least, I haven't ever seen them outside the church until the other day when they came to deliver our invitation for the spirit trial."

"Sadie must have influenced them, pushed or corralled them into helping," Amelia says, appearing by my side with the real Red in tow.

Xavier frowns. "I saw Dahlia with a string of her friends following after her. She's not doing this on her own either, Tave."

Amelia reaches out and takes my hand in hers. "We can help."

"No. Absolutely not," I say, pulling back. "I have to do this alone. It's me they hate. They won't respect me if they think you're working for me. I need to be the one to build the relationships and repair the damage done."

"Won't they?" Red says. "I think you're sabotaging yourself because you're scared to accept help... because if you do... if you have a team of people around you who all love you and are rooting for you, then it changes who you thought you were. It changes how you feel about yourself."

Her words cut deep. Something inside me breaks, and I have to inhale several deep breaths to stop myself... doing what? Screaming? Crying? Falling to my knees? Maybe all of the above.

Amelia picks up where Red stopped. "This is too serious, Octavia. You can't lose this. We all believe in you. Let us show you."

My bottom lip wobbles as I fight to hold back the tears. Xavier worries his lip as he waits for my answer.

"Octavia," Red says, and slides her hand around my waist, nudging Amelia out of the way. "Please? We are all on your side, we all want you to win this."

It takes a huge feat of mental strength for me to listen to their words. To accept that there are three faces standing before me all open, loving, willing to help.

"I... I... never..." I start, but I find myself lost and unable to actually say the words. So instead, with a shuddering voice and trembling hands I squeeze Amelia back and bend to kiss Red on the head.

"Thank you," I say.

"That's a yes!" Xavier whoops, and then he turns to the Amelia and Red. "It's go time, team. Are you ready? Because with demons approaching, we have no time to lose."

"Demons?" Amelia asks.

"The short of it is that the boundary is thinning. One attacked Red the other day—" he starts.

"It did what?" Amelia barks, grabbing Red.

"There isn't time. We think they're after me. It's weird. My best guess is they're trying to take me to the door."

"This is a lot," Amelia says, rubbing her temple.

But he's right, we don't have time to regroup on everything and definitely not if an attack is coming.

So I dish out the jobs. "Red, you use the Whisper Network, the gargoyles love you. Amelia, you're with Xavier. You two take the humans, and absolutely no compulsion. I mean it. We're going to win this the right way."

Xavier rolls his eyes at me. "Fine, fine, no compulsion. Oh wh—" he says as a piece of his mask Mother made us wear breaks off and disintegrates... "What's—? Oh, shit."

Another piece falls off.

"Fuck," Red says as both hers and Amelia's masks shed pieces.

"I knew Mother would screw us," I snarl.

"Not us," Red says. "Me. Just like the demons, she's trying to find me too..."

Amelia brushes the crumbs of her mask away and adjusts it back into position to cover what she can of her face.

Red stands tall, her face set and determined. "If we're going to be fighting demons and decaying masks, we need to get votes fast. Amelia, forget the humans, you take the hunters. I'll see if Erin can help on my way to the gargoyles. We'll regroup in an hour."

I nod, and everyone puts their hands in the middle like we're teens at summer camp. I want to lash out and tell them it's childish and a cliche, but I can't because as I slide my hand over the top of theirs, it's the first time I've truly felt like I'm enough.

CHAPTER 26

RED

After I pull Erin in to help—which, surprising no one but Octavia, she does willingly—I stroll to the club's rear door. As I make my way through the crowds, I notice more and more monks. And more and more religious types follow after them, all of them robed in the church's claret-coloured uniform. My gut is uneasy. I swear everywhere I look the club is crawling with them. No wonder Sadie is in the lead.

I reach the rear door, but the bouncer-cum-mask-distributor guy who let us in has gone. I pull the door open and halt. Somewhere in the city, a chorus of screeches pierce the air. A cold, seeping sensation crawls down my back and I shiver. The shrieking stops, then bursts to life in a harried fever pitch. It's closer than it was. Fuck. I shouldn't have stepped outside. I wonder if the demons can smell me? I need to hurry. I close the door and approach Broodmire.

"I know who you are," he says, his voice like gravel and stones grinding against each other.

"And I must ask you to keep that information secret," I say, tickling under his chin. "I'll make it worth your while..."

"I'm listening," he says, his gritty tone reverberating through my chest.

"How about I make you an even better deal..."

That makes his stony eyebrow rise. But he stays silent, waiting for me to tell him exactly what I'm offering.

"I will give you an entire vial of my blood in exchange for helping Octavia this evening..."

"How must I help her?"

"I'd like you to use the club, the whisper magic that's threaded through the building and I suspect through your veins too."

"Clever girl." He smiles.

"And what whispers would you have me share?" He yawns like he's ready for bed, so I deposit a bead of blood on his tongue to give him a short, sharp wake-up.

"The truth, actually. We want to win, but honestly. So, I'd like you to whisper the truths that you've seen. Don't endanger anyone, but I do need you to be creative when you help."

"Why isn't she asking me?" he says, chewing on something I can't see.

"She's in canvassing for votes now. But I also don't think she knows how to ask..."

"Hmm, I've seen how hard she works and how much she wants to make this city a better place. I agree to help." He jostles on the door, stretching out his shoulders like he's about to fight.

"Thank you, you have no idea how much it means to both of us."

He smiles and pokes his spiked tongue out at me. "I'll take that blood now," he says a little more seriously.

"Ahh, I think not. I'll give you half how and half after you deliver. I know how deals work."

He smirks at me, his stony-coloured eyes glinting despite their matt appearance. "Wise woman."

I place my finger over his spike and let what I think is approximately half a vial of blood flow into his mouth. I push the door open, but he calls my name.

"Red..."

"Yes?" I say, cocking my head over my shoulder.

"Your mask."

I swipe my fingers over the mask and more of it crumbles. Shit. If it completely disintegrates, I'll be visible to everyone, and then how will I get out?

"Thank you," I say and reposition the mask to cover as much of my face as I can. I brush the dust off my fingers and head into the main ballroom.

I grin as soon as I step onto the dance floor and catch sight of the glass jars. Dahlia is now in third place. Octavia's jar has climbed quickly now that there's a team of us working with her. Sadie, though, is still in the lead by quite a bit.

I spot Quinn; her mask has nearly completely deteriorated, and she's drawing attention. Scarlett follows behind her as a few people double take. Arms reach for Quinn and pull at her suit.

Scarlett bats them off, but this isn't good. It looks like everyone in here has a failing mask. Fucking Cordelia.

As soon as I think of her, I hear the first whispers... They whip around me like shadows. Secrets in the wind. I can't quite place them. As intangible and wispy as a cloud. But no less clear.

Dahlia is cheating, they say. Words wend around the room calling her a liar and a cheat and telling us all how she's placed fake blood stones into the jars. Ones that replicate.

That... may be one step too far in terms of the 'no rules' rule that Cordelia set. That's when I see them. The Chief and Cordelia marching their way to the jars. The Chief points to Dahlia's jar. If I squint, I can just about make out the replicating blood stones.

Eleanor grabs the jar and throws half Dahlia's stones out.

I catch sight of Octavia; her eyes glimmer, her lip twitches. It's like I can see the fight flooding through her system. She can do this. She can win the people over and do it right. No cheating, no blackmail. But because the people believe in her.

The whispers continue; words of truth about Octavia, about how she anonymously donates food and resources to those in her territory. About how she's got plans for unity and a new donation system so no vampire has to starve, and no human is forced to donate. On and on they whisper, filling the air with how she has plans to modernise the city, bring new technology to every citizen. But then, just as quickly, the whispers, the walls and the magic bleeding through the mansions all fall silent.

Why the hell aren't they whispering about Sadie? Why did Broodmire stop helping? I go to march back to the door and haul Broodmire out for back tracking on our deal when Sadie catches me.

"Who are you?" I say, trying to play dumb, there's several of me in here tonight, I could be anyone.

"Don't bullshit a bullshitter, I know it's you, Red. I can smell the magic on you," Sadie signs.

"Fine. What do you want?" I growl.

"Nice move with the goyles. But they won't go against me."

"And why the hell not?"

"Because they have no secrets to tell about me. All mine are silent. Duh."

I want to punch her.

"Now, now, my angry little hunter. No need to get stroppy."

"Fuck you, Sadie."

"You underestimate the loyalty of those who still believe. The church built this city. It's the foundation we have grown our society on. And I have bought the masses tonight. You might be the dhampir, but you forget your place."

"I forget nothing. Good fucking night, Sadie." I turn to leave but she grabs my wrist in a punishing grip. She yanks me to face her so she can continue signing.

"I did as you asked. Octavia is back in the competition, is she not? And if you recall, that's all I promised. I want to win, remember..."

She smirks, looking down her nose at me. Gods, I've never wanted to knock someone out more. I don't like her. I don't trust her. And I really don't want her to win. I spin on my heel and head straight to find Scarlett and Quinn because I already know if I ask Bella she'll say yes, and Remy, dominance aside, will do anything for Bella. It's Scarlett and Quinn I need to win round.

"We have a problem. There's a church in this city. And all of the congregation is going to vote for Sadie. There are dozens of monks in here, let alone the church goers. We need more people, otherwise Octavia is going to lose this."

Quinn shakes her head. "We came here to protect you, not to spend the evening helping a vampire."

"Has she done anything other than be kind and generous and utterly non-threatening to you?"

Scarlett opens her mouth, then turns to Quinn. "She technically fought by my side and then didn't abandon me when I was injured."

Quinn pouts at the pair of us. And honestly, Scarlett is the last person I thought would willingly help, but I silently thank the Mother of Blood for the mansion attack and the fact it changed Scarlett's mind.

I hold Quinn's shoulders. "Please? Do this for me."

"Let's say we agree. That means removing our masks and your magic so we can approach people as ourselves. We can't do it wearing your face. But that will leave you completely unprotected." Quinn's face is grave, sharp lines cutting her brow beneath the soft curls on top of her head.

Xavier appears then, his expression worse than Quinn's.

"What's wrong?"

"The demons have been spotted about an hour away. They're gaining speed and Cordelia seems pissed, so if we have a plan then we better execute it right the fuck now or we're not getting out of here alive, never mind winners."

I squeeze Quinn's shoulders. "I can handle myself. I'm a trained hunter, remember? But we are running out of time... Please? I'm begging you, Octavia has to win this."

Xavier glances from me to Scarlett to Quinn, his eyes widening with each of us. "Mother of Blood, please tell me you're not g—"

But Quinn nods, so I draw my hand over her face and pull the magic away.

"Oh, fuck me, Octavia is going to lose her shit," Xavier says, scanning the room for her.

"There's no time. Scarlett, come here."

I do the same to her, wiping the magic from her features.

"You remember enough from the files?" I ask. The pair of them nod at me, so I spin them to face the club, slap both their arses and say. "GO!"

"Xavier, stop standing there and fucking help. We are winning this if it kills us. Get out there." He huffs at me but stomps off and grabs the first human he sees. I scan the room, spot Remy and Bella and sprint across the room to rip the magic from their faces too.

CHAPTER 27

Look at you all, running around desperate for votes. I was here, watching you this whole time and not one of you noticed. Not one of you put two and two together.

Hell, I bet you didn't even realise it was me who let the demons out.

Sniff, sniff, Red.

I've got your blood, but the demons will come for you.

That door is going to be opened, and I will have my retribution.

CHAPTER 28

RED

We all regroup at the upstairs bar, the magicians: Bella, Remy, Scarlett and Quinn, and Amelia, Xavier, Octavia and me. We've done everything we could.

I had to stand back, my hands tied as more and more of my mask disintegrated. There's barely enough left now, but the girls stand in a protective circle around me, shielding me from every angle, though we're more concealed up here on the mezzanine. I've also used magic to morph my features just enough I don't resemble any of the posters. Although I'm sure anyone with an ounce of sense could work it out. As soon as the results are announced, we're getting out of here.

Octavia hands out shots, thanking the magicians as she distributes little tumblers with steaming liquid in them, and we all stare at the jars.

It's tight. Really tight. Cordelia descends the staircase in the middle of the club as a last group of humans approaches to vote. Tension hangs in the air, thick as blood.

Thankfully, the humans get there first and sling their bloodstones into Octavia's jar. I do a little happy dance, bouncing on my feet.

It's close, I'll accept that, but even from this distance, it's clear that Octavia has won. Cordelia strides towards the jars, her head cocked back talking to the Chief about something.

I grab Octavia's hand. "This is it," I whisper.

She trembles in my grip. Dahlia is firmly in third place. Gabriel and Xavier's jars have a few nominal stones dropped in them, mostly by people protesting the event and ardent fans. This trial was only ever about Octavia, Sadie and Dahlia.

Sadie came out of the gates too hard. She was in the lead most of the night, until the whole team banded together to support Octavia; that, and the gargoyle whispers made attendees much warier of just voting on instinct. Even though the goyles didn't outwardly help Sadie lose, their whispers about Dahlia did enough.

Scarlett sidles up to Octavia. "Never thought I'd be pleased for a vampire. But apparently, I'm chuffed for you." She clinks her empty shot glass to Octavia's, and they try and suck the last drips out of the bottom.

"Thank you, perhaps there's hope for our cities after all."

Scarlett shrugs. "I'll get Stirling to talk to Morrigan, see if we can broker some peace meetings or something. Seeing as you'll be the queen of this city before long."

Octavia grins so wide, and so delighted, her fangs descend a little. Scarlett's eyes widen, and Octavia slaps a hand over her mouth.

"Gods, sorry, how embarrassing," she says.

But Scarlett laughs it off. It's a light, fluttery chuckle, such a contrast to her brooding appearance.

Quinn gives Octavia a little bow. "Congratulations, future queen."

"Oh, stop it," Octavia says, wafting a hand at Quinn. But I can see the glint in her eye. The joy she can't suppress, lifting the corner of her plump lips into a smile. Bella pats Octavia on the shoulder, and Remy inclines her head and raises her whisky glass.

Xavier and Amelia both grin at us from the side of the bar. It's quite something, seeing us all smiling and united. Two cities working together for the first time in an immeasurable number of years. But as with anything precious, it never lasts.

The air shifts. A fracture. A sizzle cutting through the atmosphere, and in its place, whispers.

But they're not like earlier. These are fraught, screamed in breathy words. Pleads and warnings. Omens and prayers.

Demons. Demons. Beware. Help. Look out. Demons.

Everything moves in slow motion. The crowd freezes, only their heads snap around and around, darting this way and then that, trying to locate the whispers. Time elongates, only I can't seem to speed my body up. The more I try to move, the more my feet remain in position. An explosive crack that sees half the crowd slapping their hands to their ears ricochets through the club, followed by a shattering of glass like a symphony of tinkles. Then one moment of utter silence so absolute my ears roar and thunder like a stampede.

It's the ceiling that breaks first, shattering and showering brick and dust down on the dance floor like lethal rain.

Screams erupt across the room. The chandelier hanging

from the roof tilts, judders and then it plummets down, straight on top of the glass jars.

"No," I breathe, as Cordelia finally looks upon the jars a moment too late.

She didn't see. She didn't fucking see the jars. Chaos erupts, humans screaming and running. Vampires flipping out as humans are cut and injured, the huge, sudden volume of blood in the air enough to snap half a dozen into blood lust.

People duck and run for cover, the club haemorrhaging bodies like it's throwing up. And all the while, creatures drop through the roof and onto the dance floor.

"Demons," Octavia says, finally breaking out of her daze. Scarlett is back at her side.

"Get Red out, they're after her."

"No. I'm staying to fight. They'll only come after me, anyway," I bark.

"Your face," Bella says, her eyes widening.

My fingers find my cheeks, but I know without touching myself that the last of the mask has disintegrated, and in my surprise, I've dropped my magic.

Shit.

"THE DHAMPIR," someone screams from below before dropping to their knees.

It's Cordelia that breaks through the noise. "PROTECT THE DHAMPIR," she shrieks, her eyes finally finding me.

One by one, all of the demons turn their focus on me too. A sea of creatures all boring their eyes into me.

I swallow hard.

Dahlia leaps from the second floor into the middle of the dance floor.

She glances up at Octavia, a silent plea from her sister to join her, and then she lunges for the first creature.

They're all so different. One looks a little like the demon that attacked me in the street, its skin covered in a bark-like texture. But there are others with wings and fangs as long as swords, some whose skin is dark as a moonless sky and others still with grey-white skin like ghosts threaded with veins.

A group of Dahlia's soldiers appears at her back. But it's not going to be enough. Swarms of demons pour into the club.

Scarlett draws her blades, and Quinn unhooks several bottles from a belt she wears.

I grab Bella and shove her into Remy's arms. "Get her out of here. Take her back to New Imperium. Scarlett and Quinn will follow as soon as this is wrapped up," I say to Remy.

"If you think I'm leaving you," Bella protests.

"Remy..." I glare at her, and she nods, taking Bella by the back of her elbow. "We're leaving."

"Keep her safe. Use the station beneath the club."

Remy nods and Bella screeches as she's dragged from the club.

"I am warning you, do not follow me. Stay here where you're protected," Octavia snaps and leaps over the railings, landing in the middle of the fray. Scarlett follows, clearing the railings a split second later.

Scarlett's blades meet fangs and horns as she swipes and slashes this way and that. Octavia is a blur as she kicks and spins, severing demon limbs and wings. At one point, she's caught off guard and thrown back. But Scarlett is by her side and hauling her up with one hand as she draws her sword down with the other and hacks off a hand.

I glance at Quinn. "Stairs?"

"Definitely."

We race down the stairs only for me to be mobbed by monks and believers. Quinn is immediately separated from me, the swell of bodies dragging at me like an ocean current.

"Fuck," Quinn says and reaches out to me, but our fingers only brush and she's torn away.

Dahlia leaps over us and lands on a demon who spins and tries to propel her off. But she's crossed her legs under his chin and is gripping hold of him.

She pulls out a knife and slams it into his skull. The demon straightens and then topples like a stone to the ground.

I manage to duck under the hordes of bodies pushing me out towards the exit and sprint into the middle of the fight. There are people and demons and bodies everywhere. But it's clear that all of the demons are fighting their way towards one singular target.

Me.

Something lands heavy against me, a leg. Gross. It makes me want to gag. But I draw a blade from my sheath and lunge at the first demon beside me instead.

In the distance, I spot the Chief and Cordelia fighting their own battles. But I haven't got time to focus on them. The demon is fast, but not as fast as me. Dahlia appears at my back. So odd that we are now fighting side by side. An irony that isn't lost on me. I don't *want* to trust her, but she is fighting with me. She ducks as a demon swings his fist out towards her head. He roars, furious he missed her, spittle flying everywhere. She dances light-footed as I'm hauled up by the collar. The demon swings out at me, but I twist my body and wrench, shoving the blade into its eye socket. It shrieks and drops me, and I crash to the floor.

I jump up and scream as one demon knocks into Dahlia

and another drives forward with its horn-like hand aimed right at her chest. The blow penetrates her torso, and the demon keeps pressing forward until his spiked horn pierces through her back. He wrenches his arm out of her body as Octavia swings a table leg at his head.

Dahlia crumples into my arms.

And gods, part of me wants to leave her to die, really, I do. But as her skin pales, the threat of desiccation looming, I can't bring myself to do it.

"Fucksake, Dahlia." I lower her to the ground as her breathing becomes erratic, her chest arching and dropping, bubbles of dark blood forming around her lips.

My hands begin to glow golden. I dig deep, searching for as many threads of power as I can inside me, dragging them into my hands hard and fast. I've never worked on a vampire this injured. They're meant to heal themselves, but not with a wound to the heart and not without a lot of blood available.

So I do what I can, picturing the golden threads lacing around my fists sliding into her chest and stitching her bone and flesh and organs back together. The glow intensifies as I work. Heat plumes in my hands, travelling through my arms and into my chest. The faint scent of mint and lavender drifting around me. My skin tingles like lemony static. The sense of sand between toes as finally, the blood eases around her mouth right as a tabletop flies over our heads.

It crashes into the staircase and splinters. Mother of Blood, we need to get out of here.

Dahlia surges up, gasping for air. Her eyes, which are focused on something behind me, widen. She grabs me by the shoulders and flings me over her head so I slide halfway across the dance floor. I pull myself upright about to ask what the fuck, when I see her pinned under another demon.

"Fuck me!" I shout, but Octavia is already there, one of Scarlett's blades in her hands, severing his head.

Octavia extends her hand to her sister and pulls her upright. Dahlia glances at me, something washing through her gaze. She leans into Octavia's ear and whispers something, to which Octavia narrows her eyes but then nods.

There's a clear divide within the room now; by the looks, Quinn has knocked the monks out with her powders. A pile of unconscious, but seemingly unharmed people has appeared in the corner I was being dragged to.

On the other side of the room, Cordelia and Eleanor fight side by side. I spot Lincoln and a handful of other hunters caught on that side of the room too. His arms are smothered in blood, but it looks too dark to be his.

Sadie, I notice, is nowhere to be seen. Neither are Gabriel and Keir.

Octavia marches towards me, her jaw set hard. "We're leaving," she growls as yet another demon leaps across the room and lunges for me.

She spins out and drives her foot into his crotch; by the way it crumples, it is definitely male. Not wasting a moment, she stabs Scarlett's sword into its spine. It shivers and then lays still.

Scarlett and Quinn are at our sides, and with Octavia, they pin me into a protective circle as they battle our way out. I'm enraged that I can't fight with them. That I have to shuffle along, pressed between their bodies, useless. This is what I trained all those years for. But maybe if I see it from their perspective, that if I'm the target, I'm also the problem.

We make it to the corridor as Octavia and Scarlett

swing swords and sever the head of yet another demon. Quinn slams the door shut behind us, her chest heaving with great panting breaths. She unclasps another powder bottle from her belt and pours the liquid over the handle. It melts the metal and expands into the gaps to seal the door all the way around.

"Come on," Octavia says, breaking into a sprint. She leads us down into the basement of the club to the station where several abandoned carriages sit.

"Now what?" Scarlett asks.

"Strip," Octavia says to me.

"Pardon?" I say, flummoxed.

"Strip, quickly." She yanks my jacket off my back. "We're going to separate. Quinn, you take one carriage. Scarlett, you take another. Both of you will have Red's clothes in the carriage. Drop a piece of her clothing at different points in the city. Then abandon the carts and make your way back to the tunnels and get the hell out of this city.

The girls nod at her and then turn to me. "Will you use the orb thing Remy gave me to let me know you get home safe?" I ask.

"Of course." Quinn squeezes my hand.

"Remy and Bella too, hopefully they're already en route. And thank you both," I say.

"It's the least we could do, given how you helped us rid the city of Roman."

Quinn squeezes me, and Scarlett follows suit. I strip off my shirt, trousers and boots, leaving me standing in boxers and a sports bra. Not ideal, it's freezing down here. I split the clothes between them as they scramble onto their respective carriages.

Scarlett catches Octavia's eye and holds out her hand.

245

To my surprise, the vampire and magician shake, sharing a mutual look of respect. And then my friends settle into the driving seats of their carriages, flick the reins, and they're away into the night.

"Now what?" I say to Octavia, a shiver making my teeth chatter.

"You're not going to like it."

"I mean... we've just fought a legion of demons, how could it be worse than that?"

"Because we have nowhere else to go. Xavier's and my houses are compromised. We can't go to Mother's, and you can't go back to the Academy. We're definitely not safe in the church either."

My mind flashes back to the dance floor, and the way Dahlia whispered into Octavia's ear.

"Oh gods. No. Absolutely not. Just because I didn't let her die?" I shriek.

But Octavia is hauling me into the carriage and flicking the reins to make the horses move.

"We don't have a choice. It's the last place anyone would expect you to go."

"Mother of Blood."

CHAPTER 29

RED

"Well, this isn't ideal," I say, standing half-dressed outside Dahlia's mansion.

I haven't been here since the night Amelia was turned. I glance across the field at Octavia's house, wishing we could go there and knowing full well we can't.

"Come on, get inside," Octavia says, sticking her thumb over the goyle's spike and ushering me inside. We're barely through the door when Dahlia stumbles in from the other side of the mansion.

She's covered in blood, a big hole cut out in the middle of her shirt where the demon nearly killed her. She strides up to me and holds her hand out, the same way Scarlett did to Octavia. I shake her hand.

"Peace. One night only. A debt repaid. You saved me earlier, I will hide you tonight."

I release her hand. "Peace. And thank you." I offer her a small smile and she returns it. A true moment of... well, not quite friendship, but not animosity either. Dahlia's such a strange one. So violent in one moment and genuine the next. I suppose we all have our dichotomies.

"And when the Festival of Blood starts tomorrow?" Octavia says.

"Then it is what it is," she says, dragging her eyes away. "I don't want to lie to you about that. I want to win."

"As do we," Octavia says.

Dahlia glances at her sister. "So then you know that what happens out there tomorrow isn't personal."

Octavia's mouth pinches. "How do I know we're safe here?"

"You'll have to trust me."

Octavia snorts. "We don't exactly have a great track record of that."

Dahlia forcibly picks up my hand and kneels at my feet as if she were proposing or a knight ready for a queen to lay a sword on her shoulders.

"No matter how much I want to win, I am a woman of my word. Tonight, we are at peace and my home is yours. And when the door is open, my home will be open to you again."

She drops my hand and turns to her sister. "But tomorrow, when we step inside that boundary, I will come for her and I will take her from you, and then I will open that door and the city will be mine."

"A true truce for one night only," Octavia says.

"Exactly." Dahlia spreads her arms, dramatically bowing at us. "You can take any of the guest suites upstairs. I suspect Xavier will follow shortly, I saw him outside the club with your sister. Now, if you'll excuse me." She disappears into her living room, kicking the door shut behind her.

I sigh and glance at the stairs. "Shall we?"

Octavia nods and together we traipse up the stairs to find Dahlia's guest rooms.

We slip into the first one we locate, and I head to the bathroom, switching on a gloriously large rain showerhead. It takes a second before it's hot, but before I step inside, Octavia leans against the door, her arms folded, watching me.

She kicks off the wall and heads to the bath. It's one of those enormous, freestanding, ceramic tubs with iron clawfeet. It's big enough to fit three people, I'd guess. She turns the taps and runs it, adding bubbles and soap while I let the water wash away the demon grime and crusty blood.

Octavia flicks a switch and a set of lights twined around the ceiling flash one. I gasp. I hadn't noticed when I came in, but the roof of the bathroom is full of blooms and green foliage. I don't think any of them are real, but they're so lifelike they could be. Lights twinkle between the leaves like stars. It's gorgeous and kind of romantic and not very Dahlia at all.

"It's beautiful," I say.

"Get in the bath," Octavia says and then rushes into the shower herself, rinsing off the demon detritus.

I lower myself into the bubbles and lean my head against the ceramic tub. There's more than enough space in here for her, and she wastes no time joining me.

She reaches for the sponge hung around the taps and lathers it up with soap. Lifting my foot out of the water, Octavia runs the sponge down my leg, soaping me up and cleaning my skin, dropping sporadic kisses every few inches. She encourages me to turn around, and then proceeds to do the same thing again, lathering my back and kneading her fingers into my tight muscles.

"Your body is different," she whispers against my ear. The breathy words tickle as they slide over my skin.

"Stronger, and all the better for fucking you with." I grin.

She moans against my neck, kissing and licking and nibbling at my skin. I take the sponge from her and repay the tenderness, only I drop the sponge out of the bath and use my hands to caress the soap into her body. Washing the dried blood away.

When we're both clean, Octavia lets out some of the bath water and runs more warm water in. I tend to her hair, working soap through it. We're silent most of the time, both of us avoiding the elephant in the room. The fact that come sunrise, the Festival of Blood will begin and by sunset tomorrow, we'll be racing through the boundary towards the door. It will be the biggest fight of our lives, and we have no plan.

"We should talk about tomorrow," I whisper as I rinse the conditioner off her hair.

"We should, but can we have one more moment of peace first?"

I smile and lift her up and out of the bath, dropping her bottom on the lip of the iron tub.

"How about instead of talking, I put my mouth to good use?" I say.

Her eyes grow hungry, lust pooling in her gaze. I slide up the bath and push my way between her legs, cupping the back of her head and pulling her in to kiss me.

Our lips meet, soft and wet, our skin warm from the water. Hands glide over each other's soapy skin, caressing every inch of flesh we can grab. I break off the kiss, nibbling my way down her jaw and throat. I lick my way across her collar bone, peeking at her nipples as they tighten. My hand brushes each breast in turn, rubbing and tweaking until they're both hardened buds. I make my way down her body, taking each breast in my mouth and sucking the nipples until she moans my name.

"Red, fuck," she says, her head dropping back. She grabs my hand and forces it down her stomach and between her legs.

"Hmm," I hum against her nipple. "Someone's needy today, aren't they?"

"Yes," she moans. "Touch me, please."

I do as she begs and draw my fingers down her slit. She bucks at my touch, at the shock of my rapidly cooling hand against her warm skin.

I circle her clit in time with my tongue playing with her nipple.

Her hand finds its way into my hair and grips. She pulls me off her nipple and forces me down her body and between her legs.

"You know," I say as my tongue broaches her folds, "demanding little brats ought to get punished."

"Please..." she breathes, and the word is so desperate, laced with so much need, I can't bring myself to do anything other than suck her clit into my mouth and worship her.

My fingers tease her entrance, dipping in and out until they're coated with her excitement and she's practically vibrating with frustration.

I lick and lap at her clit and when I feel it swelling against my tongue, I ease off.

"Red," she pants in frustration.

But I'm having too much fun. Too preoccupied with drinking every ounce of her down. My face is covered in her, and it's divine. Sweet and moreish, I swipe my tongue over her entire pussy and moan in delight.

I pick up her feet and prop them on the edge of the bath. She wobbles but grips the edge with her hand, and then I stare at her, fully exposed and bared for me.

"Beautiful," I say.

But I lose my view and pout as she puts her feet back in the water, giving her the stability she needs. I lean in to kiss her, our mouths hungry. My fingers find their way back to her hot wetness, and I push two fingers deep inside her. She moans into my neck, her teeth brushing my skin and making a tingles spark over my skin. I thrust harder into her, letting the palm of my hand apply pressure to her clit. I sweep an arm around her waist to keep her on the tub edge and pump my fingers in and out, grazing her clit over and over.

She kisses me deeper the closer she gets to coming. My lips stroke her jaw, tasting, trailing hot breaths onto her neck, and her pussy tightens around my fingers, making it difficult to thrust inside her. I push harder, grinding my palm against her clit. My tongue licks down her carotid, my fangs dropping as I sink my teeth in and drink. She cries out, her pussy clamping and releasing as waves of pleasure wash through her.

"Oh fuck, Red. Yes," she moans.

I pump once, twice more, and then I release her neck and drop between her thighs. I want one more orgasm before we're done.

"What are you...?" she starts, but my tongue is already ravishing her clit.

"Oh gods, I can't take it," she says, twitching and bucking against my mouth.

But I'm relentless, drawing long sweeping licks over her

pussy. Sucking and kissing her clit and lapping over and over, my fingers resume thrusting inside of her. I curl them up, rubbing the spot I know will push her over the edge again.

"Gods," she moans, and this time when she crests, she grips the bath so hard, the iron buckles under her strength. Her pussy tightens and I'm sprayed with liquid as she squirts over my face.

Fuck, I love it when she does that. I lick up every drop as if I've never drunk a drop of water in my life. But she bats my head away as I try and mop up her pussy.

"I... I can't. Too sensitive."

I grin, thoroughly pleased with myself and finally relent, pushing away from her and sinking under the water.

When I rise up, she's staring at me. "If you think you're getting away with that you're wrong." She jumps out of the bath and pulls me out with her, forcing me to stand facing the bathroom wall, my palms flat on the wall. Leaning in, she kisses my neck, her fingers find their way to my extremely swollen clit. She strokes it, and I know she's not going to have to work hard to get me off. I'm too fucking aroused by what I just did to her.

She dips inside of me, pushing me up against the wall, her fingers fucking me in slow, rhythmic thrusts. Her other hand reaches around to play with my nipples as her pussy juts onto me from behind, helping her fingers grind harder into me. My body rises as waves of pleasure tingle out from where she fucks me. She spins me around and drops to her knees, nudging my legs apart.

Her tongue is hot and greedy when she takes my cunt in her mouth and pushes her fingers back inside me.

"Fuck, you're beautiful when you're on your knees for me," I say, revelling in the sight of her lapping at my pussy.

253

I rock my hips over her mouth, riding her face, looping her long, luscious hair around my fist and pulling her tighter to me. Controlling how much air she has, how much she can pull away.

"Harder, Octavia, fuck me harder."

She does exactly as she's told, driving into me harder, her other hand coming to my thigh, her nails digging in for balance and a little more for pain.

The sting as her nails cut my leg rushes over me and my pussy tightens around her.

"Fuck," I hiss as my back arches, and I come in her mouth.

"Mmm," she says, licking and kissing the last of my orgasm out of me.

She holds on to me, supporting me now that my legs have turned to jelly. Coming standing up is always brutal on the thighs.

After carrying me to the spacious canopied bed, Octavia cradles me, and I fall asleep for a few blissful hours nestled against her.

When I wake, it's to a grave expression and worry lines carved into her brow.

"What's wrong?"

"She never saw the jars... Mother, I mean."

"It's okay," I say, leaning my forehead against Octavia's. "But we know, and the people know who they voted for too. This isn't over."

"Isn't it? How the hell am I going to protect you in that boundary? We have no idea what's in there."

There's a soft knock at the door and Xavier pokes his head around.

"Hey, I figured we should talk about tonight..." he says.

I glance at Octavia and she nods. Our moment of peace is over.

"I guess it's game time," I say.

Xavier throws two sets of clothes at us. "Oh, and, Red?"

"Yeah?"

"Happy birthday." He grins and throws me a blood bag.

CHAPTER 30

CORDELIA

One Thousand Years Ago

Tonight, we believe the impossible. That we're finally free. That we've fled our families for the last time. And as Eleanor helps me astride the horse, flinging our packs on their backs and cloaks around our shoulders, hope blooms in my chest.

We're going to do this. We're really leaving.

We push the horses hard, cantering as fast as the forest tracks and night-dark skies allow. The horses whinny and rear up as the wind howls around us, but a few neck pats and slowing them for half an hour helps.

But when the wind dies, we nudge their flanks with our heels and gallop through the night. It's only when it nears midnight and both our backs and thighs ache and sweat covers our brows that we decide we've come far enough for now. They'll not be able to catch us tonight. Not with the mess of the St Clair mansion.

I pray to the witch-gods for my family's safety. Much as Mother has been awful, pushing a marriage on me, I don't want to see her harmed.

We dismount and Eleanor takes the horses to a stream a little way past the clearing we stopped in and returns fifteen minutes later. All the while, I've unpacked some dried meat and water for us.

I place a blanket on the forest floor and a second to cover us. We use our packs to lean against and curl up together; we're both exhausted. The surge of adrenaline from escaping, the intimacy in the carriage and the gruelling ride through the forest were enough to make me want to sleep for a week. But we can only afford a few hours.

Eleanor pulls me in, tucking me into her chest and wrapping her arm around me.

I lean over and kiss her. "Thank you," I say.

She smiles and rubs her nose to mine. "I will always come for you."

Eleanor falls asleep first, the soft rhythmic snuffles of her breathing enough to lull me into sleep shortly after.

Such a dull end to a love story. Truly a romance that I thought would save us both.

But that was the night that changed everything.

I'd barely been asleep more than half an hour when I startle awake, pain wracking my body.

I lurch out of her grip, everything tingling. My body shivering.

Cold infests my bones. It crawls through my veins and bleeds into my cells until I am starving. For warmth and food and something else.

My eyes find her neck, her artery fluttering in a rhythmic beat that felt like a siren's call.

I wanted it. I wanted her. I wanted to taste that glorious liquid that flowed through her body.

You know how the rest of this story goes: I fled that night, terrified of hurting Eleanor. How pathetic, how foolish I'd been. My family were protecting me from a disgusting creature. But that night, I was furious and afraid, so I chased my maker down: Isabella Montague. I found her in her house and drained her dry, leaving her to die while I stole her child away.

Two Months Later

I'm glad I abandoned Eleanor that night—in her own moment of need. She changed as much as I did, morphing from witch to hunter. A night that showed us the truth.

That we were so unalike. No St Clair should ever lower themselves to that of a Randall. I see the err of my ways now, and it's my job to set about fixing it. Fixing her... Killing her. It's the least I can do to make up for the months and years of disgracing myself. But there's time for that. First, I need to rid myself of another problem.

Someone is making creatures like me, and they are

terrorising my city. There are rumours, of course. Of monsters that dwell in the forest. Demonic, blood-drinking creatures. I know better, though. *I* am the blood-drinking monster. But as for the being in the forest, that is what I must uncover.

It's taken me three nights, but finally, I've found the village I was made in.

It's still a desolate wasteland. Bodies abandoned and decaying. Each one left to rot itself to death. The stench enough to make me gag multiple times as I stroll down the main street. Maggots infest carcasses, their abdomens writhing and wriggling in an unnatural way. My nose wrinkles as a raven plucks an eyeball from its socket, dried threads of veins and flesh dangling from its feet as it flies away.

I trace my steps back to Isabella Montague's house. It can't be her, though. I killed her. Drained her and left her for dead. Whoever is creating these creatures of the night, it must be someone else. I am only here to confirm that truth.

A cold worm winds its way around my insides, my mouth goes dry. As my fingertips brush her cottage door, I hesitate, realising her door is open, only a crack. Just enough for spiders to make it their home anchoring their webs on frame and wood.

My breathing increases, my fingers prickle. I push the door, and it creaks loud enough to startle me, my skin turning pimpled with gooseflesh.

I close my eyes, take a deep breath and shove the door the rest of the way open. My eyes fall to the kitchen cobbles and my stomach sinks.

Her body is gone. A pool of dried blood lingers in the space where she lay. And where a decaying carcass should lie, there is nothing but cobbled stone and a single sheaf of parchment written on in swirling letters.

I will come for you.
I will take back what is mine.
And then I will ruin you.

I tremble as I kneel to pick up the sheet of parchment. Blood splatters the page in pinpoint-like droplets. The page vibrates, as if her rage spilled into the ink and was absorbed by the parchment.

Fuck her. She's not having Octavia. I've grown quite fond of the little thing in the last few weeks. She has kept me sane, given me something to live for. A reason to stop the hunt for Eleanor. You know she's calling herself the Chief now? Chief of a new species. Her kind hell-bent on searching me and mine out.

The funny thing is, the more of my kind Isabella makes, the more hunters keep appearing. And I wonder what kind of fucked-up curse Isabella invoked? It's a sweet kind of irony that we're made one for one. But then magic is balance, I suppose.

I spot a bottle of oil next to the kitchen hobs. I smack it over; it topples off the counter and smashes on the cobbles.

Fury fills me as I glance at her words again. I ball up the paper, scrunching it and tossing it onto the oil spill. Then I hunt for matches. Maybe it's pathetic, childish even. But if I can't kill her this night, then I need to destroy something. I kick the kitchen chairs over. They crack and splinter. Their wood soaking with oil.

Good.

I drag a match down the pack strip, and it flares to life. I toss it onto the paper, which explodes into flames. I slide out of the house, not bothering to shut the door.

I stride out of the village and follow the road up the hill, toward Montague town. It's only then I stop and glance back down. Her cottage is in flames.

They plume so high into the sky, I know she'll see.

A threat.

An invitation.

A declaration of war . . .

Come for me if you can, Isabella. I'll be waiting.

CHAPTER 31

OCTAVIA

The carriage ride to the boundary took much of the afternoon. Xavier, Amelia, Red and I attempted to make a tactical plan.

It didn't go well.

None of us know what we're going to face once the boundary drops. And it's more difficult because Talulla isn't here, though Xavier is adamant they're only attending in name so that Mother doesn't punish them later. Neither of them is keen to step inside the boundary.

In the end, there isn't a lot we can agree on. "Two rules: we stick together"—I glare at Red—"and we don't stop for anything. We continue for the door as swiftly and directly as we can."

Red nods as does Amelia.

"Speed is the priority, especially since someone stole your blood. If whoever took it gets there first, we're screwed anyway."

"Agreed," Xavier says, and then adds, "My only rule is to

stay alive, which will mostly involve keeping the fuck out of the way of you savages. I have an orgy to plan for when this shit is over."

I'm about to cuss Xavier out, but the carriage slips, bouncing across the road. The horses whinny and neigh loud enough we all share a worried look.

"What scared them?" Amelia asks.

I poke the curtain out of the way. "Crowd."

The noise rumbles through the wooden carriage frame, rattling the window in time with their calls. The temperature plummets the closer we get to the boundary. Red shivers. Amelia's teeth chatter, even Xavier pulls his jacket tighter. The chill seeps like an icy oil slick beneath my skin until it settles in my bones.

It doesn't feel good.

We join the carriage procession making its way through the hordes of people and hands grabbing at the body of the carriage. We're tilted, swinging side to side as cheers—and jeers, in equal measure—filter in through the windows.

Red grips the roof rail and pales as I push the curtain aside just an inch to see out. The crowd is bigger than I've ever seen. Half the city must have congregated in the Montague territory. Bodies are packed together, seething like a mass of dark worms.

Up ahead, a pathway snakes through the crowds. The path only exists because a line of vampires on one side and hunters on the other push the people back, forcing the space. Strange to see hunters and vampires working together. But it does work. The crowds are shoved back, enabling us to pass.

The carriages roll down the path for a few minutes before they break into a larger cordoned-off area—which is

265

seemingly only possible because the number of vampire and hunter guards is double here.

A new vampire I don't recognise opens the door for us, frigid air rushing in as he pulls the door wide. We all climb out, nighttime drenching us with the reality of what's about to happen.

We're late; the rest of the teams are disembarked, waiting. The air seems to hum, vibrating with a collective tension that shivers down my back. The noise is painful. A garbled chorus of hollering that rings so loud I swear I'll have tinnitus for a week once this is over.

Red's brow is creased, I assume from the roaring noise. The area we're in is plain save for the boundary and a raised stage in front of us. Just a grassy area outside what was a Montague town, now hidden inside the boundary. We move towards the stage, but the press of the crowd behind us never seems to leave my back. And if all of our hunched postures are any indication, it's a heavy weight we're all carrying.

Mother and Eleanor stand before us, on a raised stage in front of the shimmering boundary. It hangs before us, reflective, like a mirror, only adding to the crawling sensation under my skin. Instead of peering inside to glimpse what's to come, we can only see ourselves and the masks of faux confidence each of us wears.

In front of the stage are monks. Dozens and dozens of monks. In fact, there are so many, I'm not sure there's any left back at the church.

"What are they doing here?" Amelia asks.

"I've no idea," Xavier whispers.

Their heads are all bowed low, their deep red cloaks shrouding their faces, and they move in a wave-like throbbing motion, almost like a heartbeat.

"This is creepy," Red breathes. I quite agree.

On the stage itself, Mother has created a fake arch, carved from a similar cream marble to Xavier's mansion. My guess is to make it look like a dramatic entrance. Both Mother's and Eleanor's greedy eyes zero in on Red as soon as she steps out from behind me. I stiffen, my body urging me on to push Red behind me, to protect her no matter what.

Their expressions sicken me. It's like they're bloodhounds with the scent of a kill on the air.

To the adoring crowd, Mother and Eleanor are close to delivering their supposed cure. And yet, I don't believe that what we're doing *is* hunting for the cure. It's not like Mother would take it, she loves who she is. What message does it give our people if one of the original vampires resigns their power and position?

I am entering the boundary tonight with nothing other than the clothes on my back and the knowledge that we are being played. I just don't know why.

Besides, for all of Mother's flaws, I'm not sure I believe the notion that she would send her children to their potential deaths in the boundary for her own goals. But with everything that's happened, perhaps I shouldn't put it past her.

Eleanor and Mother take a step forward towards Red and then freeze. They're being watched, and no matter how much they want to get their hands on Red, she's here and ready to enter the boundary. If they want to maintain appearances, they need to let us enter in peace.

Mother's fists clench and unclench at her sides. The way her gaze consumes Red tells me what I already know: she wants that door open for more reasons than she's admitting. There's no way she'll release this city without a fight, no matter what she's saying publicly. Which means I do have a fight on my hands.

I just have to hope we can get through the boundary and whatever remains of the Montague Territory alive so I can fight for the city.

I glance back at the boundary. It has a glistening sheen in the gloaming as the last dregs of burnt oranges and purples sink into the blackness of night. Stars blink into life and every so often, glint off the boundary like twinkling jewels. If you look through your peripherals at the boundary, it becomes a kaleidoscope. Rather beautiful, if you ask me, and rather a shame to pull it down. But our city needs magic, and I want to be the one to return it to our people.

Mother claps above a microphone, a thunderous crack whipping around the space. It's sudden enough the crowd startles and falls silent.

"Good evening, children, nobles, vampires, elders, hunters, and finally, humans. Tonight, we will witness a most historic event. Tonight, magic will return. The cure will be found, and we will celebrate the birth of a new city with new leaders."

I glance around, the crowd screams and cheers and boos in equal measure. We are still a divided city, and a city divided does not make for peace.

The lines of vampires and hunters on guard around the giant perimeter flex and strain against the crushing press of the crowd. How they managed to force the public back to make a path for us to exit the carriages I don't know.

Red's fingers are stiff against mine, and the way she holds my hand tells me she feels anything but safe. I glance over to the other side of the cordoned area. Sadie, Dahlia, and Gabriel stand united. Not that they're a team. But they're certainly not on ours. Next to them are Lincoln, Keir, and Talulla.

Myself, Xavier and Red stand on this side with Amelia. Talulla spots us and makes her way over to join Xavier. What I find surprising is that none of us, Sadie and Dahlia included, look happy to be here. Perhaps the reality of what we're about to do and the fact that none of us really know what's behind that boundary is setting in. Especially with the demon attacks happening in the city. Nine of us are walking through that marble archway, but none of us know how many will walk back out.

The Chief steps up to the microphone and calls for quiet once again. She raises her arms; it takes a few moments, but eventually the people acquiesce, though the monks continue their rhythmic movements.

There's a tick in Eleanor's jaw, and I wonder if it's the fact the crowd didn't quiet as quickly as they did for Mother, or if perhaps she has more of a moral conscience than Mother and is concerned for what her hunters are about to do.

The Chief clears her throat and begins addressing us, issuing instructions. "Your challenge this evening is to make your way across the boundary. We, Cordelia and I, will be following in your wake so that we are there the moment the door is opened."

Xavier's eyes slip to mine, his eyebrow raised. I bite the inside of my cheek, suppressing a barked laugh. Following in our wake? I bet they fucking will. I scan Mother's face, hunting for the truth, but find nothing. Murmurs ripple through the crowd.

Red nudges me in the ribs. "They're coming with us?"

"There's more to this than they are admitting." I rub my thumb over her palm.

"Why would they risk it? It's dangerous enough for us," Red whispers.

"They must really want the cure... or something," Xavier says.

"Or *something*." I nod in agreement. "They wouldn't put themselves in jeopardy unless there was more to it than this."

Amelia chews on her lip. "I don't like it."

"Neither do I," Red answers.

The Chief calls for quiet as Cordelia slides next to her. My lip curls; they're behaving like they're a team. It's weird. All of this is uncomfortable. It's like there's an itch under my skin I can't reach.

"Unfortunately, we did not establish the winners of the final trial due to the untimely demon attack."

A chorus of hissing and yelling rips through the crowd. It sends a flood of goosebumps over my skin. The atmosphere shifts, the ripple of a single word bouncing from faction to faction in the audience. I must be mistaken; they can't be shouting what I think they are.

It grows louder until it's frantic, screamed and shrieked, and I shiver with its ferocity.

Red squeezes my hand and grins at me. "They love you."

I pout. "They love, *you,* Red. They're tolerating me as part of the package."

But she shakes her head. "No. *Listen...*"

I close my eyes, and while it is buried under a crescendo of noise, I find a rhythmic melody of "*Octavia, Octavia, Octavia.*" My skin tightens to an almost painful level as another shiver runs down my back.

"Some of them are cheering for me?" I breathe. I can

scarcely get the words out. This time, Red tugs on my hand as she bounces on the balls of her feet.

"I told you they love you."

I have to blink back the tears. Sure, it's not the whole city; hell, it's not even the majority of the city.

But it *is* someone.

Someones, plural. My throat thickens, a heavy knot sitting right over my voice box.

I never thought . . .

This is...

This is everything.

"We're going to win this," Red says just as Mother starts talking again.

"Given we cannot determine who won, and considering the drastic loss in the trial of strength, the results of the trial of spirit, and the fact that the dhampir is on one team in particular, we have decided this creates an advantage. Therefore, Octavia and Red will start in last place."

My mouth falls open, the delightful shiver the audience gave me turning to ice.

"What the fuck?" Red barks.

This is not good.

Amelia leans closer, lowering her voice. "You'll have to move fast, it's going to give whoever stole your blood a chance to get there before you.

I pull a hand over my face, glancing at Xavier, Red and Amelia. What if it was Mother all along? What if she's sending us in to clear the way, but she's planning to open the door herself?"

Deep lines gouge through Red's brow and I, honestly, feel the same. We've come so far, beaten all the odds and even won the final round and at the eleventh hour, Mother is trying to screw me.

I glance around the clearing and out into the crowd. Despite the moonlight and the glittering stars, everything is shrouded in darkness. It's like the city is teetering on a precipice. If I strain my ears, I can just make out the chants and screams from each of the political factions.

We are broken. I swear it would only take a feather out of place for civil war to break out, here and now. I wonder whether this is what Mother really wanted to do. What she was playing for all along. War creates economy, after all. Was her goal to incite violence for her own viewing pleasure? I know she has a tormented heart, but I didn't think she was that ruthless.

"ENOUGH," Eleanor booms. Her navy hunter uniform is as sharp as her tone. When the shouts subside, she continues. "Gabriel, I believe you are refusing to enter?"

Gabriel steps forward and nods. Mother glowers at him so fiercely, it's a mystery to me how the book he's holding doesn't combust into flames where he stands.

"Fine," Eleanor continues. "Sadie St Clair, you will enter first. Dahlia, you and Lincoln will enter second. Then Xavier and Talulla, and last, Octavia and Red. Am I clear?"

We all nod in slow recognition of the shifting dynamics. Of the knowledge that all of us are going into the unknown, despite thinking we had a plan. This throws everything on its end.

"Sadie," Mother says, drawing out the amulet.

Sadie's eyes glint with the same vicious hunger as Mother's and Eleanor's. I want to laugh. Of course she became the favourite. The bloodhound in them can sense the bloodhound in her. I made the mistake of underestimating Sadie. She clearly wants to run this city far more than I realised. Perhaps the church has buoyed her up, given her the belief in herself she needs to lead not only them, but all of us.

I always thought we had a connection. I see now that I don't know her as well as I thought I did.

Sadie steps on stage and for the first time since we arrived, the crowd falls utterly silent. It's almost louder than their screaming.

Not a breath passes from a set of lips, not a whisper nor the crack of wood from the trees behind us. Even the monks still.

It's as if the forest and the people and the entire city stops breathing as Mother hands Sadie the power to change everything.

Sadie licks her lips and wraps her fingers around the amulet before turning to the crowd and raising it before them like a trophy.

A trophy she didn't win.

I don't know what she expected, but the crowd remains silent. Something hot simmers in her gaze as she glares at the assembled masses, expectant, greedy, demanding. She wants a reaction and they're not giving it to her. Just because you won Mother's favour, *Sadie,* doesn't mean you've won the people's. I, of all people, know that.

She frowns and then jabs the amulet in the air one last time. A lone person claps, a second joins them, a third until there's a disparate round of applause. It's awkward, slimy and unbearable enough that Red fidgets next to me. It's almost enough for me to feel sorry for Sadie, until I remember she's stealing my win.

Even if she does get the door open, the city doesn't love her. Fuck, they don't even know her. She might have her congregation's support, but that's only one group of people, and Sangui is a big city.

Sadie has been silent as long as I've known her. But she's not without language or a voice. She could have worked with the city, tried to connect with it, instead of hiding herself away from her family and the people, only sharing herself with her congregation.

She might have had a taste of power leading the church, but it will take more than prayers and sermons to win this city over.

Hope flickers in my belly. It's not the pretty little thing it should be, I confess. This hope is ugly and jealous and a little bitter. It writhes and squirms in my gut, making me want to keep fighting, keep pushing.

The Chief slides her arm around Sadie and guides her to the back of the stage.

Mother steps to the mic and says, "Sangui City, it's time for us to take back what was stolen from us a thousand years ago. It's time to return magic to the city and to our mansions and castles. It's time to find new leaders."

The crowd roars.

She continues. "Once the boundary has fallen there will be a two-minute time penalty for each of the successive teams. The timer starts when Sadie enters. Competitors, are you ready?"

Mother glances at each of our teams in turn. Dahlia nods along with Lincoln. Gabriel and Keir take a step back. And surprising no one, Gabe pulls out a second book from his pocket. Honestly, time and place, Gabriel.

"IN THREE," Mother bellows.

Time stops; hope blooms hot and vicious in my gut. I grip Red's hand tighter. "We can do this," I whisper.

"We have to," she says, squeezing me back.

"TWO," Mother says.

Sadie raises the amulet towards the boundary. The

shimmering dome trembles, as if it recognises the amulet, feels it calling. A circular hole appears, ready to swallow the jewelled key. I can't breathe.

This is how it ends, waiting for the boundary to fall, waiting for the moment I've dreamt of—a chance to chase my dreams and the city.

Mother raises her hand to point at the hole. "ONE."

Sadie thrusts the amulet into the gap, and everything goes mute. Noise ceases, the forest behind us falls silent. Every human, hunter and vampire in the vicinity stops breathing.

And then, particle by particle, the boundary disintegrates. A dissolution of thirty years of prophecy a thousand years in the making. It's like stardust and fairy lights. It sprinkles then swirls in whorls and eddies. The faint smell of lavender and mint coats my tongue as it permeates the air.

The particles coalesce in a violent rush of light.

A disembodied scream rips through the air, so familiar, so distant. It shatters spectacles, splinters the lectern Mother and Eleanor use, even the trees groan against the sound.

The boundary fractures, then erupts, a giant, pluming explosion that billows into the sky like a towering obelisk. And then, just as quickly, it vanishes as if sucked into a void.

I glance at Red; she's pale like she's about to throw up and clutching her chest.

"What's wrong?" I say, grabbing her.

"I… I don't know. It was… I think I felt it dying…"

I frown, a godsawful horror settling in my gut. My mind screams at me, trying to tell me something I can't quite reach. She relaxes, the tension easing out of her shoulders.

I do not. The twisting unease remains in the pit of my stomach, screaming something undecipherable.

A message.

A warning.

But it's too late because Sadie is sprinting into the boundary without a backwards glance. And Dahlia is striding up to the entrance.

Now is not the time for doubt.

It's the time for action. For forging ahead and hoping that we make it. That, after this is all over, Red and I are still standing, hand in hand.

I just wish my stomach didn't roll every time I had the thought...

CHAPTER 32

RED

Dahlia holds Lincoln's elbow, halting the pair of them to turn around on the stage. She searches Octavia and I out to give us the middle finger which she flips into two fingers that she points at her eyes and then directly at me.

I swallow, knowing that her promise of a truce only extended until the beginning of this final competition.

Lincoln gives me a sad smile as he strides in after her. At least he has the decency to shrug a pained apology as they stride through Cordelia's archway. The boundary may be gone, but the way their figures shiver and blink out tells me the magic guarding the door and the space inside the boundary has not.

I quietly wish him luck. No matter what happens, I don't want anyone injured during this. I want us all in, out, and back safely. But the tension running through Octavia's back and neck tells me she's not convinced that's how it's going to go.

The seconds crawl by. Octavia taps her foot and fidgets on the spot so much I want to yell at her to stop.

It's unnerving to see her vibrating when vampires are usually so still. But I say nothing because I'm suppressing the same tension. It's fucking freezing now. I tug my jacket a little closer, though it does fuck all to help warm me up.

Xavier and Talulla enter next, their figures shimmering and then popping out of existence. I swallow hard, realising that magic is very much still present inside that boundary. My fingers and toes go numb and tingling as I try to convince myself this is all going to be fine.

It's just Octavia and me remaining. Her grip on my hand is like steel. She doesn't want to let me out of her sight. Once we're in there, Dahlia and Sadie will come for me, and currently, we don't have a solid plan to defend ourselves. Not without seeing the lay of the land inside the boundary.

The Chief opens her arms and gestures for us to step onto the makeshift stage. We do and I swear if my heart still beat it would be hammering between my ribs. I am short of breath and sweaty and everything is bright and staticky like I'm going to pass out.

Cordelia smiles, her fingers twitching as if she wants to reach to me. It makes my skin shiver.

"Remember, you must get to the door and back again before daybreak. And if you don't, pray you find shelter. You may enter in..." Cordelia checks her watch.

I glance at my watch. Twelve hours. That's all we have. Twelve hours to make it to the heart of the lost Montague territory and back out again. Meaning we have six hours before we must turn around.

Octavia gives me one last glance, and we take the final step towards the makeshift archway. The crowd is screaming so loud I swear I can feel the pressure of it urging me forward. As if their calls and cries are hooks in my limbs.

"Three," Cordelia says.

Octavia's grip hardens on my hand.

"Two."

This is it. Everything in this city will change after this moment. I just wish I could predict the outcome.

"One. Go."

Together, at last, a team in the truest sense, Octavia and I step over the crumbled remains of the boundary and take three steps into what was the Montague territory.

We stand inside the boundary utterly perplexed. The air is dull and quiet. I glance back to the arch we just walked through. It's like the throngs and their frenetic energy are behind a soundproof curtain. The shift is disorienting.

"There's still residual magic in here," I say. I swear we've only taken a few steps and yet the scene we left seems a hundred metres away. Octavia nods in agreement.

I'm becoming aware of an odd squirming sensation in my veins. Like the territory is greeting me, pulling me in deeper, welcoming me. Or at least I hope that's what it's doing. I wonder if it's my blood. That it recognises me as the one who will open the door, with blood if not with my hands.

"So weird," Octavia says, pulling and rubbing at her ear.

"The sound? It's all muted," I say. It's like the middle of the night after heavy snowfall. Sound sucked away and muffled.

"Do you see that?" I ask, my eyes fuzzy as I stare at the atmosphere. I raise my hand and pluck a wriggly dark particle out of the air.

"What is it?" she asks.

"I'm not sure, looks like a wood shard of sorts."

"Why would it be a splinter?"

But all I can do is shrug because I'm as clueless as she is.

"Come on, I want to reach the door before Dahlia and Sadie have a chance to get to you."

We break into a run, hand in hand, pounding through the streets. I can tell the Montague territory was once grand and regal. But now it stands like the lost city it is. Derelict and decaying.

"How can it have crumbled so fast?" I ask between pants.

But my question is answered quickly as we skid to a halt. A building cracks and trembles before us. Octavia takes a step in front of me as the roof erupts.

"What the fuck?" I hiss.

A tentacle-like root whips up and out of the roof before sinking, undulating under the remains, smashing tiles and beams from the structure.

"What the hell is it?" she asks.

But I think I already know. She turns to me; I must have let out a little gasp.

"It's the door," I say, thinking back to the fine splinter I plucked from the air. Octavia frowns and brushes something off my cheek. Her frown deepens and she uses her nail to scratch it off.

"Ouch," I say.

Her nostrils flare. "It bit you," she says, holding another splinter-like thread of tree root as she wipes a smear of blood off my cheek with her thumb.

"What the fuck is going on?" Octavia asks.

"Do you remember when Cordelia described the night the door and boundary formed thirty years ago? She watched it grow. Tree-like roots and branches formed the door before she was propelled out?"

"I think the door is eating the city," Octavia breathes, turning back to the enormous root demolishing the property. And now we both stare at it, we can see it for what it is. Roof tiles are crumbling beneath its whip-like tendrils.

I take it all in, the devastation and destruction for what, just three decades ago was a thriving town. I want to do something to fix it. As if the thing writhing through my veins can sense my empathy, it wraps tighter around my insides, tugging me forward.

"Follow the roots," I say.

"Let me get this right. You want to follow the building-consuming, monster roots?"

I tut at her, "Just trust me." I pull her and we continue jogging through the abandoned town.

The deeper we go into the territory, the more roots appear and the more derelict the city becomes. We enter one street filled with broken houses, windows smashed, roofs caved in, tiles smattering the streets like paint splats. And winding their way through all the doors and windows are thick, barky roots.

"I think this is why we only had thirty years. The door is consuming the city to survive, and it's almost out of house to eat."

Octavia's face pinches as she scans the destruction. Mould and ivy wind their way up the front of the buildings, wriggling like parasites. I swear this city, despite the decay, is alive. Or maybe it's the door's veins thrumming beneath the surface. I blink, certain the ivy suffocating the house fronts tilts and turns its leaves to follow us as we pass. I shiver. This place gives me the heebie-jeebies.

The same muted air follows us, swallowing the thrumming heartbeat of the door roots as they swallow bricks and tiles and street walls. A root whip lashes out over our heads.

Octavia swears and shoves me over, knocking the pair of us down. I land on a stone, its sharp edge digging into my thigh. It would have cut me if I weren't wearing thick cargo trousers.

We brush ourselves down, our eyes skittish.

"The fuck?" Octavia says, glancing over my shoulder.

"What now?" I turn in the direction she's looking, and my mouth drops open. The monks that were congregating at the edge of the stage have made their way into the boundary.

They move in a unified, laboured procession. Their heads all bent low, their claret-coloured cloaks filling the street like blood in an artery. Despite the chill in the air, a cold line of sweat drips down my back.

"What are they doing?" I ask.

Octavia shakes her head. "I don't like it. Let's keep moving."

We move out, keeping a steady pace as we pound the pavement, dodging the lashing roots and crumbling buildings. Other than the ivy and the monks behind us, there's very little life in here. No bird song, no wind. No animal claws skittering across the cobbles. There's not a plant in sight save the dark, insidious green of the ivy suffocating the building façades and sprouting off the occasional root.

The deeper we traipse into the city, the worse the devastation becomes, as if an explosion flattened everything from the heart out. Or more likely, the door is at the heart.

I stop dead and point ahead.

Octavia freezes and glances in the direction of my finger. "Sadie," I breathe.

She's a good two to three hundred metres ahead of us. She must have gotten lost on the way because she was four minutes ahead of us and should be further into the territory by now.

I stare at Sadie, but when I blink, she vanishes.

"What the. . ." Octavia says.

"Where did she go? Why didn't she come for me?" I ask.

But before I can answer, the streets blur in front of us. I rub my eyes, trying to make them focus, but everything remains fuzzy. It's the streets themselves. When I blink again, the street refocuses. But the point in the distance I was staring at has disappeared. In its place is a derelict building.

Octavia frowns. "What the hell is going on?"

"I think the door is alive. Or sort of. Maybe it's changing the territory to suit its needs."

"There was a street right there, wasn't there?" Octavia says.

"Yeah, there was. But I have a feeling going that way would be a mistake."

"What do you mean?" Octavia asks.

I close my eyes and let the sensation drift over my skin. It's adapting, no longer crawling, but pulling.

"It's like I can feel the city," I say and wince as something scratches my neck.

Octavia sucks in a short breath and lunges for my neck, yanking what looks like a twig off me. I yelp, a stinging sensation lingers where the stick was.

Octavia's eyes widen, "Gods, it's like the roots want to consume you."

I shake my head. "Not me..."

"Your blood?"

I nod.

"Maybe I should listen to it. Let it guide me. Which way we sh—"

I'm cut off mid-sentence and this time, it's me shoving Octavia across the street, hard. I fly out of the way and crash to the ground as a giant wad of stone, tile and brick falls off the derelict building right where I was standing.

"FUCK," I shout, panting. This fucking city is lethal. My stomach knots, the realisation dawning on me that we might not get out of this alive.

"SHH." Octavia huffs as she gets up and comes over to me. "We don't want any of the other teams finding us."

I gather myself up, pat the dust off my clothes, my hand suddenly feeling naked. We're not holding hands. It leaves a bleak taste in my mouth. I grab her hand and hold it tighter, my stomach churning.

"Come on," I say, tugging her in the direction that seems to be right. We walk at a hard pace, a line of sweat forming on both our brows despite the low temperatures. It's like the roots have eaten all the warmth out of the atmosphere as well as half the buildings.

The deeper we go, the more the streets play silly buggers with us both, shifting and changing. We think we're on the right track and then bam, everything blurs. The buildings shift, and we're disoriented all over again.

Worse still are the boulders. The longer we walk, the more the buildings crumble, giant gnashing roots swinging through the air and swallowing chunks of brick and building bones. Finally, we reach the outskirts of the epicentre. I didn't think shit could get weirder.

"I swear if I have to say what the fuck one more time..." Octavia says, poking a floating brick. It spins off through the air, both of us gawping at it. While the houses and mansions are collapsing, the stones and bricks don't hit the floor. Fragments of dust, tile, glass and roots hover in the air, suspended in dust motes like time stopped.

Octavia releases my hand to brush several splints of root from my face. "You're pale," she says.

"It feels like they're leeching me of something," I say.

Octavia's mouth pinches.

The ground rumbles. A crack splinters across the building next to us. I grab Octavia's hand, but the ground literally judders so hard it shakes my bones.

Octavia is jerked backwards, her fingers ripped out of mine. I stumble after her, tripping over a stray root and collapsing to the ground. I barely manage to grasp onto her when the street blurs.

"Shit," I shriek. Octavia lurches forward to grab my arm, but it's too late.

She blurs, the air shifts, and she vanishes before me.

"FUCK," I shout and punch the ground.

My spine tingles like I'm being watched. I leap up, settling into a fighting position. Before I locate my audience, I know it's Dahlia. Sadie's energy was too focused. She was a precision-point arrow before we entered. Sadie isn't worried about revenge or fighting. Otherwise, she would have run for us when we saw her earlier. I think she wants to find the door first and guard it for when we arrive. I'll bet her thinking is why bother with me if she doesn't even know where the door is? I refocus on Dahlia.

"Such a strange mix of emotions you're wielding there, Dahlia," I say.

She steps out of the cover of one of the derelict buildings and shrugs at me. "Yeah, well, I told you it was war out here."

"I might have hidden you yesterday, but I'm still pissed that you exposed my cheating."

"There's no proof that was me. . ."

She rolls her eyes at me.

"Fine, it was me. But I can tell you're still grateful I saved your life. Tough mix..." I say, trying to make light of the situation.

Her top lip curls. There's something about the way the atmosphere clings to Dahlia that makes me shiver. A wrongness that reeks of vengeance. Iron and steel drift on the air, like she's bathed in metal and blood.

In the distance, I spot the monks, they seem to have caught up to us, or perhaps it's the shifting streets. Their slow, progressive movements jarring against the stillness inside the boundary. Dahlia snatches my attention.

"Such a shame you've been separated from Octavia," she drawls.

"We had a night of peace, Can't we work this out like adults?"

Her eyes darken. "I told you, last night... Don't mistake my honour repaying a debt owed for benevolence. I will have this city no matter the cost. It isn't personal, don't take it as such."

I swallow hard, preparing for her inevitable attack. I locate the exits, the weapons I might be able to improvise with.

"You should know, I'm not as weak as I was in that ring. I will not bow down. You don't want to fight me."

She cocks her head, examining me, a nasty sneer pulling her lips back, her fangs already on display.

"You're right. I don't want to fight. I want to win. If that means dragging your carcass to the door and letting you bleed out so I can claim this fucking city at last and take my rightful place on the throne, so be it."

"Rightful? The only one with a right is Octavia," I scoff.

Dahlia spits on the ground. "Fuck Octavia. Don't be ignorant, Red. The city thinks she's a monster. No one is ever going to let her run this place. Besides, what does she know about armies and war strategy?"

I step forward. There's no way I'm getting out of this without a fight, so I might as well be aggressive.

"It takes a monster to know a monster. And Octavia won't need an army to lead, not if she has the people."

Dahlia bursts out laughing. It's frozen and patronising. She thinks she's so much better than us, that a strong hand is the only way to lead. But all a strong hand creates is fear. We'd be no better off than we are now with Cordelia at the helm.

"She doesn't have the people, though. She never will," Dahlia snarls.

I'm done with this conversation. It's time for the city to change, and I will not fucking lose this time. I leap up while she's too busy laughing and fly across the space between us, landing on top of her and wrapping my arms around her waist and dragging her to the ground. She pushes me off with a punishing shove and I skid off her body.

I flip myself up off the floor, my ribs already aching from her fists.

"There's no Lincoln to help you today. It's just you and me." I growl.

"I don't need a fucking hunter to help me beat you."

She lashes out with her hand, rearing back and punching forward. But I'm in a position of power and dodge out of the way. I bring my fist down and smash it into her jaw. My knuckles grind against each other but in the best way possible.

Dahlia shrieks and then tilts her head to spit blood out, her teeth stained a delicious pink.

I smile.

"You'll pay for that, you little bitch."

"RED," Lincoln shouts. I glance up just as a root pierces a roof, showering the street in debris and the street shifts. He vanishes from sight. They must have gotten separated like we did.

"This is all a distraction. While we're messing about fighting, Sadie is drawing closer to the door."

Dahlia kicks out, her foot catches me and I stumble back, falling and slicing my hand open against a stray stone. Unlike like last time, I can heal just as fast as she can.

She comes straight for me. I jump up, spin and land a turning kick to her shoulder. But she braced for it and only staggers back a couple of paces.

She flings her fist out, aiming right for my jaw in a brutal upper cut.

I twist out of the way and kick out with my foot, smashing her knee in at a horrendous angle. She screams but throws her leg in a jerking movement, and the dislocation thunks back into place. The godsawful cracking sound turns my stomach.

"I told you, I'm not the weak little human you once fought." I spit the words.

"And I told you, I'm going to win at any cost..."

She lunges at me. We're a tangle of fists and feet, kicks and punches and shrieks. Dahlia manages to land a blow right in my solar plexus. I fly back, crashing to the ground gasping for air. I can't breathe, winded. I pant, panicked, desperate for oxygen. But my lungs won't work. Stars whirl around and my vision smatters. Fuck. I wasn't expecting her to land such a savage blow. My ribs spasm, my breathing haggard as I try to gulp oxygen.

Dahlia hauls me up by the collar, lifting me—despite

my increased weight and muscle tone—right off the ground. I'm defenceless as she hurls me through the air, and I crumple into a stack of demolished bricks. My head cracks against something hard and when I touch the spot, my hand comes away bloody.

But even as I touch my scalp, my healing kicks in, my lungs easing, the bone matting back together. Now, I'm pissed. I grit my teeth and push myself to standing.

"I've never liked you," I growl and charge at her. Dahlia ducks out of the way, but I already predicted her movements, so like a dance, I glide with her.

I kick her legs out and smash my fist into her nose. She's momentarily stunned as she stumbles back, struggling to stay upright. Blood pours, showering her face and jaw in blood.

"You little cunt," she sneers.

Then we're together again, all tangled limbs, balled fists and knees thrust into kidneys. She's as relentless as I am. Our blood spatters the cobbles, the roots, which hiss and vibrate and rear up when my blood sprays onto them.

Over and over, we land blows on each other. Both of us pale, our movements growing jerky and slow. Neither of us with the energy to sling insults anymore.

A familiar voice calls my name.

"RED," Lincoln bellows as he scrambles over a wall that wasn't there a few minutes ago. I'm distracted and Dahlia doesn't waste the opportunity.

Something sharp and searing stabs into my side. I scream and stagger back, pulling out what I realise is a fucking stake. Blood billows out of my abdomen, it's so pretty when it pours like that. Like a fountain.

Oh gods.

It's so much blood.

"A STAKE?" I whisper, a laugh spilling from my lips.

I'm tumbling, falling.

On my knees.

Vomit swirls in my throat. My vision smatters with grey twinkling dots. This isn't good. I know injuries, and this is serious.

Dahlia is relentless, she rounds on me, smashing my face and kicking at me until I'm bent over and only able to block the blows she's aiming at me. Everything hurts. Black speckles my vision. My body is weakening. I'm not going to make it.

Then Lincoln's above me, pushing her back, giving me vital seconds to try and heal myself.

But it's not working. My magic is waning. I think I'm burning out. I've used too much trying to heal the wounds and bruises she keeps landing on me and haven't taken in any blood. If it wasn't for this stupid fucking competition... we didn't have enough time to test the limits of my abilities, and now I'm going to fucking die before we even reach the door.

Something deep inside me wraps me in a familiar warmth. The bond. It urges me to fight. Not to give up.

Octavia.

I haul myself to kneeling. A hollow thump rips through the air, followed by a bone cracking thud. There's a beat of silence and then a shriek that chills me to my core rents the air in half.

"LINCOLN," I scream, forcing myself standing.

He's on the floor, his arm twisted at a strange angle and the same stake that Dahlia struck me with protruding from his gut.

"No, no, no. What the fuck is wrong with you, Dahlia? He's your gods damned teammate!"

"You're coming with me, Red. I don't give a shit if you're alive or dead, that door is mine and you're opening it for me."

My jaw clenches. A growl rumbles in my throat as I launch myself at Dahlia with absolutely no mind to the fact I am still bleeding out. Adrenaline and the need to keep Lincoln alive pushes me on. I fly through the air, blood streaming out of my gut.

Lincoln, bless his fucking soul, uses what little strength he has from his good arm to grasp Dahlia's leg.

She plummets to the floor instead of driving towards me. I leap up and slam my foot into her head, her skull crunching under my boot and weight. She's instantly knocked unconscious.

I turn to Lincoln. His eyes are wide with horror as his gaze flits to the wood protruding from his belly.

I glance at my own stomach. I'm woozy, but the bleeding has slowed to a gentle ooze. It's not good, and I may not fully heal, but I stand more of a chance than Lincoln. I have to focus on him.

"I need to remove the stake. But when I do, you'll lose a lot of blood."

"Maybe don't, then?" he says, his lips sheet white.

"You don't understand. You're going to bleed out either way. But I think if I remove it, I can use my healing to staunch the blood flow long enough to get you out of here." Or I hope. I hesitate, knowing my magic is struggling to heal my own wounds. But if I focus on his gut, maybe I can re-route as much as possible and give him a fighting chance. It's better than doing nothing.

"You think...?" he says, glancing up at me from the ground. His face is green, clammy. A sheen of sweat breaks out across his brow that screams organ failure and fever on the horizon.

"I mean... I've not exactly had a lot of time to refine and practice these skills but..."

"But if you don't try, I'm going to die anyway?" he says, his voice weakening.

I bite my lip. I don't want to confirm the truth hanging between us. But I don't want to lie to him either. He must be willing to take the chance.

"Just do it, Red. And try and keep me on this planet, you owe me a birthday drink."

I take a deep breath, and wince as a searing bolt of pain shoots through my torso. Fuck, my own injuries are clearly only healed surface deep. I pull my knife and leather sheath off my hip, attempting to hide the agony of movement and put it between his teeth.

"This is going to hurt, but I have to get it out before I can heal you."

He takes it between his teeth, like a horse accepts the bit, and closes his eyes, his nostrils flaring in anticipation.

I count, "One, two..."

I yank the stake out of his gut and suppress the urge to scream as blood surges up and out of his body. He screams against the blade, his eyes flashing wide.

I have to block him out, focus all my energy on pulling magic from my core. My eyes fall shut, sweat peels down my neck in thick beads. I grab the golden flow of light and ribbon-like magic from deep inside me. I hold my hands over his belly until they tingle. It's gruelling. I swear I shake. My body swaying, vision simmering between grey and blackout. As my magic re-routes itself from my wounds to his, my body screams in agony. I open my eyes and lean over to throw up not once, but twice from the lancing hot pain. But I hold tight to the desire to heal Lincoln. I will not be the reason he dies.

The electric buzz in my fingers turns to a searing heat. My hands glow brighter, the magic burning hotter, harder.

Lincoln's expression flashes, his neck corded with the strain of whatever my magic is doing to his insides. His eyes blow as wide as the moon above us. And then he slumps against the ground, unconscious.

"Fuck, come on, Lincoln, don't leave me. Not now." I shut my eyes again, pouring everything I have into his stomach. I picture internal organs matting together and meshing in healthy pink flesh. Gods, I really need some fucking training. What if I kill him because I'm making this up as I go? This is messy as fuck. There's a beat. A lost second. Three more seconds and I realise my hands have slipped from his stomach to his thigh.

Shit. Did I black out? I'm weak, barely able to keep myself upright. There's movement to my side.

Fuck. Dahlia.

She groans as her cranium reforms and heals. *Come on, Lincoln, fucking heal, you son of a bitch. HEAL.*

Dahlia groans and rolls up, a snarl emanating from her chest.

"I'm going to make you suffer before I bleed you out for the door. And for that," she touches her head, "I'm going to make Octavia watch."

And then her hands are around my throat. My grip on my magic slips, and the golden light winks out.

CHAPTER 33

OCTAVIA

T he street blurs, my grip on Red slips and I throw myself forward to grab her, but I'm too late.

Her fingers vanish, my hand swiping through nothing but dust and air. She's gone. We're separated.

"Fuck," I scream, picking up a brick and throwing it. It clatters to the street, bouncing off a tree root, which shivers in protest at the injury. I freeze.

There are voices. My skin prickles, ice flooding the air.

Not just any voice.

"Oh gods." I stop breathing. "Dahlia and Red."

I can't have moved far. I sprint for the wall in front of me and jump up, grip the edge, managing to hold myself there and peer over it.

Thank fuck. It's the street I was on. But that's the last of my gratitude because the longer I look, the more my mouth runs dry.

It is Dahlia.

And Red is all on her own.

Flashes of the thumps and whacks and hideous bone cracks in the fighting ring flood my mind. The image of her broken body in Xavier's mansion. Every inch of skin smothered in blood. The echoing wallop of Dahlia's fists landing hit after hit on her. She nearly killed Red once. My fingers go cold as I catch sight of them charging at each other. I pull myself up onto the wall ledge as the ground rumbles again.

You have got to be kidding me.

"No," I yelp as I slip. My grip slackens and I'm back on the ground, the world around me blurring and fuzzing.

"FUCKSAKE," I yell and hurl myself upright, but it's too late. The wall has already vanished and I'm in the middle of a street I don't recognise.

My lungs clamp tight enough my chest aches. It takes everything I have to calm myself and stop the panicked hyperventilating long enough to run. I have to find Red before Dahlia kills her.

I sprint down a street to the left, turn right, and right again and then round a bend. I cry out a grizzled scream when I realise I can't hear them anymore. Tightness claws up my throat, making my lungs stiff even as my breathing returns to normal. My body fizzes: adrenaline and cortisol flooding my system. I push harder, running faster, desperate to fucking find her.

I skid to a halt. I swear there was a noise. My eyes close as I strain to hear, forcing my breathing to still and quiet so I can listen to my surroundings.

There is it again.

It's them. I'm sure of it.

I break into a sprint, this time, using vampire speed to race in their direction. I careen around a corner and find the same brick wall I was on a few minutes ago. There's no hesitation this time; I run full pelt towards it and leap over it, landing in the same street as them.

At last.

But something is wrong. There's claret spilled all over the street. It bends and sweeps like the meandering curves of a river. But what chills me to my core is the fact the door roots are all creeping towards it. Their slow, writhing movements all heading towards Red. I shiver. A scream builds in my throat. Dahlia is on the floor and Red has that familiar golden glow around her hands. She's leant over Lincoln's stomach. And yet, she's stained too, a hole in her side. They're both injured.

Dahlia groans, pushing herself up. *Oh shit.* I'm too far away. Even with vampire speed, I'm the other end of the street. I'm not going to make it, and I know Red. She won't stop healing Lincoln to save herself.

I'm running before I even make the decision. My feet pound the gravel, I dig deeper than I ever have, using all my vampire speed and strength to race up the street. Step after step, after step.

Dahlia rises to a seated position.

Snarling, red bubbles froth over her lips.

Oh gods.

She stands, but I'm still too far away to reach them.

"I'm going to make you suffer before I bleed you out for the door. And for that," Dahlia touches her head, "I'm going to make Octavia watch."

Red's eyes widen and just as I predicted, she doesn't stop trying to heal Lincoln. I want to bellow at her. Holler a begged plea for her to save herself, but if I do, I'll alert Dahlia to the fact I'm coming. I push harder, force my legs to move faster. My legs pump quicker. I pant, gasping for oxygen, swallowing huge gulps of air. But I don't think I'm going to make it. I pour everything I have into moving like the wind and light. Praying to the Mother of Blood... to *my* mother to save the only woman I've ever truly loved.

Dahlia's hands move.

They're around Red's neck.

Fuck. Everything inside me howls. My muscles are hot and feverish as I force them to move faster than I'm capable of. But I can't lose her. I won't let her die for this stupid fucking competition.

The light emanating from Red's hands flickers, Dahlia's fingers tighten around her neck.

Fuck. No. Please.

I drive my arms quicker, praying to any god to just fucking help.

But Red's magic fizzles out. Her eyes widen, her skin flushes a deep rouge and then she passes out.

I want to be sick. I take one huge gulp of air, bend my legs and leap the final thirty feet. My hands landing on either side of Dahlia's head, and I twist, *hard.*

Her neck snaps in a satisfying crack, and she collapses to the street.

Not dead.

Or at least not permanently. I shove her away and grab Red, pulling her into my arms.

"Please... Please wake up..."

My fangs descend, I slice my wrist and hold it to her mouth. Hoping that if enough blood hits her stomach, it will work.

She's motionless.

Too motionless.

People say the dead look like they're sleeping. But it's not true. There's a stillness in death that is wrong; it's why vampires scare humans. We wrap death's infinite blanket around us like a weapon. Right now, it's my executioner. I lay my forehead against Red's and plead. The seconds feel like weeks. Lincoln rouses, he's pale and clammy, but I think he's going to be okay. His heart is beating a regular rhythm again.

"Stay put, you're too weak to move," I say.

"Is she..." he says, his eyes flicking to her body.

"I don't know. She doesn't have a heartbeat anymore, so I don't know how to tell..."

His expression crumbles. He pulls a hand over his brow, but the lines don't disappear.

A stray door root shivers across the broken bricks towards us. It can fuck right off. I give it a hard boot and it rears up, shaking at me like a cat about to spray, but it slopes back down and crawls away. Fucking creepy things.

We wait.

The human and the vampire, both loving the same dhampir. Both praying she returns to us. Seconds turn to a minute, which turn to two, and then three . . .

When the lump in my throat is so thick I can no longer breathe, Red sits bolt upright, inhaling a deep, noisy breath.

I can't bring myself to speak, just bury myself against her chest, tears stinging the back of my eyes. Her hands fold over my back as she rubs me.

"It's okay, I'm okay," she says, her voice weak, cracking.

"I thought I'd lost you." I whisper.

"You can't. You won't. I promise," she says.

And I let the tears fall.

CHAPTER 34

A long time ago, I told you a truth...

That any secret worth its merit is woven in the depths of midnight. Spoken in whispered promises and hapless lies. The soft, breathy words lost to the stars and buried with the moon, night after night until even the sky can't discern the truth.

This was how it happened... How my story started. How lives were ruined, and hearts were broken.

Two families sat beneath the golden glow of fire lamps, a long thin table between them. St Clairs on one side, burned and charred from an attack on their mansion.

The Randalls, equally sooty and wrapped in perpetrator's guilt, on the other.

Two families bonded by the hatred born of generations of ancestors long past. Hostility tattooed in their marrow like cancer. Spread thick and fibrous so that it was all they could breathe and smell and think. As a mansion burned, and their children ran, the night struck twelve.

They believed their hands were forced.

Lies.

Lies they stitched into their realities, made true because they chose to believe them. I begged them to reconsider. Pleaded with them to see that love could save us all.

But their hatred was terminal.

An end to all our fates.

The start of a story none of us wanted to tell.

A contract was signed. Blood prints scarred the scroll. A warning, an omen.

Too late, too late. The witch was coming.

Too late, too late, I was already there...

That's right, I came... a witch summoned like a demon... called to curse, to cut, to cleave a love in two.

And as I entered that dim-lit room, each pair of elder eyes drew over my expression. They swallowed in unison, as if they could chew down their mistakes.

But magic doesn't work that way, and neither do curses.

Cordelia's mother handed me the blade. Eleanor's mother handed me a contract.

Both their fathers sat useless, wide-eyed stares as the horror of what they were asking dawned on them. Enemies united for a goal written in blood.

So silly. So foolish.

But such is the nature of humans, never learning until it's too late. Only regretting once the error is made.

I stroked my swollen belly one last time, whispered a silent prayer that the gods forgave me for what I was about to do. And if they couldn't, then I prayed they saved my baby instead. If I had a choice, I'd never have set foot in there. But her papa abandoned us, and I needed the money. It was a lot. Gods, was it a lot. It would have kept us fed and warm for two years.

Which is why I knew I had to do it.

I took the blade and sliced my palm. Red liquid bloomed over my flesh and dripped down my wrist. I dipped my pen in the silky liquid slipping between my fingers, and I signed my name. .

.

CHAPTER 35

OCTAVIA

"Just GO," Lincoln groans, and waves a limp hand at us. His colour is a lot better than when I first arrived. But he's still pale, and even if we did try and move him, I don't think we'd get him far without assistance. Dawn is too close, and Sadie is probably already at the door. I glance around the derelict street; there's nothing and no one in sight.

"But you need a transfusion. And what if the streets change and we can't find you?" Red whines.

She's still pale. The blood I gave her is healing her enough to knit the wounds in her organs, but not enough to give her back her strength. She thinks she can hide the pain she's in, but as she moves, I notice the wince in the corner of her eyes, the way she hesitates before shifting her feet. We might not make it if the door is too far. She needs human blood.

"If Sadie opens that door before you, none of this matters. So just fucking leave. I'm alive. Alive enough to wait for help. I trust you'll find me." He pulls himself up against a large boulder, a line of sweat forming on his brow. Red grits her teeth, glancing at me, her face creased with worry.

"We're coming back for him," I say and grab her hand.

"You're sure?" she says to Lincoln.

"I swear to gods, Red, if you don't get your ass moving, I will get up and chase you all the way to the door."

"Okay, fine," she says and bends to give him a hug. "Come on then, Octavia." She pulls me away, but I only make it two steps before halting.

"Hold on... We need to bury Dahlia," I say.

"Excuse me?" Red says, cocking her head at me.

"She'll be out cold for a few hours and if sunup happens before we get back to Lincoln or before she wakes, she'll desiccate."

"And that's a bad thing?"

"She's still my sister."

"She tried to kill me... oh, wait, I forgot, it wasn't 'personal.'" She wiggles her fingers in air quotes.

I pull my shirt across displaying the circular stake wound a centimetre to the right of my heart. "Need I remind you that you tr—"

"Ugh, fine." She drops my hand and picks up the biggest boulder she can and throws it in Dahlia's direction.

It crunches down on top of her legs, an almighty crack signifying a bone break. I mean... I can hardly blame her, but also...

"Red. . . *Darling*, Dahlia is *literally* unconscious."

She stops what she's doing and glares at me so viciously that I raise my hands in retreat.

"What?" she barks. "It's not *personal.*"

There are times in a relationship that we must go to

war. And there are others when we must realise that the ship has well and truly sailed, the battle hopelessly lost, and life will be easier if we just relent.

I let her continue dropping slabs on Dahlia's body, though she is a little gentler now. I suppose Dahlia will be healed by the time she wakes anyway. When Red is done, and Dahlia still has a hand and a foot in the open, I roll my eyes at her half-arsed job and speed around picking up boulders and sealing the remaining bits of her inside. It only takes a few minutes and then we leave.

Lincoln waves us off, his colour now stable. His heart rate does pick up as we move off, but it settles when Red turns around and leaves him with a final promise to send for help as soon as we're out.

Neither of us is happy about abandoning him but even if we thought it was safe to carry him, we don't know how fragile his internal organs are. And that's beside the fact he'd slow us down.

Red leads, marching me through the decaying streets as fast as her body can. It's not quick.

Every so often, her fingers brush the place Dahlia stabbed her. I want to ask, to offer more of my blood. But I am ravenous and exhausted myself, and there is no point both of us arriving in a weakened state.

Much as she doesn't want to hear it, human blood is the only thing that really heals and nourishes a vampire. I think it's a safe bet that it's the same for the elements of her genetics that are now vampire too.

We only manage to walk for another ten minutes before the energy and atmosphere shift.

Those monks reappear, heads bent low, their slow, continuous progress forward zombie-like. They shiver out of sight, but not before I catch sight of the door ahead of them.

I freeze. "There," I say.

Red stops and glances up at where the monks just were. Her expression brightens for the first time in hours. "Let's go."

We head in the direction of the monks, and when we reach the spot they were in, we too shiver out of sight and reappear.

"The door," Red gasps.

It's still a way in front of us, but even from a distance, it towers up, glorious and welcoming. It's nestled inside a manor courtyard by the looks, but at least it's a downhill walk to the property from here.

We could have arrived in better condition. Both our bodies ache from walking all night, the fighting, the weeks of relentless stress this fucking competition has put us through. It's still dark, but the first brush of morning warmth whips around us. I glance up at the horizon, a shiver running through me.

Red checks her watch. "It's four. We're not going to make it back out in time. We need to pick up pace."

Despite the fact we're both delirious, we dig into our reserves. But like with anything inside this fucking boundary, it doesn't go according to plan.

We make it three minutes.

Three.

Red buckles over groaning. The sound cuts through me, setting my teeth on edge. She's hurting.

I slide my arms under her and haul her up; she's almost a dead weight. My stomach furls into a knot.

"What's wr—Oh..."

Those fucking splinters are all over her face and neck.

She's white, and clammy. I've never seen her look so sick. I scratch at the flakes of root, pulling and yanking them off but it leaves her face smeared with blood. Precious blood she can't afford to lose.

It takes me several minutes, but with each one I pluck off, my stomach loosens a little more. I manage to clear her face of the root shrapnel, but when I'm done, my fingers are stained with her blood, and her cheeks are mottled with smudges of drying claret. Gods, we need to get her out of here.

"Talk to me," I plead, desperate for her to say something, anything. I just need to know that she's still with me. My fingers brush her cheek, but she stiffens beneath me. It sends a prickle down my spine.

"Octavia," she breathes, her eyes wide with horror. Her fingers grip my arms so hard her nails dig into my biceps.

I turn.

Too late.

Something granite-like slams into me. I'm thrown sideways, my spine crunching against a pile of broken stone and bricks. A searing bolt rips through my back. I'm pretty sure a vertebra has shattered. Maybe a rib too. I don't have time to worry about myself, I'll heal. I'm not sure I can say the same for Red who… Oh gods. Time halts, I swear the blood in my veins stops flowing, freezing to horror-tinged ice.

She's floating two feet off the floor, a root wrapped around her waist and another around her throat.

"RED," I scream, scrambling upright. But I buckle and land on my knees as a shooting pain radiates from my spine through my ribs. Shit. Definitely cracked. I haul myself up, wincing against the pain and praying my body heals fast. I hobble-sprint towards her.

It feels like I'm moving through sludge. Every step I take is barely an inch. But like a newborn, the worst thing of all is that she's not screaming. Her mouth hangs open, her eyes moon-wide, silence flooding the air.

I drag myself across the street, my back slowly piecing itself together, with every step the pain easing. How the hell am I going to help her?

The roots don't seem to be strangling her at least. It's more that they're holding her in place. Finally, I reach her, understanding what's happened.

It's not just the thick root around her neck. There are dozens of the same capillary splinters connecting her to it. The same fucking ones I've been pulling off her this whole time. My eyes scan the thick root, realising exactly what it's leeching: blood.

"Fuck. Fuck. Fuck," I hiss. But she doesn't respond. Her eyes already dim and lifeless.

My chest tingles as I scratch and tug at the root. A branch breaks off and whips across my face, slicing my skin clean open. It stings like acid. But even as blood oozes down my skin, I'm not worried about me.

My fangs descend, I bite into the root, tearing chunks from it. My mouth fills with her blood.

Oh gods. It's not working. The root heals as quick as I slice at it.

I step back, switch tactics, and move a few paces away, following the root until I think I can get leverage. That's the thing with wood, it's thick and fibrous but it can snap. I wrap my hands around the branch, and then I wrench back with every ounce of strength I have left. My back screams, the healing slowed because of the energy expenditure and lack of blood.

I pull harder. Harder.

The root groans, cracks. But it fights back, the same spindly capillaries peeling off the root and floating through the air towards me. I move my head this way and that, trying to dodge their assault.

I dig deep, scream a roar of frustration as my spine protests. One more tug. I throw everything I have at it and finally the branch snaps. It falls loose from Red's waist, the two pieces slithering away.

I do the same to the one around her neck. Panic makes my fingers numb with tingles as I wrench harder and faster, my back desperately fighting to heal against the damage I'm doing using it before it's fixed. This root fights back too, sending more of the vile little leech roots at me. I snap my fangs and jaws at them all while hauling on the root, bending the wood in half until finally it, too, snaps.

Red collapses to the floor, eerily still, her skin an ominous shade of grey.

I drop the fucking root and run to her. She blinks. Oh gods, she blinks and it's the most glorious thing I've ever seen. She's still with me. Though that is where my hope dies.

Her mouth gulps the air as her damp eyes meet mine. Beads of sweat form on her brow and upper lip. She trembles.

"Can you move?" I ask.

But she's barely able to respond. I scoop her up into my arms, my back screaming against the weight of her and me. It's as I stand that my eyes fall upon the monks in the distance. As if she can sense my thoughts, her gaze darts across the street to their claret-coloured cloaks.

"N... N..." her words fade.

"You don't have a choice."

She opens her mouth, her fangs descending as she leans towards my arm. But I pull away.

"You can't. I'm not healing fast either. I can't give you anymore. If I could, I would, but it would finish us both."

Her jaw flexes.

"Red, please..." I glance up at the sky, "Morning is coming..."

Tears roll down her cheeks, but I'm already walking over to the procession of monks.

"Please..." I plead with her. I lay her down and grab the closest monk, whispering and begging them for their sacrifice.

And just like the monk in the arena, he nods assent and follows me. He lies next to Red and offers her his neck.

Her eyes find mine; this time, it's her pleading with me. Her silence saying everything as she shakes her head from side to side.

I hate myself, but I take her hand and whisper, "Please? If you love me, you'll do this."

Her lips purse, I know she'll be mad, but what am I supposed to do? "If you don't drink, I don't think you'll make it."

She closes her eyes, tears streaming, and when she opens them, her fangs have descended. She mumbles something I can't hear to the monk, and then she sinks her fangs into his neck.

I sag, collapsing on the ground as relief washes through me. Her throat bobs with each swallow, her skin melting from pallid grey to white to a peachy pink tone, then back to normal. The monk's eyes roll back, his body motionless. When she finally detaches, she's as still as him. My adrenaline spikes—was it not enough? Is she hurt? Just unconscious?

309

But I relax when she finally sits up. She is not, by any means back to normal. I can tell that she's carrying multiple injuries, I suspect we'd both need to drink a small village to recover, but it's enough.

"Two lives." It's the first thing she says to me.

"T—" I start.

"Two lives this fucking competition has forced me to take. Lives I'm supposed to protect." She buckles then and falls into my arms.

I hold her, stroking her head. "I'm sorry. I'm so sorry you were going to die, Red. I can't lose you."

"I know," she cries into my shoulder. "I know."

We stand like that for a while, until she pulls away, wiping her face.

"Don't," I say.

"What?"

"Hate yourself. He gave his life willingly for yours. They all would."

"I don't want them to."

I nod because what else can I do? I know it's not what she wants. "We need to leave."

She slides her hand into mine, it's a little rigid, but that's okay. She can be mad at me as long as she's still with me.

Together, we follow the path outlined by the monks until the door appears before us. We shuffle along, both weary and exhausted, holding the knowledge that there may still be a fight to come. Behind the door stands the derelict mansion of Isabella Montague, the missing original vampire, and my mother.

"Shit," I hiss, taking in the building, the courtyard and the freestanding door.

"You okay?" Red asks.

She's not asking if I'm okay, she's asking if *I'm okay*. This is where my mother lived, where I would have lived if she hadn't abandoned me. If Cordelia hadn't stolen me away. Though as soon as the melancholy ache for a place I've never known appears, I shove it away. Because this wasn't our home. My mother was poor while she was pregnant. No. This became her home only after she became a monster. Once she had power and time on her hands to build a fortune and a war none of us wanted to fight. This would never have been my home. I'd never have run from room to room holding a scruffy teddy. Because my mother *did* curse Cordelia, and in return, Cordelia stole me away. So now, I'm the thousand-year-old monster standing before the ruined remains of what once must have been a grand mansion. A mansion that must have made my mother proud. It's almost a shame that scarcely more than half of it remains. The roof caved in long ago, eaten by the same door she created. The once light-coloured sandstone bricks are stained dark, and ivy consumes what's left of the front of the mansion.

The monks have formed an enormous ring around the courtyard, their heads bent as they hum a melodic tune, their bodies swaying in simultaneous motion.

My gaze falls upon the door, which is magnificent.

It stands tall in a glorious white marble archway. The same ivy wends its way around the arch and through the wooden door itself. This close to their origin, the roots are enormous, thick trunks twining around and then away, out into the grounds and town to feed. The door seems to be made of the same twisted branches, the prophecy words etched into its skin like charcoal scars.

Behold the Door of Destiny, forged in realms unknown,

311

Guardian of secrets, in its magic it is sown.
A portal bound by time, an enigma to explore,
Yet heed this warning, for thirty years it stands, no more.
Blood of the night, a child of two worlds' embrace,
A dhampir born, a dhampir turned. The heir to unlock this sacred space.
For millennia dormant, the door now stirs.
Only the worthy may approach,
Only the true heir.
In shadows they walk, with pulse of sun and moon,
The first of their kind, with fangs that hunger and a heart that beats,
They alone shall open the door and reveal the grimoire secret within.
The prophecy whispers of this sole chance,
For the rightful heir to undo the city's dance.
But heed, oh seeker, the sands of time are swift,
Thirty years' span, and then the door shall lift.
Open the portal, reveal the truth concealed,
Or lose forever the chance for Sangui's fate be healed.

The sky, thankfully, is still inked with night, dappled with starlight speckles, but even as we walk those final feet, some of the stars are extinguishing themselves. I swallow hard. It won't be long before the sky is streaked with orange, and I'm stuck here trying to find shelter until nightfall.

"Let's do a full circle around the door before we open it," Red says.

But as soon as the words are out, Sadie appears, accompanied by two demons. Red's mouth drops open.

"Sadie?" I breathe.

The demons aren't doing anything, they're just standing on either side of her, as if on guard. In her hand, Sadie carries two empty vials. The door handle is stained, a little river of claret running down the twisted vines.

The vials drop from Sadie's hand, clattering and smashing into shards.

"It was you? You stole the blood?" I whisper.

Her face softens as she gazes at me and raises her hands to sign. "There's so much I should have told you."

I frown. "What the hell does that mean?" But Sadie doesn't get the chance to answer, because a carriage appears and draws to a halt as Eleanor and Mother step out. Their eyes flick to the door—the shattered vials and the stream of blood—and then to each other.

The demons step forward, flanking Sadie as she makes her way towards us.

"Oh gods," Red breathes as her eyes take in the sight. I am fairly certain we're all having the same realisation.

My brain moves faster than my consciousness, my body already urging me to bend over and vomit as I compute what it all means.

That the blood Red had given me—the blood Sadie stole and used on the door—isn't sufficient.

The door wants more.

It wants all of her.

It's why the roots kept coming, why every time I pulled one off, she bled.

They wanted to drain her. All of her.

Everything moves slowly. Sadie and the demons halt as Mother and Eleanor stride over. Sadie's snow-coloured hair flies loose and wispy in a gust of wind. She takes a step towards us. I slide in front of Red, my arm protecting her body.

313

"It's over," I bark at Sadie, never taking my gaze off her. I've underestimated her way too many times to take any chances. And Red isn't exactly at full strength. "It's not opening."

Sadie, moving slow as death, tilts her head to look at me. Then her eyes dance over Red's figure. The demons glance at Sadie, but she shakes her head and encourages them to guard the door. They slope away back to their positions on either side of the door.

"LOOK AT ME, SADIE," I shriek, desperate to stop her staring at Red like she's a meal. "That fucking door isn't opening."

Mother steps into my peripheral vision. "Yes. It. Is."

I push Red, stepping further away. But her body goes rigid. "Red," I hiss. But she's stiffened like rigour mortis. She won't budge despite my nudging.

"Verity," I growl under my breath.

But when I glance behind me, her eyes are glazed, unfocused, as if she's not really there. The same dazed look she had when the roots were draining her a few streets ago. She steps around me towards the door. I panic and grab her, trying to shake her. "Wake the fuck up, Red," I snap, trying to bring her back to reality.

An enormous crack cuts through the air.

Everyone jumps as a huge fracture splits the heart of the door. Red steps again, closer to the door. She is behaving like the monks. Like she fucking wants this?

It's Eleanor who approaches me, her warm hand clasping my forearm. "The door is going to crumble. We'll lose our chance, it's almost sunrise. There's no time to hesitate."

Has she lost it? Red is not giving any more fucking blood to this door. She's barely recovered as it is.

"Octavia," Mother pleads, her hand stretching out towards us.

"Red," I growl, desperately trying to push her back, but her body is like steel and utterly immovable. Her eyes are vacant like she only sees the door and everything else has vanished—including me.

I can't breathe. My lungs are so tight I'm three breaths from passing out. My vision goes spotty, the gap between my ribs tingling. How the fuck do I stop this? How do I save her?

"You have to let her go," Eleanor says and tugs on my forearm.

Sadie's eyes find me, and she raises her hands and signs, "This was always inevitable for whoever became the dhampir. I'm sorry it was her. But it's time to let go."

"Fuck you, Sadie." I grip Red's hand, tugging her, silently pleading with her to snap out of it. At last, she squeezes back.

There's another crack. The door splinters, one fracture at a time. We're running out of time.

"Octavia..." Red says. Quiet. Soft. So full of emotion.

Strange how one word can shatter your universe. Blood roars in my ears.

One word. So many meanings:

Octavia, I love you.

Octavia, what we had was amazing.

Octavia, let me go.

I shuck it all off, my body boiling. "Don't you fucking dare give up on me. Not now, not ever. You don't get to do that to me. Not again," I bark at her.

She smiles, her eyes finally focusing on me. Far too soft, far too distant. "It's calling to me. I need to go to it. At least this way, you get the city."

I scream in frustration. "FUCK the city. I don't want it. Not without you."

"The city gets magic. You get the city. I'm just one person, one life... you cannot put me above the entire city. Let me do this for you."

This time, when the door howls an almighty roar, splinters burst from it, exploding outward. Several twisted wooden vines drop to the floor.

"I am not giving up on you..." she says. "I'm giving you everything you always deserved."

She rises up on tiptoes and presses her lips to mine.

Soft, tender.

She tastes like clouds and summer. Like leather and hot skin. Summer romance and winter nights, like traces of me, and essence of her.

Longing.

Love.

But worse of all, she tastes like goodbye.

Tears leak down my cheeks. She brushes them away with her thumb.

"I always loved you. Despite everything. Through everything. Even at my worst, it was always you."

"Don't do this. I beg you, Verity, please..." Something moves in my periphery but Red has all of my attention.

She smiles at me, and I snap. I will not give up on her. "No," I growl and step in front of her.

But it's funny how your focus on one thing means it slips on something else. A shadow washes over me as a body—Eleanor's—leaps onto me, sending both of us careening onto the ground several feet from the door. Mother's hand whips out, grabbing Red and hauling her the final few steps.

I kick and lash against Eleanor. But she's wrapped her legs around my arms and pinned me in place.

"ELEANOR," I shriek. "She's like a fucking daughter to you, it will kill her."

"It won't," she says. "It's going to be okay."

I wriggle and kick, but it's no use, Eleanor, like Mother and me, is the first of her kind. The truest of all hunters and as strong as we are. Our equal, our natural balance.

Fuck this.

I rear my head back and slam it into Eleanor's nose. She shrieks and releases me. I flip myself up and dart towards Red. But Mother hears me coming. She shoves Red the final foot, slamming her into the door.

"No," I shriek and stumble back. "How could you . . .?"

"I'm sorry, fuck. I'm so sorry, Octavia, but I can't let you stop this."

"It's going to kill her. She's the love of my life. Mum, please..."

Mother steps back, one pace, two. Something glints in her hand. I lunge, but Sadie's foot kicks out, tripping me as Mother spins and slashes down across both of Red's wrists.

A hiss erupts through the air, the vines embedded in the door's wood knots peel off the slats and lunge for Red. They pierce her skin, pummelling into her one after the other. The vines shiver and glisten the colour of claret and ruby as they drain Verity of her blood.

I scream, lurch forward and slash at the branches, desperately trying to pull them off her.

"HELP ME," I shout.

But Mother and Sadie just stand there, watching, waiting.

"Eleanor, please," I beg. She glances from Red to the

vines and back to the door as the fractures that gouged their way through the wood heal.

Her eyes widen, her lips gulping at the air like a fish. I reach out and yank the collar of her shirt, bringing her back to attention.

"Eleanor, for fuck's sake, do you want Red to die?"

Her gaze refocuses. "No."

"Well, she's going to unless we get these fucking vines off her."

Eleanor steps back, her head shaking side to side. "It wasn't supposed to take this much. Fuck, it wasn't supposed to drain her. I swear."

Mother steps between Eleanor and I, protecting not me... but *her*. "It's time, Eleanor, we have to stop the cure."

I freeze. Replay her words. A chill settling in my gut.

"Stop?" I repeat.

Cordelia's eyes narrow at me. "Come on darling, you didn't think I really wanted a cure loose in the city."

She? What the hell has she done?

There's no time to tear my mother a new one. I have to focus on saving Red. Eleanor joins me at last. But the more vines we rip from her body, the more peel off the door and puncture her skin. The whole time, Verity leaks her lifeforce over the door, she keeps her eyes on me. Her mouth moving around the words *I love you*.

I love you.

I love you.

And every time she says it another piece of me shatters. I want to bellow at her to stop it.

Stop it.

Stop it.

But my entire being is focused on yanking out the stems and tendrils. Faster and faster. This is all I have.

Otherwise, I am helpless, watching the woman I have waited a millennium for die.

I can't.

I won't give up.

I have to be enough to save her.

But with every breath she takes, her body slows and another piece of my soul breaks.

Our eyes never part. A hundred things pass between us.

Silent promises.

Silent hopes.

Silent lives we would have lived.

Tears roll down my cheeks, each drop containing a million ways I should have said *I love you* back. With letters and flowers, with cups of blood in the morning, and Sunday lie-ins. With surprise vacations and art brushes, extra paint tubes and surprise date nights. With a million kisses and a million more embraces. Until her handprints leave scars on my body from holding me tight. She owns me. I'm hers to keep forever.

That is what love stories are made of.

That is how legendary love is forged.

But none of that happens. Instead, her skin pales.

"Oh gods." My heart seizes.

She stiffens, her eyes glassing over. Light blooms from her body as if she is the coming sunrise. It's the same golden glow I saw around her hands when she was healing Lincoln.

It burns brighter, erupting from her cheeks, her arms, her legs. I squint against her growing glow as I frantically pull at the parasitic branches.

Faster.

Faster.

Brighter and brighter.

Until I have to shield myself from her. She is radiant like diamonds, and glistening like star-dappled blood. Even as her eyes dim, and the door burns hotter behind her. She is still my Verity.

The wooden door splinters, finally disintegrating. It swirls and fractures and fills the air with brown shards and blood drops, a cloud made of life and violence.

And then it explodes.

Light. Blood. Dust. Wood.

Red.

And just as violently, the explosion reverses. It sucks everything in. A screaming, roaring maw. A dark void consuming everything.

Including me.

I can't see, the darkness burning my vision away. All I know is that I'm being dragged towards the open door. I howl for Red, desperately grappling with the ground, trying to reach her but all my fingers touch are rocks and dust and wooden splinters.

And then I'm yanked hard, and everything disappears.

CHAPTER 36

O ver and over, I dipped the quill in the swelling tide of red
on my palm. I drew long strokes of bloody ink across the
page. Each letter a perfect shape.

A perfect promise.

A perfect fate.

And then it was done.

My name signed in full...

Isabella Sadie Montague.

Sadie, Sadie, Sadie.

*A name I never used. A name I kept secret for seven hundred
and fifty years until I met my monster.*

The monster I made.

The monster I have to unmake.

*She thought she found me in the snow all those years ago.
But I lured her in. Tempted and teased. Always playing my
game. That bitch left me for dead, praying to my witch-gods for
salvation. She left me poor, destitute, and she stole my flesh and
blood. For seven hundred and fifty years I amassed power.*

Quietly, secretly. Always plotting. The church wasn't just a sanctuary, it was an army.

I made one mistake. I let my temper go when Cordelia stooped beside me in the snow. I'd stewed on my rage for seven and a half centuries. You can hardly blame me. I couldn't keep my fury from welling up. I bit her, took a chunk from her face.

Furious to finally meet again.

Furious that she didn't recognise me.

But it was the contract that started it all. Once it was signed, my tools laid out, it was time.

I wove and wove, drawing all of my strength and magic from my heritage. That was my second mistake. Darkness descended on the city. I tore magic from witches far and wide. I didn't know it would kill them. How I wish I could take it back.

I scarred the city for a thousand years. But I knew what was happening as the magic flooded my body. Call it my conscience, but I knew what I was doing was wrong. I needed a failsafe. So, I wove a backdoor into the spell.

Only when a worthy dhampir was born, would the door come forth. Only when enough of their blood was spilled, would the door reopen. And then it would replace what was stolen, return what was hidden, and reveal all the secrets of a witch once scorned.

It took almost a thousand years for a worthy dhampir to be born.

I just wish it wasn't her.

Anyone but her.

Because now it's not only magic I've broken, but my daughter's heart too.

CHAPTER 37

OCTAVIA

When the darkness ebbs away, the three of us: Mother, Sadie and I, are stood around a long thin table, the shadowy ghosts of two families sat on either side. The room is dim, lit by the golden glow of fire lamps and warmed by the fibrous hate riddled in the expressions of angry elders.

It's Mother who gasps first.

"Mum?" Cordelia breathes, as she steps close to the apparition of what once was. Her hand glides through her mother's image.

"It's not real," I whisper.

Sadie claps, both Mother and I startle as she signs. "This is the memory of what was." Her hand darts to her belly, holding it as if...

Pins and needles trickle into my fingers as a woman, startlingly similar to Sadie, walks into the room, her belly rounded and full. The way she winces and her belly tightens, she must be having Braxton hicks. She's ready to give birth.

Sadie glides across the room, standing side by side to the ghostly woman.

Fuck me.

They aren't just similar. They are identical, save the long, flowing dark hair the ghost has. Our Sadie's hair is white as milk, and she wears scorn like a fashion item. This vision of her is so pure, her features soft and light where our Sadie is sharp and cold. If they weren't side by side, I wouldn't recognise them for who they are...

"Oh, gods," I whisper, my eyes squeezing shut, a heaviness settling in my core. The room swims, my head dizzy as all the pieces slam together.

A thousand years.

"You," Cordelia snarls.

"Me," Sadie signs.

"This whole time...?" Mother says.

I lean on my knees and retch but nothing comes up, just the dry realisation that my mother was always here.

"Why?" I cough out.

Really, I mean so much more. Why the fuck wouldn't you tell me? Why would you keep this secret the whole fucking time? My mind washes back to all our interactions. The way she would scald me. The kisses to my forehead.

So lovely.

So fucking motherly.

The way we connected, different than Xavier and I or any of my other siblings. The way she only ever took interest in me. The fact she was always in the church, *her* church. She made herself into a fucking deity.

How the hell didn't I see it?

I gaze at her in a new light: our eyes are the same shape,

our thick hair and height. But her skin is pale where mine is tanned, an earthy bronze I must have gotten from my father, and she is svelte where I curve.

"I'm sorry," she signs. "But I had no choice. I had to get here, to this moment. To fix what I broke. That was the bargain I struck with my gods."

"YOU COULD HAVE TOLD ME," I shriek.

She shakes her head, her eyes welling. "I only got to live if I unmade the monster I created." Her eyes dart to Cordelia, who is still gawping at the shadowy figures of her long-lost family.

"You knew how much I wanted to find out who my mother was. A thousand years you could have had a relationship with me, and you chose what...? What the fuck even is this? Some millennium-old vendetta?"

I gesture at the table, the arguments clearly happening between who I now know to be the Randalls and the St Clairs.

Cordelia's mother steps up and hands the ghostly version of Sadie a blade. Another woman bearing the same ocean blue eyes as Eleanor hands her a contract. Ghost-Sadie draws the blade down her palm and dips a quill in the blood, signing her name.

Isabella Sadie Montague.

Each letter is another blow. Mother and I both gawp as ghost-Sadie signs her name. Then, together, our eyes draw up from the contract and focus on present-day Sadie.

The room shudders, the apparition fading. Mother is breathing hard, her eyes darting from Sadie to me and back again.

The last vestiges of the memory evaporate, leaving the space bare save for the table and three items on it.

A grimoire and two vials.

"The cure," Mother whispers.

"It's time," Sadie signs. "In order for magic to return, *you* must be unmade," she gestures at Cordelia.

"NO," I bark. It's so loud and so sudden that Sadie startles. I slide in front of Cordelia, ready to fight.

My jaw grinds as I glower at Sadie... my fucking birth mother. Those words will never get easier.

"You don't get to unmake her. You may have wanted me, *Sadie*," I snarl. "But Cordelia was the one who actually looked after me all these years. She may not have been the best mother, but she was *a mother*. You don't get to take her from me when you already took yourself."

A tear falls down Sadie's cheek. "I tried to protect you. I prayed to the gods to protect you, to keep you safe."

"Fuck your gods," I snap and step closer to the table— to the cure.

Sadie's eyes follow my movements.

"Please," she signs. "Please step aside. I don't want you to get hu—"

Cordelia seizes her opportunity.

She crouches low and leaps onto the table, her hands outstretched for the vials. But Sadie leaps with her. The pair of them crash into the table, knocking the vials and sending them clattering to the table surface. I lunge for them, but Sadie kicks my hand out of the way, lurching to grab them as Cordelia swings an almighty punch to her jaw. Sadie's head snaps back as Cordelia's fist collides with her. But Sadie already has the vials in her hand.

She rolls off the table, three steps from the door, placing the table between us and her.

"I killed you once, I can kill you again," Cordelia shrieks.

Sadie smiles.

It's the smile of a winner.

And then she runs, vanishing into the darkness behind her.

CHAPTER 38

RED

I seem to have a penchant for dying. It's probably not an appropriate time to joke about death, but what can I say? Dark humour is an excellent coping mechanism.

The branches that punctured my veins and drew out my life force out release me as a blinding flash of light erupts from the door. I'm catapulted forward, flying through the air and crashing into the carriage Cordelia and the Chief arrived in.

My head smashes against the wheel and everything goes black.

When I wake, I'm cradled in the Chief's arms, her wrist bleeding into my mouth. With every drop that flows down my throat, my body heals. My fangs descend of their own volition as I sink my teeth into her flesh, sucking and pulling her blood until I'm gulping mouthfuls large enough to hurt when I swallow.

Somewhere in my mind part of me is begging me to stop, but my body is working on autopilot.

When the Chief pales, her lips turning blue, I manage to wrench my fangs out of her wrist, and she collapses in my arms. I brush her hair back from her face, finally able to take in the scene around us. It's devastation. Sadie's demon companions lay motionless several feet away. The door is obliterated, and in its place stands a dark, gaping maw.

It's endless darkness. As if it's sucked life, light and everything I love into it. A prickle of panic ripples over my skin as I glance around, realising Octavia, Sadie and Cordelia are gone.

"I'm sorry," the Chief says. Her words are quiet. In fact, everything is quiet now.

"I'm sorry," she says again, her hand coming to cup my cheek.

"It's okay," I reply, not really sure what she's apologising for, but realising I may have drained too much of her. She must be hallucinating or delirious.

"I never wanted you dead. You're like a daughter to me. You were so little when you joined the Academy. I'm sorry, Red."

"Why did you do it?" I ask.

She closes her eyes, squeezing her lips shut. When she finally opens her eyes, they're bright and glassy. "I needed the dhampir to get the cure. I wanted to be rid of vampires so much, that for a while I believed that's what Cordelia and I were doing..."

The words hang in the air as I churn over everything I know.

"It was never the cure for vampirism was it...?"

"No. It's the cure for us. Cordelia and I. The antidote to the spell used to curse us."

"Fuck, but what about Octavia?" I say, trying to pull myself upright. "What the hell happens if it gets out? It could unmake her..." Blood rushes into my ears, nausea roils in my gut at the prospect of Octavia being unmade.

The Chief grips my chin and tilts it down to face her. "I don't think she will be affected; she was born not made."

"You don't think? *Think* is too much of a risk to take," I snarl, trying to lay her down and haul myself up. But she grips me hard.

"Why do you think I was trying to get the fucking cure? I want it destroyed. We... we don't want to go back." Her breathing is stilted and uneven.

"Then why not let the door go? Just let it destroy itself when no one opened it?"

"Because we knew someone else was trying to get it. This whole time, we thought it was some unknown quantity..."

"But it wasn't...?" I ask.

She shakes her head at me, her eyes rolling shut momentarily. "I didn't realise until we were here. But Sadie... she tried to use vials of your blood first. She only came for you when the vials weren't enough. That didn't make sense. Why would she do that if she wanted to win so badly? It was almost as if she were..." the words on her lips fail. But it all slots together.

"...as if she were protecting me," I whisper.

The Chief nods. "Or maybe she wasn't protecting *you* so much as the thing Octavia loves..."

My body goes cold. "Shit. Which means Sadie is—" my words are cut off by a shadowy figure looming over us.

"...The actual Mother of Blood," Sadie signs.

I flinch as I meet her gaze. If Sadie is the Mother of Blood... then, she's also Octavia's birth mother.

"I'm not going to hurt you, Red. I'm not here for you," she signs.

Her eyes slide to the Chief, who tenses in my arms.

"You're here to unmake me?" the Chief asks.

"In a way. It will make you to what you were, what you always should have been. Releasing your curse is the only way to return the magic the curse stole to the world."

The Chief scrambles out of my arms. It takes her a moment before she hauls herself standing. How she's managed it, I'm not sure. She stumbles, staggers sideways and slams into the carriage. Using the wheel to steady herself, she shakes her head. "No."

Sadie's lips press thin. "I know you don't want this. That's part of the curse, but when it's over, you will thank me."

"Over my dead body," she snarls and draws a stake, but it hangs limp in her hand.

Sadie sighs. "You don't have a choice. Don't make me hurt you..." Sadie's fangs descend, but I've already drained the Chief of a critical amount of blood. If Sadie bites her, she'll kill her for certain.

Even after everything that's happened, I don't want the Chief to die.

"Eleanor, don't..." I say, but her eyes are zeroed in on Sadie. She releases the wheel and staggers forward. This is ridiculous. I stride over, but Sadie speeds in front of me.

The Chief's eyes widen.

Sadie draws a blade in one hand and holds a vial in the other. She feints and veers towards me, blade extended.

I drive my arm up in a defensive block. But it's too late. The Chief uses the last of her strength to hurl herself in front of me, knocking me out of the way.

Sadie feints again.

I slip on a brick pebble, lose my balance and crash to the

floor. Gods, I'm exhausted, every inch of muscle aches and screams, but I pull myself up and over to them.

Sadie and the Chief are a tangle of limbs. There's no way to get between them. Despite her exhaustion, the Chief lashes out in a vicious blow. But Sadie is neither exhausted nor injured, so she dodges out of the way and throws a kick out, knocking the Chief off her feet.

It's pathetic, like Sadie's kicking a haggard old dog, and despite everything the Chief has put me through, I feel sorry for her.

Sadie elbows the Chief. Her head ricochets off the ground and then she goes still. I should reach out, stop her. Do anything I can. But I wonder if Sadie is right? I had to give myself to the door. The city does need magic.

But it's the Chief and Cordelia who are paying the price. Or maybe they paid the price for a thousand years.

I can't move, can't seem to bring myself to fight Sadie. She unstoppers the vial, grips the Chief's jaw and pries her mouth open. The liquid flows in, one long dark stream. Sadie closes the Chief's mouth and rubs her throat like she's trying to make a cat swallow a pill.

Eleanor's skin ripples, shifting from ghostly white to a deep red and fading back again. Her body seizes, trembling and shaking as thick ribbons of magic peel from her. They flow like golden threads and silken snakes from her body. The ribbons soar through the air and then plunge into the earth. Some zip off into the distance, two circle the demons and plunge into their chests. They shiver and tremble, their skin shimmering golden. One of them loses their wings, the other convulses and then settles as his skin turns pink. I frown as I realise he is human, or he was. Not just human. My mouth hangs open as I recognise the symbol hanging from the necklace he wears. Concentric circles and strikethroughs surrounding an M. Just like in Sadie's office, the same symbol on the family tree. He's a Montague. Sadie's family.

The leathery demon's skin flakes from his body, revealing flesh. This one though, looks like a monk, the cloak returning to its deep red colour. Gods.

The ground around us trembles. The Chief's body shivers as something intangible shifts in her complexion. An aged hardness finally softening. As if a thousand years are falling off her, shedding the hate, the rage, the wars. All of it melting into the air as the curse is finally lifted from her.

She lays still. I nudge Sadie out of the way and press my fingers to her throat. Her heart beats steady, though she's still unconscious.

"I had to," Sadie signs at me.

"Did you, though?"

She gives me a sad smile and then rounds on the void as Cordelia and Octavia step through.

CHAPTER 39

OCTAVIA

Sadie is my mother.
Sadie is my mother.

The words ring over and over in my mind. Mother—Cordelia—is already marching for the gloomy doorway. I speed to meet her, grabbing her wrist and pulling her to a halt.

"Did you know?" I growl.

"No," she snaps and wrenches her arm from mine.

I tilt my head to examine her expression, searching for deception. "When I asked you in your mansion foyer... was it all a lie?"

Mother's shoulders sag. "No, Octavia. The only lie I ever kept from you, was what I did to her. But I swear to you, it wasn't done with the intention of hurting you. I was mid-transition. Beside myself with hunger. All I could think of was blood and revenge. She had cursed me, broken me and turned me into this..." She gestures at herself and then tears her gaze away from me.

"I didn't even know you existed until after. It was only when she muttered your name as she lay dying in her kitchen that I spotted you in a crib."

Everything she's saying correlates with the vision the Mother of Blood gave me in the trial.

The Mother of Blood? I scoff mentally. The vision my own mother gave me.

Of course, Sadie won that trial. How could she even participate? It was her own blood she took. Her own fucking memories she was sharing. Gods. She literally gave me the vision of what Cordelia did to her. She was trying to tell me this whole time. She was right under our noses, and I was too wrapped up in my own bullshit to notice.

"I don't want to take the cure, Octavia. Please? Please help me," Mother says.

I narrow my eyes at her.

"Give me the city."

"What?" she says and steps back.

I wave my hand. "This whole competition, the trials. They were smoke and mirrors and bullshit so you could get to the cure first and prevent yourself from being turned mortal. Right?"

She purses her lips, staring hard at me and then slowly nods. "Yes."

"You were never going to give up the city, were you?"

"I'm sorry," she says, there's a hint of desperation in her tone. "Octavia, please. You don't understand. I can't go back to who I was. It disgusts me. I... we... Eleanor and I..."

"I know about you and Eleanor."

"Please. As your mother, I'm asking you to help me..."

My eyes narrow. "But you're not my mother, are you? She is." I point my finger to the blackness where Sadie vanished.

335

Cordelia's hand swings out and slaps me across the cheek. I'm so startled it makes my eyes water. Cordelia brings her hand to her mouth, stifling a gasp.

I want to take the words back, stop her recoiling away from me, but nothing comes out.

Instead, she shakes her head. "I'm so sorry. I didn't mean to. But... how could you say that? I chose you, Octavia. For a thousand years, I've chosen to be your mother every single day. I may not have birthed you, but you are mine..."

Her words crumble and she slumps to her knees, a sob ripping from her chest as she mumbles, "*I chose you, Octavia. I chose you.*" Over and over.

A painful knot cinches around my ribs, tightening my chest. But I can't help her without understanding the thing that's held me back from her for so long.

"I need to know something," I say.

She looks up, her face aged and wrinkled the way only a child can do to a parent.

"Why did you take me? That day in the cottage, when you drained Sadie."

"I am sorry for what I did to her. I was... it was the transition."

I place my hand on her arm. "I know. I've witnessed enough vampires transitioning to understand that it's not really a choice. Sadie was in the wrong place at the wrong time. It was never about that. I wasn't angry with you for draining her. What I hated was that you kept it secret. And I suppose I've always wanted to know why you didn't just leave me."

Her lips press together. She brings her hand to the cheek she slapped; this time her touch is a caress.

"Because I fell in love. I knew the moment I saw you

that you were my baby. In the moment, I was distraught and thought I was a monster. There was no one to explain what was happening to me. But you... you I understood. You were like me, and when I couldn't see the beauty in me, I saw it in you. So, I took you because you were beautiful, and I was in love, and I needed to keep you safe."

"You chose me..." I whisper.

She nods and I think I finally get it.

She's right.

She did choose me.

Sadie didn't. Sadie had a thousand years to find me and tell me the truth. Hell. She had two hundred and fifty in our family. And instead of being a mother, she pretended to be my sister. So many dinners, so many meetings, and she could have told me who she was.

She chose vengeance over love.

I kneel next to Cordelia and wrap my arms around her. She sobs into my shoulder. "I know I was cruel at times. I know I was hard, but I tried my best. And I always loved you, my darling. *Always*."

There comes a moment in every mother-daughter relationship where a line is drawn. A separation of sorts.

A moment where the daughter must let go and live her own life. It's not that she no longer loves her mother, but that she chooses to love herself. She must stop abiding by the rules of the matriarch and instead form her own.

This is my moment, the one where I choose to create my own life, born from the one my mother gave me; not the mother who birthed me, but the one who raised me.

I lean down and kiss the top of her head. "I love you too."

"You do?" she says into my shoulder.

"Of course. But..."

She disengages, her eyes furrowed as she looks up at me, waiting.

"But if you want me to help, you need to step aside. It's time, Mother. Give me the city..."

She pulls back and locks eyes with me. So much passing between us.

A war of sorts.

A lifetime of love.

Cordelia's expression flickers, her eyes drawn, jaw locked, brow furrowed as tears streak her cheeks. So many emotions as she realises I will always be her daughter, but I am no longer her child. Her body trembles as she lowers her eyes, knowing that this is it, the culmination. A moment between mother and daughter, a choice: me or the city. Me or the cure.

"Okay," she says. "Sangui is yours. It was always yours. I won't lie to you, I love this city and want to keep it for myself. But will I give it up to keep you? Always."

And that's when the realisation hits so much deeper. She *is* my mother not just because she chose me, but because she continues to choose me, even now when I ask for the thing she loves more than anything. Although, I suppose that's not really right, is it? The thing she loves most is us. Her children.

"Come on," I say and give her my hand, pulling her upright and choosing her right back.

And together we step through the darkness and back into the world.

CHAPTER 40

OCTAVIA

Morning is coming. Darkness ebbs away, the sky a liquid navy rather than the pitch of midnight; we don't have long. The monks that circle the courtyard sing louder, their hummed mantra a bittersweet melody. Their bodies rock back and forth faster as if they too know time is running out.

Sadie's face snaps to ours, her eyes dropping to where I hold Cordelia's hand. Her expression narrows, her lip curling. I spot Red and Eleanor beside the carriage. Red's alive. I gasp, my heart nearly explodes in my chest. Thank the gods. Eleanor's wrist is mangled, blood oozing from it. She fed Red?

Red stands, her fists balled, bouncing on her tiptoes, ready to launch.

"No," I mouth at her.

No fucking way is she risking herself again.

This is for us to deal with. We have to finish this, and I don't want her hurt.

"Please don't," I mouth.

Her brows tighten. "But . . .?"

But I shake my head. She raises her hands, palm up, signalling obedience as Cordelia drops my hand and runs straight for Sadie.

They smash together, fists flying, arms blocking. I dart to them, trying to force my way between their bodies. But someone, Sadie I think, shoves me back. I go stumbling and trip over a boulder and land on my arse. If I never see another brick or boulder, it will be too soon.

Cordelia swings out, landing blow after blow on Sadie. But Sadie is quick and light on her feet, almost dancing across the broken boulders and dusty gravel. She bounces this way and that, dodging and blocking. Cordelia slows, dropping her guard for a split second. Sadie capitalises on the gap, throwing her fist into the space and smashing into Cordelia's chest.

She's propelled back, stunned, wobbling on her feet.

Sadie lunges for her, but Cordelia has enough sense to kick out, knocking Sadie down. Both women are relentless, neither giving an inch. I have to end this. I leap up as Sadie lands a brutal kick to Cordelia's stomach.

Cordelia is flung backwards, careening into the carriage. It shatters around her and she collapses to the ground, scarcely missing Red and Eleanor.

Red helps Cordelia upright as Sadie stalks towards them.

I'm up, running and leaping through the air. My hands slide around Sadie's neck and lock in. I yank her back and drag her away, her heels kicking against the ground.

"Do not make me hurt you," I snarl.

Her hands come up, but all the signs are backwards

because her spine is against my chest. It takes me a moment to understand what she's saying.

"This has to happen."

"No, it doesn't, Sadie. Or should I call you Mum?"

She stiffens in my grip.

"I always loved you," she signs.

"Don't," I spit. But her words cut so deep that I've already hesitated. She—unlike me—doesn't.

She wrenches forward, pulling me up and flinging me forward until I flip over her back and thump to the ground. Her eyes widen, a flash of horror sweeping through her expression. But just like she has for the last thousand years, she chooses to pursue Cordelia instead of helping me up.

Cordelia stumbles away from the carriage, away from Red, her eyes meeting mine. A shared look, a knowing—do not jeopardise Red anymore. She's done enough.

Mother is bleeding, several enormous splinters of wood sticking out from various limbs.

She hobbles further and further away from Red. Sadie prowls closer and closer.

Cordelia stumbles and grinds to a halt as her back hits the ruined archway. Sadie, eyes focused solely on Cordelia, doesn't notice Red flinging me a broken shaft of wood—a makeshift stake.

I don't want to do this. I don't *want* to kill my birth mother. I want to know her, understand who she is, why she made the choices she did. But I also won't let her take the one mother I did have away from me.

Sadie pins Mother against the archway, her eyes boring into Cordelia's, saying everything her hands aren't.

"Open. Your. Mouth."

Cordelia strains against her. Shaking her head. Pressing

her lips shut tight. Sadie's fingers coil around Cordelia's neck. Her other hand, clutching the vial, pins her nose shut.

I step up to Sadie, the makeshift stake hovering over the spot on her back where her heart is. One shove with the stake would pierce her heart and end this all.

"Don't make me do this..." I plead. "She's my mother."

Sadie's head wrenches around, mouthing the words. "So am I," at me.

She holds my gaze, pleading, the strain carving lines into her features.

Time slows, my throat thick with indecision. Cordelia's eyes meet mine, both mothers pleading. The only thing I can hear is the roar of blood in my ears and the heavy breathing of all three of us. Both of their expressions coat my skin in guilt, fill the air with a bitter taste.

Her eyebrows pull up, pleading.

"Please, *Mum*," I whisper, my words full of desperation.

Sadie's eyes fall shut, her lips pursing as a single tear falls in a crystal river down her skin.

But she doesn't relent.

She's made her choice.

And so have I.

The stake bites into her back. I push the wood into her flesh, a scratch, a warning.

A second tear falls as she mouths, "I'm sorry."

Time swirls in odd patterns. Everything happening simultaneously, and ever so slowly, as if Sadie's last gift from the gods was a moment more with me. A moment where we should have lived an entire lifetime. Of dinners and picnics, of gifts on the holidays, and hugs beneath winter clouds and a thousand swapped stories filled with love and laughter.

But instead, the moment is filled with a bitter gaze held and the taste of a million regrets.

Everything rushes back as her head turns to Cordelia.

There's no hesitation. I shove the stake as hard as I can through Sadie's back and pierce her heart.

But I'm too late. She pulls Cordelia off the arch so quickly by her neck that the shock makes Mother open her mouth. Sadie shoves the vial into Cordelia's mouth and the force of her hitting the arch from me striking Sadie makes her jaw slam shut, shattering the glass and releasing the cure in her mouth.

The three of us stare at each other.

Three beats.

Three long seconds.

Three broken hearts.

Sadie falls first, dropping into my arms. Her hand comes to my cheek, caressing, her thumb wiping away the tears I didn't know were falling.

She smiles, and this time, it's the smile of a mother, soft eyes and warm skin. Pride etched in her brow and the tug of her cheeks.

"What have I done?" I say as I cradle her in my arms. But she's already fading. Her skin turning grey, mottled with veins. She brings her fingers up and signs two words.

"My Octavia."

And then her hands fall to her sides, her eyes dim and her body goes limp in my arms.

I lay her down, her skin already desiccating. She is lost to me, but there's no time to process. I go to Cordelia. She's spat the glass and cure on the ground.

But she's already changing.

She falls onto her hands and knees and then collapses on her side, her body writhing as the cure seeps into her system. Golden ribbons peel away from her like snakes and ribbons and rivers made of gems. The ground trembles, and cracks appear in the archway.

Shit.

I slide my arms under her and haul her back.

"Red, we have to move," I shout, glancing at the carriage, which has been obliterated. Our cover gone.

But Red's already seen what's happening and is pulling Eleanor away. More and more threads peel from Cordelia's body as I drag her away. The same threads, I realise, that are coming from Eleanor's. The ground rumbles harder, thundering with noise that finally makes the monks move. They scatter as what's left of the doorway screams.

It fractures and cracks.

I want to hold my hands over my ears, but I need to keep pulling us away.

The threads peeling off Mother and Eleanor spool and spin and swirl. Coalescing as if they are two halves of one magic. But of course, that's exactly what it is: the two halves of one curse.

"I think it's going to blow," Red bellows over the roaring noise.

The ribbons form a swelling orb, one that grows larger and larger with each passing second. Brighter and brighter it glows until it stings my eyes to look at and swallows everything in its path.

"Over there," I shout, my words lost in the wind. I point to a stone outhouse that still has a roof. The door is no longer, but there's enough porch that I'll be able to hide in the shadows if the sun rises before we get out of here. The monks have vanished up the paths and out of the courtyard. We're on our own.

I hoist Cordelia onto my back, her body still trembling,

magic still unfurling from her, and I sprint across the court-yard. Red sees what I'm doing and follows suit, though Eleanor is a little heavier than Mother and it takes her two attempts to get her on her back.

We sprint and dive into an outhouse. Red places Eleanor down, her eyes open, her face radiant with a wide smile.

"Cordelia?" she says, reaching for her hand.

Mother, barely conscious opens her eyes. "Eleanor?"

Despite the pain she's clearly in, her face lights up. I've never seen her smile like that, like she found her missing piece. Like Eleanor is summer sun and winter warmth and all the seasons in between. She smiles like she'd waited a thousand years to hear her name on those lips. And as she smiles, all the hard edges and coldness I knew evaporates away. Mother looks at Eleanor for who she is.

Her soulmate. The woman she's loved for a thousand years, and I suspect will for a thousand more.

They reach for each other, their fingertips brushing as their eyes flutter shut. Together, finally.

My fingers slip to Mother's neck. There's a beat. Thank gods. Red nods, indicating Eleanor still breathes. She raises her arm, covering her eyes as the swollen orb outside trembles.

The four of us huddle together in the corner of this run-down outhouse as the final threads of magic peel off Mother and Eleanor.

The orb expands, swelling like a bloated star.

And then it explodes.

And the whole world turns white.

CHAPTER 41

CORDELIA

Two Weeks After

I wake to thick arms wrapped around me. Warm, secure, familiar. Arms that I knew in a past life, one lost to memory for so long it became myth. I roll over and snuggle against Eleanor. *My Eleanor.*

We made it.

"Good morning," she says and kisses the top of my forehead.

"I really don't like being a middle-aged human," I say.

She laughs. "It's the aches, right?"

"Gods, it's awful. I think I slept funny and my neck hurts."

Eleanor's deep, ocean-coloured eyes smile at me and nudge me onto my front. I do as I'm bid, and she slides her hands to my neck, kneading and rubbing at my sore joints. A strangled moaning sound pours from my throat, the kind that only comes from the deliciousness and brutality of a muscular knot being massaged.

"You carry on making noises like that, and we'll never make it out of this city," she says, pummelling my shoulders.

I roll over onto my back and tug her onto my lap.

"Fuck me," I say and grab her throat, pulling her down to me. She presses her lips to mine in a bruising kiss. Tongues and lips and nibbles. Our hands pulling at each other's night clothes. My body reacting to hers, the same way it did a millennium ago.

My nipples harden, my core grows wet as she slides her hands under my clothes and over my body, stripping me naked.

I tug my hand through her curly locks, always so unruly in the mornings. Just the way I remember.

"Gods, I've waited so long for this... for you," I say against her mouth.

I peel her clothes off until we're both naked, thick bodies, soft stomachs, wet cores. This is not the firm suppleness of our twenties, but I don't care. I get one life with her after a dozen hating her. I'll take her however I can get her. And I'll keep taking her until we're old and wrinkled with memories. Until love has aged our skin and greyed our hair.

My tongue skitters over my lips as I take in my beautiful Eleanor. Finally mine.

I drag my eyes down her body to where she straddles me. I'm desperate to taste her. I want to beg, to plead with her to let me lick her the way I have every day, multiple times a day for the last week. It's been two since the curse lifted. It took us one week to heal and recover enough that we could get out of bed. The harsh reality of humanity and mortality has settled down on us once again.

And this last week . . . well, we've barely left the bedroom, a millennium to make up for.

Eleanor's hands wrap around my throat, her thumb caresses the divot between my collarbones. One little slip and she could cut my air supply off.

How surreal, that barely more than fourteen days ago she would have, gladly. She'd have given the entire Academy to choke me, stake me, just put an end to me. But now, as one thumb caresses my throat, the other reaches down behind her to find my slit. An ache blooms between my legs. She knows it too and presses her thumb a fraction harder.

I gasp, squeezing my thighs against her hand, stopping her from touching me. She tilts my chin up, dragging my eyes away from her cunt to meet her own.

"You're going to be the good girl I remember, Cordelia. Do you understand? You're going to do exactly as I tell you."

She climbs off me and hitches her way to the end of the bed.

"Spread your legs, I want to look at you. See again what I've waited a thousand years for."

I do as I'm told, my cheeks flushing at how exposed I am. How filthy I feel. Suddenly I'm not forty, I'm in my twenties, and innocent. Letting her corrupt me for the first time in that stone pavilion all over again.

"Wider," she demands. "I want to see all of you."

I spread my legs wider, barely able to breathe. Naked. Exposed. On display for her. I'm so excited anticipating her touch, her mouth on me, that wetness cools on my folds, making my core extra sensitive. A thousand years I've spent fucking my way around this city, and no one has ever made me feel the way she does. No one ever stole my heart the way she did.

"I think you like doing as you're told. I think you want me to do exactly as I please with you..." it's that same tone she uses in the Academy. Authoritative, demanding, controlling. I used to hate it, but that was just the curse. Now I crave it, obsess over it, yearn to hear her use it on me.

"Gods, yes, Use me. Fuck me. Never leave me again."

She runs a finger over my apex, the little bud already swollen with arousal. I shiver, the pressure sending a pulse around my body.

She takes her finger to her mouth and sucks on it.

"Eleanor..." I gasp.

"It's mine. I earned it. I'll do with it what I please. And what I please, *Cordelia*, is to fuck you until you can't walk. Make you come so much I drown in you. And then I'm taking you from this city and we are leaving for good."

That was the agreement. The first night after we were cured. We both knew we had to leave. Not just to give my darling Octavia a chance at leading, but because we are done here. This city has hated us; it tore us apart for a thousand years and we want a chance at something new.

A millennium ago, Eleanor was going to take me to Finis, an Academy in Ora city, located on the furthest edge of our realm. Back then, she had connections there. We decided that we still want to do that. Though it's me that has the connections now. I know the family that has run Finis Academy since its inception. I reached out and arranged for Eleanor to take a teaching role in the subject of witch magic. For now, I will study with the aim of eventually teaching there too. It's the fresh start we both need. To go somewhere neither of us are known. No history, no family, just us to make the most of however long we have left together.

Eleanor slides between my thighs, her hands curving over my legs and clutching so tight I know I'm going to be marred with prints. That thought makes me even hotter. The image of my skin mottled with bruises shaped like her fingers.

Gods, I've waited so long for this. To be free to let her touch me, hold me, mark me.

Her tongue slips between my folds, stroking top to bottom. She glides her long tongue inside me, lapping up every drop of wetness she can.

I lie back, my head resting against the pillow as waves of pleasure quiver out from my core. Her tongue does things to me that should be illegal. My hands grip the sheets, balling them in my fists as my back arches off the bed. She places a hand against my stomach forcing me back down, and then slides it between my legs to my entrance.

Her thick fingers push inside me, deliciously tight against my walls. I moan at the feeling of being filled by her.

"Touch yourself," I pant, and my cheeks flush at the words. She makes me feel young and innocent. She makes me feel like I'll live forever. Even if forever is only the next forty years.

I will gladly take one life of loving each other rather than a dozen more hating.

Her fingers curl up inside me, pressing against that exquisite spot that turns my legs to jelly.

She sucks my apex into her mouth, flicking her hard tongue against the bud and I melt against her.

"Eleanor, please. Touch yourself, I want to watch you," I moan.

I feel her hesitate, but then she slides her free hand between her thighs. The sight is exquisite. As she ravishes pleasure over my core, her own eyes melt with the first flush of orgasm in her own body.

She worships me, her tongue running relentless over my clit, hard and soft, the rhythmic lapping in time with her fingers gliding into my body. I'm swearing and cursing and crying out her name.

My body clenches and releases around her fingers as I reach the peak. For one fleeting second, I'm utterly blinded by bliss. My nipples tighten, and I rock and jerk against her mouth as my body comes apart for her.

Eventually, I come back to earth. But she is enjoying herself too much, using me to finish herself off. She moans as she licks and laps up my excitement. But I'm so sensitive, I twitch with every flick of her tongue.

"Eleanor," I whine.

"So close," she pants.

I wriggle out of her grip, and she groans as her orgasm abates. But I'm not worried, I grin at her.

"You're going to have to make up for edging me like that," she grumbles.

"I happen to have something right here I've been dying to use on you..."

"Not so innocent and sweet anymore, are you?" she smirks.

"There are a lot more toys these days. Back in our day, we only had fingers and mouths..."

Eleanor cocks an eyebrow at me and folds her arm, resting her head on her hand so she can lie facing me. "We did okay with them."

I hop off the bed and open a drawer, pulling the strap-on and harness out. "Get on your back," I say, taking control of the situation.

"Make me..." Her eyes glimmer, teasing, tempting, daring me to take charge. I grab her by the ankles and yank her down the bed. She laughs, so unused to being the one on her back, or being told what to do.

"You might tell all your students what to do, but I'm in control now."

A smile splits her face, her eyes glistening in the morning light. Fuck, she's beautiful. The softness of her skin, the faint lines tracing the corners of her eyes, her flowing curls all springy and fluffy against the sheets. I want to cry, because this was all I ever wanted. Tears sting my eyes, but I don't want to let them go and ruin the moment. "I'm so grateful we can be together again. For Sadie's sacrifice, making us take the cure even though we did everything we could not to."

"As am I... all those years... and we still love each other," she says and leans up to brush my hair behind my ears.

"All those years and we didn't give up." I kiss her hard and fast and shove her back down. She giggles as her back hits the bed. I push her legs up and lower my head between them.

My tongue finds her slit and licks from her entrance to her apex. Fuck, she tastes good. I don't think I'll ever get bored of her, or her taste, her scent. I've waited far too long. The sweetness, the hint of tang, the way she feels against my tongue, soft and swelling and soaking wet. I'd live another thousand years just to taste her one more time. She is glorious.

I stroke my tongue up and down, over and over until she's panting and her fingers find their way into my hair. But I'm not done, I want to fuck her.

I stand up and notch the cock at her entrance. "Is this okay?" I ask, and she nods.

"Everything you do is okay, Cordelia. If we never left this room, it would still be too soon."

I slide the cock in an inch, and her fingers grip the pillow under her head. She's tight and it takes me a moment to slowly push my way inside her.

"You need to relax," I say while my finger strokes her clit. I circle and rub until she relaxes and opens for me.

"Oh gods," she moans. "It's a lot."

"Mmm," I moan, heat simmering between my own legs. I've wanted to do this for so long. I drag the cock out of her, slowly, watching the way her body responds. How her nipples tighten, her mouth parts. I lift her bum from the bed, tilting her up. She moves her feet so she can hold herself there and then I thrust.

"Fuck," she cries out, and my eyes narrow, pure, unadulterated lust melting in my gaze. I hit her G-spot. I thrust again. Eleanor's mouth parts and I swear that look of ecstasy on her face is enough to make me orgasm.

My fingers stay on her clit, rubbing and circling, as I thrust in and out of her, over and over until she's panting my name.

"Eleanor..." I whisper.

She opens her eyes, and I wish I could drink this moment in forever. Her and me, our bodies gliding together. Her breasts move with my rhythm, her soft belly a tease I want to bite and suck. She's everything.

"I'm close," she whispers.

"Look at me when you come. I want to see you."

She bites her lip. "Faster, I need more."

I give her exactly what she asks for, thrusting harder,

faster, rougher. Her mouth drops open as I flick my fingers faster over her sensitive, hardening clit.

Her eyes draw closed, so I bring my hand beneath us and up to her arse, slapping hard enough it shocks her eyes open again.

"I said, eyes on me when you come."

"Fuck. Do it again," she whimpers.

So I slap her arse harder.

"Oh gods, more."

Again. Again. Again.

She grabs my rear and pulls me deeper into her, making me grind so deep I'm worried I'll hurt her. But she's unleashed something, a wild passion grips her gaze as she bites her bottom lip and a groan spills from her lips. She moves my fingers and rubs herself while I use the additional support to anchor myself and thrust into her harder and faster.

"Yes," she cries as her eyes find mine, and I know this is when she tips over the edge. Her mouth spills something obscene as she shivers, her pussy clenching and releasing around the cock until finally, she sinks to rest on the bed, a sheen of sweat glistening on her skin.

"I told you it was worth it," I purr, quietly delighted with the orgasm I gave her.

Dusk has fallen by the time we're packed and the carriage is loaded with our belongings. We're only taking a couple of suitcases. Neither of us have left the city for the last thousand years. While we're both desperate to leave, we also recognise we will miss this place. So we're not taking everything we own until we're certain that we're staying at Finis Academy.

My children all greet us by the carriage. The cure, it seems, only affected Eleanor and me. We had wondered whether it would undo the hunters' instincts and strength and return the vampires to their human forms. But it seems that the returned magic has accepted the balance that exists. The hunters now have their witch magic back and the vampires still exist. Perhaps enough of each species will survive to keep each other in line for another thousand years.

Eleanor and I don't have that luxury any longer; we need to live the years we have to their fullest extent. Gabriel is the first to say goodbye. His blood-red suit is crisp perfection this evening, a black tie cinched up to his neck.

"Going somewhere fancy?" I ask.

"I met a guy in the library," he says. "But I'm not sure it's more than a date or two. We'll see."

"That's my boy." I kiss both his cheeks. "I'd like it if you came and visited. I'm told there's an enormous library at the Academy, I think you'd like it."

"Sounds like a dream, I'll let you get settled and then organise a visit." He smiles and sidles out of the way to make room for Dahlia, slipping a book out of his pocket.

The air becomes tense. Dahlia's out of place now that Octavia has taken over. She doesn't want to work for her after everything that happened, but she doesn't particularly want to leave her home city, either. I want to meddle, the mother in me is desperate to help them resolve their differences. But I suppose I need to back out of it. I've meddled enough over the years.

"Don't go," Dahlia breathes into my neck as she throws her arms around me.

"I have to," I whisper back. "You'll be fine. Just find a nice girl, marry her and live a quiet life. Or open a fighting club, go on an adventure, you're free to live the way you want."

"I liked being a general," she sighs into my neck.

"Then make peace with your sister, Dahlia. You have choices. Go figure it out." I kiss her cheek and nudge her away.

Xavier steps up and smiles as he looks down at me. "My handsome boy."

He picks my hand up and dips into a bow as he kisses the back of my hand. "Mother." Ever the gentleman.

"Keep Octavia out of trouble," I say.

"I'll do my best." He grins and makes way for Octavia.

Even after just a week, she carries herself differently. She holds her head high, her rich crimson eyes bright even in the evening light. Her shoulders are back, and she walks with the air of a leader, a queen. Gods, she will do this city proud. I can't wait to come back in a year or two and see what's she's made of it.

She wraps her arms around me.

"I'm so proud of you," I say, "and I'm so sorry for..."

What I want to say is for everything. For not telling her about what I did to Isabella, or I should call her Sadie, I suppose. I want to apologise for stealing her away, for killing her birth mother in the first place.

"Don't say it. You are my mother. You always will be because you chose me. Sure, we did shit things, but so does every family. I love you. And I hope that Ora City and Finis Academy are everything you need them to be."

I pull her into my arms, tears leaking out of my eyes.

Part of me wants to stay and watch what becomes of the city, but the other part of me knows I need to leave and let her prosper. Perhaps, strange as it is, leaving is the first truly selfless act I've done as her mother.

She squeezes my hand and then steps back, allowing Red and Eleanor to say their own goodbyes. When they part, Eleanor slides her hand into mine and we step into the carriage.

We leave in silence, keeping the carriage curtain open a long time. Long after my children are nothing but specs of dust through the glass and we have to strain to see the castle through the darkness of night.

But eventually, when the only light we have are stars in a blanket of inky sky, Eleanor draws the curtain shut and takes my hand.

"Are you ready?" she asks.

"Ready?"

"Once upon a time, you were supposed to marry to make your mother *happy*."

I laugh and laugh and laugh.

And then I curl into her arms, and we stay entwined, knowing we won and that Eleanor is finally mine to keep.

CHAPTER 42

RED

One Month Later

I open my desk drawer and stare at the little square box. Nestled inside it is a coffin-cut ruby the colour of Octavia's eyes. I bought it off a merchant who travelled in from another city. I'm going to have it designed into a ring.

Not yet. Not today. But I will. When the changes calm down and things are settled in the Academy, I'm going to ask her to be my wife.

"Hey," Lincoln says from the doorway.

I startle and slam the drawer shut. He strolls in, cocky as ever. He healed up just fine once the medics got to him, and now he's working as my head of staff.

"A little jumpy for first thing on a Tuesday, aren't we?" He grins.

"Oh, pipe down. What news do you have?"

I swing out from behind the Chief's desk. Sorry, *my* desk. I'm still getting used to that. But The Hunter Academy wanted me back as soon as the truth of what happened came out. I couldn't, not the way it was. So, they agreed to change. Now, it's an academy of two parts: dhampir-witch training and creating a unified army whose aim is to protect the city—all the people in the city. We've broken the territories down. No more St Clair, Beaumont and Montague. It's all united. It's just: Sangui City. Octavia thought it was right, given she's technically a Montague by blood, raised a St Clair and a Beaumont in name. Now that she leads, the city needs to be at one with itself.

It's a struggle, though. We need someone to head up the army side, and the recruitment hasn't gone well in the last ten days. Granted I haven't given it my fullest attention. There's been so much work to do to reorganise the Academy, commission new buildings, source as many grimoires and texts as we could from the elders. It's been a lot. That's without helping Octavia in negotiations, her modernisation plans, tunnel re-openings. It's safe to say I'm exhausted.

Lincoln's face crumples. "Do you want the good news or the bad?"

"Start with the good," I say and tug a hand through my freshly cut hair. It's all shaved on the sides now; I figured I should have a new look for a new role. The rest of it is the same, shaggy on top. Just a little deeper undercut and a little blonder.

"Winston agreed to re-enroll and take the position of head boy."

I clap my hands in the air and let out a little whoop. "He also asked if he could come and apologise to you."

I wave him off. "He doesn't need to, I understood. I'm just glad he's coming back. Tell him I'm free this evening."

Lincoln nods and jots it down in a pad that he slides into his pocket.

"And the bad?" I ask.

His grits his teeth. "No bites on the head trainer position for the army side of the Academy."

"Shit." I slouch against the office desk. "None of this works without someone in that role."

"I know. I guess we can push the role out again on notice boards. I'll send a note to our elders to see if they have any daughters or sons who might be interested."

"Great, I'll ask Octavia the same thing about the vampire nobles, there's bound to be someone who is suitable. I just think the advertisement is getting lost in all the other city-wide communications."

Lincoln shifts on the spot, fiddling with some papers on the end of my desk.

"What? Spit it out already," I say.

"Can I knock off early today?"

I fold my arms, staring at him. "One, you are the head of staff, you don't need to ask me that. And two, why?"

"I, umm. I have a date."

I smile, broad and beaming. "Do you now."

"Oh, fuck off, Red. You don't know her. But she was one of the healers who helped me after..."

"I look forward to hearing all about your date." I can't help the mocking tone in my voice. I mean it with love though, and he knows it.

"You're such an arsehole."

"I do try," I laugh. "Go on, fuck off out of here and get your dick wet."

"You're gross. See you in the morning."

He leaves and I sit back down at my desk, pulling architect plans and funding bid papers to me. There's a soft knock at the door.

I glance up and my mouth opens.

"Dahlia? Hi. Umm... Can I help you?"

She steps inside the circular office, and then retreats back to the doorway when she realises the window blinds are open.

I get up and close them.

"Did you use the new tunnels to get here?" I ask.

She nods, and once I've closed the shutters, she steps inside the office, her eyes darting this way and that.

"I've never been to the Academy," she says.

"Well, no. It wasn't exactly a welcoming place for vampires. Everything okay?" I ask, hesitant.

We haven't exactly spent a huge amount of time in each other's presence since the events of the boundary. The healers took her in the same carriage as Lincoln. They're just about talking again. He felt, understandably betrayed. She felt like it wasn't personal. I suppose that's Dahlia for you. We've all recognised we need to leave the boundary, in the boundary so to speak. We all wanted to win. She was just a little more violent about it. Though the boulders helped work out some of that frustration on my end. She still hasn't mentioned them.

Dahlia hovers in the middle of the room, her eyes flicking to the chair in front of my desk. I gesture to it.

"Sit down, you're making me uncomfortable."

She lets out a little huff but sits anyway.

"What is it I can do for you?" I ask.

She takes a moment to inhale and settle and then looks me hard in the eye. "It's not like you can give it to anyone else, is it? Obviously, I'm made for it."

I frown. "I, umm... sorry, can we roll back a second. What in the Mother of Blood are you talking about?"

"Fucksake." She throws her hands up. "You're not exactly making this easy, are you?"

"Dahlia. Could you get to the point."

She glares at me, her jaw flexing. "Well, since Cordelia has gone to Finis Academy, and is no longer in charge of the city, there's no longer a vampire army... is there...?"

She stares at me pointedly.

Oh. Oh my gods, she wants the job... This is way too precious. Am I the arsehole? Maybe. I steel my expression, trying to suppress the smirk itching at the inside of my lips.

"That's right. We're moving towards a unified army with the Academy training it." I nod, stoic.

Her eyes widen as she realises that I have no intention of making this easy for her.

I don't know why I didn't think of it before, of course, she would be brilliant at the role. She used to lead Cordelia's army. She was their general, and for all the shit she gave us in the trials, she was bloody good at her job.

Her nostrils flare, she closes her eyes and takes a deep steadying breath. I have to physically bite the inside of my lip to stop myself from laughing. This, seeing her so deeply uncomfortable, is far more retribution than throwing the slabs on her body in the Montague territory.

"It's not like I'm going to work for Octavia, is it? I can't swallow that much humble pride."

". . . And?"

"And you require a bit less humble pie, so can we stop fucking about and you just give me the job..." She huffs again, shifting in the seat and then softens her tone, adding, "please?"

My lips twitch as I fold my arms and stare at her.

"There's a lot of water under the bridge, Dahlia. You tried to kill me."

"You crushed my body under a million stone boulders."

So she does remember. "You beat me to a pulp in a ring," I fire back.

"You would have done the same," she snaps. And she's not wrong.

I sigh, changing the game. "You gave me shelter after the demon attack."

She softens. "You saved me from a demon and hid my body from the sun."

I relax my arms, leaning over the desk. "You protected Octavia when the city hated her."

She nods. "There is a lot of history. And I think it will take time for us to trust each other. But I don't think there's anyone better suited to this role, and it gives you a vampire lead in the upper echelons of the Academy. And... and I really can't work for my sister. So would you please consider me for the role?"

I scan her face for a while, taking in the shifting emotions. Her expression is open, genuine. She's had to swallow a lot of pride to come to me.

"Okay," I say.

"No?" she says, sitting bolt upright.

"Yes, the job is yours. But there will be rules, and one foot out of line and you're out."

"Fine. Understandable even. And thank you."

"You can start Monday; I'll need to organise you an office and bits first. Is that okay?"

Dahlia nods and gets up, holding her hand out. I shake it and find it surprisingly warm. It's a sturdy grip but not so hard it hurts.

There's another soft knock at the door, and Amelia sticks her head in.

"Gods, I'm popular today. I'll see you Monday, Dahlia."

She inclines her head and retreats allowing Amelia to take her place. "I'm not here for long. I came to say goodbye."

"Goodbye?" I baulk.

"No. Gods. Sorry, I didn't mean that to sound dramatic."

"Speak faster, Amelia, for the love of blood."

"Ash. They're taking me on a romantic break. Just five days, but we're going to get out of the city and visit somewhere new. It's a surprise. But they wanted to treat me."

I smile and pull her into a hug, stroking the back of her head. "It's serious?"

She wriggles out of my grip. "I dunno. Maybe? It's not nothing. I really like them. So I just want to see where it goes. You know?"

I grin. "What about the club?"

Amelia has taken over as a kind of CEO of The Whisper Club for Octavia while she's running the city. Octavia still bases herself out of the club, mind you, which means Amelia can lean on her as it's an enormous step up in her career. But it seems to be working, and she's holding the fort with a little help from Erin and Broodmire.

"Erin is going to deal with the drink deliveries, and it's only five days. I've organised the weekend's events, it should be fine. We're not opening any of the club's new functions this weekend, so should be business as usual."

"Then I suppose all that's left to say is have fun."

She beams at me and kisses both my cheeks before darting out of the office.

I watch her go, and then move to the arched windows. She'll be in the tunnels beneath the courtyard and heading back into the main city. But I picture her prancing through them, her delighted smile. It was the right choice, not forcing the cure on her. Not that I'd have been able to, given there were only two vials. They were always meant for Cordelia and Eleanor. But I'm glad I decided against it anyway. It would have broken us. I see that now. Amelia's so happy with Ash and her role in the club. There are moments when I flinch at some of the savagery that comes with her vampire nature. But then my own nature is changing too.

I feed from humans occasionally, mostly at Octavia's request, because she is wildly turned on watching me feed, the visual of my fangs sinking into throats.

I think I'll always wrangle with that piece of me, the morals I had to question and then break to become who and what I am.

But I like who I am now. The power I have. It's still growing and shifting inside me. The more I learn, the more I develop new abilities.

Of course, it's new to all of us, but I'm working with the hunter elders, perhaps I should call them dhampir elders now that magic has returned to our city. Our buildings all possess the power they were made to hold.

I'm excited for the future. My gaze flicks to the wedding invitation on the shelf for a few weeks' time. New Imperium here we come. What a way to break the ice. Scarlett and Quinn, Remy, Bella and all the girls will be there, of course. They've visited since everything went down. To my surprise, and Octavia's, both she and Scarlett seem to be something of kindred souls. It's the predator in them, I think. It was either going to end in bloodshed or besties. I'm just glad it was the latter.

But I'm also excited to see what we can learn and

uncover about our magic now that it's returned. We'll have to do it together, of course. Me and all the hunters who've finally had their magic restored. And as for the city, we're united at last, prospering without the burden of a curse. Without the secrets and lies and stolen memories and fucked-up trials.

It's just me and Octavia, free to love each other, now, today, tomorrow, and for the rest of our days.

CHAPTER 43

OCTAVIA

Three Months After

Much of that day is a blur now. Red and I hid until midday when Xavier appeared with more carriages. It was easy moving Mother and Eleanor, of course, they are human again and fine under the sun, so Red helped them to the carriage. We had to manoeuvre the horses and carriage as close to the door as possible to get me out. One speedy leap into the compartment and I escaped with only a tiny blister on my hand the size of a small coin.

We scattered what was left of Sadie in the grounds of Castle Beaumont. While she was wrong, she still birthed me, and I wanted to acknowledge that. That's why I was determined to unite the city as one territory. It was Red who pointed it out: born a Montague, raised a St Clair, and a Beaumont by choice. I *am* the city, all three pieces. Only I could unite it, so that's what I've done. Funny how after all these years of rejection, I am the one to bring us together. The Montague territory sustained a lot of damage, but we're repairing it. It will take time, of course, but now that magic is flowing through the land and we have practitioners who can use it, things are speeding up.

I'm not sure I've really comes to terms with what happened with Sadie. There are so many questions I wanted answered, so much I wanted to know.

Why did she do it? Why didn't she just tell me? And perhaps I'll never know. I do take comfort in the memories I have of us, though. I take them out every so often—metaphorically, I mean. And sift through the encounters, wondering if I missed something, trying to tease information, clues, anything I can from our conversations. Red tells me to let it go, to accept that our parents aren't always who we want them to be because they're just as broken and fallible as we are. I'm trying to accept that. Trying to move on, but it takes time.

Mother and Eleanor have been at Finis Academy a couple of months now and are settling in just fine.

As for Red and I...

The city is ours, at last. And my gods, is it prospering. Remy is coming back today to finalise the implementation plans for the RuneNet, which the people of the city voted for en masse. I knew modernisation was the way forward. And the civil wars have thankfully ceased.

As for Red, she's settled into her role as head of the Academy— the Chief. She's managing it with Lincoln and Dahlia at her side. Not a match I thought I'd see, but stranger friendships have formed. Like Scarlett and me. I'm rather fond of the assassin. I do believe she's what I'd call a friend. A real one.

Red seems to particularly love the name *Chief*. And has taken to demanding I call her it, but only in private.

There's a knock on my office door. Much as I should probably take different office quarters, especially now Amelia is so embedded in the club, I can't quite bring myself to leave the Whisper Club. It looked after me when the city hated me. I want to look after it, now the city loves me.

"Enter," I say.

"Two tasks this evening, your royalness," Xavier announces.

I scoff a laugh and smile. "Hello, favourite."

He swaggers in, takes the seat opposite my desk and flicks his feet up onto my desk.

I raise an eyebrow. "Do you mind?"

"I don't, as it happens. Your secretary asked me to tell you to be ready in an hour. You have two jobs today."

"And why, pray tell, are you delivering this message instead of him?"

He waves a lazy hand at me. "Fucked him senseless and now he's sleeping it off."

"Delightful," I drawl and wait... and wait... "The tasks, Xavier, the tasks...?"

"Right, yes. Sorry. Seems I'm in a little bit of my own post-orgasm fog. Something about visiting Sadie's office."

"The church demolition? Fuck, I forgot." I gather my belongings together, nudge his feet off my desk and tip him out of his chair.

"Wait, what about the other thing?" I ask, herding him out.

"A wedding?" He frowns. "That doesn't seem right."

"Wedding?" I stop as I reach the stairs.

"New Imperium? Mother of Blood, I forgot about that too. It's in two days. We need to leave tomorrow."

"New Imperium, that was it." He nods sagely like he knew all along.

"I don't know why you're so chill. All of us have been invited. Dahlia and Gabriel too. It's the new queen's way of initiating peace between our cities. So, you better get your shit packed up too as we'll be there for a few days, peace talks and what not. And given you are now my right-hand man…"

"And delightfully charming…" He winks at me.

"Xavier, I swear if you use anything but your natural charm, I will—"

"—No compulsion. Got it."

"Can you please tell our siblings to pack?"

"Yeah, yeah. Oh, and your lover is here. Now, I'd better be off. I have some border-talk discussions to mediate between Lord can't-remember and elder so-and-so…" He yawns.

"Am I paying you?" I ask.

He snorts. "Not nearly enough for me to remember their names."

I groan and shove him down the stairs and out the front door where Red greets us.

She's tickling Broodmire under the chin and he's chuckling and purring at her. Strange little goyle. I press my finger to his tongue and his skin shivers pink before settling back to stone.

"Hey," Red says.

"Hey, yourself."

Xavier tips his head at the pair of us and speeds off into the night.

"Thought I'd accompany you tonight—" She cuts

herself off and frowns at something over my shoulder. I glance around to find a woman standing behind me.

"Can I help you?" Red says.

The woman is a little taller than Red, her hair shaved on the sides. It's spiky on top and jet—the colour of darkness. Her eyes though, are a cold blue that reminds me of winter.

"I know your mother," she says.

"Which one?"

She frowns at me. "Cordelia St Clair."

I narrow my eyes at her. "You're from Finis Academy."

She shrugs, neither confirming nor denying.

"What can I do for you?" I ask.

Red, though is seething. She stands beside me, her arms folded, glaring at the newcomer. I get it. The woman standing before me is gorgeous, masc and she clearly wants something from me.

I can't lie, Red's jealousy is kind of hot. But I don't want to poke her tonight. Not when she's come to accompany me to the demolition.

"We have a problem. Your mother specifically sent me to see if you'd be willing to consult on the issue." She turns to Red. "Both of you, actually."

Red and I glance at each other, her shoulders soften a touch when she realises the girl wants help, not to sit on my face.

"Can you wait a few hours?" Red asks. "We have to be somewhere right now, but Broodmire here, will let you into the club, and Erin, the tall bouncer, will keep you fed and watered. Tell her we sent you."

The woman scratches her temple but nods. "Sure."

Red climbs into the carriage, but I turn and ask, "Hey, what was your name?"

"Midnight," she says.

Red frowns, but Midnight doesn't elaborate, so Red says, "Nice to meet you."

Midnight smiles, and it's bright like the moon, like trouble and hunger. Whoever she is, there's a story behind the glint in her eyes. But she's obviously not going to tell us tonight.

"See you in a couple of hours," I say and climb into the carriage.

R ed sits with her legs crossed, her sketch pad on her knees, her fingers drumming the cover.

"Stressed?" I ask.

She shifts in her seat, but finally shoves the sketch pad at me. "I made you something."

I cock my head at her. "Thank you?"

Her neck flushes pink, and she kneads her knuckles. I don't think I've ever seen her this uncomfortable.

"Just open it already," she says.

I peel open the cover and my eyes instantly well. "Wow," I gasp.

It's three portraits. I'm in the front, head and shoulders, my long hair flowing around my face, and behind me, on either side, sit my *two* mothers. Sadie to the left, Cordelia to the right.

"It's beautiful," I say, barely able to get my words out.

She's captured our likenesses so well. I carry Sadie's refined features, her eyes and thick hair, and her height too. But my nose belongs to someone else, my full lips too. Cordelia, though, while we share no genetics, bequeathed to me her desire, which shows in my expressions. We share the same relentlessness and somehow, Red managed to capture it all in her sketch.

"There's something else," she says.

"Oh?"

"I've been working with the hunter elders, the ones who can trace their lineage to the dhampirs of old. They've been letting me borrow their family grimoires and as they all retrain, they've been teaching me what they know."

"Okay..." I say.

She rubs her fingers together, whispers something under her breath and her hands glow. The sketchbook grows so hot in my hands, I have to put in on the booth seat next to me.

The pencil sketches glisten and shimmer and then lift from the page. I gasp again as the faces of the three of us float above the page like grey ghosts. They spin, connected to the page by a thread.

"You can choose to either hang it as a flat sketch or I'm learning how to solidify them as 3D renderings, so you could put it in a Perspex box and keep them like this. I just need a bit more practice." She grins at me.

"You're amazing," I say and kneel at her feet. I'm about to kiss her when the carriage draws to a halt.

"Damn, and I was hoping for that kiss." She smirks.

"You'll get it, don't worry," I say and tug her out of the carriage.

As we stride across the Church of Blood's courtyard, several kids smile and wave and call out 'Octavia' as they're herded back behind the demolition safety lines.

I smile and wave. Funny how children are so full of love. They were the first to open up and stop seeing me as a monster. The kid's festival I threw in the middle of the city with candy and vampire clowns may have helped.

Of course, there are still people who see me the way I was. But the city is evolving and so am I.

The changes I'm implementing are helping. We've already opened the tunnels to other cities. The trade routes are flourishing, Montague is being rebuilt, and the economy is thriving. That has gone a long way to changing the way people see me. And once the New Imperium wedding is over, we'll be fostering relations there too.

Red slides her hand into mine as we traipse around the back of the Church of Blood.

We reach the back door, and she leans against it, blocking my way. "You were about to get on your knees..." she says, lust pooling in her gaze.

"Here? Red, really?"

She pouts.

"You're incorrigible. We don't have long either, we're supposed to get in, scan the rooms and get out," I say.

She folds her arms but doesn't budge an inch. *Honestly*.

But like I'd turn down Red offering herself to me. I slide my hand around her neck and press my lips to hers. Her arms loosen and curl around my back as she deepens the kiss. I slip my tongue inside her mouth. Her hands tug at my shirt, finding their way to my skin, to the buckle of my trousers.

I bat her away. This is all about her. I pull at her trouser button until it's free and I can loosen the zip.

She breaks the kiss. "I wonder if we'll be arrested for fucking against a church wall."

I laugh. There is no church, not anymore. With Sadie gone and revealed as the witch god they'd been worshipping, the monks lost their purpose and decided to disband the organisation. There are a few die-hard believers still desperately protesting the demolitions and swearing that she will return as a deity. But even if she did, this is my city now.

I reach behind Red and unlock the back door. Even though we still fuck openly in the club, there are children running around out here.

The door swings open and Red topples back. I scoop her up into my arms and she swings her legs around my back locking them in place. I carry her to the sanctuary and lay her down on the altar table. While most of the church is empty now, there are a few odds and ends that haven't been cleaned out, including some candelabras and stubs of half used candles.

"How's your magic training going again?" I ask.

She glances at the candles and flicks her hand out in a whipping motion. They all flash to life, flames emanating a dim glow. I run my hands up Red's trousers, my fingers hovering over her crotch. I grin. Red catches my eye, knowing exactly what I'm about to do.

"Octavia," Red growls. "Don't you d—"

I slide my nail into her crotch and slice, giggling to myself the entire time.

"Gods dammit, I only bought these last week," she says as I shred the crotch and push her legs open.

"Just for old time's sake." I'm smirking but she lays there decidedly unimpressed.

I tug on her top and pull it up over her head, sports bra too. Until she's laid there topless with shredded trousers.

"We're going to hell for this," she says as her nipples pebble in the cool air.

There are two types of candles, regular long-stick church ones and then blood-coloured flowers, which seem to have melted quicker than the white ones. I narrow my eyes, wondering if one of the monks had a penchant for wax play.

"Top, blindfold," I demand. She glares at me, but eventually does as she's told, wrapping her shirt sleeves around her eyes.

I take the flower candle and lean it over her stomach. It pours out in delicious blood-red droplets. She hisses as the wax drips onto her skin, her back arching off the altar. I slide my other hand to her crotch, and push through the torn fabric until I find her slit.

"Fuck, Octavia," she moans as I run my finger through her folds all while raising the candle higher, dripping the wax over her nipples and breasts.

I glide over her core and stop to circle her entrance. She rolls her hips, forcing my finger inside her cunt.

I pull out. "Needy tonight, aren't you."

"Yes, gods, just fuck me already..."

I glare at her blindfolded head.

She must realise so adds. "Please."

For once, I give her exactly what she asks for and slide my fingers inside her pussy, fucking her in long, hard strokes, all while dripping the candle over her body.

She moans and writhes on the table until my fingers are coated in her excitement. I'm way too thirsty to sit this out. I strip my trousers off and climb onto the table. Red pulls her makeshift blindfold off, peering at me.

"Is the altar going to hold us both?" she says as it wobbles while I readjust my position.

"We'll soon see." I lay on top of her, sliding my pussy back until it hits her mouth and then I lower myself to her soaking cunt. I shred her trousers open a little wider for good measure.

She tuts against my folds and mumbles something about buying her new ones. But I shut her up with my tongue. She tastes like wildfire and summer, like sweet temptation and forever love.

I lap at her pussy, the same way she licks mine. Long lavish swipes, both our clits swelling against tongues. I angle my body so I can slide a finger inside her, curling up until I find the fleshy mound inside her pussy, and I rub over and over.

She rocks against my mouth in quick jerks, her tongue's movement becoming sporadic as she moans. I suck as much of her into my mouth as I can get, moaning my own melody of pleasure as I take her, fuck her, lick her clean.

Her taste is divine. I could ravish her while the building came down around us and never stop.

The first rush of tingles soars into my pussy. She holds herself back, waiting for me to meet her on the edge of orgasm. I grind into her mouth, her tongue darting across my folds, into my entrance and back to my clit. Waves of pleasure radiate out, flowing into my thighs. The exquisite taste of her on my tongue while she laps at my clit is a heady concoction I can barely keep control of.

"Fuck, Red," I moan as both of us climb higher, higher. Lick quicker, faster, harder.

Sex is so much more these days, our bond solidifying and growing roots. Our bodies become one, especially in moments like this. Her breath is my breath, her pleasure, my pleasure. She is everywhere. Under my skin and in my soul. Our hearts grown as one, our veins matted like tree roots.

"I'm going to—" she cries as her pussy clamps around my fingers. Fuck, I love making her come. Which is why knowing my mouth is causing her filthy moans is enough to throw me over my own blissful precipice. I come hard, drenching her face, blinded by pleasure as I grind out the last waves of orgasm onto her mouth.

I pull my finger out of her pussy and lick her folds clean all while she giggle-protests, begging me to stop for how sensitive she is. I give her one last lick and relent, climbing off her and helping her up.

I survey the area. The candelabras shattered on the ground, the candles rolled halfway across the sanctuary and the altar looking decidedly worse for wear. Flames lick at a wooden pew.

"Yeah, we're going to hell," I agree.

Once we're both dressed, we make our way through the church, checking offices and rooms for anything that should have been removed. The place is empty and anything that has been left isn't important.

"This is the start," Red says suddenly.

"Of what?" I ask.

She smiles as me. "Everything."

And I know exactly what she means. It's the start of us —no more memory stealing, no more secrets, no more hating. But more than that, it's the start of a new life, a new city, a new reign.

We stop outside Sadie's office.

"You sure you're ready?" she asks.

I nod. "It's time."

I will always live wondering why, and what if. But I've come to accept the fact that Sadie did what she thought was best. It wasn't just me she duped. It was the whole city.

We're all floundering in the shattered pieces of the city she left behind. Our society was built on a lie she propagated. Maybe none of us will ever really know who she was.

I can either choose to let that crush me, or I can choose to move on... Build a new city based on the truth.

I open the door, my breath suspended. It swings open. I don't know what I expected, but my heart sinks. The office is empty save for a single sheaf of paper on the desk.

A letter. I glance at Red and she shrugs, clueless as I am. I approach the desk and glance at the note. My whole body stills as I read the words scrawled in Sadie's looping script...

Dearest Octavia.

CHAPTER 44

Dearest Octavia

If you're reading this, I'm already gone.
I'm using what little magic I have to enchant
these words to reappear upon my death. I hope
the magic is strong enough that the letter finds
its way to you when you're ready to read it.

I don't know where to begin. It's hard
knowing these will be my last words to you, but
I suspect you have so many unanswered questions. Questions I won't answer until, I fear,
it's too late.

Let me start with the end.

I've known for a thousand years that I
was going to die.

That if I undid the curse, one way or
another, it would unmake me too. A sacrifice I
was more than willing to give to rectify the

380

wrong I've done.

I've lived too many years, even a hundred is a lot of life. But I've lived ten times that length, and so recognising that the end is near when I've had so long and not nearly long enough with you, is hard.

I see now that my mistake was living with a singular focus: releasing the cure and paying penance for my mistakes.

I hope you understand that I never wanted to destroy magic. I never wanted to create monsters. I was just trying to earn enough money to keep us warm and safe. But it seems that I had the wrong focus all these years. I should have left it all and been with you, made a life for us. But even now, as I write this, mere hours from the Festival of Blood beginning, I realise I cannot stop. I want to, believe me, I want to give it all up and just tell you who I am. But a thousand years pursuing the same goal is a hard thing to let go of.

I want to say I'm only human, but I'm not. And yet, I am just as fallible.

Just as weak.

Just as flawed.

It's okay for you to disagree with me, to hate me for what I'm doing and the choices

381

I'm making.

I don't expect you to forgive me, but I do want you to know that you are loved.

Gods, Octavia, you are so loved. You were always enough. What I'm doing, the choice to pursue the cure isn't about you. And I know, I know. That's selfish of me, and mothers shouldn't be selfish.

But why not?

Why shouldn't we put ourselves first for once? Perhaps my issue is that I put myself first too often, too much and for that, I am deeply sorry.

I made so many mistakes, lived so many years by your side wishing, pleading with myself to tell you. It was cowardly to watch from the sidelines as Cordelia parented you in a way I never could. Sure, she had her own faults, but from what I can see, she did a good job and she loved you. Cordelia is a better mother to you than I can be. And that makes me hate her a little bit more.

I made a bargain with the gods themselves, so whether I want to or not, I must fulfil my duty.

Perhaps that will be too much for you to excuse. I will go to my death knowing that you may never forgive me. But I will also go praying that despite our differences, you can find at least a little piece of you to love me.

I want you to know that no matter how much the curse twisted and gnarled at my soul, all I ever wanted was to have you in my life.

Those months you grew in my belly were so joyful. We had nothing and yet every day, I was so proud to be growing a tiny baby. Those first few days I got with you were everything. Even a thousand years on, those memories are fresh and rich. The way I held your tiny fingers and toes etched into my mind forever. I would have been a good mother, I think. Perhaps in another life I can try again.

But I want you to know, that even though I kept my identity from you, I was always by your side.

I watched you grow in secret. I fumed when that man spread those lies about you as a child. I seethed as the city hated you. But I was always there.

Just like I watched you fall for Red, your love blossoming. I held every memory precious, even if it was from the sidelines. That is the sacrifice a mother makes. I could only have you from afar, so I took the pieces of you I could and treasured each one. Even though the pain of having you from afar was agonising, I endured it willingly.

I know you, Octavia. You don't realise it, but I do. I know the way you hide in a club full of people, and still feel alone. I know the yearn you have to make our city better. I know the hurt you carry because of me.

Believe me, I bore witness to the pain I caused you and it is the one regret I will take to my death.

My darling Octavia... all parents are fallible. Perhaps one day, if you have the blessing of children, you'll understand everything I did to make this city a better place was for you. It's going to be yours, the city, I mean. The people will love you because you were born for this.

We're close now.

I'm going to fulfil my duty; unmake the monsters I created. It hurts to realise that in doing so, I'm losing you in the process.

It seems that in the end, my mistakes didn't matter.

You mattered, Octavia.
To me, to the city, to Red.
Forgive me.

Isabella Sadie Montague
Your loving mother in blood and bonds, this life and the next.

Do you want to find out what Midnight's story is? Preorder *Architecti* now. www.rubyroe.co.uk/architecti

If you'd like to read a free prequel to my *Girl Games* series, full of just as many lesbians and just as much spice, you can do that by signing up here: rubyroe.co.uk/signup.

Last, reviews are super important for authors, they help provide needed social proof that helps to sell more books. If you have a moment and you're able to leave a review on the store you bought the book from, I'd be really grateful.

ABOUT THE AUTHOR

Ruby Roe is the pen name of Sacha Black. Ruby is the author of lesbian fantasy romance. She loves a bit of magic with her smut, but she'll read anything as long as the characters get down and dirty. When Ruby isn't writing romance, she can usually be found beasting herself in the gym, snuggling with her two pussy... cats, or spanking all her money on her next travel adventure. She lives in England with her wife, son and two devious rag doll cats.

The Girl Games Series

A Game of Hearts and Heists
A Game of Romance and Ruin
A Game of Deceit and Desire

instagram.com/sachablackauthor

tiktok.com/@rubyroeauthor

Printed in the USA
CPSIA information can be obtained
at www.ICGtesting.com
LVHW091708061224
798423LV00002B/352